Ellen
in
Pieces

Ellen
in
Pieces

A Novel

Caroline Adderson

Patrick Crean Editions

An imprint of HarperCollins*PublishersLtd*

A Patrick Crean Edition published by
HarperCollins Publishers Ltd

First edition

HarperCollins Publishers Ltd
2 Bloor Street East, 20th Floor
Toronto, Ontario, Canada
M4W 1A8

www.harpercollins.ca

Library and Archives Canada Cataloguing in
Publication information is available upon request

ISBN 978-1-44342-678-7

Printed and bound in the United States of
America
RRD 9 8 7 6 5 4 3 2 1

The author would like to acknowledge the
support of the BC Arts Council

BRITISH COLUMBIA
ARTS COUNCIL
An agency of the Province of British Columbia

Parts of this book were previously published in
slightly different forms.

"I Feel Lousy" appeared in *Eighteen Bridges*, Issue 5,
Winter 2012.

"Poppycock" appeared in *The New Quarterly*,
Number 121, Winter 2012. It was reprinted in
Best Canadian Stories 12, Oberon Press, 2012.

"Ellen-Celine, Celine-Ellen" appeared in
Canadian Notes and Queries, Number 86,
Winter 2012. It was reprinted in *Best
Canadian Stories 13*, Oberon Press, 2013.

"Your Dog Makes Me Smile" appeared in *Numéro
Cinq*, Volume III, Number 26, October 2012. It
was reprinted in *Best Canadian Stories 14*, Oberon
Press, 2014.

Chéri by Colette, translated by Roger Senhouse,
Penguin, 1954.

"Not Waving But Drowning" by Stevie Smith,
Andre Deutsch, 1957.

"Lady with Lapdog" from *Lady with Lapdog* by
Anton Chekhov, translated by David Magershak,
Penguin Classics, 1964.

In memory of my father

In this way she would be spared, for many years, the degrading listlessness of women past their prime, who abandon first their stays, then their hair-dye, and who finally no longer bother about the quality of their underclothes.

—COLETTE, *CHÉRI*

Ellen
in
Pieces

Act One

I

I FEEL LOUSY

...

That was as much as Ellen could get out of Yolanda as she hovered above her in the bathroom, holding back her golden hair while she retched.

"Maybe you should stay home," Ellen said.

Yolanda lifted her face out of the toilet. Pink with misery, she let Ellen apply a cool damp cloth. "I can't skip Inorganic Chemistry, Mom. It's unbelievably hard."

"Fine then. Just don't spread it all over campus."

Later, Ellen wondered how she could have been so dense.

ELLEN had finished. She'd seen her daughters into adulthood, Mimi far too early, slinking off to child-unfriendly places, fearless in the dark. Yolanda she'd had to drag, but anyway, she'd done it, raised her two girls all on her own, except for that nine-month blip when Yo was seven and Mimi ten and Larry came back. Before that, he'd been out sowing his wild oats, which he kept in a little bag between his legs.

It had always been so. They'd met at a house party during university. Larry was just slipping out of one of the bedrooms, closing the door behind him, when Ellen appeared in the hall on her way from the bathroom. Larry followed her to the living room where everyone was bouncing in a circle to The Clash. Later, a rumpled girl appeared and, in dismay, looked around the room for him. Ellen pegged her instantly; she'd been behind the door that Larry had discreetly closed. In the bed. The girl saw Larry tight on the couch with Ellen, his silvery charms back on display, and ran out heaving sobs.

Did Ellen sympathize? Did she foresee in this girl's public misery the personal shaming in store for her?

No. She'd married Larry.

They heard about this place, Cordova Island, an hour's ferry ride from Vancouver Island. It was the 1980s, but might as well have been the 1960s on Cordova. Ellen and Larry absconded there in search of freedom, both of them growing out their hair (Ellen wore hers, auburn and thick, in a braid down her back; Larry, a dark ponytail and beard to match). To be free in a place where deer and feral sheep roamed the forest trails, the locals, too, because it was quicker than the road. Free like the Free Store, which was really just a glorified recycling depot. Anytime you looked up, anytime you consulted the sky, there would be a bald eagle or a turkey vulture high above in a tree, watching your every move, like God.

BUT that was twenty years ago. These days Ellen's elder daughter Mimi lived across the bridge in East Vancouver with two roommates she loathed. She worked at Kinko's and hated that too. Mimi had a talent for dissatisfaction. Yolanda was in pre-med, still at home with Ellen in the house she'd grown up in North Vancouver, a cedar split-level high up the side of Grouse Mountain. Ellen and Larry had bought it just before their marriage self-destructed, bought it with the outrageous fortune he'd suddenly started making in L.A. On rare clear days there was a gasp-inducing view—oh, the silver-plated ocean!—as far as the Olympic Peninsula.

A few days ago Yolanda had begun experiencing flu-like symptoms. Now they had settled into a regular pattern. Violent vomiting first thing in the morning. Violent vomiting if she didn't eat. Violent vomiting if she ate anything but bread, potatoes, or mushy, Dalmatianed bananas. She walked around the house with these offensive bananas tucked under her arm. While studying, she kept a bunch within reach.

"So what do you plan to do?" Ellen asked from Yo's bedroom door.

Yolanda glanced over her shoulder at Ellen and immediately shrunk down, like she was still a little girl fearful of her mother's rages—despite the fact that they were never directed at her. Or rarely. Unlike Mimi, Yolanda had been a model child.

"I'm going to have an abortion," she said.

Just like that.

Ellen bowed her head in case there was any sign on her face of what she was feeling. What *was* she feeling? A lot of contradictory things. Relief, for one, but also a painful, almost menstrual spasm.

"Okay. Have you made an appointment?"

"Not yet."

"Well, you have to get on it, don't you think?"

"I've been studying."

Ellen threw up her hands, and even this small gesture set Yolanda wailing.

3

"Tell me what I should do!"

"Isn't there a clinic on campus? Make an appointment. Get a referral. For God's sake, you're in pre-med!" Ellen stormed off, sure now of what she felt.

Two hours later she came back un-angry. Something about the matter-of-fact way Yolanda had communicated her decision troubled Ellen. It sounded like she'd been chanting it to convince herself. Or maybe *he* was making her do it. The culprit, whoever he was. Either way, Ellen wasn't going to get involved. But she thought Yo could use a hug, and she was right. Yolanda was still bent over one of the massive tomes that threatened to pop the pegs of her IKEA desk, feverishly highlighting whole paragraphs, flayed banana peels strewn everywhere. She turned in her chair and flung her arms around Ellen's waist. Her glasses were smeary. She was too preoccupied to clean them, or she'd been crying.

"You'll come with me when I do it, won't you?" she whimpered.

And a great cloud of fruit flies lifted off the half-rotten bananas and swarmed them both.

ELLEN phoned her old friend Georgia with the news. In the background Gary, Georgia's husband, the last Marxist left standing and an inveterate eavesdropper, asked, "What now? Mimi's up the pole?"

Georgia shushed him. "For once it's not Mimi."

Ellen heard the processor grinding. Georgia and Gary were in the kitchen. They cooked together, which Ellen envied. Ellen cooked alone. She pictured them, petite, delicate Georgia with the phone lost in her sproingy hair, circumnavigating Gary—a fat man—at the counter. Their afterthought child, the boy genius Maximilian, four years old, would be reading out the recipe. Their

4

older son Jacob was away at McGill. Jacob was mild and average. But Maximilian? At two, he would stand on the coffee table during parties and recite "Religion is the opium of the people" to guests who were either shocked or delighted, depending on whether Georgia or Gary had invited them.

To Ellen, Georgia asked the obvious question, the one Ellen had refused to ask Yolanda because of her non-involvement stance. "Who's the guilty party?"

"I have no idea," Ellen said. "She's never even had a real boyfriend. Not that I know of. Last year she took the smartest, gayest boy in the whole school to Grad."

"Can Mimi find out?"

"I don't want to involve Mimi. Also, do I need to know who did it?"

"But you think she might have been coerced? Or is being coerced?"

"I hope not. But it's not like I want her to have it either. Because I'm the one who'll get stuck with it. I know I will. What do I want a baby for?"

"They smell so good," Georgia said. "I'd have another if I could. But I can't."

"I had my tubes tied," Ellen said. "Ten years ago."

"What I mean is, I need to know that the kid I currently have is going to be all right before I commit to another."

"He'll be fine!" Gary called from across the room.

"I don't multi-task with my maternal responsibilities. How did you, Ellen?"

"I made a lot of mistakes," Ellen told Georgia, "as you well know."

• • •

ELLEN remembered something as soon as she hung up. How when Mimi and Yolanda were in elementary school they kept coming home with lice. The school was good, Rayburn Elementary, and right in the neighbourhood, two blocks away. A good school but lousy at the same time. Every year, four or five notices would come home requesting a scalp check.

"*Fuck!*" Ellen would roar, which cued the girls to duck and cover before she hurled the comb. Every infestation a toxic ordeal, a nit-picking torture. Both had silky Rapunzel tresses that took hours to properly delouse. Mimi screeched and writhed, but Yolanda would sit quietly, her back to Ellen, paging through a picture book.

During one of these sessions Ellen noticed that Yolanda had been crying the whole time. Her chest was bibbed with tears. "Oh, honey," Ellen said. "Am I hurting you?"

"I feel so sorry for them."

"For who?"

"The baby lices."

SPRING, the window partially open, letting in a bright green scent. Yolanda tossed and sighed in the dark.

"You seem uncertain."

"Do I?"

"Well, yes."

They were in Ellen's bed, where Yolanda sometimes liked to come and cuddle in the middle of the night. She had only started doing this last year, after Mimi left. Mimi, who had once slept between two loving parents, while Yolanda, fatherless at birth, had been banished to a crib.

After a long silence, Ellen asked how she was feeling.

"Awful," Yolanda answered, and Ellen gathered her up.

It felt strange to be holding a smaller adult in her arms. How many men had she invited into this bed? Too many. Very few who counted and none recently.

"Yo? You don't have to. You can do whatever you want."

"Can I?"

"Of course. But I'm not raising it. That's the last thing I'll say about it."

"What about school?"

"What about it?" Ellen said, meaning a baby was an inconvenience, not an obstacle. All over the world women squatted in fields and pushed them out, then strapped them to their chests and hoed the afterbirth into the ground. Look at Ellen, a single mother. Larry kept up payments on the house for those years, but that was it. He contributed shelter; Ellen food, clothing, allowance, dance lessons, drug rehab. She'd started Ellen Silver Promotions when Yolanda was a baby and Mimi three. Before cell phones! Nowadays any woman could run a successful business from a playground—but back then? No.

7

But telling Yolanda this would be getting involved, so Ellen held her tongue. Also, it would sound like she wanted Yolanda to have the baby, which she certainly did not. If Yolanda had that baby the door to Ellen's life, which had only just swung open letting in this delicious, irresponsible breeze, would slam shut for eighteen more years.

Periodically, Ellen would evaluate herself in the bedroom mirror. Shoulder-length hair, still mostly auburn. A nice nose, long with a slight bump below the bridge to make it interesting. Blue eyes. The thin lips were treatable with lipstick. A B+ face. With a good night's sleep, even an A– face. Below the neck, though, where gravity had rendered her one-time best asset a defect, her average (and her assets!) declined precipitously. Ellen was juggy. Her hips were wide, her ass too—could it be otherwise? But on the positive side again, she was only forty-one and only twenty pounds overweight. She was going to tackle the excess poundage, really—and then, who knew? Who knew what delights awaited her? Unless she had Yolanda's baby to look after.

"How could I keep going to school?" Yolanda asked.

"No comment."

"Have you ever?" Yolanda asked.

"What?"

"Had an abortion."

Ellen winced and changed the subject. "You weren't forced or anything? Tell me you weren't."

"No."

"No you won't tell me, or no you weren't raped?"

"I wasn't raped!"

"Okay. Then I don't need to know anything else unless you want to tell me about the man."

"What man?" Yolanda said, and Ellen let go a sigh of her own.

Actually, in the case of Yo, it could have been Immaculate Conception. She seemed so innocent. Also stupid, the way really smart people sometimes are. Socially hopeless and befuddled and shy. Not that she didn't understand sex, far from it. Ellen had made sure of that, always tucking condoms in with the sanitary supplies.

Finally, Yolanda clued in. "Oh, him! You mean *him*? He was just a boy."

• • •

YOLANDA slept with Ellen the next night too, and the next, so Ellen reasoned that, since sharing a bed *was* de facto involvement, she might as well make an appointment for Yolanda to see the doctor. Apparently Yolanda was too busy studying to do the responsible thing herself.

The day of the appointment, Ellen went in first to explain the situation, leaving Yolanda in the waiting room. "She says she wants an abortion. Obviously we have to act quickly because— Well, you know. And see what you can find out. How this happened. I'm appalled."

"Ellen," said Carol, the doctor whom Ellen had been seeing for so many years they were practically friends.

"What?"

"She's eighteen."

"She sure doesn't seem it. I mean, if it wasn't for her scholarship, I'd think she was retarded."

Carol fixed a look on Ellen. She was a long, sinewy woman with a stare like a mink. Her cropped brown hair even resembled a pelt. "Go," she told Ellen. "Tell her to come in. And by the way, you are way overdue for a mammogram."

While Yolanda was in with Carol, trying to determine the date of conception, Ellen opened the biology textbook Yolanda had brought along. The highlighter pen was stuck in the chapter on ferns. Ferns, she read, reproduce with spores instead of seeds. The diagram showed the released spores developing into pretty little heart-shaped gametophytes. Gametophytes had both male and female sex organs. Convenient! There were photographs, too, that filled Ellen with verdant memories of those hidden paths that criss-crossed Cordova Island and sometimes opened into spectacular waist-high ferneries.

"I'm ready."

9

Ellen looked up with a start. Yolanda stood there, smeary, twisting her hands.

"Hold on. I want to talk to Carol again."

Ellen found her in the hall reading her next patient's file. "What did she tell you?"

"No," Carol said, waving Ellen away with the file folder. "You are incorrigible."

This forced Ellen, who really did not want to get any more involved, to ask Yolanda outright when they were in the car driving home. "So? So?"

"She did an examination," Yo said. "She made me pee on the stick just in case."

"It's not the flu then?"

"Ha ha." Yolanda opened her textbook and resumed reading.

Ellen asked how far along she was. She asked when the office would call about the referral. Between her monosyllabic replies, Yolanda uncapped the highlighter with her teeth.

"What else did she say?"

"We talked about being a doctor. How important experience is compared with knowledge. I feel like I have a lot of knowledge, but almost no experience."

"That's funny," Ellen said. "I'm the opposite."

Abruptly Yolanda groaned and hugged the textbook to her. The highlighter bounced off her lap and onto the floor mat.

"Oh, honey!" Ellen said. "Do you need a banana?"

"It's why I did it, Mom." Then she was sobbing her heart out.

Ellen pulled over into a loading zone, cutting someone off. She answered his reprimand, a honk for a honk, and turned to Yolanda, collapsed over the dash. "What are you saying, honey? Please. Tell me what's going on."

• • •

YET Ellen hadn't told Yolanda what had happened to her. To her, Yolanda was a daughter in trouble confiding in her mother. They were not yet two grown women sharing private aspects of their lives. It was still a one-way street for Ellen, a street Yolanda had driven up in the wrong direction, causing the two of them to crash.

A decade ago, when Larry and Ellen had already been apart—separated, then divorced—for seven years, Larry phoned.

Normally, Ellen called him. She called so that his daughters could have contact with their father. She would pass the receiver over to them, or suggest he invite them down to L.A. Even though Ellen felt humiliated when Mrs. Silver II answered, she called. Estranged from her own family and suffering because of it, she swallowed hard and dialled. She dialled for the sake of her girls.

Now Larry phoned out of the blue and asked to come back. His marriage to Amy was over. Some new woman he'd been besotted with had dumped him at the same time the television series he wrote for was cancelled. Raw with these failures, Larry wanted to be with his children.

And Ellen allowed it. Watching him get out of the cab a few days later, seeing his overgrown black curls, his wrinkled chinos and sad pouched eyes, the way he set down his suitcases and checked every pocket of his pants and jacket to come up with the fare, drawing out a wadded bill here, a bit of change there, she immediately forgave him. Forgave and swelled with a physical ache to have him inside her body and life again.

And Larry forgave Ellen, though he had much less to forgive.

Ellen thought they were happy, like during those two crazy, hippy years on Cordova Island living off the grid. Larry had *seemed*

11

happy the nine months he lived with them in North Vancouver. They had great sex. He and the girls formed an instant mutual adoration society. He even made their lunches—better lunches than Ellen's, cheese melts with raisin faces, Rice Krispies squares that weren't square but stamped out with cookie cutters.

Before Larry's return, the girls used to walk themselves to school. Ellen was working, the only mother who didn't escort her kids, and for her negligence she received a wide range of disapproving looks, from askance all the way to deploring. But now Mimi and Yo had a father to walk them and pick them up. In between, Larry fixed up the house and wrote his play and pulled the phone out of Ellen's working hand and fucked her in the afternoon. He stood at the stove stirring Rice Krispies into the marshmallow goop, muttering snatches of dialogue. He'd written plays before getting sucked into television. Ellen told him he didn't need the money anymore. Ellen Silver Promotions was thriving by then so he could be true to his art again.

"You make me puke," she told him when he announced he was going back. "To Amy?"

"To L.A." He rose from the bed and left her in it, closing the door softly with a hand behind his back.

Within twenty-four hours, he was packed and out of their lives.

At the time, Ellen had been hired to promote an American novelist on the Vancouver leg of his West Coast book tour. She got the girls up, dumped their cereal in and around their bowls.

"When's Daddy coming back?" they asked. Again, again, again!

They couldn't understand his inconstancy. Mimi was too young the first time to remember he'd abandoned her before. Yolanda had been unborn.

Ellen lost it. "Daddy isn't coming back! Daddy's never coming back! Daddy used up all his chances!"

That went over well. It was one of the few mornings she walked them to school. Well, she dragged them, sobbing, Ellen in tears herself, saying, "I'm sorry. I'm sorry. But I have to be downtown in twenty minutes. Believe me, I would like nothing better than to stay home with you and cry."

She met the American novelist in the restaurant of the Hyatt to review his schedule. Interviews, bookstore signings, then the grand finale, the Reading. He asked straight out, "Did you love my book?"

"I did," Ellen said. She'd only read the beginning and the end and some of the middle bits. "It's brilliant." It was middling, actually, but you don't feed two children on honesty. "Before I forget." She slid her business card across the table to him. "Anytime you need to, call."

13

He looked at it. "'ESP.' Cute."

Ellen sighed. "Silver isn't even my name anymore. I'm back to McGinty. I'm divorced."

How it seared, that admission. Why had she told him? She looked down at the coffee spoon on her saucer and contemplated gouging out her eyes with it. *I'm not crying,* she would tell the surprised novelist, *I'm not. It's just that, when you blind yourself? Your eyes water.*

And so the American novelist's reply didn't register at first. Ellen was on autopilot, not only contemplating self-harm but miserable for having shouted at the girls that morning. All through the meeting she'd kept picturing herself hauling them, wailing and unbrushed, into the school.

What he'd said was "Good."

Now she looked up and really saw him, the antithesis of Larry. Tall, even when seated. Also full of himself, though that was more a point of commonality. He would have been gorgeous but for the blond hair ebbing off the promontory of his forehead. But who was Ellen to be critical? Parts of her were too prominent. Fortunately, she was sitting on two of them.

"Do you have ESP?" the novelist asked.

The business was done, his breakfast consumed, their coffee cups thrice refilled. Ellen relaxed. "Let me see." She closed her eyes and touched her temples. Under the table, the novelist placed a foot over hers, implying not pressure but closeness. A shudder ran through her, half-thrill, half-warning. She felt very slightly ill. "The bill will come," she intoned, "and you will offer to pay it. But I will insist and you will succumb."

"Succumb?"

The waiter appeared. Just before she closed her eyes, Ellen had noticed him in her peripheral vision making his way across the room. The novelist threw back his head and let go a weird, high-pitched laugh, almost a seal's bark.

"I'll get it," he said before the waiter even opened his mouth.

"I insist," Ellen said, reaching for her purse.

The novelist laid the back of his hand across his Gibraltar forehead, behind which all his novels were plotted—his conquests, too, no doubt. "Oh, I succumb!"

Had his publicist in San Francisco succumbed? In Seattle? At eleven-thirty in the morning? She shouldn't do it. Why did she always do it? To spite Larry? He wouldn't care. To prove to herself that she could collect lovers too? That she was still desirable even though Larry didn't want her? Or just to keep opening her wound? She felt so wretched afterward. She always felt so lousy.

"We could go upstairs. But I warn you, I'll want to hear more about my book."

"I could read it out loud," Ellen said.

"While I do delicious things to you."

The waiter, who had vanished with her credit card, returned with it on a tray just in time to hear the novelist in mid-seduction. He quickly stepped away. Ellen, blushing, leaned over the bill, dizzy with embarrassment and desire. Desire could be so wonderfully distracting. Her desolation was lifting, even as she calculated the tip. Fifteen percent, plus five for discretion.

Click.

Something dropped onto the bill, right onto the blank line she was staring at. A crumb, or a speck of dirt.

She hoped.

Not alive. Not a living thing.

Yes. It definitely moved, was probably on its back, kicking its imperceptible legs in the invisible air. You needed the magnifying glass that came in the nit kit to actually see their legs.

In an instant her whole scalp was crawling. She glanced at the novelist to see if he'd noticed—no. He was signing her copy of his book. Ellen swept the tray onto the restaurant floor, oopsed and picked it up.

"Excuse me. I'll be right back."

She barely reached the bathroom in time. Vomited, rinsed her mouth in the sink, scratched her whole head hard enough to draw blood. With the comb, she made herself presentable again.

Back at the table, she told him. "Sorry. Suddenly, I'm not feeling so hot."

On her way home, she stopped at the drugstore for delousing shampoo and a pregnancy test. Now she lay in the tub in the middle of the day, suds dripping down her shoulders, over her breasts.

It took ten minutes to kill the lice. Then you had to comb out the corpses and the eggs.

Deep inside her, a factory was churning out cells. Of course she would have to have it, the assembled product. A sister or a brother to her girls. A living thing.

Except Larry would accuse her of doing it on purpose. To lure him back. She didn't have to tell him. She could claim it wasn't his. Thank God she hadn't slept with the American novelist or she'd have him to contend with too.

But how could she have another baby on her own? She wouldn't be able to work for months. Larry had no money. She didn't qualify for Employment Insurance. She'd have to sell the house. And, as if the judgmental looks she received at the girls' school weren't bad enough, imagine her waddling in, pregnant, with no obvious father around? She didn't care for her own sake, but it wasn't fair that Mimi and Yolanda should be stigmatized.

That had to be ten minutes. Eyes watering, stomach twisting from the smell, she slid down, just her face and knees out of the water, legs bent like she was already in the stirrups.

It was her only option. Then she'd start volunteering on Hot Dog Day.

AFTER Yolanda's collapse in the car on the way home from seeing Dr. Carol, Ellen sat her down in the living room for a proper talk. She brought her a piece of bread, a glass of water. Yo, cross-legged on the couch, swollen from crying, tore off the crusts, rolled some of the soft part into a pill, and washed it down.

"Come on," Ellen said. "Tell me what's going on."

Yolanda lifted her face, which was so pretty, yet always naked and defenceless. Only the glasses protected her. "I thought I should know what it was like."

"What?" Ellen asked. "Being pregnant?"

"No. Having sex."

"Don't tell me you didn't use a condom. After how I brought you up?"

"It broke."

Then the inevitable complications. She liked him. Especially after the sex. "I read about it," Yolanda said. "Your body releases a hormone during sex to make you bond."

"Maybe he likes you too," Ellen said.

"Men don't have that hormone."

"Ah," said Ellen. "That explains a lot."

Yolanda rolled herself another bread pill. "Also, I hardly know him."

"So what do you want to do?"

"I've never had any kind of operation. It would be another experience. Except, I have . . . I have these *feelings*." Her glasses misted over again.

"That's hormones too," Ellen said.

"I already love it," Yolanda announced.

Ellen remembered her glass of wine on the kitchen counter. When she came back, Yolanda's UBC T-shirt was hiked up, her hand on her belly, which looked more sunken than anything. Ellen set the glass down and light moved through the wine and shone on a magazine, the opposite of a shadow, a burning spot so fierce it seemed the magazine would ignite. Why can't we feel that purely? she wondered. Why was there always mishmash and contradiction? She wasn't a sentimental person. She really believed that Yolanda should have the abortion and get on with her life. Yet when Ellen was in the same predicament, she hadn't been able to do it either. The hospital had called with the date of her procedure and she'd cancelled it in a gush of tears.

"What should I do, Mom?" Yolanda pleaded. "What would you do?"

Ellen took a sip of wine. "No comment."

"I know it will be hard. Raising a kid on my own."

"Try raising two," Ellen said.

"I know. I know how hard it was for you, Mom."

Ellen stiffened defensively. "Do you?"

"You seemed so angry."

"I *was* angry!" Ellen said, causing Yolanda to shrink back. "You would've been angry too. You don't know the half of it. And your sister. Your *sister*! Have your baby! If it turns out like your sister, then you'll see!"

"I wasn't accusing you of anything," Yolanda whimpered. "I was trying to be . . ." She started to rise off the couch. "Sympathetic."

Abruptly she bolted, a hand clapped over her mouth. Ellen set down her glass and went after her.

Yolanda made it as far as the bathtub, where she disgorged the thirteen bananas and half a slice of bread that she'd eaten that day. Ellen sat on the edge of the tub and stared down at the beige sludge. It looked remarkably like baby food.

She wet the cloth, wrung it out, wiped her daughter's face. "I'm sorry. I was yelling."

"You were always yelling," Yolanda said without meeting Ellen's eye.

"Always?"

"At Mimi. Not me. That didn't make it any better."

"Look at me," Ellen said, and she lifted Yolanda's atrocious glasses off her face. "I shouldn't have said what I said. What I should have said was this. I wouldn't have changed anything about you. Not for the world. You were, are, perfect. And if you have that baby? It'll be perfect too."

A *buttinsky*. Where did that come from? Probably Esther, Larry's mother, Ellen's former mother-in-law, an odious person, yet charmingly stuffed with Yiddish *bons mots*. "I'm *curious*," Ellen said in the car, in her own defence, to no one. What mother wouldn't want to get a gog at the boy who had deflowered her daughter? Who had *impregnated* her?

She found parking just off campus, then asked directions to the liquor store. Right next door was a café. "You call it Tall," Ellen told the girl behind the counter, "but it's actually Short. It's Small, yet you call it Tall."

The girl sighed.

"I'm just saying," Ellen muttered. "Some people have it figured out."

She took her coffee outside and, at one of the metal tables, pretended to read *Pride and Prejudice*, holding it upside down for fun. He wasn't there. Yolanda had said he always was. After a few minutes she turned the book the right way up and that was it. Completely absorbed by the Bennet family's delightful problems, she forgot the stakeout.

In the middle of Chapter Three, a sound like a train clacking over the rails returned her to her proper task. Him for sure, pirouetting to a stop. The skateboard took flight, its coloured underside flashing. He caught it in one hand. Tan dreadlocks, dirty jeans barely clinging to his hips, a bad cough. His name, Yolanda had said, was Sean.

From behind *Pride and Prejudice*, Ellen watched. He rooted through his backpack. Out came crocheted juggling balls, a cigar box. To warm up, he flipped two balls in each hand and coughed. A university liquor store was not the most lucrative place to ply his trade. While his coloured balls orbited, frat boys went in and out for beer, ignoring him. "Hi!" he kept saying. "Hi!" The cough sounded like a chair being pushed out, scraping the floor.

Occasionally he'd cajole someone into tossing him a set of keys, or an apple, for a few turns with the balls. Or he'd look at his watch without altering his rhythm. "These balls have been in the air for thirteen minutes. Only your generous donation can keep them going."

Yolanda must have donated. Ellen pictured her scooting past, hurling change in the Romeo y Julieta box. The bus stop where she always waited was just across the street. When you see a person every day, you start to feel connected. You start to worry when they're not there, or when their cough won't go away.

Ellen gave him a twenty, which was stupid, because he watched it flutter down on the mosaic of pennies and dimes in the bottom of the box, then looked at her, amazed. And smiled. Very boyishly. All the while the balls kept circling. Blushing, her cover blown, Ellen slunk off.

"Hey, awesome! Thanks! Good karma to you, lady! That lady just gave me twenty. I didn't put it in myself—"

He broke off hacking.

LATER that night, delivering rotten bananas to Yolanda at her desk, Ellen noticed she was highlighting every word in *What to Expect When You're Expecting*.

So, she thought. So.

She made no comment.

But then *the feelings* jackbooted in and they were not at all what Ellen had expected. Almost faint with them, she took to her bed with a cold cloth over her forehead and a box of tissues balanced on her stomach. She wasn't angry. She wasn't even relieved that Yolanda had finally made up her mind.

Back then—ten years ago, when Ellen had been pregnant for the third time by Larry—she'd been all business. She'd had no time to feel anything but nausea. She'd taken on extra contracts, written grant proposals for arts organizations too, just to earn enough money to get them through the year after the baby was born.

Ironically, it made her an even worse mother. Where once she'd rationed the TV—thirty minutes a day, no more—now it babysat Mimi and Yo. Or she farmed them out shamelessly to Georgia and picked them up late. No time to patiently comb every strand. Off to her hairdresser they went, the girls bawling in side-by-side chairs while Tony, making a face, lopped off their infested ponytails and tossed them on the floor.

"Remember?" he told Ellen. "I did that to *you* when you came over here from that"—he flapped his little hands—"that *island* where you never bathed."

Even lopped, Mimi's and Yo's hair still grazed their indignant shoulders. Not good enough. "Mia Farrow in *Rosemary's Baby*," Ellen told him. "As short as that."

Afterward Mimi had said, "Mama? I'll hate you forever and ever now."

Little did Ellen know she would hear those words so often they would eventually have no effect, but that was the first time and they felt like a wrecking ball to the chest. Back then, in the

21

sunshiny world of childhood, where forgiveness was dispensed like lollipops, she made everything right just by taking them to get their ears pierced.

At twelve weeks, Carol sent Ellen for an ultrasound. Ellen shuddered, remembering how the technician had buried the transducer so deep into Ellen's fat that it hurt. She suggested a transvaginal scan instead. For this Ellen had to clamber off the table, dress, and go empty her bladder, which she'd painstakingly filled on Carol's orders.

"Well, that was a relief," she told the technician after she had dumped all those cups of tea. "This? Not so much." She meant being penetrated with a cold, K-Y Jelly–slathered rod. What could you do at a time like this but crack a joke or fake an orgasm? Except the technician seemed humourless.

Because the fetus was dead.

She didn't say that, though. She called it *blighted*.

Later, on the phone, Carol had advised Ellen that she could wait until she miscarried naturally, or she could have a D&C. Really, Ellen shouldn't have cared. She'd been ambivalent anyway. Yet after the *procedure*, after Georgia drove her home from the hospital, Ellen had made Mimi and Yo peanut butter sandwiches and an enormous bowl of cheese popcorn. She set a travel clock on the TV and started the cartoons blasting.

"When the alarm rings, come and get me. But don't come until it rings. No matter what."

"What if we're hungry?" Mimi asked.

"Eat something."

"What if we're thirsty?"

"You know how to turn on a tap."

"What if the house catches fire?"

"Run out the back. Don't worry about me."

She shut herself in her bedroom and sobbed until, hours and hours later, four hours to be exact, Mimi and Yolanda crept in and woke her up.

"Mama," they whimpered. "We thought it wasn't ever going to ring."

Somehow Ellen had managed to put that grief away. For a decade she'd forgotten it completely. She'd also taken measures to ensure she would never feel it again.

And she hadn't. Until now, with the cold comfort of the cloth across her forehead and the tissue box on her belly, weightless as the very thing her body would never again contain.

23

THE next time Ellen went, the boy remembered her.

"Last week."

"No," said Ellen.

It was actually just four days ago. Yolanda had an exam today and Ellen had offered to drive her. She had to drop off some posters anyway. She wanted to take another look. Birthmarks, eye colour, et cetera. Things she hadn't looked for the first time, when she'd been merely curious.

So there wouldn't be any surprises.

So she would know what to expect.

"Do you want something from me?" Sean asked.

"Absolutely not!" Ellen said.

"But you gave me a twenty last week too."

"I must have a doppelgänger. This tall? Big hips? A lot of money to throw around? I'm taking it back."

She retrieved the twenty, and when she straightened he was laughing. The chair pushed out in his chest, scraping his lungs, yet the balls didn't fall, or even slow or falter. She was impressed. Quite won over. She noted blue eyes. Larry's eyes, nearly black, had trumped hers. Larry had blotted the blue right out of his daughters. But this grandchild of hers? It had a chance.

"What else could I do for twenty dollars?" he asked.

Ellen, normally unfazable, drew back.

"I give a good back rub. Or I could teach you to juggle."

It would seem Oedipal if he touched her, even if by "back rub" he actually meant rubbing her back. Juggling? Ha!

They went for a walk.

"How does your meter work?" Ellen asked. "Am I paying by the minute, or the mile?"

"I'm easy," he said.

A nearly eight-hundred-hectare forest grew right up against the university. In Ellen's day, when she was an English major here, it had a different name. Barely anything on campus was recognizable. Over there, a familiar building—Chemistry?—but it lacked all context. What context! She'd met Larry here, got pregnant, dropped out, ran off to Cordova Island.

They turned onto Westbrook Mall, Sean clacking beside her on the board, clacking and coughing. The hospital looked the same but the old frat houses had been torn down and replaced by frat condos.

When they reached the forest, Sean stashed his skateboard in a tree. It was easy to get him talking then. His whole story he offered up, how he'd got pneumonia while tree planting and ended up in hospital. Afterward, he didn't want to go back home.

"Where's home?" Ellen asked.

"Back east. My brother's there but he doesn't give a shit about me."

Orphan, Ellen noted with a pang. Also, weak in the lungs. "Are you living on campus?"

He flipped back the dull ropes of his hair and smiled. "For now. I was staying with friends, but they went planting again and sublet their place. What about you? Where do you live?"

"The North Shore."

"Mountains. Awesome. Here. Let's go this way. I want to show you something."

He tried to take her hand, but she plucked it back. Had he led Yolanda off the marked trail like this, into the thick of the green where no one would hear them? Ellen followed, freshly appalled at Yolanda's stupidity. Yet moments later here was Ellen with no idea where she was. She stepped over logs, kicked through salal. The ground, wet and humusy, sponged underfoot. Eventually they came to an enormous cedar, its limbs shagged with moss. Great hanks hung all over it like green tangled hair. What interested Sean was how the tree had grown over a fallen log, its roots partially above ground, elongated, like a pair of straddling legs.

"Doesn't that look alive?" he asked.

"It is alive."

"I mean, doesn't it look like it could walk and talk? It's the fucking *Lord of the Rings* in here. There's nothing like this in Sudbury. I can tell you that much."

All around, ferns clumped, their outrageous crowns like giant Copacabana headdresses. Ellen turned over a frond and saw the tiny regular circles roughing up its underside. They were pale green now, but as the spores matured they would darken to a powdery brown.

"So sperms and eggs are, like, floating all around us?" Sean asked when she explained it.

25

"Yes."

He gazed up, squinting, and the dreadlocks slid heavily down his back. Ellen looked up too, at the light penetrating the canopy of branches. Something moved. A very fine filament, a silken tail, tracing an otherwise invisible trajectory. Then the molecular burst of connection.

Probably a spiderweb. Probably a water droplet snagged on the afternoon.

Sean said, "Awesome."

And it was. It filled her with awe until she remembered that she'd only paid the parking meter for an hour.

"This way," Sean said, striking off ahead of her. "It's faster."

"Would you say you're generally a happy person?" Ellen asked.

"I'm really happy," he said, coughing.

"That's so comforting to know. One of my daughters gets low. Because of her father. Of course she blames me. Takes it out on me."

He pointed deeper into the trees where he had rigged up a tarp, green to camouflage it. "There's my pad."

"Can I?" she asked, and he gestured for her to go ahead.

Ellen bent and peered inside the plastic shelter where Yolanda had probably lost her virginity and gained more experience than she'd counted on. Butane camping stove, sleeping bag, mildewed paperbacks. Some things in garbage bags—but the rest damp looking and not very clean.

"Cozy," she said, though already she was fretting about his cough. This was a rain forest. What he really needed was to dry out. And the other thing—she'd been avoiding thinking about it, trying not to notice how often he wormed a finger through the dreadlocks to scratch his scalp.

As he sauntered ahead of her in the tree-dappled light, a song

26

came to her. A song about a forest boy with shy, sad eyes. An enchanted boy. Her mother used to sing it when Ellen was a little girl.

"Is there a place you can shower?" she asked.

Nature Boy.

"The pool's too expensive," he told her. "I found a shower in one of the science buildings. Then, last time? I got caught."

He lifted one arm and sniffed. "Sorry."

SOME people have it figured out, but there's no shortage of schlemiels either. Back at the car, a sixty-dollar parking ticket decorated Ellen's windshield. Plus twenty for Sean.

"You don't have to pay me," he said. "You're letting me use your shower."

She stuffed the bill into the pocket of his T-shirt, over one weak, rattling lung. "We have to stop for some bananas on the way."

"No problemo."

You can never go back home. Well, *she* wasn't. So it wouldn't be the same story twice. Different people, different story. Maybe a happier ending this time. Maybe a perfect one.

What would Yolanda say when she got back from her exam? Ellen would deal with that after she made some calls. She was going to phone a few old friends and see if anyone had an empty cabin. He could chop wood, do some construction. He was probably strong when he wasn't sick. Or he could teach juggling at the Waldorf School. Almost everyone had a cabin out back on Cordova Island, or a shack they'd lived in while they built their permanent place.

A lot of people still owed Ellen. They owed her for the oats they let Larry sprinkle in their beds.

27

2

POPPYCOCK

...

Now Ellen was alone in the North Vancouver house, blessedly alone at first, then lonely. Yolanda and Sean and little Eli, Ellen's grandson, had been living on Cordova Island for the past four years. Ellen, a grandmother to a five-year-old? Maybe she'd dreamed it.

Once a month now, instead of every six weeks, she made her pilgrimage to Tony's salon so he could camouflage the years.

Briefly, Mimi had moved back in, making teeny-mouth all day long, that sour, lip-pursing expression that drove Ellen mad. In fact, mother and daughter so irritated each other that in the end Mimi had packed herself off to Toronto, which was, she claimed, "As far away as I can get."

"There's Antarctica," Ellen had muttered, only to be ambushed by guilt.

Alone again.

So Ellen decided to sell the house. Sell just as soon as she unloaded her twenty-plus years of crap. Already she'd given up on boxes and garbage bags, the pretense of logical sorting. The morning her father called, she was ruthlessly heaping everything to one side of the rec room, as though to douse it all with kerosene. Her wedding pictures, for example. Into the pile they went.

The phone rang and Ellen emerged from the crawl space like a miner from an underground shaft and ran for it.

"It's me, your father."

She blinked, the cordless in her hand. The voice was not so much older as entirely unfamiliar. Sort of tremulous.

"Are you there?"

"Yes," she said.

"I'm coming to see you."

"Really?" Ellen said.

"Tomorrow. Monday."

"What? Okay. Would you like me to pick you up?"

"I was hoping."

"All right," Ellen said and, still stunned, she wrote the flight time and number on a box flap and ripped it off. "Where are you staying?"

A long silence unfolded between them, though not as long as the last one, which had gone on close to twenty-three years. This time Ellen cut it short.

"Okay," she said.

WESTJET from Calgary, direct. Ellen waited empty-handed in the terminal. She'd considered bringing something welcoming, but what? All she could think of was that sickening candy in a cardboard can with some kind of flower in its name. The whole long drive from North Vancouver, across the Lions Gate Bridge, through downtown, over the Burrard Street Bridge, along fifty car-clotted blocks of Granville Street, then over the Arthur Laing Bridge to Richmond where the airport was, she'd alternated between her mantra, *Driving sucks*, and trying to remember the name of that caramel-popcorn-and-nut confection. Her mother used to buy it for him every Christmas. Even as its flowery name eluded her, Ellen could picture the cylindrical outline in the stocking, a blockage. Passengers trickled, then surged into the baggage claim area and the luggage carousel jerked to life. Ellen stalled on *petunia*.

Eventually the area around the carousel cleared, just a few unclaimed bags going around for the ride. She wondered if she'd got the time wrong, but had left the box flap with the details in the car. Then it occurred to her that her father must have walked right past her. They hadn't even recognized each other. People change. She'd changed.

Well, there was an understatement.

She checked the taxi stand outside. From the matte and colourless sky, planes kept sinking down, one after another with just a couple of breaths between, each a surprise. The last time she saw her father, she'd been a slip of a girl. No. She'd actually been enormously pregnant with Yolanda. In fact, Yolanda was almost the same age Ellen had been at Jack McGinty's fiftieth birthday party.

Back inside, by the carousel, where those same few bags were going nowhere fast, a uniformed woman came pushing a man in a wheelchair.

"Excuse me?" Ellen said. "I'm looking for the WestJet counter."

"Ellen," croaked the man.

Wide panicked eyes under outrageous brows. The jaw working, working, blood all down his chin.

Poppycock.

• • •

THE next seven hours blurred by. Jack McGinty barely spoke. Not in the car bleeding and tremoring all the way to the hospital, not in the limbo of the waiting room. In the plane somewhere over the Purcell Mountains he'd bitten his tongue and it just wouldn't stop bleeding. Apart from that, he refused to explain his deterioration, or why he'd come. Ellen kept thrusting tissues at him, which he lifted in a wad to his mouth. The tremors were so bad they did the daubing for him.

They'd been waiting three hours when the nurse finally called, "Jack McGinty?"

He took a typed note from his breast pocket and handed it to Ellen, which was when she noticed the mechanical pencils. Her whole childhood he'd carried those pencils in that pocket, up against his mathematical heart. Now they made her tear up.

I am sorry. Love, Dad, the note read.

"What's this?" Ellen asked.

He looked at the note and, frowning with his bloodied mouth, took a second slip of paper from his pocket, which he traded for the first. The tremors made him seem impatient.

It was a list of medications, also typed. Many medications. Ellen was alarmed by how many there were.

"Give it to them," he said.

Four hours after that, Ellen drove the car into the garage at home and parked. Jaw clenched, she helped her father out. Anger, her default emotion, not always appropriately. For example, when her mother died. Later she'd felt all kinds of things, but right off the top of any given situation, she was usually blistering.

"This is a nice place," Jack remarked, as though Emergency had never happened and they'd come directly from the airport.

Ellen turned her exhausted eyes to him. "I'm selling it."

31

She led her spasming father inside, snapping on lights as they went. Usually she left one on; she hated arriving to darkness. "I made up the room downstairs," she said, because, with him in this condition, she wasn't sure if he could handle stairs.

"Downstairs is fine. It's a very nice home, Ellen."

Arm in arm they reached the bottom, he clutching the paper bag containing the Senokot they'd stopped for. The spare room was off the rec room, which was half heaped with the past she planned on disposing of. He didn't even see the mess. His eyes were fixed straight ahead on the open bedroom door, as though with sufficient intensity of gaze he might transport the twitching mass of his body as far as the bed, visible there with its fresh linens and cascade of little pillows.

After running every conceivable test, extracting his fluids, X-raying every inch of him, tapping his juddering body with their rubber hammers, the doctor had clipped the X-ray to a square of light on the wall.

"This is how far the stool is backed up."

"He's shaking and champing because he's *constipated?*" Ellen had asked.

Or he had Parkinson's disease, but that was beyond the purview of Emergency. So with a referral to a geriatric specialist and a list of laxatives in hand, Ellen, seething, had brought her father home.

THAT first night she couldn't sleep for the downstairs toilet flushing, the French doors rattling, Jack going out in the cold October night, and coming back. She wasn't angry anymore, only worried. Parkinson's? She'd have to look it up.

Flush!

With her father in the house, her teenage self came sneaking back, long-forgotten and reckless, a leggy force. *That* Ellen used to lie in bed like this, but with her nightie over her clothes until she was sure her father and her older sister, Moira, were asleep. Then, joyfully, she would fling the nightie off and escape the stifling house. Some boyfriend would be waiting in his truck halfway down the street. Bush parties were the thing. Bonfires in the country, girls swilling pink gin then puking in the woods.

This must have been when her mother was in the hospital. Ellen distinctly recalled asking if she was going to be all right and her father saying, "She'll be fine." It was a lie.

One night Ellen crept back in reekingly drunk. Caught! Her dad and Moira were up. The hospital had phoned. Her mother had *died*.

Ellen was furious, of course.

Nothing was the same with the heart ripped out of their family. Moira stepped into their mother's shoes for a few years, but she hadn't been able to control Ellen. And every time they fought, Moira renewed her disavowal of Ellen. Because she hadn't been there the night their mother died. Hadn't Ellen been punished enough, losing her only true ally? Her father was around, but he always seemed so stiff and remote, like he only knew how to love one person, the one who used to sing "Don't Get Around Much Anymore" and "Embraceable You." The one who sang "Let's Call the Whole Thing Off" for Ellen to fall asleep to.

After she died, Jack never seemed to say a word.

AT five the next morning, Jack McGinty was flushing the toilet again. Then a series of mysterious whirrings and buzzings started,

33

which Ellen listened to forever, curled resentfully in her bed with the pillow over her head, teeth gritted, thinking he'd better explain himself. He'd better explain what he meant by coming here. By the time she'd identified the sounds—electric shaver, electric toothbrush—she was too angry to fall back to sleep.

She found him in the kitchen, dressed and brushed, with the pencils lined up in his pocket, swaying like a man standing in a canoe. "Good morning," he said, and a bit of pink showed in the corners of his mouth.

Poof! Un-angry.

"How's the tongue?" Ellen asked. He stuck it out, hideous and inflamed, a purple crescent at the end where his teeth had cut through. She shuddered. "What do you want for breakfast? Cereal, toast, eggs?"

"Don't go to any trouble."

"I won't. Just tell me what you want."

"Cereal's fine."

"It's fine or it's what you want?"

He said he wanted it, but who could tell? Maybe he wanted Oysters Rockefeller. Why couldn't people just say what they meant? This was Ellen's downfall. She said what she meant (thereby offending nearly everyone) and assumed everyone else did too, assumed that "She'll be fine" signified she would in fact be fine.

In the hopes that at future 5 a.m.s her father might take the initiative to feed himself, Ellen directed him to the cereal cupboard and went to dress.

He was tissuing orange juice off the seat of the chair when she returned. So much for sitting him down for a talk. She hurried over with the cloth. "There. Sit, Dad."

Dad. After twenty-three years, her mouth had formed the word.

He obeyed, staring wistfully at the cereal box until Ellen filled his bowl for him. She watched him eat, saw how most of the cereal never completed the trip to his mouth on the wildly shaking spoon. Pity wrung her out the way she'd wrung out the sticky cloth a moment ago.

"I heard you up in the night," she said.

"I'm sorry."

"Don't be. Can't you sleep? What about your pills? Wasn't Zopiclone on that list? It's for sleeping. Does Moira know about the pills?"

She hadn't meant to bring up her sister, Moira, but she was, after all, a nurse. Presumably they were in touch. Presumably. How did she know?

He burst out, "All of this is Charles's fault! She should never have listened to him!"

Charles, Moira's husband. Ellen's brother-in-law. Ellen took a backward step, wondering if Jack meant *her* and Charles. Also, Jack McGinty was not a yeller. He was, practically speaking, a Trappist.

And now that he had humiliated himself enough with the Shreddies, he thanked her for breakfast and went downstairs to rest.

"You do that, Dad. I'll see you later."

Ellen still didn't know why he'd come.

SHE phoned the geriatric place. It had a two-week waiting list. She called her own doctor, but hard-line Carol did not accept out-of-province patients.

Then her realtor called. "Ellen? Brad Wheeler."

It was a strain for Ellen not to reply, "Brad Wheeler-Dealer?"

Brad was ramped up and ready to roll.

"Ready to roll up the ramp?" Ellen asked.

"You bet," he said. So Ellen's news could only disappoint. "How long's he staying for?"

"I wish I knew. I'll call you."

"It's a seller's market, Ellen. Don't put it off too long."

Downstairs, Ellen peeked in the bedroom to see if her father was awake. He was, sort of, lying on his back masticating at the ceiling, hands going *abracadabra abracadabra* against the bedspread. "Are you all right, Dad?" she asked.

"Fine! Fine!"

For Christ's sake, this was *not* fine. It was alarming and weird. "I'm just going out to the store. Do you want anything?"

"All-Bran!"

"Okay. Anything else?"

"Regular All-Bran, not the flakes."

"Okay. I'll be back shortly."

"Fine!"

She ran upstairs to google Parkinson's disease. *Diagnosis depends on the presence of one or more of the four most common motor symptoms: resting tremor, rigidity, postural instability, and bradykinesia.* Bradykinesia? Google said: *Slowing of movements, short shuffling steps, sudden stopping of an ongoing movement.*

As in the empty spoon at breakfast, poised in mid-air, and Jack staring at it in complete bewilderment.

She phoned again. "I talked to you about a half-hour ago? About my father? Jack McGinty."

"Oh, yes."

"He's got Parkinson's. For sure he's got Parkinson's. He shuffles. He sways. He's got bradykinesia. Now he's just lying there convulsing."

"Convulsing?" the receptionist squeaked.

"Pretty much. The thing is, we can't wait two weeks. Can't, can't, can't."

People said Ellen was pushy. All those years as a publicist, "pushy" was what she heard. That she knew how to get what she wanted. As if *not* knowing how to get what you wanted was better. Besides, had she really gotten what she wanted? What *did* she want?

She could hear the woman clicking the computer keys, checking the schedule one more time. "I'll squeeze you in next Wednesday morning at eight," she said.

"That's a week and a day away. Is it the best you can do?" Ellen asked.

"Yes."

"Then I thank you. I thank you from the bottom of my heart."

She made a list. All-Bran, bread, prunes. Poppycock! She wrote *Geriatric appt* on the calendar and under it, in big letters, *Flowers for the receptionist.*

No one could say Ms. Pushy Face didn't show her appreciation.

"I'VE started to forget things," she told Georgia on the phone that night. "People's names. Nouns. I stood in that airport saying 'petunia, petunia, petunia.' It took five minutes to come up with 'rose.'"

"How old are you?" Georgia asked.

"The same age as you," Ellen said. "Forty-six, right?"

In the background, Gary asked, "How old is Ellen?"

"The same age as me," Georgia told Gary, who was probably tucked up in bed beside her reading the parts of *Das Kapital* he hadn't memorized yet. He sounded very close and it was after eleven.

"You look better," Gary said.

"Tell him I heard that!"

Oops! No yelling. No yelling with an insomniac in the house. Besides, it wasn't strictly true. Georgia *was* better, no question— kinder, sweeter, more tactful, loyal. (Ellen too could claim loyal. She could sew that badge on her sash.) Unlike Georgia, Ellen updated her look now and then, and wore adult clothes and, despite her ambivalence about her body, she carried it front and centre. Georgia worked with children and it had rubbed off. Also, she seemed about sixty percent hair. Gary probably meant Ellen was *fatter* than Georgia, who had the advantage of being a former dancer.

"Am I fat?" she asked Georgia.

"Is Ellen fat?"

Gary of the meaty circumference was going to pronounce on Ellen's BMI? "Don't ask Gary! I don't care if *Gary* thinks I'm fat!"

"Ellen is hubba-hubba," she heard him say.

"Put that darling man on the line," Ellen said.

"Tell me about this long-lost father of yours, then let me go to sleep," Georgia said. "Some people have jobs."

Ellen finished recounting the airport episode of the day before, how she had failed to recognize her own father, he was such a wreck. She described the seven pointless hours in Emergency.

"They weren't pointless," Georgia pointed out. "You found out he might have Parkinson's. Were there any cute doctors?"

"It was horrible. The only good thing about yesterday was I realized I'm not that fat. Because the last time I saw my father? I was twenty-three and weighed one-ten. Well, I weighed one-forty, but thirty of that was Yo. I weigh one-fifty-three now. That's less than two pounds a year."

"What are you going to do?"

"Stop eating cheese. Just for a while. *Rip Van Winkle!*" Finally, the synapses connected. "That's who my father's like. He doesn't know anything that's happened to me in the last two decades. Tonight I found out he thought I was still with Larry."

"Do you know what's happened to your father?" Georgia asked.

"Yes," Ellen said, for surely Jack McGinty had plodded on exactly as he had before turning fifty on that disastrous July day, living in the house by Nose Hill, working until he retired from teaching high school math. After retirement, there would have been news watching, tub caulking, yardwork, perhaps some symphony going. Also pill taking. He probably ate dinner every Sunday with Moira and Charles and—she could barely remember the kids' names. Jenny, and the boy with a girl's name, Sandy. The oldest was something with a C. Charles. No, *he* was Charles. Her niece and nephews would be grown up now. They would be finished university and working as accountants or computer programmers.

"Does your sister even know he's here?" asked Georgia.

"Good question."

"You should phone her."

"I can't," Ellen said. "She hates me."

EARLIER that night, Tuesday, Ellen had gone down to tell her father dinner was ready. She'd waited, embarrassed, for him to finish in the bathroom, the steaks cooling on the plates upstairs, the little Parmesan popovers she'd taken so much trouble over, deflating.

He shuffled out, champing.

"Those laxatives are working, I guess," she said.

"Did you go to the store?"

39

"Yes. I bought steak. Alberta steak. I remembered you like it. Do you still?"

"Fine! Did you get toilet paper?"

"There's tons of toilet paper, Dad. Don't worry about that."

"Where's Larry?"

She froze at the bottom of the stairs. What was that called? The Brady Bunch. Bradybunchkinesia. What to say about Larry? He left me on your fiftieth birthday? If that day came up, she would die.

"Larry moved back to Cordova Island."

"You still have that place?"

They were climbing the stairs now, laborious and slow. She and Whatshisname. The guy who fell asleep under a tree for twenty years.

"No," Ellen said. "He built another house on the other side of the island, near Yolanda. We're divorced, Dad. He remarried."

She decided not to mention Larry's third wife, Amber, his child bride (as Ellen liked to call her), Yolanda's best friend, half Larry's age. It was too confusing and Jack seemed not to be listening anyway as he reached the top of the stairs and lurched single-mindedly toward his dinner, feeling all over the chair back before he sat.

"Didn't Moira tell you Larry and I divorced, Dad?"

"No."

"I used to run into Whatshername, who lived two blocks from us in Calgary. That poor girl with the moles? Remember? She was a friend of Moira's. She lives out here now. No doubt she kept Moira apprised of my goings-on."

"I don't listen to gossip."

"Thank you," Ellen said.

The cutlery shook in his hands but the fork steadied once he got it planted in the meat. Ellen was about to broach the subject again—*why are you here?*—when both utensils shot out of his grasp and the entire steak skidded off the plate and onto the tablecloth, trailing all its juices.

She sprang up. "How long have you been like this? How long?"

He hung his head, a bloom on a parched plant. "A couple of months."

"*Months?* Why didn't Moira help you? Is that why you came? For help? I'd like to kill her! Leave it! Let me cut it! What was I thinking? Steak! What an idiot!"

She cubed the meat savagely, scarring her sister for life. Again. Then, flinging the knife and fork down, she wept hot, self-hating tears into her napkin.

"I'm sorry," Jack said.

"What for? *I'm* sorry. Can you eat? What about your tongue? I forgot."

"It's fine."

"Eat then." She blew her nose and poked at the popover, which was a letdown, and cold.

When he finally got some steak in his mouth, the unceasing jaw movements blended heroically with the chewing. He swallowed, paused, started the whole agonizing procedure again.

"Who's Yolanda?"

So he had been listening.

"My daughter," Ellen said.

"It was another girl then?"

"A girl. Yes."

He didn't ask any more questions and neither did Ellen. It was like those meals after her mother died, chewing and scraping the only sounds, certainly no small talk, no big talk, no talking back.

41

Ellen could have talked back but there was nothing to talk back to. The angel of silence had claimed her mother's chair. How hard it was for Jack to eat off that vacillating fork now, what heartbreaking effort it took just to get through the meal.

Maybe then as well.

SHE popped a Zopiclone from her own stash and closed her bedroom door. Every night she would need to do this or she wouldn't survive until his Wednesday appointment.

When the alarm rang the next morning, she felt coated in a sticky residue of unease, as though she'd slept through something important, something everyone but her knew. Like when she found out Larry had been cheating.

Her father was up, his dishes already in the sink, which she took as a good sign. Also, the file folders spread across the table.

Ellen put on the coffee. "I was thinking last night." During the five minutes before she plunged headlong into dreamless oblivion. "Would you like to meet Yolanda? And—surprise!—your great-grandson? They could come over on the ferry if Yo feels up to the trip. She's pregnant again."

Under Jack's crazy eyebrows, the veins in his eyes were like cracks in a china cup. "Do you have a lawyer?"

The coffee machine started dribbling, reminding Ellen, as always, of an imbecile child in a Southern novel. "I did. Once upon a time. Why? Now can you tell me what's going on?"

It was all in the folders. The Power of Attorney. He was making his bank accounts joint.

"With me?" Ellen said. "What for?"

"It's shutting down," he said.

"What is?"

"My whole system's shutting down."

"You're constipated," Ellen said. "Wednesday you'll see the doctor. Unless you want to go back to Emerg." She hoped he didn't.

"We have to get this done," Jack said. "Before it's too late."

Oh God, thought Ellen. Coffee, coffee. She poured them both a mug and, after a large swig to brace herself, began again. "Why aren't you doing this with Moira?"

"She's married to that idiot! This is all his fault!"

"Charles? What did he do?"

"He got on the computer and looked things up! He said I didn't need this medication! I didn't need that one! Then Moira got involved! They're in cahoots with my doctor! Now my system's shutting down!"

43

"Can't you wait until your appointment? They'll sort out your meds at the clinic."

Jack couldn't wait, so Ellen opened the folders. He banked like a squirrel with a half-dozen accounts in different institutions. After an hour phoning, she managed to schedule all the appointments and find a Yellow Pages lawyer whose name she liked. Lawyers, wine, men—she chose with her ear and gut, despite the mixed results. Meanwhile, Jack paced the kitchen, from chair back to chair back, chewing the air.

Moira, of course, would take this as a threat. If only Ellen had her e-mail address, Moira wouldn't have to talk to her, or even reply if she didn't want to.

"Do you have Moira's e-mail?" she asked.

"Don't bring her into this," Jack barked.

Then, a horrible thought. "You're not changing your will, are you?" Moira would kill Ellen if she inherited anything.

"It's the same will," he said. "Fifty-fifty."

"Dad," said Ellen, cringing. "Don't. I don't deserve it."

"Why not? It wasn't your fault. It was that idiot, Charles."

HE blamed Charles. Fine, thought Ellen, let Charles be the scape-goat. What was Charles to her? Nothing, despite the fact that she'd slept with him. Well, not slept. She hadn't even closed her eyes.

Oh Christ. She wasn't going to get off as easy as that. She had a conscience (disputed by Moira), and she couldn't let it stand. How to set her father right, though? She could hardly give him the sordid details of the day he turned fifty, when, inconveniently, Ellen had been seven and a half months pregnant with Yolanda, and Mimi terribly two.

While her father vibrated on his bed the rest of Wednesday, Ellen drove to Lonsdale Quay for dried porcini and a pound of oys-ter mushrooms, singing "The Sunny Side of the Street" *fortissimo*. She was giddy. Giddy with happiness. Because he blamed Charles, not Ellen. Because everything was fifty-fifty. Not the money. Ellen didn't give a damn about the money. Wine. Nice crusty bread. She waltzed over to the cheese kiosk, remembered she was fat, and turned away.

His love, equally divided. Right down the middle. That's why he came.

Something soft for a sore tongue. Something that would stick to an unsteady spoon.

But her risotto, a lump of grey goo on his plate, barely regis-tered with Jack McGinty that night. He didn't care what he ate, Ellen realized. He probably didn't even taste it. Afterward, he heaved himself out of the chair while Ellen dashed to the counter for the can.

44

"Look, Dad! Poppycock!"

"Fine! What time are we leaving in the morning?"

"About nine."

He thanked her for the meal and headed back downstairs, the Poppycock under his arm.

He loves me, Ellen thought. My father loves me.

She heard the can strike the carpeted stair, then bounce the rest of the way down, rattling all the way.

"Of course he does," said Georgia when Ellen phoned her, the only person who knew that Ellen's father had re-entered her life.

He'd come in through a door labelled Heartbreaking Loss. Ellen could take that sign down now, but she didn't want to tell Yo and Mimi just yet. Not until Jack was in better shape.

In the background, Gary asked Georgia, "Did she meet somebody?"

"Her *father* loves her."

That night, despite her father's prowlings, Ellen resisted the Zopiclone. So what if she was strung-out tomorrow? How often did this zingy feeling come along? She lay in bed basking in the zing and, the next day, exhausted, cheerful, utterly magnanimous in downtown traffic, she chauffeured Jack from appointment to appointment, meeting all those boring bankers, signing all those tedious forms. So illegible was his signature, he may as well have signed with the pen between his teeth. Even when Evelyn Letendre turned out to be less sympathetic than her name, Ellen shrugged it off. She was forgiven! Her father, her one remaining parent, loved her!

"Why didn't you call me before?" Ellen asked in the car.

"What?"

"What took you so long?"

45

He put a shaking hand over his face. "I thought you would call me."

"I did! I did call you! You hung up!"

"Did I? Your sister must have been there. You should have called again."

All these years she'd thought he hated her for what she'd done to Moira, he'd merely been cowed. He loved her, and Ellen felt all that love now, retroactively, felt dunked in it, slathered with it, emolliated with the parental caring she had longed for all this time. Though not when she looked over at him in the passenger seat, head bowed, fingers rolling imaginary pills. Then she felt sorrowful and sick.

"Where's the ocean?" He asked this out of the blue not five minutes after they had crossed the Lions Gate Bridge, where, if he'd looked up, he would have seen the waters of Burrard Inlet diligently lapping at the edges of the city. Since his arrival three days ago, there had been nothing but view-obfuscating drizzle. Driving around in the car, he'd mainly focused on his lap.

"You may as well see it if you're here. How about we go down to Lonsdale Quay tomorrow? We could even take the SeaBus across to downtown. For fun. If you're feeling up to it."

He lifted his head now, interested in something for the first time. Another good sign. "SeaBus? You mean a ferry?"

"Sort of."

He wanted to go right now.

"You're too tired, Dad. I can tell. And you must be starving."

He insisted, so Ellen took the Lonsdale exit. They could have lunch at the Quay.

But no sooner had she parked and got him out of the car than he took a cursory glance around and changed his mind.

"Take me home," he said.

• • •

WHILE the disintegration of Ellen and Larry's marriage took place in one day on the July long weekend at Moira's in Calgary, the marriage itself lasted two and a half years, most of them spent on Cordova Island because land off the grid was cheap and they could live cheaply on it while Larry wrote his plays.

Cordova Island was also where Ellen discovered pottery. She'd been pregnant with Mimi when they first arrived and needed an outlet herself. The island so teemed with creative types that you didn't really fit in unless you batiked, or made driftwood furniture, or wove lampshades out of kelp. Ellen took lessons with an island potter, Mary Bourne, who encouraged her. Apparently Ellen had an instinctive feel for the possibilities of clay, not to mention strong hands. It made her ludicrously happy to take what was essentially a lump of dirt and transform it into something useful.

But along came Mimi, demanding Ellen's full attention. When Ellen wasn't tending to the baby, or the garden, or the chickens, or milking Stinky, the goat, she was scrubbing diapers against the painful corrugations of a washboard. Water warmed continuously in a vat on the wood stove for this purpose. Larry saw to that at least—chopping the wood and exorcising his dramaturgical frustrations at the same time. This division of labour worked well for him. Ellen, though, made little progress in her craft after giving birth. She carted the same box of pots and knick-knacks down to the Cordova Island Saturday market, stationing herself behind her foldable card table spread with her amateur wares, Mimi in a sling across her chest, nursing on demand. The tourists would come, though not that many. Most made the difficult trip for a different kind of pot.

With her second pregnancy, it became too much. A wave of morning sickness hit and she would stagger outside and retch in

47

the grass because the outhouse was too far. "Please, Larry," she would say, supplicating with chapped hands. "I just can't do it this way anymore."

Larry liked island life. They would probably have stayed, except that something happened that entirely changed their lives.

They'd been subsisting on an allowance from Esther, Larry's mother, and the modest royalties of one of his plays, *Talking Stick*, the one that had won a Jessie and a Chalmers award and had even enjoyed a short run in an L.A. little theatre. A producer saw the L.A. show and contacted Larry through his agent, offering to fly him down to talk about some projects he needed writers like Larry Silver for.

Larry used the diaper water to shave off his beard. "Oh my God," Ellen told him afterward. "You looked like a rabbi. I never noticed."

He kept the ponytail, but when he got back a week later, the first thing he did was get Ellen to cut it off.

"So we're moving?" she said.

They put the Cordova Island cabin on the market, bought the house on the North Shore, Larry's future earnings easily qualifying them for a mortgage. He already had script meetings, so it was up to Ellen to pack and petition friends to take the animals. After L.A., Larry would fly to Florida to visit his mother for a few days. He'd join Ellen and Mimi in Calgary for Jack McGinty's fiftieth birthday party on the July long weekend.

By then Ellen had entered the most frustrating phase of pregnancy, when desire supplanted nausea. This desire, she knew from carrying Mimi, would only increase in direct proportion to her swelling.

"Some men find pregnant women incredibly sexy," she told Larry. "They place ads in the paper. That's what they want."

"And some men think they look like a certain farm animal."

Larry gave her permission to answer an ad. He had a TV pilot to write.

"It's *your* throbbing cock I want inside me," she whispered.

Larry said, "Nice try."

The dreams were shocking. Larry may not have desired congress with an animal, but Ellen had it with a grotesque cliché of a bull, a great heaving beast with a bracelet through its nose. Weirdly, she was off the ground, clinging to its underside, somehow hanging on. Even Tom Green, the captain of the Cordova Island ferry, made an appearance. About sixty with stumpy legs, he was a physically unappealing man. Ellen couldn't meet his eye when she and Mimi boarded to cross to the mainland and catch their flight. Troll-like Tom lifted Mimi off the dock so gently. Ellen, remembering his way with her the night before, blushed.

49

Even after they touched down at the Calgary airport, Southern Alberta seemed one vast cloud-piled sky. Ellen could see things in those clouds like she used to as a child. Now though, instead of elephants and ducks, there were clefted buttocks, pillowy vulvas.

Cocks.

The two sisters, who had only been grudgingly in touch since Ellen left home, were now grown women with something in common—husbands and children. Moira, three years older than Ellen, already seemed middle-aged with her mannish, no-nonsense haircut and her golf clothes. In Alberta, they added fluoride to the water system, a practice scientifically linked to Conservative values. Or so Ellen joked. But now Moira was being exceptionally solicitous to her frazzled, hippy sister. She seemed to want to make up for their soured adolescence.

"You look tired, Ellen," she said the afternoon they arrived.

"I'm hot. I'm preggers."

"Go lie down. Jenny and Sandy will watch Mimi."

So thoughtful! Now Ellen could masturbate.

They'd come a few days before the big birthday party specifically for the cousins to acquaint. Moira's younger two doted on Mimi, petting her wispy hair and kissing her fairy hands. With all the attention lavished on her, Mimi's rages simply ceased.

The eldest boy was uninterested. He read a lot and wore braces rigged out with coloured rubber bands. Something in the way the elastics stretched and retracted unnerved Ellen. It was exactly the sort of detail her subconscious might erotically repurpose.

Desperate, she phoned Larry in Florida and got his mother.

"Out where, Esther?" she asked.

"At the grocery store. Is there a message?"

"Just tell him I called. He'll know what it's about."

She didn't hear back until the next day, when Larry delivered the frustrating news that his mother had twisted her ankle. On purpose, Ellen assumed. He was staying an extra day to drive her to her appointments.

"How about I take the extension in the bedroom?"

"Oh, please," Larry said.

Calvin. That was the eldest boy's name. Thankfully he stayed away at night. It was his father who ventured into the lurid playroom of Ellen's dreams. Soft-spoken, uxorious, not-her-type-at-all Charles. Charles who was about as sexy as Tom Green.

But look how Tom Green had pleased her!

• • •

AND now Jack McGinty had been staying with Ellen in North Vancouver for five days. Friday, the morning after the banking marathon, Ellen found mail for him in her box, several pieces, each with a yellow sticker indicating it had been officially redirected. How odd, she thought. When he first phoned, he'd asked for her address even though she'd offered to pick him up. Did he want to stay?

Maybe she wouldn't sell the house. Maybe she'd keep it and live here with her father. If he had Parkinson's disease, she would have to. It wasn't as though he was any trouble. He only came upstairs to eat and apologize for being so much trouble.

She took his mail downstairs. The bedroom door was closed. She'd already seen his breakfast dishes in the sink, heard the whir of the shaver and the higher-pitched whir of the electric toothbrush. Now all was quiet so, leaving his mail on the seat of the stationary bicycle, she went to augment his toilet paper from her Costco hoard.

Ack! Splashed all over the bathroom mirror, *brown flecks*. On closer inspection it turned out to be All-Bran flung off the toothbrush. She cleaned the mirror. All the while it niggled at her that the bedroom door had never been closed before.

"Dad?"

She opened the door and looked in, saw the empty bed tidily made with shaking hands. On the dresser lay his note.

I am sorry. Love, Dad

It took a few minutes to figure out where he might have gone. She remembered the day before, his head rearing up at the word *SeaBus*, and then she was flooring it down Lonsdale Avenue in the rain, swearing and honking, fingering everybody, arriving just in

51

time to see her father at the ticket counter fumbling with his wallet. He acted like he didn't even know her, this coatless Fury, his own daughter.

"What did you mean by that note?"

The jaw wagged.

"I'll go with you." She turned to the girl behind the counter. "Two tickets."

Jack McGinty walked away. "Where are you going?" Ellen shouted. "Come back here right now!"

"What's your problem, lady?" the girl asked.

Ellen swept after him, took his arm less than gently. Outside the terminal, she pulled him in the direction of the car. He almost stumbled, which set Ellen shrieking.

"What were you going to do that you would leave me that note? Run away? In this condition? Where?"

Strangers had stopped to watch. Some of them circled Ellen and Jack McGinty, umbrellas open, trying to decide whether or not to intervene.

The SeaBus. The ocean. The ocean. Then she knew.

"No, Dad. You weren't going to do that. There isn't any deck or anything."

She began to wail. "If I take you to the hospital, will you tell them what you planned to do? Will you? Because then they'll have to help you."

And that was what happened, five long days after he arrived, a bloodied, tremoring mess.

It felt like five months to Ellen, who, after another entire day spent in Emergency, staggered into her dark house alone and turned on all the lights.

She was wresting the cork from the wine bottle, about to make an earnest start on it, when the doorbell rang. Too exhausted to think, she answered it.

Two people with blacked-out eye sockets stood on her porch. For mouths, crazy crimson gashes.

Halloween. She'd completely forgotten.

"Do you think he really would have done it?" Georgia asked the next day on the phone.

It was in his eyes already, something dead in the cracked bottom of the china cup.

Ellen said, "I told the admitting clerk he was suicidal. That he planned to throw himself off the SeaBus. She said to let him speak for himself."

"And?"

"He nodded."

"I'm so sorry," Georgia said and, for once, Gary, who was probably right there listening, butted out.

"Then this inexplicable behaviour once he gets admitted. He turns all jolly, chatting up the nurses, telling his life story. Things I'd never heard. After the nurse leaves, I explode, of course. 'What do you mean you're fine? Are you fine? Did you come here because you're fine? If you're fine, they'll send us home and, frankly, Dad, I don't know what to do with you.'"

Georgia produced the sympathetic clucks she could always be counted on to produce.

He had done exactly the same thing with the beautiful red-sweatered psychiatrist with the Polish name. This time Ellen had interrupted the cheerful chit-chat. "Am I going to get a chance to talk?"

They left Jack and headed down the stretcher-jammed corridor.

"Old people groaning," she told Georgia. "People covered in blood." She thought of the pair at her front door. "Blind, teeth kicked in."

"No!" Georgia cried.

"I was already telling the whole story to Dr. Polska, begging for her help. Meanwhile, all those eyes were saying, 'Help us too!' Why is there so much suffering, Georgia?"

"Oh, Ellen. I don't know."

They found the room—bare of wall, ugly of chair—whose purpose, Ellen surmised, was to assemble loved ones for the delivery of devastating prognoses.

The doctor was committing Jack McGinty.

"What do you mean committing?" Ellen asked. "I thought he had Parkinson's."

YET Ellen McGinty herself was no stranger to mental distress. She'd had her own brushes with despair. Her mother's death, for example, when Ellen was at an impressionable, confused age. And when Larry left her, Larry with whom she'd been ruinously in love, for whom she'd changed her name because from the moment she met him she'd wished only to expunge her McGintyness and let Larry plate her very essence, which was restless and hungry to live.

And Mimi! Miss Teen Druggy, Lady Permastone. She might as well have jammed a stick of dynamite between Ellen's ribs, blown her heart right out of her chest, then tap-danced across the bloody, strewn bits.

"At least you have a mother to hate!" Ellen used to yell at her.

Yes, Ellen had been wretched and sometimes she hadn't wanted to get out of bed, sometimes hadn't, but made the thousand phone calls that put the food on the table *from* her bed, weeping in between them. But now when she thought of her father's tremors, the castanet of his jaws, she understood that something black had seized his every fibre and was shaking him from the inside.

Imagine, she thought. Imagine *always* coming home to darkness.

The day after he was committed, the city descended bleakly into November. All Souls' Day, Day of the Dead. Ellen stood at the window, depressed—well, not really, she knew now—sad, hungover, staring at the forbearing cedars dripping in the yard. Her father had only just returned and already he was lost to her again.

Later in the afternoon she visited his tiny cupboard of a room in the psychiatric assessment ward. While he quivered silently in his bed, Ellen perched on the chair with a fruit basket in her lap. Now that she knew what was the matter with him, it seemed so obvious.

"I still miss Mom," she told him. "Every single day. There are so many things I wish I could have talked to her about. Sometimes I do talk to her. Sometimes she even answers. Once I was complaining about Mimi. You know what she said? She said, 'She's just like you were.' I heard her, clear as anything."

Ellen looked over at her father. His eyes had rolled back in his head, like she'd shot him.

Earlier, walking into the hospital, Ellen had tripped. Some of the fruit had spilled out of the basket. She got up now and went over to the little basin in the corner, filled it with soapy water. Every piece of fruit she washed then dried with paper towels.

The human heart is about the size of your fist. Where had she learned that? About the size of a Macintosh apple, all dented and bruised to mush.

"He's there, isn't he?"

This was Wednesday, the day Jack McGinty was supposed to see the geriatric specialist. Ellen had just left a message cancelling the appointment she'd finagled. Assuming it was the clinic calling back, she'd answered without looking at the call display.

Moira said, "I thought you were going to stay out of our lives. I thought you were going to leave us alone. What do you mean by this? You are not to interfere! Do you hear me? You are not to get involved! Put him on the line! Put him on right now!"

"He's not here."

"Liar! We all still hate you!"

Her sister breathed hard, catching her breath for the next round.

"How do you really feel, Moira?" Ellen asked.

Moira hung up.

But now Ellen had the number, not unlisted at all, right there on the call display.

Jack McGinty's fiftieth birthday party, August 2, 1983. Larry had insisted on cabbing from the airport.

"How much is that going to cost?" Ellen had asked him on the phone, before remembering that Larry was making real money now.

She wanted to pick him up. She wanted to get out of her sister's house and away from Charles.

In her dream the night before, she'd encountered Charles

somewhere innocuous, the backyard or the garage. He was doing something with his hands—what, she couldn't tell. In waking life Charles's hobby was making and flying model airplanes. That was the boyish kind of man he was, the kind Larry scorned. In fact, she dreaded that Charles would invite Larry to fly one of his planes and that Larry would pretend enthusiasm and later mock his brother-in-law in a play, or worse now, in a television sit-com that Moira and Charles would be more likely to see. Would Larry ever write another play? She hoped so. The best of him came out in his work, the part she loved best, the humour and the tenderness. The best went to the play, and what remained was Ellen's.

In the dream, Charles must have been working on a model, but as the details were released to Ellen intermittently throughout the morning in mortifyingly erotic little fragments, the toy plane eventually disappeared and only the screwdriver remained.

"For God's sake," Ellen muttered to herself.

Then even the screwdriver vanished and she and Charles were entangled in coitus. It was very, very good, exquisite even. Because of his cock. There was something special about Charles's cock, something ecstasy-inducing, but Ellen couldn't remember what. In the kitchen kneading raw onion and garlic into a bowl of ground beef, she both wanted to remember, because she was curious, and didn't.

At just that moment, with Ellen torn between curiosity and embarrassment, in strolled Charles. Ellen yelped, tossed her head so her braid swung over her shoulder, then fled, awkwardly, her smocked belly leading the way to the bedroom, her arms up—*don't shoot!*—because of the hamburger stuck all over her hands.

She closed the door with her hip. She'd only been standing there

57

a second when a car pulled up outside. The cab. Mimi, playing in the front yard in an inflatable pool with her cousins, started singing, "Dada, dada, dada!" Ellen heard her through the window and, relieved, opened the door again.

Charles! Right there in the hall. He was a tall, pointily featured man who wore dress socks with sandals, and now this look of wounded bafflement. Ellen brushed past him.

"Ellen?" Charles bleated.

She ducked into the bathroom.

With Yolanda performing a vigorous *in utero* callisthenic routine, Ellen scrubbed the E. coli off her hands. She heard everyone troop inside, Moira directing Larry to the spare bedroom, asking about the trip, and the besotted cousins chasing Mimi back outside under the suggestively clouded sky.

One of the not-best things about Larry was his moodiness. Later, after Ellen started in publicity, she came to realize that most artists walk a zigzag between pathetically insecure and egomaniacal, except for the really good ones, who are quite normal. That day, preventing Larry from acting like an asshole with her sister overrode her fear of running into Charles. She stepped into the hall again and, thankfully, he was gone.

"Baby," she said from the spare room doorway.

Larry was sitting on the bed talking to Moira. He looked up at Ellen, cringed. He'd forgotten she was pregnant, just like she'd forgotten he'd cut his hair and shaved. But while he looked better for this—tanned, dark curls held back by sunglasses on top of his head, a linen suit jacket she'd never seen before over a T-shirt she'd also never seen—after a ten-day separation Ellen only looked more of the barnyard.

Ellen came over and they kissed, her dissatisfied tongue stirring in her mouth. A good little tongue, tucked behind her teeth. Then she remembered the hamburger on the counter.

"I'll put it way," Moira volunteered.

As soon as Moira was out of the room, Larry stood and emptied his pockets onto the bureau. He tossed the linen jacket on the bed.

"This is nice," Ellen said, sitting carefully beside the jacket, but not touching it lest she wrinkle it further. It was hard to believe that Larry had purchased this jacket, but of course he had meetings. He couldn't schlep his scripts around L.A. dressed like a hobo.

She settled on her side and arranged her top so as not to look like a nursing sow. Or a cow. Larry hadn't specified which farm animal. "How was the trip?"

"Exhausting," Larry said. He stripped while Ellen watched.

"How's your mother?"

"Good."

"It wasn't broken?"

"What? No. Sprained."

"Come here," she said.

"I really need a shower. Where is it?"

"Down the hall."

How quickly showers became essential when for two winters he had uncomplainingly sponge-bathed in diaper water. When in summer, they'd hooked a hose to a tree.

Larry stepped out of his jeans and there it was, his cock, so longed-for and pink, seemingly innocent, like something you'd cradle in your palm and feed from a dropper. He moved toward the door. Ellen gestured severely to the clean towels folded nearby on a chair and Larry, smiling for the first time, covered his nakedness and left.

59

And she remembered what was so special about Charles. He had two.

Two cocks.

She got off the bed, cumbersomely, and began to gather Larry's clothes off the floor, also cumbersomely. She sniffed the T-shirt, but it hadn't absorbed his scent, not even in the armpits, which smelled like deodorant. Honestly, though, she was weary of pong. She wiped the door handle with a tissue, then tidied the bureau strewn with his passport and wallet and various paper scraps including his boarding pass, which she looked at twice before the inconsistency registered.

He returned, hair dripping, face shiny from Moira's Lady Schick. Ellen was still holding the boarding pass. Strangely, she wasn't angry, not yet.

"You didn't even go to Florida. Is that why you didn't want me to pick you up?"

Larry, using the towel from around his waist to dry his hair, looked like an abashed schoolboy. "I was going to tell you, babe. Really. I just thought that we should get through this party first. Can we?"

So for the first time in more than twenty years, Ellen phoned her sister Moira. She phoned in the middle of the day, when everyone was likely to be at work. "The good news is they've already moved him to this other ward. For geriatric cases. It's much, much better."

In the psychiatric assessment ward all the other patients had been young. Jack McGinty, who would not leave his cupboard, had seemed worse off than them, except when Ellen ventured to the open kitchen to make herself a cup of tea and saw all the apocalyptic drawings fixed to the fridge door with ladybug magnets.

Someone has spent the last thirty years trying to make me crazy and they have more or less succeeded!!!!

But yesterday the friendly nurse with all the piercings told her Jack McGinty was upstairs in the Geriatric Psychiatric Centre. Ellen found her father there, glassy-eyed but miraculously sitting up.

"Oh!" she said.

"They gave me something last night, I don't know what. It sure worked."

For the first time in nine weeks, he'd slept more than two consecutive hours.

When Jack McGinty was better, Ellen told Moira's voice mail, she would put him on a plane to Calgary, if that was what he wanted. But first she needed to know what had happened to reduce him to such a state. No doubt that would set Moira screeching. She also apprised her sister of the Power of Attorney, the joint accounts, the unchanged will, so Ellen wouldn't be accused of anything underhanded. It took three calls to say all this because she kept getting cut off.

"What do you mean by accusing us?" Moira called back to yell, not screech. (The hatred in her sister's voice had diminished several decibels from that first call.) "Who's been looking after him for the last twenty years? Not *you*, that's for sure."

"I would have," Ellen said meekly, "if someone had told me I was allowed to."

Moira huffed.

"You can't have it both ways, Moira. You can't expel me from the family then say I never helped."

"We don't want anything to do with you."

"I understand and respect that. And let me say one more time that I'm sorry. I said it then. I wrote you fifty letters. I'm saying it now. I'm sorry. But the fact is, Dad's here. If we could cooperate on this? That would be big of you. Huge. I'll never ask for anything else."

"You took everything already," Moira said.

"Did I? I mean, Moira, come on. Are you still married to Charles? Dad says you are. Am I married to Larry? No. I'm married to nobody."

Ellen took off her glasses and squeezed the bridge of her nose. She hoped she didn't sound pathetic or manipulative. She was startled by how matter-of-factly she had said it. *I'm married to nobody.* She flinched, but she didn't howl.

62

A long pause followed. Ellen expected Moira to hang up, but she didn't. She let Ellen sit alone with her pain. Eventually it passed, like a contraction.

"How's Mimi?" she finally asked.

"Good."

"I heard she got into drugs."

Ellen sighed. "She's fine now. She's in Toronto. She's a dancer. Yolanda has a five-year-old. There's another on the way."

"Jenny had a baby too! Finally!"

Ellen looked at her watch. Four minutes and Moira was still on the line.

A whole team combined forces to get Jack McGinty back to normal—psychiatrist, psychiatric resident, social worker, O.T., not to mention the cheerful army of nurses in their coloured Crocs, dispensing laxatives. And Ellen McGinty, who came twice a week. With this gap of days between visits, his improvement showed; the jaw movements grew less ferocious, his hands a little steadier. These were withdrawal symptoms, Dr. Tung (older, Chinese, moderately cute, she noted for when Georgia asked) explained. *Nortriptyline, Felodipine, Quetiapine, Loxapine.* Ellen knew she should try to understand the pharmacology, but after this ordeal, she wasn't going to suggest taking him off anything.

Soon Jack was taking his meals in the dining room. One afternoon she found him there with three crones, the women slouched at one end of the long table, walkers and canes stationed nearby, Jack at the other suddenly seeming the junior to everyone, flush-faced and alert, a box of tissues within reach. He brightened when he saw Ellen and she reciprocated.

"You've got mail." She waved it.

It was a knife-free ward so she used the handle of a plastic spoon to slit the envelopes. The first contained a cheque.

"It's a reimbursement from my drug plan," he said.

"You're rich," Ellen said.

"Put it in the TD account."

Ellen tucked the cheque back in the envelope and wrote *TD* on it. Jack blew his nose.

"Do you have a cold?" she asked.

"I'm fine." He handed her the tissue.

"I should deposit this too?"

"Moira called. Tell her not to call here anymore. It's long distance. I'm fine. Tell her not to come."

"She's coming here?" Ellen said, astonished.

"I don't want her to. I'm fine."

"She told me Charles had nothing to do with switching your meds. She says it was her. She thought it was time someone updated them."

"It was *Charles!*"

Ellen leaned away from her father's vehemence. Just then a silver-haired man with a showy belt buckle breezed through to announce gold was up. The three crones did not react.

"Thinks he's a big investor," Jack whispered. "Hogs the TV. Always checking his stocks." He passed her the cable bill. "Pay that."

"Please?" Ellen hinted.

How annoying Jack was today, she thought as she nosed the car out of the hospital parking lot into rush-hour traffic. Do this, do that. Empty the dishwasher. Clean your room. His old, order-barking self. What was she, his secretary? And why did he keep blaming Charles? Poor Charles.

64

It got dark so early now. Clouds, shiftless, loitered over the city, accumulating moisture, then sidled off to drop their load on the North Shore. After she sold the house she was going to move into a mirrored downtown tower high above all weather systems. She'd get rid of the car too, but in the meantime here she was, peering through the liquid smear, hoping vainly to merge onto the highway.

She Morse-coded with the brake lights: *dot dot dash dot - dot dot dash*. F.U. Would no one let her in? Ever?

Finally, one of those yacht-sized American guzzlers slowed. Ellen gunned it, merged, then waved broadly to communicate her thanks. All she could see of her rescuer in her rear-view mirror was white hair.

He was old. Old and chivalrous.

YES, Jack McGinty was on the mend. He was becoming himself again—brusque, taciturn, but not unloving, it turned out. Growing up, Ellen had misinterpreted his stiffness. She felt profoundly sorry for him now, for how do you express love when in a perpetual state of emotional incapacitation? Emoting for her was effortless. The opposite—holding her feelings inside—impossible. Even thinking of it made her curl up in a cramping ball.

No laxative for that.

He'd loved her mother, that was for sure, and on his fiftieth birthday he'd still looked young. Why didn't he remarry, she'd wondered that summer when she took Mimi to see him in the Nose Hill house.

Yet just a few days later, when Jack showed up for his party, Ellen barely glanced at the guest of honour. She'd just found out that Larry already had an L.A. mistress. She didn't know yet that he'd also bedded half the female population of Cordova Island, including friends of hers. Larry would tell her that later, when she insisted their actions cancelled each other out—what Larry had done with that slut was equal to what Ellen had done with Charles—so they should just forgive and forget and get on with their marriage.

Larry didn't want to. He didn't want to be married to Ellen anymore.

When her father came through Moira's door the day of the party, Ellen hugged him. Her belly, taut with life, pushed into his and he recoiled. Larry stepped forward and shook Jack's hand, clasped it warmly, more warmly than he ever had before because he'd probably never see the man again.

"Happy birthday, Jack," he said.

Moira touched Ellen's shoulder, beckoned. In a trance, Ellen followed.

"What's wrong?" Moira asked.

65

Instinctively, Ellen clutched her unborn child. "What do you mean?"

"Charles thinks you're mad at him."

The dream, forgotten in her shock, came back, the two cocks and their mysterious configuration. Side by side, or forked with a single shaft for the two heads?

"I'm not mad," said Ellen, who was just now thawing, feeling the first tingles of a stupendous rage.

"Did he do something?" Moira asked.

"No!"

"So go talk to him."

"I don't want to talk to him!"

"You *are* mad!" Moira said. "You seem really mad. What did he do?"

"Nothing!"

Ellen left Moira in the living room and went to find Mimi, who was in the backyard on her faithless father's lap, stroking his smooth face. All her life Mimi had had his long beard to tug and scratch; now he was a new, fascinating toy. Jack sat in the matching Muskoka chair, Charles on the swinging love seat with the awning because he sunburned easily, the three men with beers already in their clasp, failing at small talk. Ellen came across the grass in her bare feet, feeling exactly how Larry thought she ought to feel, like a cow that had broken through a dozen suburban fences to end up here.

Jack and Charles stood. Charles said, "I'll get you a chair, Ellen." He sounded bashful and eager to set things right.

"I'll sit here beside you." She smiled at him. It must have been an evil smile because he dropped his gaze in confusion. As the love seat set sail under them, a bit of urine gushed from her. Still no one spoke except Mimi, cooing, "Dada soft, Dada soft . . ."

Ellen stared desperately at Larry, but he refused to meet her eye. Then, without really meaning to, she glanced at her brother-in-law's crotch where the khaki fabric was bunched up. Another gush. She was turning to liquid, the milk collecting in her readying breasts, the crotch of her panties dampening even more.

"Oh God!" she cried, and finally, Larry looked at her. Coldly. A warning. She struggled to get up, but couldn't with the love seat swaying.

Charles sprang to his feet and offered his hand.

Ellen passed Moira as she stumbled through the kitchen. "Charles, did you light the briquettes?" Moira asked.

In the bedroom, Ellen shut the door and, leaning against it, tried not to scream.

On the other side, Moira said, "Go in and talk to her. Go. Are the briquettes lit?"

Charles knocked. Ellen felt it in her back, his timid tapping sending out ripples of lust, and this combination—lust and fury—propelled her to the middle of the room. "Yes?"

Pink with embarrassment, or sunburn, Charles entered.

"Close the door," Ellen said, and he closed the door.

"Come here."

He came over. Why didn't I fall for this kind of man, Ellen thought, the kind who does everything you ask?

"I dreamed about you," she said.

"You did?"

She seized his ears and drew him angrily to her mouth. Naughty, naughty tongue. And Charles, in his astonishment, kissed her back.

Ellen snatched his hand, like she would snatch Mimi's away from something dangerous. But Charles was allowed and she

67

employed him, used his hand the way she'd been forced these last months to use her own. He let her, then took over, kneading her breasts, stroking her round belly, a fortune teller fondling the future. He touched her wet cunt through her clothes and said her name.

She unbuttoned his shorts.

"Ellen?"

"Shh." She yanked the shorts down hard, like she did with Mimi when trying to get at a soggy diaper. An erection bulged in the briefs, singularly, and as Ellen freed it from the elastic waistband, she used her other hand to wriggle out of her shorts, urgently, like in the dream. Like she was in the grip of a furious maenadic ritual, Charles backing away, she moving forward until she trapped him against the dresser.

68

"I can't, Ellen, I can't."

She ground against him. He was panting, she was panting, Ellen naked below the waist except for her underwear ringing one ankle, pulling on his ordinary cock like it was an elastic she was stretching out long, long, and bringing back. Between them, Yolanda floated upside down.

"I can't," Charles groaned. "Your stomach. You're too big."

Ellen sank to all fours, tugged his leg. He whimpered as he knelt. "I want to. But we shouldn't."

Ellen shoved him onto his back and, straddling him, pushed down once, hard, hating Larry.

"Oh, Ellen," Charles whispered. "*Vroom. Vroom.*"

On the third or fourth push, Ellen realized he had withered and was already out of gas. He scrambled out from under her, sat there glistening and limp in his remorse. Ellen had not experienced a release of any kind, but Charles was crying.

"I'm sorry. I'm so sorry. You're pregnant and everything."

"Don't tell Moira," she said, though she had every intention of telling Larry.

WHILE Jack McGinty was still in hospital, Ellen called Brad Wheeler-Dealer. December wasn't the best month to put a house on the market, what could they do?

Ellen hadn't actually met Brad in person, had only seen him smiling boyishly out of bus shelters. (She'd picked him for his name, because he sounded like he would rake in the biggest bucks.)

He showed up the next day to do the walk-through. "This lino, Ellen? If you replace it with cork or ceramic, you'll recoup the expense tenfold, I guarantee it. Same for the cabinets."

"I should redo my kitchen for a stranger? I don't know, Brad."

He'd already fixed sticky notes to half the furniture, little yellow flags that meant *get rid of it*.

She felt angry. Why? If, over the years, she'd learned a thing or two about herself, one of them was just to stop. Stop and try to figure out the real source of the rage. If she did that, it would usually dissipate.

"I feel like you're judging me, Brad."

"Judging you? Never. It's just a house."

Ellen sighed. Because, of course, if she didn't do so many stupid, impulsive things, no one would have any reason to judge her.

"At the very least, Ellen? Paint. And this sort of thing"—he gestured to the fridge papered over with recipes and photographs—"it will cost you thousands. I'm not kidding."

She ripped it all down. Baked Alaska. The list of fruits and vegetables most likely to be pesticide-tainted. Here, under several layers, was a three-year-old mammogram reminder. Brad was chuckling.

"What?" she asked.

"Nothing. Who's this?" He pointed at the picture of Mimi in front of the CN Tower, toothful smile, nose ring. She told him. "Really?" he said. "I thought she was your sister."

"Come on."

"For sure. We could have a drink sometime after all this is over. To celebrate."

Ellen tapped the broad gold band on his finger. "I don't think so."

"No hard feelings," said Brad Wheeler, who evidently didn't feel things very solidly. He left a stack of papers—the contract, stat sheets on houses in the area and what they'd sold for.

So here was Ellen, chucking again. Chucking crap so the house would show well. On all fours in the downstairs crawl space, pushing more boxes out into the light. Mildewy cardboard boxes all over the rec room. Opening the softened flaps of one, she discovered school-work. Such comical spellings! In the drawings, no one had a neck. How could she discard this precious record, proof that no matter how she beat herself up about it now, her girls had been happy?

At the bottom, a smaller box. She lifted the lid, shrieked, and dropped it. The disgusting contents spilled out onto the floor. Something had chewed its way into the box and expired. A very hairy sort of rodent. She bent to inspect it then, gingerly, picked it up. By the blunt end, not the flowing end.

Larry's ponytail.

Oh, she was evil. Wicked. She put it in a padded envelope addressed to *Larry Silver. General Delivery. Cordova Island.*

She knew the address by heart.

ON the first of December Jack McGinty was released from hospital. He stayed with Ellen for a week, enjoying her cooking now, taking short walks in the neighbourhood with her. Ellen kept him company during the evening news, which she normally didn't watch because she interacted too much with the television. Jack coached her through several minor repairs, such as replacing a broken switch plate in the hall; he couldn't do the work himself because his hands still shook, though not half as much.

Brad Wheeler-Dealer's stat sheets scandalized Jack. He couldn't believe the price of real estate.

"The more expensive, the better. I've got plans."

What plans? her father wanted to know.

"I'm tired of publicity. It's all self-promotion now anyway. Social media. Do you remember I used to make pots?"

Jack didn't. He'd probably never seen one of her pots.

"Back when I was married to Larry. When we were living on Cordova Island. I'd like to take it up again. I'm going to sell the house and live off the proceeds. Sign up for some classes. Maybe rent a studio."

"You'll have more than enough money," her father said.

Every night Moira phoned to talk to him and exchange with Ellen a few civil, then gradually warm, words. That day twenty-three years ago, when Charles ran straight to Moira and foolishly confessed because he couldn't wait until the party was over like everyone else—it seemed to evaporate. The fact that there was no party in the end, only confrontation, screaming, Jack McGinty leaning back in the Muskoka chair gripping the armrests like he was travelling too fast in it. The flurry of confused packing, Ellen fleeing with Larry and Mimi and not even saying goodbye to her father. It had all happened so long ago—did it even matter?

"How are you holding up with him?" Moira asked. "Is he driving you crazy?"

71

"Does he drive you crazy?" Ellen asked.

"Of course! He never talks. You never know what he's thinking. Mom did all the talking. Remember?"

"Yes," Ellen said, suddenly tearing up. "I do."

The night before Jack was supposed to fly back to Calgary, Moira said over the phone, "Ellen? I always thought Larry was a jerk. You did everything for him, but what did he ever do for you? We watched that program of his. It wasn't even funny. We didn't get it at all."

"Thank you," Ellen said.

The next morning, since Ellen and her father were both up anyway and it was unexpectedly clear and sunny, she suggested that they leave for the airport early and take a walk on the jetty. Jack attended fully to the drive, seeing the city for the first time in his seven-week stay, the city herself finally showing all her coloured feathers. The mountains were two-toned with snow, the fields around the runways a shimmery green. When Ellen asked him what he thought of it, he said, "It's fine."

They parked. For five kilometres the jetty stretched out into the ocean, an elevated road to nowhere, banked with boulders. Under it a pipe led from the sewage treatment plant. Jack had sure put that pipe to the test.

High above them a plane traced a U before landing. Jack watched, then did the same, took Ellen's arm and turned back toward the beach. At the water's reedy edge the sand was flecked with broken shells and glass and plastic. He managed an unsteady squat then, placing both hands in the icy water, waved them, like he was Moses trying to coax the sea apart.

"There," he said, once she got him standing again. "Now let's go."

His bags were half stuffed with Poppycock. She helped check

them in, then he insisted that she leave. He was fine. He would get a cup of coffee. He would have his seashore-besmirched shoes shined.

"What was the name of the place you just took me to?"

"The Iona Jetty," Ellen said.

She was meeting Brad Wheeler-Dealer back at the house, so she said goodbye. She hugged her father and he actually told her, maybe for the first time in her life, "I love you, Ellen."

When she looked back, he was still standing in front of the taxi stand, watching her walk toward the parkade. Like in that poem, not drowning, but waving. She smiled and waved back.

But during the long drive home, as she strained to remember the name of the poet, the lines came back to her.

I was much too far out all my life / And not waving but drowning.

She'd misremembered it. She only realized what it meant later, when she and Brad sat down at her kitchen table.

Because the first thing she saw was her father moving his hands in the water, testing the temperature, and the typed note on top of all the papers.

I am sorry.

"What's the matter, Ellen?" Brad asked. "What's this all about?"

3

ELLEN-CELINE, CELINE-ELLEN

. . .

So Ellen had found herself alone with a two-year-old in a near-empty, perpetually cloud-scarved house halfway up the North Shore mountains, eight months pregnant with her second child. All those years ago.

Only twenty-two and already divorcing.

As desperate as she'd been to leave Cordova Island, population 357 born-again hippies, aging draft dodgers and sundry arty types, now Ellen missed it. Ellen and Larry had been passionate members of that close community (Larry too passionate, it turned out), contributors to its potlucks and Friday-night jams in the tiny island hall, users of its Free Store and babysitting co-op. If you met somebody on the road on Cordova Island, you stopped and talked for half an hour about your garlic crop and your aura. That's the kind of place it was.

But now when Ellen took Mimi to the park, she felt she was from a far-off country, a land of long-tressed, naked-faced women and bearded, huggy men, she a resident alien among the feather-haired and Lycraed North Vancouver natives, all of whom chatted in tight circles around the playground equipment, snubbing her. It was 1983. Mimi teetered then fell on all fours in the sandbox. Ellen marvelled at how she simply thrust her diapered bottom in the air and boosted herself up. "How do you do that?" she asked, for she, Ellen, was in mid-collapse and would never, ever right herself.

Every few nights she called Larry in California and asked him to please, please, just come back for the birth. He kept telling her, "Amy wouldn't like it."

Amy was the slutty L.A. actress who had stolen Larry from her.

At her core Ellen was resilient and practical—no crisis could override that—so one day she took the bus down to the Health Unit and signed up for pre-natal classes. Tuesday evenings for four weeks, babysitting provided.

In the second class they practised breathing exercises on mats. Ellen had to pair up with the instructor, which caused the pity level in the room to soar. Afterward a ringlettey woman, who was so petite and muscular her pregnancy barely showed, intercepted Ellen and asked if she wanted to go for coffee sometime. That was Georgia.

"Oh, thank you!" Ellen gasped.

When they met up later in the week, Georgia brought along Celine, the glamorous one who all through the class ostentatiously stroked her belly like she was accompanying them on the harp. She was much taller, massively pregnant, but only from the front and side. From the back, you couldn't tell. (Ellen just looked fat under all her loose hippy garments, so no one offered her a seat on the bus.) By chance Georgia had run into Celine at the Park Royal Mall, recognized her from the class, and invited her along. None of them really knew each other.

Georgia, who seemed tactful and shy, might never have asked, but Celine did, the second their coffee mugs were set in front of them. There was a boldness to Celine, a right-to-knowness that, combined with her overall perfection—clothes, hair, skin—would have smacked of bourgeois entitlement on Cordova Island.

"So?" Celine asked Ellen. "Are you doing this on your own?"

Ellen fiddled with her hair, still long then, more chewed-on rope than braid. Here in the city, her hair added to her pathos, but she hadn't realized it yet. "Apparently," she said.

"What does that mean?"

The interrogation obviously pained Georgia. She stared into her mug, then shot Ellen a lifeline kind of look. Ellen ignored it. Bobbing far out beyond her pride, she wanted, needed, Celine's sympathy more.

"I *was* married. Until about a month ago."

"That's brave," Celine said, taking in Mimi too, squeezed onto what little remained of Ellen's lap, sucking on the crayons the waitress had brought. "I'm not sure I'd leave Richard in my condition. Not that I have reason to."

"It wasn't my idea," Ellen said.

"He left *you?*" Celine said, and both women, Georgia too, instinctively and together, reached for Ellen. "What a *bastard!*"

Ellen wished Larry could hear how she limped to his defence. "He had his reasons, I guess." Then, without volunteering the fact of her own slip-up, she started weeping.

Georgia squeezed her hand; Celine hugged Ellen hard. This was the sisterhood they had celebrated in the Cordova Island Community Hall once a month when the Women's Empowerment Group met, but which had proved to be a lie. Who would have thought she'd find it here, in a yuppie café on Lonsdale Avenue?

It was Celine who answered Ellen's call when her labour started, who took Mimi to Georgia's and coached Ellen all day, rubbing the small of her back, timing contractions, reading out from her notebook the pertinent passages they had covered in class. Who drove Ellen to the hospital six hours later and remained steadfastly with her in the delivery room while Ellen, squatting, screamed out her agony, "I hate your fucking guts, Larry Silver! I hate you so much!"

For here was another lie: contrary to what they'd learned in pre-natal class, the crowning of the baby's head is not necessarily a moment of pure joy. Ellen was, in fact, at her lowest then, the most biblically wretched creature that had ever crawled the clodded surface of the earth. No one could feel more abandoned, more utterly abject, than she, Ellen Silver, in her final push.

Two thousand kilometres away the father of the child ripping mercilessly through her body was probably screwing his slutty actress girlfriend *right that minute*. What could be worse than that?

Something. What happened to Celine was worse.

77

"ARE you on crack?" Tony, her hairdresser, asked in 2007, the week before Ellen left on her trip to France with Celine. "*That* Celine? The quack? The one you complain about *every time* you come here?"

"Every time?" Ellen asked, surprised and a little ashamed she could be so consistently disloyal.

To her relief, Tony moved on to the subject at hand, Ellen's roots, how the grey was already showing again so how about something *dramatique*? He danced around the chair, running his tiny hands upward from the nape of her neck to her crown. These days Ellen wore her hair to her shoulders. The ungrey ends slithered between Tony's fingers. He tocked his head from side to side, a dashboard ornament, formulating improvements.

Recently, Tony had softened his own look. Because he was small, he seemed ageless. Not a perceivable minute had settled on him since 1983, when Ellen first sat in this chair. Now he'd turned himself into a tousled schoolboy just leaping out of bed, an effect that probably took hours to create.

"I could do something to you today, Ellen, that I guarantee will draw those horny Frenchmen to you like, like— They will *oo-la-la!* They will fall on those shit-covered French sidewalks trying to get a glimpse up your skort." (Ellen had brought her new skort in a bag to show Tony.) "They will curse that skort. *Merde, merde, merde*, they will say. I thought it was a skirt, but I can't see *anything!*"

"Skirt plus shorts. Skort," Ellen said again.

"It will put them into a frenzy, the skort together with what I could do to your hair, if only you'd let me. If only you would *laissez-faire* your hair the way you have your life."

"Don't fuck up my hair, Tony."

"You take chances, Ellen. You'll probably screw fifty horny Frenchmen over there. Or you could. If you'd let me do this one little thing."

"It's tempting," Ellen had said.

Now here she was! In France! In France, writing a postcard to Tony so he would get it before her next appointment. Until they adjusted to the time change, she and Celine were renting a six-hundred-year-old house in a tiny village in the Luberon Mountains. Celine, a practising herbalist, was all messed up. She'd locked herself in her room. But Ellen had been liberal with the Zopiclone, even on the plane. (If it went down, she preferred to sleep through it.)

Ellen, in France, with her *café au lait* and chocolate *croissant* that she had ordered herself using actual French words, sitting in a village square waiting for a horny Frenchman she might claim in the postcard to have screwed to come along. Wild iris crowded the base of the fountain, *à la* Van Gogh. Chocolate bittersweet on her tongue. Then the bells in the eleventh-century church began to ring.

Oh my God, thought Ellen, clutching her head. *Sonnez les matines! Ding dang dong!*

It was almost too much, too beautiful.

She wrote on the card to Tony, *Who needs a man?*

HER relationship with Celine was complicated, more complicated than with Georgia, who, like Tony, had also expressed trepidation when Ellen told her about the hiking trip. Ellen and Celine had a long history together, yet this history, full of tribulations for both, as well as minor triumphs, did absolutely nothing to change Celine's attitude toward Ellen. Celine was (Ellen thought) frozen in the big-sister role she had taken on when they first met, a role that Ellen frequently resented, especially now that her actual sister, Moira, was back in her life.

After their father's inexplicable suicide last winter, Moira had barged in on Ellen's grief and taken control of practical matters— the funeral, returning the body to Alberta to be buried beside their mother. Ellen, named as executor of his will (again, inexplicably), still had many tedious and terrible tasks to perform (his taxes, for one). But she had put it all aside with Moira's blessing for this rejuvenating trip with Celine.

All those years ago Ellen had been lost and desperate and she would never forget Celine's kindness to her, which was probably why they were still friends. (She wasn't so disloyal after all!) She just didn't want to be treated like a woebegone child at the age of forty-six.

This wasn't Georgia's take on it. Georgia said, "You're exactly alike."

"What? I'm flakey and judgmental?"

"Not flakey," Georgia conceded, which shut Ellen up.

Every cell in Georgia's body was powered by honesty and loving-kindness. She was entirely without ego or wiles. Georgia deserved her own constellation.

The proprietor of the six-hundred-year-old house had stocked it with tourist brochures. Discovering it was market day in a nearby village, Ellen left a note for Celine then drove off in the rental car along narrow winding roads, past tidily arranged vineyards and olive groves. Even on the curves dozens of lead-footed Provençals, heedless of the dividing line or death, overtook her. Of course they could die. They'd already been to heaven, which, Ellen soon realized, was a Provençal market. On the return trip the hatch of the Clio was stuffed with proof—a waxy yellow chicken, black and green tapenade, four kinds of chèvre. Baguettes. A pink, frilled, bridal bouquet of a lettuce. Two bottles of Châteauneuf-du-Pape. She would have bought more, but they were leaving in two days and she would have to carry it all on her back.

That evening, with still no sign of Celine, Ellen set to cooking in the three-year-old kitchen in the six-hundred-year-old house, happily into the wine, so happy for the first time since Jack died, which was the purpose of the trip, Celine had claimed. To cheer Ellen up. She sang to herself, rubbing the powdery *fleur de sel* into the puckered skin of the bird. Sang and sang.

Until Celine shouted from her bedroom down the hall. "Can you be a little quieter in there, Ellen, for Christ's sake?"

• • •

Two days later Ellen was packed and ready and waiting for Celine. Waiting for Celine to finish her yoga routine, then waiting while Celine reorganized her backpack so the heavier things would be on the bottom. There were no heavy things in Ellen's backpack. It was practically weightless with newly purchased, featherlight, scrunchable travel clothes, including a wrinkle-free peony of a little green dress that Ellen adored.

But for the first day of their hike she had put on the skort. She turned a circle for Celine. "What do you think?"

"Slimming," Celine said.

The remark deformed in Ellen's ear. She'd already lost ten pounds. That was the only good thing about her father's suicide. When you take to your bed with the covers over your head, you don't eat so much. But she was still too fat for Celine. Celine was too thin. Ellen suspected fasting and (shudder) herbal colonics zealously self-administered.

Finally, finally, Celine was ready. Bidding *adieu* to the hilltop village, they drove off to return the rental car in a town forty minutes away, Celine at the wheel because she'd been to the area several times and knew the roads. On the way, she pointed out various landmarks. "See that château? It belonged to the Marquis de Sade." "That crossroads? That's the exact spot where Beckett got the idea for *Waiting for Godot*. Later in the week we'll come to the town where Camus died. We can picnic on his grave."

"Why didn't you tell me this before?" Ellen complained. She hadn't even considered *Justine* or *Molloy* or *L'Étranger*. She'd brought Colette.

The rental car office was closed, not just for those two-hour French lunches. According to the handwritten message Celine read on the door, it was shut for the whole long weekend.

"Is it the weekend?" Ellen asked.

"This is outrageous." Celine stormed over to the Clio, snatched the Europcar contract from the glove compartment. "It says we return it here. Today. Saturday, May 24."

They found a pay phone a block away outside the train station. Celine bought a phone card, then called in her complaint in French. Ellen didn't think Celine sounded angry enough, stammering like that, so she muscled her aside and grabbed the receiver.

"Do you speak English?"

The woman did, about as well as Celine spoke French, giving Ellen the upper hand. Yet this lackey didn't crumple the way her North American counterpart would have done if blasted with consumer discontent. She didn't even apologize, merely explained in a charming accent that they should drive to the TGV station in Avignon, where one of their offices was open. The two friends stomped back to the car, arms linked, for there is nothing more unifying than a common grievance, except maybe love.

After the two-hour wait in Avignon for the forty-minute train trip back to the same town they'd failed to return the car in, then a costly thirty-minute cab ride, they arrived at the trailhead. It was in another hilltop village, this one partially abandoned, long-weekend tourists elbow to elbow among the ruined castle and the tiny ruined houses and the restored sixteenth-century church. The reinhabited part was full of shops. Ellen wanted to see the pottery before they left.

"I have a plan," she told Celine, poking through the brightly glazed touristy stuff. She'd hoped for *faïence*, a kind of marbled pottery from the area. "I've worked for years promoting creative people. I'd like to be creative myself."

"How?" Celine asked.

"I'm going to start making pots again."

"It's so hard to start a small business, Ellen. Take my advice."

"I'm less interested in the business part than the pottery part."

"How are you going to live?"

"The house is worth about ten times what we bought it for. Plus, my dad socked his money away all his life."

"Well, *that's* lucky," Celine said. "Can we start now?"

Again, Ellen felt that twist. She was lucky that her father had killed himself? Was that what Celine meant? When Ellen would give up every cent she had to buy him back to life?

She tailed Celine out of the shop, frowning, careful that her pack didn't knock the tchotchkes off the shelves.

By then it was four-thirty in the afternoon.

Before this trip, Ellen hadn't known that all of France was netted with walking trails. Celine showed her a red-and-white blaze on a wall, consulted the map, pointed straight ahead. Ellen tightened the straps of her pack (which was not, by then, weightless, but fairly heavy), and followed Celine along what was at first a cobbled medieval road, then an ascending footpath. They'd already talked themselves out on the train, venting their mutual anger, and now Ellen let Celine's comment in the shop pass. No particular emotion replaced that umbrage for some time. Up they walked, through a forest ringing electrically with cicadas. At their feet were wildflowers of the sort Ellen cultivated in her own garden at home—candelabra primula, candy tuft, Lenten rose, muscari, euphorbia, daffodil—all in miniature. Even the trees seemed stunted. The insects, on the other hand, were gargantuan. A bee the size of her thumb bonked her on the temple. It felt like a stoning's introductory blow.

On the treeless crest, a wind reared up and almost blew them over. They bent into it, scrambling over the rocks, moving slowly,

83

hair whipping around their heads. Below was the town where they had a reservation for the night, a manageable distance away, not that far, ten kilometres by the map. It would be easy now that they were going down, but down by the most up-and-down route possible, it turned out. Sometimes they missed the trail markings and had to backtrack. Or they stopped to consult the map, then argued about which way to go. If they took Celine's suggestion and met up with a bold red X on a rock, she wouldn't admit fault. She'd say, "Oh, not this way, I guess," despite how she had insisted they take that turn. If Ellen was wrong, though, Ellen would say sorry.

Meanwhile, Ellen was in pain. Feet, knees, back. "You've done this hike?" she asked.

Celine had not. "I told you that, Ellen."

She'd only admired these mountains from a safe distance. Compared to *their* mountains back home in North Vancouver, these were barely foothills, she'd told Ellen, another French miniature, which was technically true but ignored the fact of the very challenging terrain.

The thing about walking is that it frees the mind. Ellen's mind, freed, was inclined to brood. To brood about her father these days, how the last time she'd seen Jack alive he'd told her that he loved her. The alarm bells should have sounded right then, but no. Ellen had been *pleased*. Pleased, too, that he'd come out of the airport to wave goodbye. And Ellen, in a hurry that day, had waved back, then turned and strode away. Except he wasn't waving to her. He was flagging a cab, which he then rode to the Iona Jetty for the purpose of drowning himself. Any remotely sensitive daughter would have picked up on these clues. But Ellen hadn't.

She would have liked to share these dark thoughts with Celine as they walked, but after Celine's comment in the gift shop, Ellen was wary. Celine was just as likely to reinforce Ellen's self-blame as she was to lift it off her shoulders. So on Ellen trudged, wordlessly self-flagellating herself in hindsight.

Dusk fell around eight, by which time Ellen had finally managed to shift the focus of her brooding to something Celine could sympathize with. The outrage perpetrated on them by Europcar. This was when Celine let slip a shocking fact: the office had been open.

"It's too bad we didn't get there before noon," she said.

"What?" Ellen roared. "I was ready to go by nine! We could easily have gotten there if you hadn't taken two hours to pack your stuff!"

"There you go again, Ellen. Don't. Don't start with this blaming stuff."

"Why shouldn't I? It's your fault."

"Am I blaming *you*?"

"For what?"

"For dawdling in every one of those shops even though they all sell the same Provençal crap. We could have been on the trail an hour earlier."

"So you *are* blaming me."

"I'm saying you bear some responsibility too. I choose not to blame. Blaming is toxic."

This was *exactly* Ellen's complaint to Tony: Celine's passive-aggressive tendencies. "You blamed Europcar!" she shrilled.

She itched, just itched, to kick the skinny Lululemoned ass she'd been forced to look at for the last four hours—the ass she ended up looking at for two more, or rather, could barely make out in the dark as they stumbled into the town and found the guest house and roused the owner, who, as he showed them their room, confessed that he'd lost hope they would show up.

85

"J'ai perdu l'espoir."
Even Ellen understood that.

ELLEN didn't kick Celine's skinny ass. She couldn't because Celine's baby died all those years ago when Ellen's and Georgia's babies were born healthy and lusting for life. It had squirmed in its incubator for two days, and then it died. It had no brain.

When Ellen woke the next morning after eight hours of undrugged sleep, she remembered that terrible time, Celine's milk coming in for nothing, her tranced shuffling around her house of grief, belly still huge with the dead space the baby had left in her life. And Ellen's heart went out to Celine snoring lightly in the adjacent twin bed. Celine, her dear friend whom she loved. Celine, who was not half so annoying when unconscious.

At breakfast, Ellen asked, "How far today?"

Celine showed her the map. Twenty-five kilometres. At least they would be on the trail in good time. They agreed to rest more frequently, to eat more, to be kinder to each other.

"I'm sorry I lost it yesterday," Ellen said.

Celine said, "Oh, Ellen. Never mind."

Stiff from the day before, they hobbled back through the stone town, stopping for the baguettes they stuffed arrowlike in the quiver of their packs. Celine, a vegetarian, waited outside the *boucherie* while Ellen bought herself a donkey sausage.

Every muscle screamed. The tender spots on Ellen's feet pulsated, despite the moleskin. Two hours of slow, silent climbing back up the rock-studded, thyme-scrubbed side of the mountain, the descent of which had wrecked their knees the night before. Gradually, Ellen felt herself detach. It was as though she was already out of this situation telling someone about it later. Who? Georgia?

Tony. *En garde-ing* in the mirror with the scissors, rolling his eyes. She was telling tell him about the trip, how Celine hadn't come out of her room the first two days, how bossy she'd been with the map.

"A country of what? *Sixty million?* And you couldn't find *one single* horny Frenchman to screw you?"

They rested on some boulders next to the trail. While Celine drank her boiled water, Ellen, taking an advance on lunch, joked about Tony's hopes for her. Celine's lips tightened.

"Don't be such a prude," Ellen said, poking her with the gnawed-on baguette.

"I'm just not into those types of relationships. You know that, Ellen. I would find it demeaning."

Celine got off the rock she was sitting on, swung her pack onto her back. She was visibly shorter with it on, three inches at least. "You charge at men," she said.

"I used to," Ellen said. "I haven't for some time."

This was less because she'd stopped waving the red cape of her need than because no one came near enough to see it.

"They don't respect you and you don't respect yourself."

"Okay, okay," Ellen said, holding out her hand. Celine helped her up, Ellen groaning loudly, not just for effect.

"Let's sing," Ellen said, trying for a lighter tone. "Let's make a joyful noise."

They didn't know the same songs, so they took turns. Celine's repertoire was meagre, Ellen's vast—all the jazz standards her mother used to sing, the hippy songs from Cordova Island. ("We Shall Overcome" seemed particularly apropos.) Soon Ellen was doing all the singing, and when she realized it, she stopped, thinking that maybe she was annoying Celine. Maybe Celine was at that moment far in the future complaining to Georgia about how Ellen wouldn't stop singing on the trail. How she actually wasn't that great a singer. Ellen couldn't tell what Celine was thinking, since her back was to Ellen as she set their bovine pace.

"Moo," Ellen said.

Celine looked over her shoulder. "What's that supposed to mean?"

"Nothing. I was just mooing." Never had putting one foot in front of the other seemed so gruelling! "Celine? My feet? My metatarsals? They're aching like you would not believe. I don't think I've ever experienced pain like this. Childbirth was nothing." And her shoulders—so tight. It wasn't hot, the temperature was, in fact, perfect—everything so fucking perfect!—yet she poured out sweat.

After lunch, when precious energy had been diverted toward digestion, when jet lag struck again (it had not been vanquished after all, only temporarily staved off), Ellen's default switch tripped to the brood position. If she'd only given her father a second glance, she would have seen him getting into that cab. She could have raced back and hopped in one herself, given chase.

That scenario played out over and over until— *Stop it!* She swigged some water. Slogged on. Her bra was saturated. There were wet patches, like when she had nursed her babies.

Larry's abandoned babies.

And then she was brooding again over those early months in North Vancouver, with a newborn and a two-year-old, Ellen doing most of it on her own, in the rain. It never stopped raining, a fact no one had mentioned before they bought the house. Ellen had only two friends at that time—Georgia and Celine. Georgia had her own newborn. Celine couldn't help Ellen. Celine's baby was dead.

Meanwhile, Larry was in sunny L.A., writing his crap TV show and screwing Amy.

"I get so angry!" Ellen said.

Vainly, she wished for Celine to say the right thing.

Celine sighed. "Issues, Ellen."

"I know I have issues. I'm trying. Don't you ever think of Richard?"

Ahead of her Celine stiffened, reclaiming her three lost inches. "No."

Ellen herself hadn't thought of Richard in years, could barely picture the effete-looking man of the pre-natal classes, the stunned one from the funeral. Before the baby, Celine had been a meat-eating, middle-class suburban wife with a government job. Richard hadn't made it into the After frame of Celine's Before-and-After life. Larry, though, was still very much in Ellen's life, because they had children. Also, Larry had moved back to Cordova Island—a surprise to everyone. Ellen saw him whenever she visited Yo and Sean.

There had been an additional, private surprise for Ellen—sex. A couple of times over the last few years she and Larry had found themselves alone and atingle with nostalgia, and so they'd reached out for old times' sake. Last Christmas they'd coupled in Larry's office while Amber, his child bride, was tucked upstairs in bed. Ellen blushed, remembering. What did it mean, these intermittent reunions? Not much. After all they'd been through, Ellen and Larry were simply connected, for better or for worse.

Celine and Ellen were walking in the woods now, which seemed eerily quiet for a holiday weekend. They'd encountered no one on the trail. When eventually they came to a gravel road, Ellen looked at Celine. Hair sticking to her pale face, Celine was obviously suffering as much as Ellen, maybe more, just not complaining about it. She pointed her chin up the road. Ellen deferred. Moments later, they saw the rude red X on a tree trunk, turned and headed the other way.

"Oh, great," Ellen said, pointing at another X.

"It must be here," said Celine, walking straight into the trees on the other side of the road.

Ellen had no opinion now, was simply stumbling along behind Celine. Celine could lead her off a cliff if she wanted.

The trees were deciduous. Ellen marked each syllable with a step. *Dee-sid-you-us.* She sensed them, these trees, their straight grey trunks so evenly spaced in her peripheral vision. *You-us. Dee-sid.* And something flipped. She and Celine were standing still and the trees were advancing on them, surrounding them. But trees didn't have feet. (Oh, not to have feet!) She turned her head and saw this was silly, the trees weren't moving. Someone was watching them and had been for a long time.

Not the trees, *from* them.

But no one was there. All Ellen saw was ashen bark, the bright green coinage of leaves. How old were they, these French trees? Young. Someone must have planted them after the war. Which war? They'd had so many. Also this terrible massacre of a Protestant sect a few centuries ago. Ellen had read about it in the guidebook.

She came to enough to ask if Celine had actually seen a marker.

"Just back there," Celine told her, and Ellen, believing her, plodded on because if she stopped she would never start again.

"I haven't," she said after a while. "I haven't seen any marker for a long, long time."

It was dead people. Centuries of them. The dead were watching them from the trees. Just then Celine sank down on the path, as though she'd had the same realization, and the weight of her pack tipped her onto her side and held her there. Out of her rose a wrenching, leaf-stirring sob.

Ellen looked down at her. "I shouldn't have mentioned Richard."

"Shh!"

"I'm sorry, Celine."

Ellen undid her own pack and let it thud to the ground. The relief was exquisite, but short-lived. When she knelt to unfasten Celine's buckles and liberate her, a burning pain ripped up her thighs.

Celine sobbed. "I thought you could use this trip, Ellen. That's what I thought."

(Was he here too? Her father? Ellen looked around.)

At that moment Ellen simply gave up. She lay down and curled in a ball on the forest floor among the tiny wildflowers and the super-sized bugs. She closed her eyes. She didn't give a flying fuck what happened next.

Which was that they both fell asleep.

When they woke, they were cold and stiff nearly to the point of paralysis, and utterly alone.

Somehow they struggled to their feet. Celine's face was streaked with mud. Dried leaves and dirt decorated her hair. Ellen pulled some from her own, then lifted Celine's pack for her to put on; Celine lifted Ellen's. Equally burdened, they limped back to the road, where they turned in unison and carried on downhill, right past the X, completely in sync, as though they never, ever disagreed on anything.

"We're too old for this," Ellen told Celine from her twin bed that night, when it all seemed funny. "I mean, we're middle-aged. Didn't that occur to you?"

91

Celine said, "Speak for yourself."

"We might have died out there. Now I've bonded with that boy. He saved our lives. I'm in love with him."

"His name is Oog," Celine said.

"What?"

"That's what he said."

"That's unfortunate."

Celine rolled over so her back was to Ellen. She giggled.

"What?" Ellen asked.

"I'm surprised you aren't screwing him right now."

"I would! *He* wouldn't. I'm too old."

Ten minutes down the road they had come to a riding stable. "I'm stealing a horse," Ellen said, but when they staggered into the barn a young man was there brushing the animals. Celine asked in French for a phone to call a cab. Despite her exhaustion, Ellen got the gist of what he told Celine in reply, that he was actually a prince, not a lowly, well-built stable boy, that he had been waiting a hundred years for them to stumble in and break the cruel spell that had been cast on him.

Celine turned to Ellen, tears shining in her eyes. "He's going to drive us!"

His van was white, further proof of his enchantment. Celine immediately claimed the passenger seat, because she spoke French. Ellen hoped this didn't mean that Celine got to marry him. No, Ellen did, because the prince offered his hand for Ellen to climb in the horsey-smelling back of the van that had no seats, just a foam mattress. Ellen was Cinderella. He threw in their packs, and his, and a rolled-up sleeping bag.

With just one touch, her pain had vanished.

Up front, Celine explained their predicament. "Ellen? He says he can drop us off in Lourmarin, or we can go where he's going. Another town a little farther. He has a friend there who runs a winery with a campground and a *gîte*. A hostel. He says there's even a pool."

Ellen said, "I go wherever he goes."

THE next morning Ellen woke alone in the cramped room at the top of the stairs. Two twin beds separated by a night table. A wardrobe for their things. Stiff, battered, she limped to the window. Celine was down in the vineyard, saluting the Provençal sun, her purple yoga mat unrolled between the vines.

A twenty-minute walk in sandals brought Ellen to the large stone reservoir surrounded by plane trees in the centre of town. Café tables clustered on one side. Here she sat for the rest of the morning in perfect contentment with her *café au lait* and *croissant*, writing postcards to Mimi and Yolanda, notifying them that they had very nearly been left motherless. Then she poked around the town buying delicacies for lunch.

On the way back to the *gîte* she spotted the white van of their saviour, Oog, in the adjacent campground. The stone house, bearded with ivy between bright blue shutters, was divided, one side the elderly proprietors' residence, the other the *gîte*. Despite the campground being full, Ellen and Celine were the only guests. It was normally only open in summer, Celine had translated the night before. They had made an exception for Celine and Ellen, since they had come with Oog.

Now a truck about the size of a moving van was backed against the barnlike building that stood at a right angle to the house. Celine and the old woman were sitting together at one of the picnic tables under the trees.

"They're bottling the wine," Celine told Ellen when she walked up. "And his name is Hugues. *Hugh*. It's pronounced differently in French."

"I'll say."

The old woman's filamentous hair suggested illness; it barely concealed her pink scalp. She smiled at Ellen.

"*Bonjour*," Ellen said. "*Comment allez-vous?*" This malpronounced greeting unleashed a long gravelly reply, which Celine had to translate.

"She's asking how you slept."

"*Très bon.*"

Ellen sat down with her provisions at her feet, but gave up on the conversation. She was still deeply tired and the French floated around her in the scented air with the strange insects and the masculine voices in the barn and the machinery sounds. Now and then she understood something Celine said to the old woman. *Divorcée*. The old woman gestured to the barn, got up, and went into the house.

"She's making their lunch," Celine said.

Ellen went into their side of the house to do the same, to the *gîte* kitchen. She cooled the bottle of rosé in the freezer while she assembled a tray, then brought lunch out to Celine. "I am going to be so fat when this is over."

"Don't eat so much," Celine said.

"What would be the point then?"

Ellen shook the water off a lettuce leaf, dipped it directly into a saucer of walnut oil, salted it. As she ate it some of the oil ran down her chin and christened the front of her little green dress. She opened the wine. Celine wouldn't drink in the daytime. She would only eat the lettuce and a bit of baguette and chèvre.

Though Ellen's back was to the barn, she could tell from Celine's face when the men came out. "You're blushing," she said.

Hugues walked right over in his undershirt and pirate bandana, bringing the son of the old couple, who looked in his early forties. He had fine brown hair, rolled sleeves, and glasses with thick frames. Hugues nodded to Celine and said, "Hélène," by way of introducing her. Ellen he called *Celine*.

"Actually, *I'm* Ellen," said Ellen, shaking the hand the son extended to her.

"Jean-François," he said. "John-Frank."

"Ah," said Ellen. "Someone I can talk to."

"Not today, I regret. We are embottling the wine."

Hugues and Jean-François entered the house while the other workers washed at an outside tap then gathered at a picnic table across the yard. The food came out in several trips, carried by the old couple and Hugues and Jean-François—an armload of baguettes, two casserole dishes, cheeses, three bottles of wine. The old man, very Cézanne in his straw hat, waved to them. Now and then Ellen glanced over her shoulder to admire the unselfconscious way the men ate, bowed low over their plates, tearing at the bread, swallowing the wine like water.

"We're ahead of schedule now," Celine said. "Do you want to stay a day or two and rest up?"

"Do you?" Ellen asked.

TUESDAY after the long weekend the campground emptied out— no more screeching children, no radios playing American rap. The bottling was finished and the enchanting Hugues drove off in his white van, stirring up clouds of dust and yearning. The next few

95

mornings glided into routine: Celine drank her herbal tinctures, yogaed, swam in the pool, while Ellen walked to town for *petit déjeuner* and postcard writing and a few chapters of *Chéri* by the reservoir. In the afternoon, they hiked with day packs. Afterward, the old man, who was born in the area and something of a naturalist, would look at the pictures on Ellen's camera and name all the bugs and flowers in French.

They came across the bizarrest sight on Thursday. A trail of caterpillars almost two metres long, each holding onto the caterpillar in front. This prompted a long incomprehensible story from Monsieur Cézanne. (They were calling him this to his face now and he liked it.) He got Celine and Ellen up, Celine's hands on his waist, Ellen's on Celine's, and they marched around the yard, laughing.

"We're getting along better here," Celine told Ellen when they were tucked into their twin beds that night.

"That's because you're not being such a bitch," Ellen said, and Celine laughed again.

Neither mentioned getting back on the trail.

THE following morning a car pulled alongside Ellen as she was walking to town. "*Allô!* Celine!"

"John-Frank," said Ellen, recognizing the emphatic glasses more than the rather vague driver. "I'm Ellen."

"Hélène! Sorry!" he called across the empty passenger seat. "You see, in French they are confusable names. *Say-leen. Ay-len.*"

About as similar as *Hyoo* and *Oog* were different. She told Jean-François, "We don't even look alike."

Jean-François drew back in surprise. "You do. Let me drive you, Hélène."

"I'm supposed to be on a walking holiday. Thanks, though."

"Celine isn't walking," Jean-François said, still matching her pace in the Audi. "I saw her in the vineyard. Exercising."

"She's like that," Ellen said. "Where did you learn English?"

"Canada."

"Really? Where?"

Actually, he'd learned it in university but spent six months in Canada last year helping friends set up a winery. "You probably don't know this place. Kelowna."

"Of course I do. I'm from British Columbia."

"No!"

Then a funny thing happened. In his amazement Jean-François let go of the wheel. There was no verge. Ellen was on the very edge of the road next to some prickly sort of hedge. As the car veered toward her, she instinctively put out her hand, as though she could actually stop several thousand pounds of machine from running into her. And when that didn't work, she smacked the hood hard.

Jean-François braked just in time, seemingly unaware he had nearly killed her. "I wonder. No." He shook his head.

Ellen bent to look in the window. "What?"

"If you know my friends. Mireille and Réné Vardon? No, see? I always expect too much. Still, it's amazing you ended up here, don't you think?"

Ellen resumed walking, still accompanied by Jean-François. No one honked. She hadn't heard a single horn in France. Traffic swerved around the crawling Audi and eventually Ellen and her escort reached the reservoir, where Jean-François parked the car on the sidewalk and leapt out. At one of the café tables, he pulled out a chair for her and hurried inside, returning shortly with two espressos.

97

Ellen felt a tiny bit annoyed. Because this life wouldn't last forever and she wanted it *just so* for as long as possible, the ritual of her *croissant* and bowl of coffee. She wanted to order it herself, to say out loud what were practically the only French words she knew. Then she thought, why not have coffee with him? Jean-François wasn't good-looking, but he wasn't bad-looking either, especially now that Hugues was gone. He had a sexy, hyphenated name and a sexy accent, particularly the way he said "the Okanagan."

Ellen had been to Kelowna once and thought it was a dump.

"What's a dump?" Jean-François asked.

"You probably don't have them here," Ellen said.

He picked *Chéri* off the table and studied it. "How long are you staying?"

"Actually," Ellen said. "I might never go back."

"That would be pleasant," Jean-François said, still looking at the book.

A fluttering started inside Ellen that was very pleasant in itself, like a cloud of butterflies inhaled. She looked at Jean-François to see if he meant what she thought he meant.

Smiling, he pointed to the plain orange and beige cover of the book with its jaunty little penguin. "*Chéri*. Darling."

Flutter, flutter.

Jean-François didn't live with his old parents, but in an apartment in town. He went back and forth all day. When Ellen said she was picking up groceries, he offered to meet her back at the car in an hour. "I'll take your food for you. So you can have your walk."

It seemed only right to ask him to dinner.

• • •

ON their hike that afternoon, Ellen and Celine passed a vineyard where a tractor was spewing a greenish powder over the rows of vines. The breeze shifted and the cloud about-faced and headed for the path Celine and Ellen were on. Celine clapped a hand over her mouth and nose and ran.

When Celine told Jean-François about it at dinner, he grew indignant. They did not apply pesticides or antifungals to their vines. As soon as he said this, Celine took a bolder sip of the wine he'd brought, pronounced it delicious, then went on to have two full glasses—about half what Ellen had been drinking every night. Celine's unlined complexion often seemed translucent (*pallid*, Ellen thought, when she felt uncharitable), but the wine made this rosier Celine laugh freely, with her head back so her hair, blond camouflaging the grey, brushed her narrow shoulder blades. Yet every time Ellen glanced across the table to see the effect Celine was having on Jean-François, he smiled at Ellen.

He had two children who lived up in Lyon with their mother. He turned to Ellen. "You are divorced too."

"Who told you that?" Ellen asked.

"My mother," he said.

Ellen could have said that there were three people sitting at the long table whose marriages had failed, or who had failed their marriages, though afterward she was glad she hadn't, because it had been a perfect evening. Jean-François didn't seem to want it to end. Ellen served lamb, massaged, kneaded, and spanked until the thyme she'd gathered on the trail had penetrated the flesh. Jean-François praised it, and while Celine ate only the lentils and the salad, she told Jean-François that Ellen was spoiling her with her cooking. And it seemed to Ellen that whenever she left the common room and went to the kitchen for another course, she could feel Jean-François's eyes, darkly framed by the glasses, following her.

She was wearing the green dress.

Eventually he looked at his watch, heaved a Gallic shrug, rose. Celine and Ellen walked him out to his Audi, where he kissed them each three times—left cheek, right cheek, left cheek.

To Ellen he said, very tenderly, "*Bonne nuit, Celine.*" And to Celine, "*Bonne nuit, Hélène.*"

Both women burst out laughing.

Going up to their room, Ellen stumbled. She would have screwed Jean-François if Celine hadn't been there. If Celine had gone to bed instead of yawning on the floor of the common room with her long legs twisted into the lotus position. Why hadn't she? Celine didn't want to screw him anyway. She would have found it demeaning.

Ellen shook a Zopiclone out of the bottle, squinted at its turquoiseness.

"Are you sure you want to take that, Ellen? After all you drank? I can prepare you a remedy that will work just was well."

SURPRISE, surprise, she was angry in the morning. Angry and hungover.

Celine was still in bed, sleeping holistically after her temperate evening, until Ellen asked, loudly, "Why do you have to tell everyone I'm divorced?"

Celine's eyes flew open.

"It makes me feel like a failure," Ellen said.

Celine sighed. "You're not a failure, Ellen. Larry's a failure."

"Larry's a failure? Larry is the most successful person you know." She clutched her headache. Why did she defend him all the time?

"Ellen? I've said it before. Here I go again. Larry is a jerk. He screwed everyone. Forget about him."

"Did he screw you?" Ellen asked.

"I wouldn't let Larry near me."

"Then what do you know about it?"

"You told me!" Celine said, throwing back the covers and springing up. "You've told me so many times!" She turned her bony back to Ellen, stripped off her pyjama top, struggled into her bra.

"You seem defensive," Ellen said.

"Oh, shut up."

"You are. You're defensive. So did you sleep with Larry or not?"

Celine drove one leg, then the other, into tiny cotton panties. She yanked them over her enviably skinny ass.

"Why aren't you answering me? Yes, or no?"

Celine grabbed her clothes and her yoga mat and walked out.

Angry, actually.

101

As soon as Ellen got to town, she bought a postcard for Georgia. At the café, she wrote: *Sitting beside a reservoir. About to fling myself in.* Like her father had. *Then this holiday will be over!*

She felt like it. She really did.

Instead, she opened Colette, dragged her eyes down the page. It didn't make sense. Léa loses her young lover, her darling Chéri, to her rival's daughter. Now she looks in the mirror and sees *an old woman, out of breath . . . what could she have in common with that crazy creature?*

What crazy creature? Ellen turned the page. *The End?*

She gathered up her things and went inside to pay. They would never come out. You could die at your table, your face on the plate, flies swarming above you, and they wouldn't come out.

In the café bathroom, she combed her hair, which she had apparently neglected to do before leaving the *gîte*. She picked the grains of sleep out of her eyes.

The walk back helped. Twice, she dropped Colette because she had to keep hoisting her stretched-out skort. Each time she bent over to pick up the book from the dusty roadside, her mood relaxed its hold a little. By the time she reached the campground, it was dawning on her that she had behaved badly.

Surprise, surprise.

Celine was in the pool. It was unheated, too cold for Ellen, she had discovered the first day when she dipped her hand in. Celine, though, was made of stiffer stuff, and there stood Jean-François, watching her ply the waters. Ellen watched him watching her friend's long lithe body glide the blue length of the pool, his glasses trained on her, magnifying her, bringing her closer. Who could blame him? Celine looked thirty under water.

Jean-François glanced up and, seeing Ellen, hurried over. "There was a dead mouse in the pool this morning. I didn't have time to get it out. I came to tell her. But maybe I shouldn't now. What she doesn't know? *Ça ne la blessera pas.*"

He followed Ellen away from the pool. "What's wrong?"

"Nothing."

"You are crying."

She blinked through the sudden tears. She was ashamed of how she had goaded Celine that morning—Celine who was like a sister to her. "It's nothing. It's stupid." Her skirt was hanging low on her hips. She yanked it up and Colette fell to the ground again. And Ellen remembered the last line of the book and her own harried face in the café mirror, uglier for never, ever being in the wrong.

"I finished my book," she told Jean-François as she bent to pick it up. "I didn't bring another."

"We have books!" Jean-François guided her by the elbow toward the *gîte*. "English books. People leave them."

In the common room where they had eaten the night before, he pulled something off the shelf. Dean Koontz. He squeezed her shoulders, ran his hands up and down her bare arms as she clasped both books to her chest. When he kissed her, it was full on the lips, not alternate cheeks, and for a long time. He tangoed her against the bookshelf and lapped inside her mouth. And Ellen kissed him back like she had nothing to lose, which was true.

Jean-François searched his pocket and came up with a scrap, a receipt it looked like. "Write your e-mail address. Here." There was a jar on the shelf. "Here is a pen."

When she'd written her address, he took the receipt. Then he took her book, kissing her wrist as payment. "I am going to read this book about Colette."

"Actually, it's about Chéri," Ellen said.

"It will be good for my English. Now I have to go back to work. You're not leaving yet? Will I see you later?"

"I sure hope so," Ellen said.

Upstairs, the shower was running, meaning Celine had probably walked right past the open door of the common room. Ellen lay on her bed. She could still feel it, the ridge of the bookshelf impressing itself into the small of her back, the fullness of two tongues in her mouth.

The shower turned off. A few minutes later, Celine came in. Seeing Ellen, she made a sound. Disgust maybe. Or hurt.

"I'm sorry," Ellen said.

"Oh, right," Celine said.

"I am."

Celine applied some kind of balm to her lips. When she finished, she asked, "Do you want to go or stay?"

"What do you want to do?" Ellen said.

"I don't care either way."

But Ellen could tell that she did.

"Let's go then," she said.

THE last four days of the hike were on flatter terrain, much of it on roads. They felt almost merry, walking along, Ellen suffused with longing the whole way. She couldn't stop thinking about the kiss and that maybe Jean-François would write. How glad she was that they'd left before she screwed him. Because sometimes a kiss was enough. The bittersweetness of it. He had picked her. Picked her like a fruit.

In Ellen's experience, the promise of love was usually more pleasurable than its fulfillment.

She told Celine, "Thank you for bringing me here. I love it. I would come back in a second."

On the roadside, frequent casualties—*les papillons* (another word she knew!), their wings a startling blue, or variations of orange and brown. *Flutter, flutter.* All along the way, she took pictures of the inch-high daffodils and the bizarre beetles they encountered on the trails. She used Celine's hand as a frame of reference.

Otherwise no one would believe her.

TONY got her postcard.

"I *kissed* someone," she told him at her next appointment.

"Doesn't that count? Against a bookcase. I almost slipped a disc. And Tony? It was a *French* kiss."

Tony said, "*Oo-la-la!*"

Two weeks after they got back, Celine phoned to say that Jean-François had e-mailed.

"I didn't realize you exchanged addresses," Ellen said, perhaps in a give-away tone, because Celine clammed up after that.

"What did he say?"

"Nothing. Just hello. Anyway, I should go."

"Thanks for telling me," Ellen said. She was already checking her own e-mail. Nothing from Jean-François, just a long complaining message from Mimi in Toronto.

Georgia called fifteen minutes later. Ellen was still at her desk, rooted there in shock. "What happened on your trip that you didn't tell me about, Ellen?"

Ellen had wanted to savour Jean-François a little longer, to keep him a secret, to see what might happen if she didn't charge at a man for a change. But it had never been secret. Celine was in on it, though she hadn't mentioned, or even hinted at, seeing Ellen and Jean-François kiss.

"Celine just phoned me," Georgia said. "She's got a thing going with some guy there."

In the background, Gary called, "Get the details!"

Obviously, Jean-François had kissed Celine too, in between ogling her in the pool. He had wooed Ellen in town, then driven back to the *gîte* to woo Celine. That kiss, which Ellen had cherished as a rarity, a curiosity, a delicate and precious wonder, it meant nothing.

"He was nothing," she told Georgia. "Just French. It made him seem more attractive than he really was. And you know what? I'm never travelling with Celine again. She has to have her way with everything. Where we stayed, where we ate. But she's never up-front about it. You discuss it and, lo and behold, you're doing what she wants every time. She's the same here. All because of a dead baby."

There. She had said it. And shuddered in triumph.

"Ellen," Georgia said.

"You know it's true. Even now when I mention Mimi or Yolanda, she tenses up. How dare I remind her of her loss! Unless it's something bad. Mimi's drug troubles? It was all Celine could do not to rub her hands together in glee."

"What happened to Celine was awful."

"And it was a long, long time ago. Enough is enough. What was it called? What it died of?" Ellen, still at the computer, tried to type it in.

Mr. Google said: *Did you mean* anencephaly?

"And Ellen?" Georgia said. "I got your postcard. What did you mean?"

A picture of an anencephalic baby popped up on the screen, a little saucer-eyed alien, its head flattened just above the eyebrows, staring out at Ellen. Ellen stared back, unable to close the window or turn away. Grotesque, piteous, the creature looked right into her empty place. And Ellen shuddered again to think what it saw there. Yet the body was normal and human. No, look. Oh, Christ! The poor little thing had no fingers. No fingers on its tiny little hands.

She pressed her forehead to the cold desk. "Georgia. I'm hanging up. I can't talk about this anymore."

• • •

"JEAN-FRANÇOIS believes in destiny. Like I do," Celine told Ellen later that summer.

"Oh, puke," Ellen said. "You hardly know the guy."

"We e-mail every day. Several times."

"You should be careful," Ellen said. "You can get cancer from too much screen time. Horrible tumours all over your face."

"You'll find someone too, Ellen. As soon as you renounce your negativity. So will you come, or will you stay home and pout?"

"I think I'll come and pout," Ellen said.

She goes to Celine's dinner party even though she doesn't like Celine's food. Once Celine served three different potato dishes in the same meal, another time fried-tofu bologna. Anyway, Ellen is trying to keep off those eight pounds that she unexpectedly dropped on the trail in France, and the ten she lost after her father killed himself, so why not? She brings two bottles of Châteauneuf-du-Pape.

Jean-François leaps up from the couch when Ellen comes in the door, bestows the triple kiss—left cheek, right cheek, left cheek. Unfortunately, he looks better than she remembered, mostly because she's been downplaying him in her mind all day. The unflattering glasses, the beige hair. Dean Koontz! In her imagination his hair had thinned more and more until his not-so-innocent scalp shone through, which only makes his hair seem thicker now. Also, his glasses are new, the frames smaller and rounder, she thinks. He looks so plaintive.

Georgia and Gary were invited too, so the conversation turns political. Luckily, Jean-François is a Green, which keeps the shouting to a bearable level. European politics—left, right, left—who can figure it out? Ellen sips her wine and smiles, pleased by how little she actually feels after her day-long snit. Every time her eyes and Jean-François's cross paths, she forces herself to blink.

107

Before dessert, she comes out of the bathroom—"Ah!"—to find Jean-François lurking in the hall.

"Sorry," Ellen tells him. "You should have knocked."

"I was waiting," he explains. "Waiting to speak with you."

Ellen is a little drunk. In the bathroom, she was wondering whether, if she stopped drinking now, she could still drive home.

"I thought I was writing *you*," he says.

He means *help me*, and glances back down the hall to the dining room where Celine is dishing out rubbery squares of tofu cheesecake.

"I gave you my address," Ellen hisses.

"I lost it! I had to look for it in the guest book!"

"What guest book?" Ellen says. "I didn't sign any guest book."

Jean-François lifts his shoulders, his Gallic, tragicomic shrug flowing into a lean. He leans into Ellen and she responds, so they meet in the middle of this terrible gap of geography and misunderstanding. Then, instinctively, she puts out her hand. Drunkenly, with a strength she doesn't even know she possesses, she smacks it flat against Jean-François's chest, pinning his eager heart beneath her palm.

This way, she holds him back.

BECAUSE, when Yolanda was born, Celine was the first to cradle her, even before Ellen. Celine, who kept sniffing the top of the baby's head, the dark, pasted-down fluff. Celine was a week overdue then.

She told Ellen, "I can't wait. I just can't wait."

4

DIVINATION

...

The triplex Ellen moves into that September is old. Eighty years old, even a hundred (what is time?). Three shops stood here once, but now they're artists' studios, green-shingled with large windows, in the heart of Kitsilano. Time has played a trick on the neighbourhood too. Once Kits was the Cordova Island of Vancouver, a hippy paradise, but after four gentrifying decades only pockets of this patchoulied past remain.

The studio is about a quarter the size of Ellen's former house in North Vancouver. She's had to sort and cull her life's artifacts down to a cruel minimum. Unloading her car that first day, backing up with a box of books she couldn't bear to part with, she crashes into her new neighbour Gerhard standing too close behind her. She bounces off him, one of those large, incompressible Germans with a shaved head, unnerving blue eyes, and chains. Jangling, he stoops to gather the fallen books, then carries them into the studio half filled with her scant cardboard-boxed possessions.

And won't leave. He stands like a monolith in the middle of the empty space, talking about his work. Ellen, flustered, locates the espresso machine in a box, fires it up. She knows by the display in his window that video is his medium, the wilderness his muse, as it often seems to be for Germans. (Ellen, who has never been to Berlin, where Gerhard says he's from, pictures it in black and white with beautiful soot-dark buildings, a city without chlorophyll.) The video monitor in Gerhard's window shows a forest clearing, static except for the occasional meanderings of a squirrel or the winged interruption of a bird. This may draw crowds in Berlin, Ellen thinks, but here?

After she brings out the coffee and they settle on the floor to drink it, Gerhard explains the significance of the penises.

Ellen says, "What?"

She leaves him sitting cross-legged, a position he struggled into, the espresso cup in his big hand like a part of a doll's tea set, and goes outside to look in his window again. There they are, rearing up from a dozen trees, wooden phalluses that she somehow missed on first glance. She wants to watch longer in case a hiker or a school group accidentally stumbles into the clearing, but she can't; she has company.

When she returns, Gerhard's lengthy, blue-eyed appraisal causes her to blush. Can he see it? Forty-seven years piled on her face, her nervousness making this move?

"And you, Ellen McGinty?" he finally says. "Tell me about your art."

"I'm a potter."

Is she even allowed to say that when, except for last summer's refresher at the community centre, she hasn't actually thrown a pot for twenty-five years? She points across the terrifying studio space, past the tiny kitchen. There's a tumble-down garage out back.

"I'll mostly be working in the garage. That's where I'll put the wheel and kiln. I'll sell the pots here. Make some kind of window display, like you have. It'll be wonderful. Every day, heaven."

"HELL," she tells Tilda, months later.

Tilda is a fabric artist, a knitter of iconic Canadian wildlife, who lives on the other side of Ellen in the triplex. Big round glasses on a gaunt face emphasize her waifishness, as do her hands, perpetually chapped from the wool. Tilda looks like a thirty-year-old Joyce Carol Oates who knits, rather than writes, compulsively.

For Ellen, after the initial excitement of the move came the inevitable letdown: such is the human condition. Since then she's been, creatively speaking, funked. On the plus side, she has some furniture now and a broad knowledge of Japanese penis temples, Thai penis amulets (Gerhard's are displayed in small velvet-lined boxes), and the famous penis park in Korea. Thanks to Tilda, she knows the difference between a Townsend's vole and a Short-tailed shrew and how one is much harder to knit. But the pots are giving her trouble. They are the irritants in what would otherwise be the life she saw in dreams.

"I like your pots," Tilda tells her.

"Even in the way you say that. You might have said, 'I like cabbage.' I thought I would feel fulfilled. Creative. I'm just bored. Also, no one buys my pots."

"What is your problem?" Gerhard asks, carrying in from the kitchen a large bowl filled with water.

They're in his studio awaiting the new year. He sets the bowl on the coffee table in front of the women, checks his watch. "There is art and there is commerce. Which is making you unhappy? That

111

no one buys your product? Or that you are not creating the art you yearn to create?"

"Is it too much to ask that I create beautiful art that lots of people want to buy?"

"Yes," Gerhard says.

"It sometimes happens," Tilda says. "But do you need money, Ellen?"

"Not really. I sold my house, remember?"

She doesn't mention the inheritance from her father. Her years as publicist taught her that people in the arts can be resentful. Such, too, is the human condition when everyone is desperate for a grant.

"What is your problem then, Ellen?" Gerhard asks on his way back to the kitchen.

"I feel my pots are worthless if no one wants them. And if they're worthless, I'm worthless. Also, there's a space issue. Where am I going to put them?"

"You are confused!" he calls.

Gerhard returns with a lighter and a long, perfectly innocent beeswax taper. Ellen holds out her wineglass to be refilled. Tilda covers hers with her hand (headaches).

"What is this thing you call 'worth,' Ellen? A perception. Make your worthless pots and sell them for a thousand dollars. More people will buy them than if you charge ten bucks. But are they worth more because of that? Are you worth more as a person?"

"I would feel more successful," Ellen says.

"What is success?" Gerhard asks.

"Why is it so hard to talk to Germans?" Ellen asks Tilda.

"Answer me. Is success only to be measured in terms of money?"

"If you knew how poor I was twenty-five years ago. Larry, my ex? He left me when I was pregnant. I had a two-year-old. I didn't know how to do anything but read a book. Well, I knew how to throw a pot that wouldn't wobble. You can guess how much use that was."

"Wa-wa-wa," Gerhard says, rubbing his gargantuan fist in his Aryan eye. "Wa-wa-wa."

He can be too blunt, cruel, and his forceful, *über*-correct English makes the unilingual Ellen wither. But there's a truth in what he's saying too. She's been holding onto that sob story for years. Even she's tired of it.

When he has finished mocking her, he says, "It's almost time. Put on your hats."

Gerhard created penis hats for their first New Year's Eve as side-by-side neighbours. They get along, the three of them, so much that Ellen turned down several invitations in order to stay home tonight. No doubt Gerhard will go out later, but he has chosen to be with Ellen and Tilda at the crucial moment.

The unicorn horn of the *papier-mâché* erection juts from Tilda's forehead. It looks to have been constructed around the cardboard tube from a roll of paper towels, as does Gerhard's, while Ellen's is obviously built up from a measly toilet-paper tube.

"Why is mine the smallest?"

Gerhard checks his watch again. "Now is the time to count. Ten, nine . . ." Ellen frowns. Gerhard tells Tilda, "Trade with her."

Tilda, bless her, does.

Five, four, three, two, one. Happy new year! They cheer and clink glasses, and Ellen tries to fit them, penises and all, in one picture while holding the camera out at the end of her arm.

Gerhard lights the taper, lets it burn for a minute. When the wax is flowing, he passes it to Ellen, who leans over the pot of cold water with the taper angled so the molten wax runs into it. On

113

Gerhard's signal, she hands the taper to Tilda. Their penises knock together, giving Ellen the idea to engage in a little swordplay. Even Tilda, who generally looks on the verge of tears, laughs. Gerhard tells them to grow up.

All three take a turn. When Gerhard determines that their futures have solidified (if they handle them too soon—*Bleigiessen* they are called—they may deform), Ellen scoops out the hardened shapes. Gerhard snaps off the light.

"And now we read them."

He sets up the candle just so, while outside in the rain-washed night, the newborn year, pots bang on and firecrackers screech like shrapnel.

Something's gone from his wall, Ellen can't recall what. Now there is this white space on which their shadowy futures will be projected, interpreted, accepted or denied, all without influencing the actual events to come. Or so thinks Ellen, who is having a lot of fun. She's reached the stage in her drinking where she laughs through her nose.

Gerhard holds his *Bleigiessen* between the flame and the blank wall. "Some shapes have traditional meanings. A bell, an egg. They mean good news. *Das Kreuz*—a cross—it signifies death. Ah!" he declares to the shape on the wall. "A spider. *Die Spinne.*"

"What does a spider mean?" Ellen asks, already sensing Gerhard, like everyone, is seeing what he wants to see.

"Happiness hangs in the balance," he says.

"Okay," she says, pushing away his hand. "My turn."

And the dark shape of Ellen's destiny silhouettes itself on the blank wall, a Rorschach divination. Ellen tries. She strains.

"I see a heart," says Gerhard.

"To me?" Ellen says. "It looks like a lump."

• • •

THIS she completely forgets by morning when she wakes in the grey light of the new year. The year she will finally become a potter, which, ironically, will make her less inclined to call herself one. "I mess with clay," she'll say, because that's what it feels like to carve away most of a pot's substance until it becomes a container for light and air. The year she stops caring about success, or what anyone thinks she's worth.

Well into January, though, she's still in her funk.

The day of her breakthrough, January 21, Ellen is especially irritable. It seems that she's forgotten something, which is in itself normal. For the last few years even people she's known for ages have devolved into "Whatshername," entire countries to "that place," objects to "thingies." This morning, though, there's some kind of urgency to the unretrievable memory, a sense of jeopardy sparking around its edges. It torments her as she disgruntledly pokes at the clay.

She's making anuses. It's a nostalgia exercise more than anything, for she used to make anuses years ago on Cordova Island when she was first learning to throw a pot. To make a pot, you slap a lump of clay on the stationary wheel, enclose it in wet hands, and start it turning. The clay needs to be worked before it accepts its proper form. It needs to warm up. Gently, you squeeze until it rises into a column, then, with the palm of your hand, press down to make it squat again. Draw it into a column once, twice, three times. Then dig in your thumbs to make a hole.

It's hard work. You need strong hands. In the beginning Ellen's hands tired—not to mention her back (she was pregnant with Yo at the time)—and she would let the wheel spin to a stop so she could rest. There, sitting on the wheel, was a narrow cylinder with a hole down its middle, a sea anemone with its tentacles withdrawn.

Or an anus.

She cut it off the wheel with the wire and set it aside to dry. She made another. And another. Three weeks later she carted a dozen pink-glazed anuses to the Cordova Island market.

"Pencil holder?" someone asked.

"Ouch," Ellen replied.

She made a little sign: ANUSES. At the Christmas bazaar: AN ANUS FOR THE ASSHOLE IN YOUR LIFE!

Needless to say, she couldn't make them fast enough. Here she is, a quarter century later, trying to unfunk herself with anuses even as she understands you can never go back and, anyway, it's childish—though Gerhard will like his, she's sure.

All the while, it needles her that she's forgetting something. Finally, she thinks to look in her date book.

Leaving in a hurry, she runs into Tilda, who is just scurrying back from the store clutching her cloth bag as though it's filled with acorns and nuts, clearly sorry to have met another person, even Ellen. She only wants to get back inside and knit.

"I can't stop, honey," Ellen tells her. "I have a whatsit at the you-know-what."

An hour later, bibbed in the hygienist's chair, wearing the plastic sunglasses that protect her from flying chunks of her own tartar, she realizes the dental appointment isn't it. The important thing she's forgetting is still waving its arms in her peripheral vision, but she's not in any position to turn her head and look with the suction tube gurgling in her mouth and the hygienist's rubber-gloved hands in there too, wrist deep.

"Okay?" the hygienist asks, taking a break to pat Ellen's lips with the bib.

"Do you like your job?" Ellen asks.

"I love it!"

"Love it?" Ellen says before opening wide again.

Now she's really twisted up. This woman leaning in to scrape accretions off Ellen's molars, lifting out on her hooked tool a rotten shred of lettuce that, having somehow eluded the toothbrush, has been composting in Ellen's mouth for days, wiping it on a gauze pad and (here's the kicker) *smiling*? She loves her job.

Ellen hates her job, if she can even call it a job. Even if she didn't hate it, if she was contented instead of bored, Ellen, who once yearned to be an artist, is back making anuses. Anyway, pottery is so dead. Plastic killed it. Her days would be better spent flogging Tupperware.

The hygienist interrupts Ellen's downward spiral. "Your saliva has a really lovely consistency."

117

Accepted here: flattery, compliments, affirmations, praise however faint. Ellen is not just distracted from, but pulled right out of her funk by these words. She raises one finger in the air, signalling for the hygienist to remove her tool so she can speak.

"It's not too stringy?"

"Oh no!"

"Because I sometimes think it's overly viscous. When I spit, it won't let go. It just dangles there. I feel embarrassed."

"Don't be embarrassed," the woman says.

It's a mystery how art happens. Patience, hard work, coincidence— in some combination. Quantities need not be exact, but it's more work than anything. The other really crucial thing is to reach zero. To be abject.

That morning Ellen McGinty sat at her wheel, sat for ages until, erupting in frustration and rage, she attacked the anuses.

Clawed and squished until they extruded, shitlike, between her fingers. She howled and, howling still, staggered out of the garage behind the triplex and into her studio, where she threw herself onto the foldout couch, careful not to smear it with clay.

Sobbing, sobbing, sobbing. Ellen emptied out.

Afterward, she washed her hands in a trance and put on the kettle. On the windowsill, a dead plant and, beside it, her lumpy *Bleigiessen* from New Year's Eve. While she waited for the water to boil, she pushed a finger into the powdery soil of the plant. Water, water everywhere, and not a drop to drink. The leaves had sun-bleached to a linen-textured translucency, held together by fibrous veins.

Which was when Ellen thought to check her date book and saw she had a dental appointment.

She dressed in a rush, thinking that the life that was behind her showed like a dirty slip. All she had wanted was a fresh start.

Now she's in the dentist's chair, feeling flattered and affirmed, grateful for, and touched by, the words of the bright-toothed woman leaning over her with her tool. The sight of the tool and the hygienist's kindness coincide (the coincidence) with Ellen's months of frustration (the hard work, the patience). Ellen remembers the dead plant and how the light shone through a part of it that should have been opaque. The negative space. How it opened to the light. At that moment, stretched out long in the chair, relinquishing herself to its embrace, Ellen breaks through.

Afterward, in the liquor store, the clerk scanning her bottle says, "You're happy."

She's seen him before. He's a liquor-store lifer, slightly grizzled, eyes pouched. He probably gets a discount.

"I'm *very* happy," Ellen tells him. "I just had an epiphany at the dentist."

"No kidding."

Not only that, she finally remembered that elusive thingy. Driving her eye along the shelves, looking for a label that she liked, it came to her in a flash, unheralded, and not so important after all.

Her eye parked on a bottle of Fat Bastard and Ellen remembered. January 21. Today's date. Larry's birthday!

When she gets home, she'll give him a call.

"An epiphany," the clerk says. "And what is that again?"

"Halfway between an orgasm and an epileptic seizure."

NINE months later it's fall again. The purple whatchamacallits are in bloom, also the yellow whatsits. Ellen slips out midday to buy coffee, which she discovered she was out of when she woke, but hasn't done anything about until now because she's working on a new pot.

These days her work absorbs and enthralls her, so much so that when passersby drop into the studio (which they do more often), when one of them actually wants to buy a pot, Ellen feels protective of it. She looks the prospective buyer up and down while probing for the sort of information that is usually asked of people adopting pets. (How many hours of the day will the pot be left alone? Are small children likely to be handling it?) This way she has inadvertently bartered up her price. She can get as much as two hundred and fifty dollars, but she will also give one away if she thinks it will be particularly loved.

Her studio window has changed too. In the beginning there were those stolid, cabbagey pots she used to make. Then, for the months that she was teaching herself new techniques with porcelain, it was strewn with broken shards of the old pots with a couple of cabbages tossed in. Plenty of people stopped to comment on that. And now there is just one small white pot on a wooden pedestal in the window heaped with carded fleece that she got from Tilda. The pot is rising out of a cloud.

Another thing that's different: her vintage dentist's chair bought in an antique store on Main Street.

The sign on her door shows a clock. She moves the hands to say she'll be back in ten, then heads off in the direction of Fourth Avenue.

On this day, Ellen McGinty, forty-eight, has reached the point where she would give herself away if she thought she would be particularly loved. From the outside, it seems as though she's been doing this her whole life. There have been a lot of men since Larry, short-term boyfriends, one-night stands, but they always shared her with Larry, a person they may not have known existed. Why this should have been the case, and why it suddenly isn't any longer, Ellen can't say. She's just enjoying the fact of it.

She buys a pound of coffee, returns home to grind it and make herself an espresso. The dead plant still sits on the ledge above the sink and beside it, her *Bleigiessen*, which has been changing shape all summer, softening and spreading.

In the main studio window a white curtain hangs. Ellen leaves it open during the day. She throws her pots out back, but does the carving here at a workbench in the corner. She felt isolated out there. Here she sees it all—who admires her wares, who walks right by. Right now a man with a takeout coffee in his hand is looking in, first at the pot in the window, then right into the studio. Because it's so bright outside, and because Ellen is standing at the rear of the studio, in the kitchen doorway, he probably can't see her. But she can see him, backlit, autumn sunshine all around his edges.

He's just a shape now, but somehow familiar. Who? She leaves her cup of coffee on her workbench and starts toward him. It's Whatshisname—no, Whosit. The closer she gets, the less sure she is because the years keep dropping off him. A few steps across the studio's battered fir floor to the dentist's chair and he's already a younger man than she first thought. By the time she reaches the door, still unnoticed by him, he's a young one.

In a moment she'll open the door and he'll fall back in surprise, as if she has caught him red-handed in some subterfuge. This will be quickly overridden by a powerful mutual recognition. The widening of his sleepy eyes, the way he pushes the heavy waves of hair off his forehead, revealing the whole of his face, which has a sweetness to it—baby cheeks, fleshy nose. She knows this face, yet can't quite place him.

"Come in," she'll say.

Shyly, he'll step inside and look around. Ellen will point to the small case in the corner where three more pots are displayed, then settle back at her workbench. She'll unwind the damp cloth from the new pot, take up her tool again. This is the moment when visitors to the studio either thank her and slip out, or ask her a question to signify their interest in actually making a purchase. Either way is fine with Ellen, who will have commenced the delicate scraping of the semi-hardened clay. She'll forget all about this vaguely familiar visitor.

When she pauses for a sip of lukewarm coffee, he'll be there still, watching her. And Ellen will ask, "Do I know you?"

"In the café. Ten minutes ago. I was in front of you in line." He'll lift his paper cup in the air, as though toasting her. "Matt."

Now Ellen will remember. The tag of his shirt showed, the side with the washing instructions. The nape of the neck is such

121

a vulnerable place. (When her daughters were babies, she loved to nuzzle them there.) Impulsively, she tucked it in, which caused him to turn around, a young man in shorts who might have been offended to be touched by an older stranger, who instead said in a startlingly deep voice that did not match his baby face, "Your hands are cold."

"Cold hands, warm heart," Ellen chirped.

"I can see that."

At her age flirting warms her cockles. She left the café pleased.

She'll reswaddle the pot and rise from her stool with her coffee cup in hand. "Do you want another, Matt? Mine's cold. I'm making more anyway."

"Sure."

"I'm Ellen."

He'll follow her to the small kitchen in the rear with its geriatric appliances and knobless cupboards. He'll say, "What's going on next door?"

"What do you mean?"

"Those trees with dicks."

Laughing, Ellen will bend to knock the puck of old coffee out of the portafilter basket into the compost.

When she straightens, he'll wave the empty paper cup, say, "Can I toss this?" and lean in to drop it in the garbage can. He'll be close enough then to kiss her, and will.

When he pulls away, he'll say, "Sorry. I wanted to do that in the café. I was kicking myself that I didn't."

In a moment all this will happen. But not yet.

Ellen is still watching him, a stranger, through the glass door as he gazes at the pot, which is actually less a pot now than the filigreed outline of one, the clay scraped away with the pin tool or the fettling knife and sometimes actual pins or nails. In the beginning she copied patterns she found on the Internet, jewellery and lace, even a surprisingly beautiful pattern in a tumour, discovered by Googling the word *filigree*. (Needless to say, she did not tell this to the person who bought it.)

Lately, though, she just lets the pattern flow out the end of her tool, following it, instead of leading. So far she's been pleased. She works her way around the pot, liberating its negative space, creating the pattern that she somehow senses was always there in the clay, waiting for her. Sometimes it meets up perfectly where she started.

Sometimes it doesn't.

123

5

ERECTION MAN

...

In the fall Matt's girlfriend, Nicole, spent six weeks up north doing fieldwork for her thesis. When she returned, she asked Matt to go to a craft fair. She said it was famous, this huge craft fair at the Convention Centre, as famous as the Christmas train through Stanley Park, the carol ships in the harbour, the bridges and construction cranes outlined in coloured lights. Matt, heading into his first sodden coastal winter, concluded that Vancouver had a snow complex. When you have the white stuff, you don't need convention-sized craft fairs in early November to get you in the mood. But he went. Nicole wanted him to. Not for one second did he imagine Ellen would be there because he'd forgotten all about this other thing she did, this thing that had nothing to do with him.

He'd seen the sails of the Convention Centre before, while biking around the seawall. Ten white tentlike peaks. The day of the craft fair he looked up at the ceiling and realized where he was. Not across the water from this canvasy structure, but inside it. When he levelled his gaze again, he was looking right at Ellen. Just the day before he'd frolicked nakedly in her loft, yet it took a full second for the seismic shudder of recognition to move through him. He nearly fainted and popped an erection at the same time. Nearly collapsed on the red industrial carpet, a tent rising in his pants.

Nicole touched his sleeve and pointed into the crowded maze of booths. His eyes felt weird in their sockets, like they were floating in brine; he wondered if they looked weird to her.

"I'll catch up," he said, and she glided away, right past Ellen, without giving her or her wares so much as a glance.

Three of Ellen's filigreed pots were displayed on their own small wooden boxes. She hadn't noticed him yet. Her face was turned away, as though to avoid the stream of shoppers, while on the other side of the black fabric partition a grinning woman in a Santa hat offered candy canes to anyone who stopped to smell her soap. Ellen's booth was undecorated, just her and the pots, a black velvet cloth, and the pedestal boxes. A crease ran from the side of her nose to the corner of her mouth, previously unnoticed by Matt. It made her look angry. Or older. Or as old as she really was.

Matt came over and stood in front of her and she raised her eyes to him. The blankness in them was so wounding! Remember *yesterday?* It was just *yesterday* that I pounded my love into you. Then something happened on her face. The context he didn't belong in—the vaulted ceiling, the whole teeming fair beneath it, the ear-worming carols, and the thousand things beaded, turned, spun, and stitched—it all began to fall away, crumbling to bits around him, inconsequential, irrelevant.

EVER since Matt and Nicole got together four years ago, they'd spent Christmas with her parents. When they were at the U of A,

125

no one mentioned this arrangement; holidays didn't matter so much when you could see your family whenever. But now that Matt and Nicole lived a plane ride away in Vancouver, there were tensions. On the phone his sister Patty had said, "Why do *they* always get Christmas? Why can't *they* take Boxing Day for a change?"

"Nicole's an only child," Matt said. "Mom and Dad have you and Carl. And now the baby too. And I was just out there. Remember?" He'd come home for a week in September to see his newborn nephew, his sort-of namesake, Cody Matthias.

And so on the twenty-sixth, after French-press coffee and homemade scones at Nicole's parents' place, they headed out to the Grove. It was an ugly Kal Tire–Tim Hortons kind of drive with only blowing snow to soften the fact of it. Already, after just five months on the coast, Matt was questioning a whole life spent in a place like Spruce Grove, in a house like the one he pulled up at, its double garage doors the focal point, implying the most important thing in Spruce Grove was that you owned two cars.

"Well," Matt said. "I guess it's Christmas cake again."

Last year Nicole had choked on the fossilized Christmas cake. She'd excused herself from the table to go dig the package out of the garbage. Later, vindicated, she'd shown the best-before date to Matt.

"It might be the same cake as last year," he said now, and Nicole laughed. Easy to joke about his family out in the car, but the second he walked through that door the sluggish pledge he carried in his veins would start to flow.

The sheers parted in the window and a bloated face looked out. Patty. She made an obscure gesture with her hand, not welcoming at all, more like a push-off. Typical Patty: love ya, get lost. Then

Carl, Matt's brother-in-law, reared up hugely in the window with a more definite sign. He was telling them to go around the back.

"What's going on?" Nicole asked.

They left everything in the car and went around the side of the house, the minus-30-something outside air a psychic shock. Carl met them at the back door, clasped Matt's hand bro-style. Matt clasped back. He liked being related to this body type. Normally if a hulk like Carl came toward Matt? He crossed the street.

"Don't make a sound," Carl told them. "Don't say a word."

They slipped off their boots and crept to the living room still wearing their coats. Patty was stationed on the couch nursing the baby, which had tripled in size since September, just as Patty had tripled with her pregnancy. All you could see was the infant's veloured back and bald spot as he reclined on the C-shaped pillow around Patty's stomach. She wiggled her fingers at Matt. His dad, Alden, was there too, having given up his recliner for Nicole, squeezing Matt's shoulder as he limped past, coming back a minute later with a can of beer to shove in his hand.

It was eleven o'clock in the morning. All the presents under the tree were unopened.

"Alden?" Matt's mother, Anne, called from upstairs. "Where are you?"

Patty buckled over, trying not to laugh. The baby was nearly squashed.

"Down here!" his dad called. "We're waiting for Matty."

"Is he here?"

"Not yet."

First her socked feet appeared, one finding its place on the stair before the other moved down to join it. In silence they watched her slow, banister-clutching descent. It seemed cruel to Matt and he

127

had to look away. When she finally reached the bottom and started into the room, she walked almost normally except for her arms, which she bent at the elbows as if carrying an invisible tray.

She stopped. "Matthias?"

"See!" Patty shrieked at the same time Carl and Alden let out a roar. "See! She always knows!"

"Should I change my deodorant?" Matt asked, going over to his mother, who turned to him for a hug. In September she could still see him. Couldn't she? He waved the unopened beer in her face, but she didn't react.

"Matty's here," she whispered in his ear, as though he were someone else.

He pulled away. "Mom. I should get the bags."

Coatless, he sprinted out the door to the car, the cold pummelling him all the way.

When he burst back inside, Carl called, "I hope those are the presents. I want my presents."

"You should have gone ahead without us," Nicole said.

"We didn't want to," Patty said in a long-suffering tone. She lifted the baby to her shoulder, drummed his back. He sounded hollow.

"Can I see him?" Nicole asked, just as Alden appeared carrying a mug with a spoon sticking out. "Here's your tea, dear."

Anne was right behind him. "Did you ask her what she takes in it?"

"What do you take in it, dear?"

"Milk," Nicole said.

"No sugar?" Anne asked Alden.

"Just milk," Nicole said.

"Alden, take it back and put some milk in."

"I'm on it, Mother. I'm on it."

Carl, on his hands and knees under the tree, began passing presents around. "Patty. Patty. The Hickey Machine."

"Oh, he's so cute," said Nicole, taking a seat next to Patty on the couch. "Hi, Cody. Hi. Let me know when I can hold him."

"He feeds, like, all the time."

There was a PhD thesis to be written on what came out of his sister's mouth, Matt thought as he settled beside Nicole. Differentiating the layers of grievance—Boxing Day, the countless tactless things Nicole had unwittingly blurted over the years—then sorting the grievances from the sharp way Patty expressed her love.

Carl read a tag and tossed a present. "Matty. Feels like a mouse pad."

129

"Okay, here she comes," Alden announced, limping in with the tea.

"Did you take out the bag?" asked Anne, who still hovered between the living room and the dining room, turned slightly away from everyone, looking old and odd.

Alden turned and limped back out.

As soon as Nicole got her tea the way she liked it, they started on the presents, everyone turning first to Matt, who opened the mouse pad. It was custom printed with a picture of his nephew.

"I'll keep it in my wallet. There's plenty of room. Not like there's any money in it." He took the wallet from his back pocket and feigned jamming the mouse pad in.

"He has a finger pad on his computer," Nicole explained.

"Oh, sorry," Patty said.

Because of Matt's lack of funds, Alden, Patty, Carl, and the baby all received a can of Kokanee. "B.C. beer!" Alden said. "That'll make for a change."

Carl and Patty seemed touched that the baby had got his first beer at three months. "Hey, Hickey Machine!" Patty said, jiggling the can over his head while he nursed. "Look what your uncle gave you!" She said the outrageously overpriced booties that Nicole had bought at the craft fair were "Nice."

"I hope you didn't get beer, dear," Alden told Nicole, who laughed and shook her head.

"Where's the other two beer then?" Carl said. "Anne, did you get *two* beer from Matty? No fair."

"It's smaller than beer," Anne said, lifting the box into her lap.

As well as the mouse pad, Matt got a Walmart sweater and Oilers memorabilia, Nicole a Walmart sweater and bath beads. She pulled the pink atrocity over her head, seemingly oblivious to the fact that it had been purchased for her by his sister out of sheer hostility, not bad taste. Or not only bad taste. Her static-charged hair rose like feelers in the dry air.

"Acrylic is so warm," she said.

"What does it look like?" his mother asked.

"It looks okay," Patty said. "What did Matt get you, Nicole?"

Nicole said, "A water bottle."

"What!" Carl roared. "*We* all got beer!"

"It's a hydration system," Matt said. "I'll show you." He went to the door where their bags still were and brought it back, a red nylon pouch with a long clear tube dangling down.

"What does it look like?" Matt's mother asked.

"A douche bag," Patty said.

"I was going to say whoopee cushion," Alden said.

"Pass it here," said Carl. "I'll sit on it."

"Don't," Patty told him. "You'll pop it. Then she won't be able to drink her water."

"Okay, okay," said Matt, seeing Nicole's face pinkening to match the sweater. He took it and shoved it down into Nicole's overnight bag again. "It's for hiking. We're hiking a lot out there."

Alden said, "You're up, Mother. Go ahead."

Anne turned the present in her lap, feeling for the folds in the paper. Matt had used too much tape.

"I'll do it, Mom."

He leapt up but Patty waved him back. What was worse, fumbling with something in front of everyone or being denied the chance to? Anne finally tore the paper off. Now she was feeling the box, but would never get inside it.

"Here, Mom," he said, taking her hands in his. He righted the box, positioned her thumb in the notch on the lid. "It slides open."

"I see," said his mother, even though she didn't.

She lifted the tiny pot out of the straw it was packed in and held it an inch from her eyes. For some reason this made her seem stupid. "What's it for?" she asked.

Not—what is it? *What's it for?*

This was the kind of people they were. His father, who suffered chronic back pain, kept on running his carpet-cleaning business anyway. Until just a few years ago, when her eyesight got too bad, Anne used to go on rounds with him; now she booked their dwindling appointments. (Laminate had cut their business in half.) Carl was a manager at Canadian Tire. Patty had cashiered at Safeway since she was sixteen. In Matt's family, you worked and the things you bought with your hard-earned money had a purpose, like beer. No one was the least offended to receive beer for Christmas, but everyone stared at the pot Anne was turning in her hands and their unease was palpable.

A pot too small to put anything in. A pot full of holes. She

131

couldn't even see it! Everything they feared for him had come true. He'd given up a job offer to go live in a city so soft it didn't even snow, where he had no other job lined up and still hadn't found one despite his unpaid-for university degree. He'd followed Nicole without marrying her, Nicole who hogged him every Christmas and was getting a PhD in a subject they couldn't remember or understand. All of it, embodied in this inexplicable gift.

And that was only the half of it. They didn't even know that Matt was sleeping with the woman who'd made the pot.

BACK in mid-October, after Nicole left town, Matt met Ellen at the coffee place on the corner. A woman in loose clothes, older than him; women his age dressed in yoga bondage.

The way she stood in the line—claiming her full allotment of space, confident she deserved it—attracted Matt, who every second second-guessed himself. He should have been earning 2.3 million Korean *won* a month plus the completion bonus at the end of two years, living in free housing supplied by the *hakwon*. He should have been eating kimchi. Nicole had agreed he should go and clear up his debt. And if she wasn't accepted in any of the PhD programs she'd applied to, she would come to Korea too. You didn't need the TESL certificate, just earned more if you had one.

But she *was* accepted, and it turned out that she couldn't bear to part from him, and he her, in truth. Normally, they didn't do the dirty enough to satisfy Matt, not by a long shot. Anticipating their parting, they did it all the time, and Matt thought, okay, this is worth 2.3 million *won*. He cancelled his contract.

Two months later Nicole went up north, leaving Matt in Vancouver following strange women around. Why not? He'd followed Nicole here. He would pick a woman at random and tail her until he was in danger of being noticed, picturing himself and her in an alternative life. In bed, yes, but other things too. Carrying her shopping basket, lifting the fallen chain back on her bike. It seemed conceivable then, that he could be with anyone, and if he could—be *with* anyone—he could *be* anyone.

That October day the game had ended almost immediately. Ellen lived a block from the café in an old triplex of artist studios. He followed Ellen home like a lost dog and when he got there, what was in the window? A pot.

And a different game began.

AFTER present opening, the lacuna of waiting for dinner, the life sentence of every Christmas afternoon. Matt tried not to watch his sister nursing the baby, but there she sat, letting it all hang out. Ellen had large dark aureolae while Nicole's were pale pink, almost flesh-toned. Patty's were somewhere in between, nipples elongated from the sucking. When Ellen lay on her back, her breasts tumbled into her armpits. When she knelt with her elbows on the bed, her nipples brushed the sheet. He'd never, of course, get Nicole in that position. She often found intercourse painful. And Ellen's bush was so extravagant; he'd been startled at first.

Carl was playing Wii with the sound off. He nudged Matt with his foot. "That's your sister, buddy."

Matt blushed, but Patty said, "I don't care. I'm just a dairy producer now. Hey, who wants to hold the Hickey Machine while I pee?"

"Me," Nicole said.

She had disappeared upstairs right after the presents were opened. Now she'd returned with a book under her arm. She must have slipped away to read, except her eyes looked puffy and her brief glance in Matt's direction seemed freighted with reproach. He couldn't think what he'd done.

Patty made like she hadn't heard Nicole's offer, or maybe she hadn't. She heaved herself off the couch and deposited the baby into Matt's unready arms. With wide, surprised eyes, the baby regarded him.

"Hi," Matt said.

Cody Matthias pitched forward in a swoon and proceeded to nuzzle Matt's neck. "Help," he said to Nicole.

"He sucks," Carl said. "Sucks, poops, cries. It's quite the life."

Nicole seemed happy to take the baby, but she also frowned at Matt during the transfer. Because Patty hadn't given her the baby in the first place? Matt shrugged and got up.

In the kitchen his mother was patting down the uncooked turkey. "There's Froot Loops," she said the second he stepped in the room.

Shaking his head, Matt poured himself a bowl, then watched as Anne performed a cavity search on the bird.

"What is *that*?" he asked.

She had extracted something penile and flayed. The neck, she claimed.

"How did it get up its arse?"

On the phone, Alden was saying, "Not possible. Tomorrow would work, first thing. In the meantime, salt. Sifto or what-have-you."

He was wearing Anne's apron, Matt noticed. He'd never seen his father in an apron before.

"What next, Mother?" he asked when he hung up.

"I can help," Matt said.

Then Patty came in cupping both breasts.

"And what is that about?" Matt asked her.

"I'm trying to figure out which one is fuller."

"Where's the bread?" Anne asked.

"Right in front of you, Mom." Patty snatched up the Wonder Bread and bopped Anne on the head with it.

"Get out of here, you two," Anne snapped. "You're just in the way."

Matt dropped his dirty bowl in the sink and followed Patty out. "That's a bit harsh," he said. "Hitting Mom."

Patty swung around. "Matt, she wants you to treat her the same."

"Did she say that?"

"She said it to Dad. She can take a joke. She just can't see."

135

"Not at all?" Matt asked, pained, but Patty was already waddling away. So fat! Was she going to stay like that? he wondered.

In the living room the Hickey Machine was grousing, Nicole pacing with him, trying to forestall full-blown wails. Every time she passed in front of the TV, Carl leaned sideways in his chair so he wouldn't total his Ferrari. Patty plopped down on the couch, horseshoed herself with the nursing pillow, held out her arms for the baby. The way she whipped out the breast and plugged it in made Matt grimace. Carl saw and guffawed.

Nicole sat beside Patty again and, ignoring her book on the coffee table, picked up the *Cosmopolitan* beside it. She indulged in these kinds of magazines herself, mostly when she was depressed. She would curl up in bed with *People* and a carton of Häagen-Dazs.

"'Your Sexual Horoscope for 2009!'" Matt read off the cover. "Hmm. I wonder what's in store for Gemini."

Nicole ignored him. So. Definitely mad. To Patty, she said, "This is great. I don't have time to read trash anymore."

Patty's thought-balloon broke off and hovered above her. Apparently, only Matt could see it: *Trash?* She asked, "How come you don't have time?"

"A PhD is so gruelling. I had no idea."

Patty's thought-balloon: *Ha! Try having a baby!*

And it seemed to Matt, not for the first time, that Nicole couldn't possibly be smart enough for a PhD.

"First Matty. Then Matt-a-tat-tat. Which became Machine-Gun Matt. Machine-Gun Mutt. Doggy. Dogbone. Boner. Erection Man, or just E.M. Then, for some reason, Dr. Dog. Dr. Love. Loverboy."

"Loverboy?" Nicole said, still staring straight ahead. "Really?"

He had made her come for this drive. "Clay Franks lived here." Slowing, he stared at the house. Snow-blown driveway, its banks waist-high. Two-car garage. Vinyl siding. Amber glass on either side of the front door. Same as every other house.

"A.k.a. Frankster. Frankenfurter. Weiner. Weenie. Teenie-Weenie. Then just Teenie, though the guy was, and probably still is, huge."

Nicole finally broke her silence. "It's so sad about your mom. She's much worse than last summer. She seems completely blind now."

"We got mad at him and put a bag of dog shit in his mailbox."

"Charming."

"Next door there? That was Tommy Gerken's place. He tried to make Blake Wineman grab Teenie's balls. 'Grab them! Grab them!' I guess he was gay, but we didn't think of that. He was unbelievable on defence. Later he got called up from Juniors. Played two games for the Flyers. We all went over to Winey's to watch."

He glanced over. Nicole seemed to be pouting now. She was wearing a tweed newsboy cap that left the tips of her ears exposed and a long muffler wrapped twice around her neck. She lifted her chin so he could see her mouth better.

"What?" Matt said.

"I don't find this particularly interesting."

"I went shopping with you."

"When? You mean with my parents?"

"The craft fair."

"Oh, the *craft fair!*" She crossed her arms over her chest and stared out the passenger window, right at Penny Barber's house. Penny Barber—Barbie, Barbell, Barbarella—was the first girl Matt ever asked out. She said no.

"What?" Matt said.

"You're just so weird around your family."

"Weird?"

"I get the feeling you're embarrassed by me."

"What?" He accelerated at the same time he slapped the wheel, like the car was a horse. "You're embarrassed by *me!*"

"I am not!"

"'Matt prefers Tim Hortons,'" he mocked.

"What was I supposed to say? You stormed out of Starbucks."

"There was a huge line. I just went across the street where there wasn't one. What's the matter with that?"

"Can you look at the road when you drive? This car belongs to my parents."

"Starbucks is overrated. And I hate"—he took his hands off the wheel to scratch air-quotes—"'French-press' coffee. It tastes like sludge. Your parents' French press?" Hands up again for the quotes. "It's made in China."

137

They drove in complete silence for several blocks, along the winter-locked streets of his banal childhood, the stomping ground of his appalling ordinariness, the inspiration for everything he would eventually not become. Not even come close to becoming. Nicole wouldn't look at him, but finally she said, "I know you must be sad about your mom. I know because you gave her such a nice present."

THAT was what she was upset about. He didn't realize it until the end of the day, not even when he found her crouching by the artificial tree peering inside the little wooden box.

138

She said, "You bought this at the craft fair."

But before that there was Christmas dinner, Patty and Carl spelling each other off, treading a circle around the table with the bawling Hickey Machine. Matt had seen the kid's face but once the whole day. Other than that, his strange tonsure was always turned toward them.

Anne wouldn't address Nicole directly, which Matt was beginning to wonder about. She must be mad, too, like Patty. She stabbed at her plate, hit china. A few times she actually pushed pieces of food onto the tines of her fork with her fingers, hunkering down, trying to be surreptitious. But everyone noticed. Everyone stared, it was so sad and bizarre. Nicole must be grossed out, Matt thought.

Nicole was telling them about Hazelton, where she had researched her thesis. "Eagles everywhere. I got to interview the elders. I felt so privileged."

She wasn't grossed out. Matt was grossed out.

"What exactly are you studying again, dear?" Alden asked.

"Case and agreement in Gitxsan. Gitxsan is the language they speak up there. I'm trying to figure out why there are these two very different sentence types with different agreement patterns."

"I have an agreement pattern," Carl said. "I agree with everything Patty says."

"You had to go all that way? Why not pick up the phone?" Alden asked.

"They can't tell you. They don't know. Just like you probably can't explain why we say 'thieves' instead of 'thiefs,' for example."

"Do we?" Carl asked. "Thiefs. Thieves. Thiefs. Thieves."

Matt dreaded someone would use the word *Indian*. When they'd had this same conversation the night before, everyone said "First Nations." Nicole's parents had praised her to the skies for working to preserve a dying language, while Matt sat with the paper crown from the Christmas cracker on his head, a linguistic imperialist with a TESL certificate.

Also, at Nicole's they'd had trifle.

Nicole filled the hydration system while they were in the bathroom getting ready for bed. She squirted Matt and more water came out than expected and soaked his shirt.

"What did you do that for?"

He only had two shirts with him. The rest were back at Nicole's parents' place. He peeled off the wet one and, shoving the towels aside to make room, hung it over the rack.

Nicole said, "It was just a joke. Lighten up. You're the one who gave me a crappy present."

Ah, he thought, welling with tenderness. So that was it? She was jealous. Jealous of his mother, thank God. But how to explain? He couldn't have given Nicole the pot. He wasn't a complete cad.

He folded her against his bare chest. She was taller than Ellen, but much slighter. There didn't seem to be enough of her, while he could grab pieces of Ellen in his hands. These kisses were so different as well: tentative, regretful.

"I wish we could sleep together," Nicole said when they separated.

"We'll sleep together tomorrow night at your folks' place."

"But I want to sleep with you tonight. I miss you. We sleep together in Vancouver. They know that. Why can't we sleep together here?"

"It's just the way they are," Matt said, digging out the toothpaste from her makeup bag.

"Well, it's silly."

"Sorry they're so silly."

"Me too," Nicole said, and something in Matt twisted.

"Sorry my family isn't hip, like yours," he said. "Sorry they're low-class."

"I didn't mean that."

"You thought it."

"I never once thought it!"

"Sorry you had to buy the plane tickets. Sorry I'm such a lousy boyfriend. Sorry I don't feel like sleeping with you tonight."

She was behind him in the mirror, her eyes filling with tears. Then she wasn't.

THE basement bedroom was cold even in the Walmart sweater and Matt couldn't sleep. He lay there thinking about his conversation after supper with Carl, the two of them on the back deck sharing a cigar, the double cloud of smoke and breath, while Patty and Nicole cleaned up.

Matt had been fully accoutred: parka, hat, gloves. He stomped his boots as he smoked. He-man Carl wore a hoodie.

"There's this glut of ESL teachers in Vancouver. Half the schools shut down after 9/11. I'm on all the sub lists but, so far, nobody's calling."

"So what're you doing with yourself every day?" Carl asked, manipulating his jaw to expel the smoke in perfect rings of diminishing size.

Matt, who had consumed a lot of beer by then, was going to tell him. About the following game and how, surprise surprise, it had brought him to Ellen. He and Carl didn't normally exchange intimacies, but Matt remembered that he'd married Patty in a Catholic church. Carl might understand about guilt and the warped things it made you say and do. But in that long pause, while Matt's dulled brain sorted the pros and cons of a confession, Carl changed the subject.

"I'm first in my hockey pool," he said.

Nicole was in Matt's old room upstairs. He should go to her and apologize, slip into bed with her, sneak down in the morning.

He considered phoning Winey or Teenie, but according to the clock it was two in the morning. "Hey, it's me, Loverboy. Dr. Dog. E.M. What's happening, man? Long time no see. Yeah, I'm living in Vancouver now. Yeah. Fuckin' ay, man."

He could have looked them up any of the hundred times he'd been home during university, but he never had.

When he finally got out of bed, it was because he remembered the *Cosmo* on the coffee table and the tantalizing information it contained. To know his sexual destiny, or even get a hint about where this business with Ellen was heading, would help him sleep. If not, there were the models, all of them super stacked.

The Christmas tree had been turned off but the lamp next to the couch was on. He didn't see her until she spoke.

"Matthias?"

But he'd been quiet! Absolutely soundless. So how did she know? How could she not? She'd given birth to him, nursed him. (He'd probably suckled her the way the Hickey Machine suckled Patty, like a workaholic leech.)

All day Matt had been avoiding his mother. He was afraid of her blindness. Now he stood before her, mortified. She knew he'd come upstairs for the magazine. She knew he intended to jerk off with it. She knew everything: when he was in the room, when he felt ashamed.

He felt ashamed.

"Here I am," he said.

She patted the place next to her; he came and sat beside her on the couch. His gift to her was in her lap, he saw now, out of the wooden box. She fumbled for the light, snapping it off and plunging Matt into darkness with her, but only for a second. When the light came back on, an intricate pattern sprang out from the ceiling and walls, kaleidoscopic, as she turned the pot.

"Can you see it?" she asked.

She was holding the pot over the bulb. Above and all around them, its negative spaces filled with light. Lacy, sensual, vaguely Arabic, or like some arcane script no one knew how to decode, the shapes frolicked and wrote themselves.

"Can *you* see it?" Matt asked.

"That's all I see. Lights and darks."

He tipped back his head to watch. Anne found his hand, found and squeezed it. Matt squeezed back.

This was what the pot was for.

• • •

IN the Convention Centre, the crowd pressed around them but they might as well have been alone. He and Ellen stared at one another, each surprised the other existed outside the universe of Ellen's bedroom loft. That was what Matt was thinking anyway. Finally, he picked up one of the pots, only to discover it was mainly made of air. Afraid it would crumble in his hand, he set it down.

"Take it," she said.

"No. I want to buy it. How much is it?"

She pointed to the small clear sticker on the box. One hundred and fifty dollars. He must have winced because, again, she invited him to take it. Then she looked away. With her face turned, he saw her crease again.

Ellen asked, "Who's it for?"

He hadn't got that far in his mind. He was only being gallant. But she misunderstood his hesitation and quickly scanned the crowd. It ruined everything, this acknowledgment that other people existed, one in particular who was unknowingly involved and very, very close to being hurt.

Ellen fished under the table for the Visa machine. She took his credit card, impersonally, made the imprint and handed it to him to sign.

Matt signed. He watched her pack the pot in the little wooden box, nestle it in the straw, slide closed the lid. She put the box in a string-handled bag and passed it to him.

"I love you," he said.

Ellen said, "Oh, come on."

FAR ahead, Nicole perused some knit goods. Over the top of the partition she could see on display in the next booth pictures jigsawed from inlaid wood. When her eye fell on one of an eagle, she was back in Hazelton again, walking by the river with a tiny, wiry elder in a trucker's cap, trying to ply out words. She got the feeling he was only pretending not to understand her questions, so she stopped asking, and when she did the river's palaver came to the fore. Stones grated underfoot. And something else, a sound like a very angry person cleaning glass. The elder pointed to a tree.

An eagle? Really? Its call was so high-pitched and girlish.

She heard her name and turned. Matt was weaving through the crowd. In the weeks since her return, she'd grown used to the silent language of his resentment. All her beautiful memories, like the one she'd just been enjoying, tainted with his mood. But here he was, coming toward her now, shining all over. The old Matt.

She smiled and dangled two pairs of booties. "For the baby. Which ones do you like?"

Then she noticed the bag hanging on his arm and, curious, said, "You bought something. Can I see it?"

Matt said no, which pleased her more than anything.

144

6

YOUR DOG MAKES ME SMILE

. . .

So in her forty-eighth year Ellen took up with a man-boy in his twenties who wore shorts in any weather. She couldn't believe her luck.

At first Matt had hours (all day in fact; he was unemployed) to lie around with Ellen, who, living off her savings, was queen of her own life. Queen Ellen spread out in the loft on the hot twisted sheets, inhaling the tang of their exertions, while Matt scampered naked down the ladder to do her bidding. He brought her a glass of water, a wad of tissues to wipe the milty puddle off her belly, a cheese plate from the fridge.

One afternoon he fell back, curls fanning across the pillow. "I need to ask you something really personal. I've never asked anyone before. I need the honest truth. Please."

"What?" Ellen said. "What?"

"Is my cock too big?"

This went on for three glorious weeks that autumn while even the weather seemed to announce the return of love. The horse-chestnut trees burst into flame, the Japanese maples dripped red, burgundy, carnelian. It didn't rain.

And then it did. Lashings of it, the wind tearing off the last celebratory leaves. The trees stood around, undressed and shivering, clotted with crows' nests.

Now Matt brought his cell phone up to the loft and left it turned on. Ellen pretended she didn't see it tossed onto the clothes he'd so urgently shed, but there it lay, connecting him to someone he'd failed to mention.

She pulled the sheet up to cover her body. Too much information.

Let the suffering begin.

146   ACROSS the street from the studio was a corner store. This time of year Christmas cacti, poinsettia, and little bonsai pines crowded the board-and-cinderblock shelves out front. Plants, cigarettes, and lottery tickets were the store's main business. Ellen, worried the place would go under, occasionally scooted across to buy something she didn't need. Another plant to ignore to death. A can of corn. There was little else. The Frosted Flakes looked archeological.

She ran across in sweats and an old loose T-shirt scabbed with drying flecks of clay. A dog was shivering in a newspaper-lined box beside the till. She couldn't tell its breed. The black kind with a goatee and plaintive eyes.

"Where did it come from?" she asked.

The owner of the store said, "My brother. Driving from Chilliwack? He saw it on the road. You want it?"

"I just came in for some corn." Ellen set the can down, leaving fingerprints in the dust on top. "Maybe you should take it to the SPCA."

He waved his arms back and forth like an aircraft marshal directing a 747 with batons. "Too busy!"

"Oh. Do you want me to take it for you?"

Ellen tucked the niblets in the box with the small black dog and carried both across the street. Halfway, the dog reached up and licked her face.

"None of that now," she said.

Hardly anyone got Ellen at first, but this dog did. He beat his feathery tail against the side of the box and smiled. When she shifted the cardboard carrier onto one hip to open the door, he leapt right down, dashing circles around the studio, sniffing everything—Ellen's workbench where she carved her pots, her dentist's chair. He jumped onto the couch and tossed the cushions aside with his snout. Then he did what Ellen always did when visiting someone for the first time. He flounced over to the shelf and read the spines of all her books.

147

MATT didn't come that day, or call. Normally this meant long unfocused hours tied up in knots of hope, then, when Ellen could no longer deny he was a no-show, her dejected release from these self-wound coils. How pathetic to be waiting all day for a man as young as her daughters. Tear-stained, humiliated, she fashioned little monsters out of clay, then flattened them.

Today she put aside these pitiful recreations. She had to get a dog to the SPCA. To do that, she needed a collar and leash. One thing led to another and, come evening, the dog was still there sniffing Ellen's books.

She too loved the smell of old paperbacks, that particular, melancholy odour. It only followed then that the dog should have a literary name. (She had to call him *something* before she turned him in.) Tintin? Tintin was the boy, not the dog. What was the dog's name? She Googled it. *Snowy.*

Snowy would not do.

Chekhov's stories were right there on the shelf, perfumed by dust and sadness. The moment Ellen settled in the dentist's chair with the book, the dog sprang onto the footrest, gingerly walked the double plank of her outstretched legs, then curled into a polite ball and fell asleep. A dog in the lap of a lady reading "Lady with a Lapdog."

In the story the dog appears in the opening paragraph, trotting along the Yalta promenade. No name, just a breed. A white Pomeranian. (This is ironic, for Dmitry Dmitrich Gurov thinks of the women he seduces as of *the lower breed.*) How many times had Ellen read this story of a passing affair that swells to a grand passion? Many, many times, and every time reminded her of her first reading at seventeen or eighteen, when she'd sobbed. With each rereading, the sob returned, a ghost in her chest, lodged too deeply now to release, her own heartaches grown around it. She'd been living with that impacted sob ever since. *Catharsis interruptus.*

Tonight though, she felt nothing. Something rang false.

A few days after noticing Anna Sergeyevna, the lady with the lapdog, Gurov seats himself close by at an outdoor restaurant. He wags his finger at the Pomeranian, and, when it growls, appeases it with a bone off his plate. It's a ploy, of course, to secure Anna Sergeyevna's acquaintance.

After dinner, Anna and Gurov take a long walk, just as Ellen herself had done that afternoon when she returned home with the leash and collar and a hundred and twenty dollars' worth of dog food and paraphernalia. What happened with Ellen was that the dog—the black one, the flesh-and-blood, tongue-and-tail one—made straight for the nearest tree and began to circle it, forcing Ellen to leave the sidewalk and slop around on the saturated verge. It was as though he were searching for something he'd lost in the longer grass at the tree's base, something he was desperate to recover. Finally, he found it, this precious thing invisible to Ellen. When he did, he lifted his leg and pissed all over it, then romped ahead to the next tree where, evidently, he had also left something in the grass.

After ten minutes of this Ellen grew impatient and tried to pull the dog along. He stiffened his legs, effectively putting on his brakes, and stared at her, ill-done-by. She had to coax and herd him, then pick him up and carry him. In other words, the entire walk had been about getting the dog to walk instead of sniff. More than once she became tangled in the leash, or he did.

149

Yet when Gurov and Anna Sergeyevna go strolling after dinner, talking the whole time, marvelling at the way the light falls on the sea, the dog isn't even mentioned. Presumably he was there, or had they left him tied up back at the restaurant?

A week later, Gurov and Anna Sergeyevna retire to her hotel room to consummate their affair. Again, no reference to the Pomeranian. Does he object to their lovemaking? Is he jealous? Have they shut him in the bathroom? It doesn't say. In fact, the dog is only mentioned once more in the story. Months after they both leave Yalta, Gurov finds he can't forget the lady with the lapdog. He travels to her town and loiters in front of her house until, after a miserable hour, an old woman comes out with the Pomeranian.

Gurov was about to call to the dog, but his heart began to beat violently and in his excitement he could not remember its name.

Here Ellen lifted the real nameless dog out of her lap so she could return the book to the shelf. It was the first time the story had failed her.

An hour later while brushing her teeth, she realized something: the story was in Gurov's point of view! It wasn't *Chekhov*, but *Gurov* who was indifferent to the dog beyond the purpose it could serve him in seducing a young woman. Whatever Chekhov may have felt about the canine species, Ellen knew this: if the story had been from Anna Sergeyevna's point of view the dog would certainly have had a name. And a patronymic. And a diminutive too.

So she settled on Anton. The resemblance was obvious by then—the longer black chin hairs, the compassionate tilt of the head. Tony for short, in honour of her dog-loyal hairdresser.

150

THE next day Matt was out front getting rained on when Ellen and Tony returned from their walk. Her heart stuttered at the sight of those bare knees. According to the clock with movable hands on her door, Ellen was late. This clock had proved useful in their affair, which was being conducted strictly on a drop-in basis. Now it provided Matt with a grievance.

She pointed to her goateed excuse, though Tony's goatee was not so obvious with the wet sock hanging down.

Matt asked, "What's it got in its mouth?"

"A sock. Isn't that cute?"

Before the door was fully open, Tony bolted in ahead of Matt, who threw back the dripping hood of his Gore-Tex and sampled Ellen, her mouth and neck. After they separated and shed their rain gear, he asked whose dog it was.

"Well," Ellen said.

She told him the whole story of bringing the dog home and the trip to the pet store. She might have been reading a script. Did he hear it? This was how she lived now, hovering above her own life, watching herself so that later, when she recounted her day to Matt, he would be amused.

He checked his phone.

"You would not believe what they had in that store!" Ellen babbled. "See? Party-balloon poop bags! I can coordinate Tony's poop bag to my outfit. Or I can say, 'I'm feeling existential,' and take a blue one."

Everything was in the box Tony and the can of corn had come across the street in. Matt reached for the plastic banana, squeaked it. Tony snapped to attention.

"That's a lot of stuff to take to the SPCA, Ellen."

"And I hate shopping. I don't know what came over me."

"Let's go up," he said, starting for the ladder to the loft, pulling on her sleeve.

Ellen sashayed over to the sign and turned the hands of the clock forward another forty minutes, remembering how, not so long ago, their pleasure hadn't been so stingily meted out, yet still feeling grateful, so very grateful.

SHE walked Tony to the vet, paid for shots, deworming, and the flea treatments she had to purchase in a six-month pack. Wheaten terrier, the vet thought, with a dash of Labrador. Maybe even a little corgi. He lectured her on neutering.

Ellen said, "The thing is, I'm not keeping him."

She should have been churning out Christmas pots, but couldn't settle at her wheel, not since that debilitating conversation with Mimi the day before.

"You're not coming home for Christmas?" Ellen had asked.

151

"I hate Christmas."

"Say the word and I'll buy you the ticket, sweetheart. All of us together for once, even your dad."

"Who?" Mimi said, and Ellen sighed.

"Listen, Mom. I'm not in the mood for this. I just had my pubes waxed. I'm dying here."

"You *what?*" Ellen asked.

She was practically shaking with mortification when Mimi finished explaining. "Everyone does it, Mom. No one would ever go around all hairy *down there.*"

Another thing for Ellen to fret about: her wild bush. If she went and had it done now, Matt would notice. Boy, would he notice.

She started training Tony out of library books, glad to have found a use for all that corn. Tony was gaga for niblets. Within days she had him sitting and lying down for niblets, though no inducement would endear him to the leash. He was a free spirit and, respecting that, Ellen let him sniff along behind her.

On YouTube, she watched Pumpkin the beagle read. It really seemed that he could. When shown a picture of a cat and offered a selection of words printed on cards, Pumpkin selected C–A–T one hundred percent of the time.

Some old competitive streak surfaced in Ellen. She opened another can of niblets.

Finally, finally, Matt dropped by. "Sorry," he said.

"What for?" Ellen chirped.

"I couldn't get away."

Ellen pictured the girlfriend, not her ineffable face, but her tidy little Chekhov mound, pristinely waxed. All her thinking about the Russians had brought her to this unflattering comparison, that, pubically, Ellen was in the Tolstoy camp.

Matt said, "And I'm going home for the holidays. Did I mention that?"

One of the dog books explained stances, tail positions, barks. Ellen had noticed that though Matt always said "I," when he really meant "we" he cast his eyes down and to the right. And if she told him how desperate this news made her, would he ever come back?

"And where is home?" she asked.

"Spruce Grove. Outside of Edmonton."

She feigned nonchalance, said she was going away herself.

"Cordova Island?" he said. "Where's that?"

"I used to live there a long time ago. When I was married. My younger daughter Yolanda lives there now with her partner and their kids. She dropped out of pre-med to relive my life. The weird thing is, then my ex-husband moved back."

"Oh," Matt said. "Should I be jealous?"

Ellen laughed, but he didn't. His face folded up in a way she hadn't seen. He was always so uncreased, so playful, except when lamenting his penis size or paying obeisance to his phone. It frightened her into blurting, "Oh! We've got something to show you!"

"We?"

It seemed Matt had forgotten Tony until Ellen called him. His black head popped up among the couch cushions.

Ellen selected three books from the shelf—*Lady with a Lapdog, The Portrait of a Lady, Anna Karenina*—books the average undergrad couldn't tell apart. She stood them up on the floor. Tony waited, shifting from side to side, licking his lips, which Ellen knew now was a sign of anxiety. She showed Matt the index card with its neatly printed question: *Which book did Chekhov write?*

"Read," she commanded, holding the card in front of Tony.

He pranced over to *Lady with a Lapdog* and brought it back to

153

Ellen. For this, she rewarded him with a palm full of corn. Then she turned to Matt so he might—she hoped—claim his reward too.

Bus to Horseshoe Bay, ferry to Nanaimo, bus upisland to German Creek. Ellen pulled her suitcase—stop-start, stop-start—stones jamming the wheels, through the gravel parking lot to the government wharf where the ramp was angled at eighty degrees. And she remembered how, all those years ago, whenever they left Cordova Island or returned, it had seemed so difficult. Inevitably it would be low tide like this and Ellen would have to negotiate the ramp with all their groceries and bags, and Mimi, just a baby. Ellen had needed a sherpa. And where was Larry? Why couldn't he sherp?

She let the suitcase go first, clutching its strap and the railing, inching her way down, thinking of Tony pulling on the leash. She'd left him with Tilda.

It was the same ferry, a metal tub with a covered freight area, rows of wooden benches inside. Ellen loaded her suitcase on. Eventually other passengers began arriving with backpacks and Rubbermaid bins filled with provisions or the Christmas presents they'd come to the mainland to buy, stacked on foldable dollies. A group of strangers. It used to be that whenever she took the ferry, she knew everyone and they knew her and half of them, it would turn out, had slept with Larry.

Last year Ellen had slept with Larry at the Winter Solstice party at Larry and Amber's house. Amber had gone to bed early. "Cramps," she'd announced to the room. The island was full of secretless women, their menstrual cycles public knowledge. Ellen used to be one herself, though last year she had taken this information to mean that Amber's body, if not Amber, accepted that these intermittent reunions between Larry and Ellen were Ellen's only opportunity for sex.

That was Ellen's point of view anyway, that she threatened no one.

And this year? This year Ellen was besotted with Matt, who kept coming around. If he had a reason apart from sex, it was his secret.

The ferry backed out of its berth. A seal watched, head and shoulders out of the water, then ducked. Gulls screamed in a wheel above the dockside fish store. Ellen had forgotten the Solstice Party until now. At the end of Ellen and Larry's marriage, when she'd learned that friends of hers had slept with him, she'd sought them out, shrieking, "How could you?" Very easily, it turned out. As easily as Ellen slept with Matt, rationalizing all the way. Ellen didn't know the girlfriend. She was young. She would pity Ellen if she knew.

But Ellen knew Amber. She was practically related to her.

Tossed in the bag with the Christmas presents, *Lady with a Lapdog*. During the crossing, Ellen took out the book and sniffed it, ran her fingers over the dog-Braille inside the front cover. She'd intended to reread the whole thing, but instead found herself back with poor Anna Sergeyevna, stuck in love with Gurov, a man who classifies the women he sleeps with according to three types: *carefree, good-natured women, whom love had made gay and who were grateful to him for the happiness he gave them; those who made love without sincerity, with unnecessary talk, affectedly, hysterically; and two or three very beautiful women whose faces suddenly lit up with a predatory expression, an obstinate desire to take, to snatch from life, more than it could give.*

This last type were *no longer in their first youth.*

155

And Ellen? Which type was she? Grateful and utterly sincere, yes. But it was true, too, that she was chatty in bed and freely voiced her pleasure. And that in two years she'd be fifty.

Then she felt it, the sob that could never be released, pressing hard behind her ribs. She put both hands over the place at the same time she glanced out the window, glanced at that precise December moment out on the open ocean with the solstice approaching when the colour of the sky and the colour of the water merged and there was no light anywhere to orient her. The great grey middle of her life.

The sob absorbed back inside her body. Next time she looked, it was night.

156

HER son-in-law, Sean, picked her up in the truck. They drove the main road companionably, Ellen shocked by the winter darkness. Off the grid, the island shut down on these long, overcast December evenings. They passed the Post Office, the Community Hall, the Free Store; Ellen couldn't see these structures, only the forest in the headlights. She marvelled that Sean knew onto which rutted lane to turn. They bounced along, cedar boughs brushing against her window, spookily, like the memories of her former life here clawing to get in.

Eli ran out of the cabin when he heard the truck. "Nonny!" He was almost seven, with wild clown-hair he'd got from his dad. Sean, though, had sheared off his Medusa dreadlocks and reinvented himself—toque-wearing father, entrepreneur.

Taking her hand, Eli dragged Ellen inside. Sean followed with her suitcase. Eli looked from it to Ellen.

"Did you bring me a present, Nonny?"

Yolanda came over from the stove with baby Fern in a sling on her back, tsking at Eli, her glasses half fogged from cooking, exhausted and angelic in her half-hearted ponytail. She'd thickened from having babies, the way Ellen had. That's what motherhood did, puffed you up, then beat you down.

"Give me that baby right now," Ellen said in the middle of their hug.

Yolanda loosened the knot on her chest. Ellen waltzed Fern over to the couch lumped with sleeping cats. "Eli, come here," she called. "I have some news. I have a dog staying at my house. His name is Tony. And you will not believe this, but it's true. He can read."

Yolanda, back at the stove, said, "I thought we were cat people."

"Where are our presents?" Eli asked.

"Don't give in to him. He has to wait."

"Why should you?" Ellen whispered. "Bring me that bag next to my suitcase."

In it was *Lepus arcticus*. Arctic Hare.

At dinner, Ellen told them about her neighbour Tilda. "She knits Canadian wildlife. She spins the yarn herself." The white hare slouched on the table dangerously close to Eli's bowl of chili. "That's why he's so soft," Ellen told him. "He's got real bunny fur mixed in with the wool." She didn't want to say what the hare and the tiny Townsend's vole she'd bought for Fern had cost. "They're not really toys. They're works of art."

Yolanda said, "The Solstice Party's at Mason and Spirit's place this year. And Amber invited us over tomorrow night. Do you want to go?"

Likely Ellen blushed. She fanned her face, pretending the chili was too hot. If she said no to Amber's invitation they would wonder why.

157

Sean was trying to get Fern to eat a bean, washing the sauce off in his mouth, spitting out the bean, and feeding it to the baby by hand. At the same time, he glanced at Ellen and smirked.

"What?" Ellen said.

"Amber alert!" he cawed, flapping his hands on either side of his toque. "Amber alert!"

Yolanda slapped him on the shoulder.

"What does he mean?" Ellen asked, but Yolanda wouldn't say.

Before bed Ellen read to the children and tucked them in. Then she stumbled in the starless dark to the outhouse and back. Calling good night to Yo and Sean, she retired to the tiny, frigid room, the one too far from the wood stove, less a bedroom than a pantry lined with dried beans and canned preserves. The cats joined her, bed-warmers, slipping out later to kill.

Last year she'd lain in this same rack of a cot listening to the ocean's restless exhalations, wondering what would happen between her and Larry. This year, the ocean was still exhaling, but the hands Ellen imagined moving over her were young.

"WHEN I say *walkies* he grabs something that smells like me. A sock. Once he headed out with my panties."

Yolanda asked, "Are you keeping him or not?"

"I didn't plan on it. Now I'm in something of a situation. Because I care about him. I can't stop thinking about him. Like now. Talking about the dog counteracts the pointlessness I feel going for a walk without a dog."

They were following a rocky trail through the woods down to the beach, Fern in the sling wearing a bright Peruvian cap with ties, twisting her head back to look at Ellen, Eli marching ahead pretending to shoot things, while Yolanda intermittently called out, "Cease-fire!"

"I should give him up. I'm not getting any work done. I feel like I'm being dragged around by the hair."

"Sounds like you're in love," Yolanda said.

Ellen halted in the middle of the path with her mouth open, her hand clutching her heart. Was she? The other hand reached for the support of a tree. She leaned in, pressing her forehead to the rough bark.

"Mom?" Yolanda hurried back and slipped an arm around Ellen. "What's wrong?"

Fern's small hand patted her head. It felt like the touch of a crow's wing, over and over.

"Are you depressed?"

"No."

"Last night I thought you looked so beautiful when you came into the cabin. You seemed so happy."

Ellen glanced up. "Did I?"

"Yes. Sean even said so. He said you looked hot."

"I love that man," Ellen said, wiping her nose on her sleeve. "I'm—"

No, she was too embarrassed to confess.

"I know," Yo said. "It's the holidays. They get me down too. Maybe we shouldn't go tonight." Her lips brushed Ellen's cheek.

"Go where?" Ellen asked.

YOLANDA went ahead with the kids in the truck while Ellen and Sean walked over with flashlights, Ellen hugging the ditch. Any old draft dodger with one headlight and a medicinal marijuana permit could round the bend, but Sean strode fearlessly up the middle, the way he would, on a dry day, streak down it in a death-defying crouch. He custom-made longboards and sold them online, or bartered with them. Somehow the boards, their Child Tax Benefit payment, and Ellen's occasional cheques sustained them, the way Larry's plays and Ellen's pots and her mother-in-law's handouts had sustained Ellen and Larry all those years ago.

The glowing glass lantern of Larry and Amber's house appeared through the trees, the opposite of Yolanda and Sean's cabin. The opposite, too, of the shack where Larry had once lived with Ellen. This house, architect-designed, cathedral-ceilinged, powered by the sun, was built on sitcoms. You walked right into the heart of it, where Larry's big, sturdy child-bride Amber stood at the stove talking to Yolanda, but falling silent when she saw Ellen come in the door.

Amber had changed her hair, sheared the sides and beaded the long part on top.

"Nice," Ellen said, smiling and opening her arms.

On Cordova Island the standard greeting was a hug. You hugged the postmistress when she handed over your mail. You hugged the man who filled your propane tank. But Amber turned away from Ellen.

Bewildered, stung, Ellen tried again. "What are you making?"

"Latkes." Amber transferred one out of the pan onto a paper-towel-lined plate.

"I have the best latke recipe," Ellen said. "Grind the potatoes in the food processor. Then they're fluffy instead of rubbery and don't look so grey. Do you have a food processor?"

"No," Amber said.

"Are we doing Hanukkah?"

"No," Amber said.

"Can I help?" Ellen asked, sincerely.

"No," again, just as a latke slapped the floor. When Amber bent to pick it up, the not-too-small of her back showed, along with her thong.

"I see London, I see France," Ellen said, and Amber straightened with such a look of undiluted hatred, Ellen backed away.

All the way to where Yolanda had escaped to nurse Fern in the big armchair by the fire. She sank down on the hearth. Amber was never really warm with Ellen, understandably. Her best friend's mother was also her husband's ex-wife, but they'd always muddled through. Now Ellen, who had only expected, along with the usual awkwardness, the guilt anyone would feel returning to the scene of a crime, was confronted with a hostility whose source she quailed to guess at. Amber was the one who'd invited Ellen. Yolanda had said so. Why would Amber do this if she knew what had happened between Ellen and Larry last year?

"Where's your father?" Ellen asked Yolanda.

"I don't know. Sean's checking on Eli in the bath."

They came over once a week for this purpose, Ellen remembered, trying not to panic. Because Sean and Yolanda would take a bath, too, probably together, while Larry hid in his study—like now, leaving Ellen alone and defenceless against Amber.

"Sure you're okay, Mom?" Yolanda asked, touching Ellen's hair.

Larry didn't show himself until dinner. Unshaven, in slippers and a stretched-out cable-knit sweater, the kind on offer in the Free Store, covered with pills, he finally appeared. At the sight of Ellen, he drew his head back sharply, which confused her. Also, she didn't know if she should hug him with Amber right there carrying in the plate of latkes, and, instead of setting it down on the table, letting it drop the last two inches so it clattered.

161

Ellen decided to behave normally and hug Larry before he sat down. It was awkward and his sweater was pungent with old wood-smoke. Strange how different his once-loved body felt when for all these years it had been everyone else's body that felt strange. All those lovers who weren't Larry.

Last year, and the year before, over the last quarter century, in fact, when she knew she would soon see Larry, she would always be in some kind of state. Excitement sometimes, often rage. At any rate, some form of passion would carry her away. But this year? This year all she felt looking across the table at the delicately made, silvering man who had ruled her heart for decades was a mild irritation that he couldn't be bothered to put on something presentable.

She raised her wineglass high in the air. "Cheers, everybody."

"It's not you," Yolanda told Ellen after they had got through the incredibly strained meal, made bearable to Ellen only by her own inane chatter. No one else would step up to the plate and talk. Except the children. Fern had blatted her few words, then guffawed as though she'd cracked a joke.

Ellen, with much nervous lip-licking, had explained how to teach a dog to read. "Take soap. Rub it on the card with the correct word. Rub the corresponding picture or object. Leave the other pictures unsoaped. What the dog is actually doing is reading the smell. That's what smelling is for them."

Eli asked what grade Tony was in.

(Lying with Matt, listening to Tony singing at the bottom of the ladder, she had used *Lady with a Lapdog* to teasingly fan his face. "Aren't you curious how I taught him?"

"I know how you did it," Matt had said. "That's the book with teeth marks all over it.")

Amber wouldn't make eye contact, even when Ellen complimented her on the latkes, which were in fact rubbery and grey. Neither would Amber look at Larry. Instead, she shot secretive glances at Yolanda as though the two of them were teenagers.

Afterward, Ellen volunteered to do the dishes. Yolanda offered to dry.

Two rubber duckies, one with a bow tie, the other in a flowered bonnet, perched on the window ledge above the sink amid the driftwood and shells and coloured bits of beach glass. Ellen wondered about the pretty detritus, the shells and glass, things you'd pick up on a beach holiday to take home as mementoes. What possessed Amber—it had to be her—to gather and display things so commonplace to island life? Ellen pictured her moping down at the beach, noticing a shell, and stooping. And in her mind's eye Ellen saw the thong again, the world's most uncomfortable undergarment, and was glad, very glad, no longer to be young.

Yolanda whispered, "So Dad told Amber—"

The plate Ellen was washing nearly slipped out of her hand.

"—that he didn't find her *very interesting*."

Ellen untensed. "Why is she mad at me, then?"

Yolanda said, "It's not you. She's mad at Dad. See how the boy is facing straight ahead?" She pointed to the duckies. "That means Dad wants to make up. But the girl has her back to him. So Amber is still pissed off."

"Are you serious?" Ellen asked.

Yolanda picked a dripping plate out of the rack and, covering her face with it, giggled.

• • •

WHEN the dishes were done, Yolanda went out to the greenhouse with Amber, ostensibly so Amber could smoke. Sean was in the bath with Fern. This left Ellen and Larry effectively alone, except for Eli, who was walking on Larry's back.

"Why do you like to get stepped on?" Eli asked.

"It's what I'm used to," Larry said.

Ellen snorted. Soon Eli lost interest and scampered off to look for his Arctic Hare, leaving Larry face down on the rug.

"Those are great kids," Ellen said. "It's nice you see so much of them."

"I'm wanted for my indoor plumbing."

She laughed and went to the kitchen for more wine, found Eli crouching behind the island counter with the hare that had cost her three hundred and fifty dollars, its face stained with chili now. He'd discovered chopsticks in a drawer and was carefully inserting them between the stitches into the animal's body.

She returned with a glass for Larry too. By then he'd resurrected himself and was stoking the fire, stabbing the burning logs with the fresh one.

"Did you lose weight?" he asked.

"No," Ellen lied.

Larry closed the fireplace doors. "You seem happier."

"You don't. And your sweater is ugly."

She felt sorry for him, the way after seven or eight readings she had begun to feel sorry for Gurov, shackled by bitterness. Every new affair inevitably grew *complicated* and problematic; love always became an unbearable *situation*. When Yolanda moved here to be with Sean after Eli was born, Larry visited them. His visits to his own children had been infrequent, but now that he was a grandfather, he came. At some point he decided to move back, possibly when he met Amber. Ellen had never asked why, but now she did.

There turned out to be a story. The way Larry offered it up made Ellen think he had been waiting a long time for someone sympathetic to lend an ear, and that no one had until now. Until Ellen. It concerned a play Larry had gone to see in L.A. five years before.

"A play everyone was raving about. By a young playwright."

"A woman."

Larry nodded. "It was pretty good. I liked it. The playwright was there so afterward I went over and introduced myself. She didn't know who I was."

Ellen sensed what was coming. She disguised her cringe with another sip of wine.

165

"I told her about *Talking Stick* and the awards it won and my TV projects."

"*Talking Stick* was a great play," Ellen said. "Your best."

"I only wrote two plays," Larry said.

"That was my favourite."

He looked at her. Larry had a look like a Taser—it disabled you with feelings of stupidity and self-doubt. But Ellen had been looked at by Larry so many times over the years she was as desensitized as a lab rat. "And?"

"That's it," Larry said. "I told her who I was. She didn't have a clue. She'd never heard of *A Principled Man*. It ran two seasons. I was head writer. *Curve Ball*?"

"The baseball show," Ellen said, being kind. She'd never seen it. She'd never watched a baseball game in her life.

"*Curve Ball* drew a blank too." He scratched his stubble, then admitted that he had asked the young playwright to go for a drink sometime, not necessarily that night. "'To talk about your play.' I said I had a few suggestions. Well. She took *gross* offence. It was unbelievable how she overreacted. Like I'd just said her play was shit, when I'd said the opposite."

"Unbelievable," Ellen said, thinking of Tony in full snorkel mode at the base of a tree. Now that she'd read all those dog books, she knew what he was so desperately seeking there. Some other dog's three-week-old piss to dilute with his own.

Amber appeared out of nowhere with Yolanda behind her. "I'm going to bed," she announced.

"See you," Ellen sang. "Thanks for dinner."

Larry looked at Amber and it had its intended effect. She swung around and stomped off like a giant little girl, her beads clacking.

Yolanda said, "I'm just taking a quick bath, Mom. Do you want to walk now with Sean and Fern or come later with me and Eli in the truck?"

"We're talking," Larry told her.

"Well, don't talk too much," she said to Ellen.

"Gotcha," Ellen said as Yolanda left.

"The last time I wrote something decent was when we lived here," Larry said, as though those discomfiting walk-throughs hadn't happened. "That's your answer. That's why I came."

"So how's the play?" Ellen asked.

"There's no play," Larry said, and he turned and opened the doors of the fireplace and slammed another wood chunk in.

"Did you tell Amber about last year?"

Larry said nothing.

"Larry? You shouldn't have. She'll tell Yolanda if she hasn't already. And now she hates me. Is that why she invited me? To show me that she hates me?"

"It's a test," Larry said.

Ellen threw up her hands. "It was nothing."

"Was it?"

The way Larry looked at her then was entirely unfamiliar. There was a softening in his eyes that seemed more than the creases of middle age. She saw his pain too. His back, and now his play. Larry had always had a tortured process.

"My therapist?" Larry said. "The one in L.A.? He used to say I was addicted to Act One."

"What does that mean?"

"I like beginnings. When I lived with you? Here? That was the only time I ever finished a play."

Ellen stared at him. The sweater made him seem shrunken. He pressed both hands to the small of his back. Also, now that his legs were stretched out in front of him, she saw two different coloured socks, brown and black.

Larry stood. Last year she'd followed him to his office, to his battered leather couch calicoed with the stains of former conquests. Not then, not during any of the other times that they had coupled up for old times' sake, or relief, had he ever indicated that she might be his muse.

Now he limped out, leaving Ellen by the fire in the lonely cathedral of the room, wondering where everyone had got to and how they'd ended up this way, so miserable. Well, the children were all right, and Sean too. Yolanda was just tired.

"Nonny!" Eli called.

Ellen had forgotten he was behind the kitchen island. She hurried over. Eli held up the hare, impaled with chopsticks now—a voodoo doll—and Ellen sighed.

She lifted him off the floor, set him on the counter next to the sink.

167

"Look at these two," she said, showing him the duckies on the windowsill. She made the girl ducky fight the boy ducky, and Eli threw back his head and laughed.

It *was* laughable. *Pathetic.*

Then she turned the girl ducky so it faced the boy ducky, so it seemed to be nuzzling the boy ducky's neck.

SOMETHING happened just as they were leaving that changed the entire holiday for Ellen. Larry, when summoned by his daughter, shambled out to be hugged by her, then Ellen. After helping a squirming Eli into his coat, Ellen pulled her gloves from her pocket. And something fluttered to the floor, something orange that Larry bent, wincing, to pick up. To her amazement, and Yolanda's apparently, he straightened with a smile, his first that evening—for all Ellen knew, that year.

A poop bag.

"I know what's different about you, Ellen," he said. "You got a dog."

IN the truck, as they drove away, Ellen told Yolanda, "I love him."

"Who? Dad?"

"My dog."

She came to her decision then. She would forget Matt. Forget Larry. What had they, or any man, ever done for her? She was always giving, giving herself away. No more, she decided. No more. She would get Tony neutered and live with him instead. Long slow walks in the morning, reading together every night. In between, a little bit of squeaky banana and some fetch. The second half of her life unspooled before her like a newsreel, its headline blazing: CONTENTMENT! CONTENTMENT!

After that, Ellen just *had to* talk to Tony. She used Yolanda's phone to call Tilda.

Tilda said, "Yesterday there was so much corn in his poo. Today he's better."

"Have you been practising with the Henry James?"

"Um," Tilda said.

"Where is he?"

"Right here. He's sleeping."

"Put him on. Tony? Hi, Tony! Whatcha doing? Do you miss me, Tony? I sure miss you. What's he doing, Tilda? Does he know it's me?"

"He's wagging all over the place."

So who was Ellen's grand passion? She wondered this after she hung up. Of course it was Larry. It had always been Larry, her Gurov. (But this was only her point of view. Larry, of course, would have a different opinion. He always did.)

Then this past October she'd found herself standing in line behind a young man whose shirt tag poked out the back of his collar. She'd tucked it in. He'd turned and said, "Your hands are cold."

Your hands are cold. Your hands are cold. Let me. Warm them. Let's go up.

She hadn't told Larry about Matt, though she'd planned to. She'd planned to say, "See? I, too, can *snatch from life* all that it can give."

Then, what with the Winter Solstice party, and Christmas, and visiting old friends who still lived on Cordova Island, Ellen did forget Matt. She barely thought of him after that night at Larry's. Things were getting complicated between them anyway, especially now. Now that she had Tony.

• • •

WHEN she got home to Vancouver, he was waiting for her. Tilda opened the door and he leapt against her legs and dervished all around her. The whole dog wagged. He wagged for Ellen.

She threw her bags inside and out they went. Tony sniffed and peed, sniffed and peed. Reaching the end of the block she turned; he was far behind. But all she had to do was call his name and he ran right to her, tongue out.

A child's pink purse lay in the gutter in front of the corner store across the street. Ellen wiped it on the grass and showed it to Tony, who took the handle in his mouth.

In the next block, an elderly woman came along. "What in the world is he carrying?"

"We're just coming back from Saks," Ellen said. "Gucci's on sale."

"Well, he is cute."

"Smart too. This dog can read."

The woman's face crinkled all over when she smiled, in a way Ellen found very beautiful.

Back home, the mail was in a drift behind the door. She unpacked her suitcase first—she had bones for Tony—then checked her phone messages.

"Ellen? Are you back? It's Matt. I've been calling and calling. I really have to see you. I *have to*."

She pressed the phone against her ribs, pressed it hard, but it wasn't any use. It had been building all this time. And out it came. Out and out and out.

Tony laid back his ears and cocked his head to one side, *but both of them knew because both of them had read the story. The end was still a long, long way away and the most complicated and difficult part was only just beginning.*

7

IT'S ALL YOUR MOTHER'S FAULT

. . .

Back in fifth grade at Rayburn Elementary in North Vancouver, Mimi had felt her first cruel stirrings of love. They were for Mr. Clark—lanky of limb, hair tucked girlishly behind his ears, the same navy blazer every day with a chalk line across his butt from leaning against the board ledge. Not during class, but whenever they happened to pass each other in the hall, Mr. Clark would sing out, *"Che gelida manina!"* Though Mimi had no clue what it meant, it sounded beautiful ringing off the walls, almost as beautiful as "(Everything I Do) I Do It for You," by Bryan Adams, though not quite.

Another thing she remembered. How Mr. Clark brought in a mechanical model of the solar system and set it up on his desk.

"An orrery," her counsellor Kevin said seven years later when she was being treated for her interesting life. Kevin was Mr. Clark's opposite—blocky, his shaved head parenthesized by large ears. She hated him for saying "orrery," the way she hated him a minute ago for saying, *"La Bohème?"* As though that could possibly compute for a seventeen-year-old.

"That's what it's called. You turn the crank and the planets move?"

She made teeny-mouth. Outside the window, the Red Riding Hood woods pressed in around the rehab centre.

"Sorry," Kevin said. "I'll be good."

Mimi waited a full three minutes, waited until he stirred in his chair. It was Ellen who had named teeny-mouth and revealed its effectiveness. "I just want to grab you by the face when you do that."

"Do what?"

"Make that teeny-mouth."

Mimi hadn't even known she was!

She didn't actually want the session with Kevin to end; she was her own favourite subject back then. Just before he gave up on her, she relaxed her mouth.

"How did you even get this job?"

He laughed. "You were saying?"

Back at Rayburn Elementary, Mr. Clark asked who wanted to help work the orrery. Though every hand shot up, he naturally picked Mimi to walk the long aisle between the desks and stand by his side at the front of the room. She only reached his blue-blazered chest, though, to Mimi, their height difference was irrelevant.

The gears started stiffly, but once the two of them got going, Mr. Clark's moist hand over hers, they really flew. Faster and faster, the nine planets Tilt-A-Whirled around the bright orange ball of the sun. Before the astonished class, Mimi and Mr. Clark made time. That was what it amounted to, this dizzying choreography, the earth pirouetting on its axis, reeling through its orbit: days, months, year after year. She was ten, she was seventeen, she was twenty-seven and still trying so very hard not to have an interesting life.

• • •

EVENTUALLY Mimi escaped—not rehab, but her family. Or more to the point, Ellen. Ellen who blamed Mimi for everything that had gone wrong in her own life.

Mimi headed for Toronto, where she rented the first place she looked at, an apartment in a house on Davenport Road with an old yellow one-speed stashed on the porch. The landlord said she was welcome to use the bike. The previous tenant was unlikely to return for it, having gone off to join a convent.

The apartment smelled funny. Mothbally nun's habit, Mimi thought. Nevertheless, she stayed for the two years that she worked at Future Bakery. When she left that job for BioLife on the Danforth, she moved across town to a brick co-op. It was a sublet, thankfully; she wasn't expected to be co-operative. All that time she'd been writing long frustrated e-mails to Ellen about not dancing and not being able to work up the nerve to audition, and receiving not-very-helpful e-mails back.

Then Georgia, Mimi's childhood dance teacher and Ellen's good friend, set up an audition. But this only meant that when Mimi was invited into the company—semi-professional, no big deal—it felt like a favour to Georgia. Mimi ended up making teeny-mouth all the time. Sarcastic e-mails flowed out of her. The bloody commute to Scarborough, how the show was stupid, a musical comedy about nuns. *Nuns are following me everywhere*, she wrote. She was still riding around on the old yellow bike from the first apartment.

One morning she woke swollen and immobilized. Get out of bed? How? She was on the phone so fast to Ellen, who, of course, didn't believe a word she said.

From: emcginty61@shaw.ca

Sweetheart,
    Please don't hang up on me. I'm only trying to help. Go to a doctor. Get a referral for physio. Can you skip rehearsals for a few weeks?

Mom

From: mimiredshoes@gmail.com
    DON'T YOU GET IT????? I AM IN PAIN!!!!!!

174

"DON'T touch it!" she shrieked.

The doctor cocked a skeptical eyebrow that her flowered hijab seemed to neutralize. "You have to show me. I have to know there's really something wrong."

"Of course there's *really* something wrong! I can't bend my leg! It hurts like hell!"

"Hop up." The doctor patted the table, making the paper crackle.

"I can't."

"Then pull your pant leg over your knee."

Mimi did and the doctor said, "Okay. I see what you mean." She knelt on the floor and gently prodded the tender grapefruit of Mimi's joint, causing her to wince.

Rest. Elevation. Ice.

"Can you give me the name of a physio?"

"That's all you want. A physiotherapist?"

"Yes," Mimi said.

The doctor wrote down a name and Mimi took the torn-off sheet and turned to go.

"And the pain?" the doctor asked.

The scarf bowed over the pad again. Mimi accepted the prescription, folded it in half, and limped out without saying thanks. Yet she was tingling all over and the pain in her leg had temporarily vanished. Just from a word written on a piece of paper.

"It gives me powers," she'd told bald, sticky-out-eared Kevin, all those years ago in his office in the woods.

"How so?"

175

"It makes the pain go away. That's what it's for, right?"

"If you use it correctly. If you don't, it causes more pain. Pain for everyone in your life."

"That's what I mean," Mimi said. "It gives me powers."

She quit rehearsals. After a week Sebastian, the director, called. "I'm only phoning you, honey, because Georgia e-mailed and asked me to. She says you hurt yourself. Did you hurt yourself?"

"Yes."

"That's a nice tone of voice to use on someone who's phoning out of concern."

"You're concerned about Georgia, not me."

"Correct. But she's concerned about you. And you're lucky in that. You're a very lucky girl. Georgia is one of the kind souls of this world."

"I'm twenty-seven."

"Meaning?"

"I'm not a girl."

"You act twelve. If you want to help out until your leg gets bet-ter, come. But you have to commit and be responsible. You have to fix your broken attitude. Are you coming back?"

Mimi hung up.

She couldn't ride the yellow bike now, had to take the streetcar to work. Boarding, she placed her right foot on the first step and straightened the leg to bring the unbendable left one up beside it. And again. The driver stared, then looked away. Mimi made teeny-mouth as she dropped in the fare.

On Broadview, they passed an old brick church that previewed its sermons on a sign out front. That day it was about counting the hairs on your head. She would remember the quote later because for much of the ride she puzzled over whether this was even pos-sible when there were something like a hundred thousand strands on the average human head. She'd read that somewhere.

At BioLife they tried to accommodate her injury. They let her sit on a stool behind the register. The earnest, long-skirted man-ager recommended glucosamine and fish oil capsules; she reminded Mimi of her employee discount. Mimi tucked the bottles under the counter. The next afternoon they were gone, reshelved, and Mimi knew the jig was up. How could she work there if she didn't believe in the healing power of Nature?

For Mimi, there was really only one thing that worked.

"DID you ask for it?" Ellen said on the phone, her voice tight with panic. No, probably anger.

"She offered it to me."

To Mimi's surprise, Ellen started pleading. Back when Mimi was using, Ellen had only pleaded as a last resort. She was the adult, Mimi the child. But now they were even.

"Don't take it, sweetheart. Don't give in."

"Why not? I can't dance. Every time I try to get back onstage, I hurt myself. Oh, and I'm quitting my job. They're giving me the stink eye because I wouldn't buy their forty-dollar supplements."

In the long, ensuing silence, Mimi thought she could hear her mother writhe.

Secretarial (Etobicoke, ON)
    Reply to: job-5cjjq-2236343801@craigslist.org
    Filing and organizing for retiree. 416-688-1532 $10/hr

Way over on the other side of the city in the opposite direction of Scarborough. Wherever Mimi needed to go, it would be far.

THE first thing she saw coming out of the subway station into the heat was the TEMPORARILY OUT OF SERVICE sign on the litter bins out front, the clear plastic wrap that had swathed the lids already torn away. The bins erupted greasy takeout cartons and swollen diapers.

After a ten-minute limp up a long, mansioned street, she arrived at Mr. D'Huet's all sweaty. The house looked vaguely Shakespearean except for the Cadillac in the driveway with a pugged front grill. She rang the bell. Eventually he answered, a shirtless old man with wild, flossy hair.

"Ah!" he said.

"I saw your ad. On Craigslist? I got a text back right away."

His fingers disappeared inside his white mat of chest hair and his face, open a moment ago in surprise, took on a conflicted aspect. Mimi had hacked out a bob the night before with manicure scissors and troubled herself into something secretarial; she was buttoned to her chin so her tattoo wouldn't show. Not making teeny-mouth was killing her.

"Come in then," he said, gesturing toward a chandeliered dining room stacked with cardboard boxes. Boxes on the floor, on the table, on the brocade seats of all the chairs. In another room a phone was ringing.

Mimi hobbled through the cardboard obstacle course, glancing back at Mr. D'Huet, not so mobile himself, using the furniture as crutches. He motioned for her to carry on through a door that led to a bright, unclean kitchen. By then whoever was phoning had given up.

There were boxes everywhere here, too, and a girl with butterscotch hair and heavy bangs sitting at the table evaluating Mimi through mascara-clotted eyes. Some relation, Mimi thought, a granddaughter or a great-niece, yet vaguely familiar.

"Sit down," the old man said.

"Take off your shirt," the granddaughter deadpanned.

Mimi did a double take and the girl giggled. Mr. D'Huet missed the quip. He introduced himself, then the girl. Glenna.

"And you are?"

"Mimi."

Only when she'd pulled her resumé from her bag and slid it across the table to Mr. D'Huet did Mimi realize this sooty-eyed Glenna had actually come for the job too. Because there already was a resumé on the table. Glenna unslouched herself so she could better read the exaggerated facts Mimi had bulleted on hers. She grinned, and the collusion Mimi saw on her rival's face spooked and offended her. Mimi placed Glenna then, not by the grin with its childish gaps, but the zeros in her eyes. Not Glenna per se. Her *type*.

After that, Mimi avoided all contact with those ciphered eyes.

The old man donned a pair of smeared glasses to consider the two documents. Even before he'd finished reading, the phone on the wall started ringing again. He looked at it in desperation, cuing Glenna, who sprang out of her seat to answer it. Until then Mimi had assumed no contest between her and a girl who was soaring before 10 a.m.

"If the job's already taken, I'll go," Mimi said.

Mr. D'Huet blinked through the smears. He covered her hand with his. "But there's so much to do."

"It's taken." Glenna hung up. "So how about I turn the ringer off?"

Mr. D'Huet had never heard of Craigslist. He didn't even know what Mimi had meant by texting. His son had placed the ad, then left town on business. He wanted the boxes dealt with before he returned at the end of the week.

Some of them were decades old, filled with brittle articles pressed in yellowed folders. Various passions had absorbed Mr. D'Huet at various times, most recently the life-giving properties of peanut butter that had saved him after the devastating loss of his wife three years before. Also the D'Huet family tree, regimental beer steins, and astronomy. He'd retained every warranty certificate for every appliance he'd ever owned, every airline ticket and boarding pass for every flight he'd taken. One box was for Christmas cards, one for completed crossword puzzles, and many were dedicated to his son, Brent—report cards, artwork, certificates of merit. Forty years of his wife's sewing patterns.

179

Glenna and Mimi were supposed to sort through everything, cull the important from the absurd and discard the latter.
Mr. D'Huet gave this order himself, passed on from his son, but
in practice he made it difficult to carry out. When Mimi limped
into the living room seeking permission to chuck a folder of articles
about the reinstatement of Pluto as a planet, Mr. D'Huet's sympathetic expression, brought on by her awkward gait, converted to
alarm. But it was so interesting! And this was the secret to a long
and happy life—to be *interested*. And to eat peanut butter.

At the end of the day he paid them in cash, though little had
been accomplished, certainly nothing in the living room, where
Glenna had perched on the couch next to Mr. D'Huet squeezing
her wrists between her knees and prodding him to tell her more
and more about his beer steins.

They left Mr. D'Huet's together. From the corner of Mimi's
eye Glenna looked on the scrawny side of sixteen, though was
probably twenty, like the girls Mimi had hung with ten years ago
in Vancouver, ageless within a range, able to project innocence or
sophistication, depending on their purposes. Mimi had got in deep
with them, shared and shared alike, crushed the pills together and
took turns licking the spoon.

Eyes like that little Orphan girl in the cartoon.

Glenna said, "Easy, hey? I bet he's a nudist. He just puts on
pants for company." She fished for lip gloss in her bag. "He's dia-
betic."

"How do you know that?"

"Wow, she can talk." Glenna bumped against Mimi chummily.
"I saw the stuff in his bathroom."

All Mimi had seen was a container on the kitchen counter
among the bread heels and the peanut butter jars. Seven small

lidded compartments, one for each day of the week. Through the semi-transparent plastic, the ghosts of different coloured pills.

She had yet to fill the prescription the hijab doctor had given her. Instead she'd tucked it in an envelope, sealed it, then closed it in a patterned soap box, an Ellen gift. She'd tied a string around the box, knotted it twice, and buried it in a drawer. Now all she had to do to feel its charge was draw alongside the dresser.

"There's some good stuff in one of the upstairs bathrooms," Glenna told her. "I should have taken it. Oh, well. Tomorrow."

What outraged Mimi was that this girl she didn't even know, this *Glenna*, imagined she, Mimi, would want to know about the good stuff. Mimi had lived inside her abstention, tested it, and won—she had a prescription!—yet she was still, all these years later, sweating some pheromone the zero-eyed sniffed out. The same thing had happened at Future Bakery, so she'd left.

"I love these jobs with old people. Their bathroom cupboards are, like, stuffed. They don't even know what's in there half the time."

"So this is what you do? Steal from old people?"

"I don't take anything they'd miss. This is a great gig. Usually I have to wipe their asses. Is your leg real or fake?"

Mimi didn't reply.

"You live over near the Danforth, right?"

"How do you know that?"

"I read it on your resumé. Notice how there isn't any garbage around here? Rich people drive their garbage to Muskoka. In their Beemers. Or they come over to Parkdale and dump it."

But there was garbage, right where Mimi stopped, in front of the subway station, the teeming contents of the bins fermenting in the precocious June heat. She pretended she wasn't going home by subway, because Glenna was. "Are you going back?"

181

"To Mr. D'Huet's?" Glenna said. "Aren't you?"

"That depends if you are or not."

"For sure I'll go, then," Glenna said. "Maybe we'll have some fun, hey?"

Sweetheart,

This is just a little something for that crummy commute when you're back rehearsing. The extra thing is because Georgia says to build your leg up with walking. Nothing strenuous. Enjoy.

Love, Mom

182

P.S. I hear there's a garbage strike out there. Ugh!

Mimi tossed the card aside on the bed where she was icing her knee. She already had an iPod. Typical Ellen with her memory issues. Especially annoying was her self-serving habit of blanking on everything bad—Mr. Clark, for example.

Back in rehab, during their family sessions, Ellen's constant tactic had been to deny, deny, deny. Poor Kevin would press his prayer hands to his lips to keep himself from interrupting her. (Or maybe he *was* praying. Pseudo-godliness suffused the place, from the New Age music piped into the post-and-beam lobby, to the whispered talk about giving yourself over to a higher power.)

Once Mimi had said, "I can count on one hand the times I felt loved as a child."

"How, sweetheart?" Ellen had asked in a tremulous voice.

"I felt loved when I had lice."

Everyone recoiled, Ellen and Kevin, Mimi's younger sister Yolanda, huddled in the corner weeping behind her glasses.

"That was the only time you ever gave me your undivided attention," Mimi said. "Your fingers in my hair? I needed that."

Of course Ellen didn't remember it the same way, but at least she remembered. "You screamed bloody murder all the way through it."

And they both turned to Kevin so he could choose between their contradictory recollections, Kevin who was praying hard that they could just get through the hour.

"Is attention the same thing as love?" Ellen had asked him. "Because I loved her so much. I do. But I had to earn a living. I didn't always have time to spend with her."

"You had boyfriend time," Mimi had said with a triumphant glance at Kevin.

Anyway, Ellen *had* sent something Mimi didn't have, a sensor to Velcro onto her running shoe. The tape had been peeled off the hard plastic case the iPod came in; Ellen had already opened it. And charged the iPod, Mimi saw when she lifted it out, shiny and metallic green. And downloaded two dozen songs. Billie Holiday. Ella Fitzgerald. Louis Armstrong. Charles Aznavour. The corny music Ellen loved.

Mimi twiddled to the bottom of the list.

"(Everything I Do) I Do It for You."

183

THE next day she showed up at Mr. D'Huet's early. While she waited for him to get to the door, she checked the pedometer. One thousand and forty-three steps.

"Hello! Thanks for coming!" He waved her in. Foam tracked one side of his wobbly face. He was shirtless today, too, dressed in sport socks and slippers and khaki shorts that grazed his hairy knees.

"Should I continue with those boxes in the kitchen, Mr. D'Huet?"

"Start anywhere you want. There's so much to do. I'll be down in a few minutes." He clutched the banister.

Mimi waited, watching him ascend the white-carpeted stairs, an ancient trudging up Everest, until he safely reached the summit.

The first box was stuffed with opera and theatre programs, another with old phone bills. She dumped it all into a plastic garbage bag.

Mr. D'Huet reappeared. "What am I supposed to do with the bags?" she asked. "There's a garbage strike."

"Really?" Mr. D'Huet said. "This is the first I've heard of it."

When the doorbell rang, Mimi volunteered to get it because Mr. D'Huet was just taking a loaf out of the old-fashioned breadbox and searching for a clean knife.

Glenna jittered on the front steps. Cut-offs and toffee pigtails. Her gapped, complicit smile.

"He doesn't want you anymore," Mimi said.

Laughing, Glenna stepped forward. Mimi slammed the door and locked it. Glenna rang again.

"You're fired," Mimi whispered through the mail slot.

"Fuck you!"

While Glenna pounded, Mimi limped off as fast as she could in case Glenna snuck around and tried to insinuate herself in the back door.

Mr. D'Huet was sitting at the kitchen table with his bread and peanut butter, bobbing a teabag in a mug. "What was that all about?"

"UNICEF."

"Oh," he said. "Too bad. I'd like to get in touch with them."

Mimi dragged the garbage bag filled with opera programs

through the French doors, kicked it down the deck stairs with her good leg, then limped to the far railing, where she peered along the side of the house. No Glenna. She waited a few minutes just in case, staring out at the overgrown back garden.

Mr. D'Huet was paying a breeder to develop a rose in honour of his late wife. He told Mimi this when she came back inside and complimented him on his roses, roses being the only flower she could identify in his garden other than dandelions. Later, she found the file of correspondence with the breeder. Also the resumés, hers and Glenna's, on a pile of grocery delivery forms.

Mimi got through twelve boxes that second day. The most interesting contained old black-and-white erotic postcards. She kept those but chucked the takeout menus. A few times Mr. D'Huet wandered in to talk, out of loneliness or because he wanted to check on what she was throwing out. Personal questions she deflected with questions right back.

"So what are you going to call the rose?"

As she was leaving, Mr. D'Huet counting the bills into her hand, she said, "You keep your doors locked, don't you? Because you should if you've got cash lying around."

"It's not lying around. It's in my desk drawer."

She couldn't believe he'd told her that.

Then he asked something weird. "Are you a churchgoer?"

"What? No. Why?"

"You're always humming. It sounds like a hymn."

"I don't know any hymns," Mimi said.

"It's quite pretty, whatever it is. Mabel was Anglican. I went along for the ride. Are you coming back tomorrow? Good. Good. I wonder what happened to the other girl."

He tipped her a ten because she'd worked so hard.

185

On the steps, Mimi turned on the pedometer. Two blocks away, she checked that it was counting. Fifty-two slow steps.

Somewhere in the trees the telephone bird sang, the one whose call sounded like a ringing phone. She remembered hearing it at Mr. D'Huet's throughout the morning, but now it dawned on her that it hadn't been the bird. It was the upstairs phone. Yesterday Glenna had turned off the ringer in the kitchen. If Mimi went back to tell Mr. D'Huet, it would mess up the pedometer. Also her leg hurt. She could feel it stiffening as the fluid built up.

She limped on, humming "(Everything I Do) I Do It for You."

As soon as she heard herself, she made teeny-mouth and picked up her pace.

186

Sweetheart, I meant nothing by it. I just remembered you were so crazy about Bryan Adams. Remember how you taped pictures of him all over your room? I put it on for fun. I'm sorry. Take it off. Just delete it. How's the new job?
Mom

"Mr. Clark was like the sun to you," Kevin had said during rehab. "All you kids were the planets moving around him. Did you see him as a father figure? Your own father had just left you. He was absent most of your life. Then he came back, only to leave again."

"Haven't you been listening to a single word I've said?" Mimi replied. "I loved him. I wanted to get married to him."

But how had a song by Bryan Adams attached itself to Mr. Clark? Mr. Clark who liked opera? Mimi had attached it. A child's soundtrack is different from an adult's; adult motives obscure, their movements uninterpretable. She didn't know that at ten. For a long time Mimi actually believed the teachers slept at the school. She couldn't fathom that they had a life outside of teaching her.

She deleted the song from the iPod, but she couldn't clear it from her head. When you delete files, they're still there, the same way the past is always there. In rehab, under Kevin's patient guidance, Mimi had figured out Mr. Clark was the real reason she started using percs. Kevin helped her get over the pain of what had happened, but he hadn't deleted Mr. Clark.

Now she was humming the song all the time.

The next day, Wednesday, she was okay. She focused on the sealed envelope in the soap box, how she had resisted it. She kept on resisting until Thursday afternoon when she came to Mr. D'Huet with a question.

The owl folder in her hand, Mimi knocked on the open door. Mr. D'Huet looked up from his desk, vaguely owlish himself in his glasses. He was writing to the United Nations and the Red Cross and any other humanitarian agency he could find the address for. Could Mimi help with that too? Could she drive? Since they'd revoked his licence, getting to the library was so difficult.

"Don't you have Internet?" Mimi asked.

"I don't believe I do."

She asked about the owls.

"The name D'Huet derives from *chouette*, which is French for 'owlet.' No, keep this. It's interesting." He bent over the old manual typewriter again and continued two-fingering his peanut butter testimony, showing Mimi the feathery hairs on his back. Then, as she turned to go, he asked, "Do you want to look at Mabel's things? In case there's anything you fancy?"

Mimi heard the *whoosh whoosh whoosh* of air through feathers. Her resistance growing wings and flapping off.

She dropped the file on the stairs, stepped up with the good leg, straightening it to lift the other, until she reached the top. The bedrooms were on the upper floor, three of them as unlived-in as museum displays. The exception was the small plaid room that must have been Mr. D'Huet's, the twin bed tousled, stuff piled everywhere. A nozzled machine sat on the bedside table. Yesterday Mr. D'Huet had refused to part with an article on how playing the didgeridoo reduced the symptoms of sleep apnea. Mimi pictured him in the bed gasping for breath in the middle of the night, the mask and nozzle attached to his face, a shrivelled old elephant god.

In the bathroom at the end of the hall syringes and swabs in plastic packaging cluttered the counter. She moved on to the master bedroom, where dark furniture stood around on a soundless white carpet, a carpet like snow with a perfect set of tracks leading to the ensuite bathroom. A wintery stillness filled this room, a palpable sense of expectation coming from furniture kept behind heavy drapes. The furniture was waiting for something to happen and now, finally, something did.

Mimi followed Glenna's tracks. When she opened the medicine cabinet, bottles and bottles rolled out and tumbled into the sink, their clattery warning drowning out her curses.

"DID you find something you liked?" Mr. D'Huet asked.

She patted where it hung by her hip. An Indian shoulder bag embroidered with little mirrors, the pill bottle in it.

"Oh," Mr. D'Huet said, peering. "Was that Mabel's?"

"It was in the closet."

"I guess it was, then. I'm glad you found something. Let me get your money. Will I see you tomorrow?"

Outside, the bag's tiny stitched-on mirrors ignited in the sun. Mimi dragged her stiff leg along, making resolute fists. People had started leaving their garbage where there were city bins, creating these impromptu mini dumps. Passing the one in front of the Old Mill station, she held her breath.

Down on the platform, a just-departed car inspired her. Mimi twirled, then collapsed against a pillar like some martyr in a painting. A man jogged down the tiled stairs and leered. Her button had come undone. Mimi covered the tattoo—the outline of a hand with the lines of significance drawn in. She'd found the picture in a book in the spirituality section at BioLife, torn it out, and brought it to be needled onto her chest. Her real hand pressed the tattooed hand and the subway screeched in.

189

The things Mimi used to do! Back then, if a man had leered then followed her into a subway car? *Come along!* she'd have sung.

She got off a few stops before hers and so did he. She felt him tailing her. When she emerged into the sticky, sour air of Bloor Street, she swung around. "Do you see zeros in my eyes?"

He wore hipster glasses and an untucked dress shirt over shorts. Maybe he wasn't the same guy from the Old Mill station. "Um. I do not see any zeros, no."

"Good." She limped off, energy pulsing from the Indian bag like it was decorated with little windows, sparks shooting out.

Don't take it, sweetheart. Don't give in.

The hipster had let her get ahead. He was half a block behind her now, not within speaking range. Yet she'd heard those words.

A bar. Brown tables, brown carpet, brown walls. Brown coffee that the bartender set in front of where Mimi perched on a stool. Mimi was the only one breathing the brown air, except for the bartender, a lady-wrestler type with long grey hair, rolling coins from the till.

"What's that look for?" she asked.

"I just heard my mother talking to me. I swear I heard her like she was right there."

"Is she dead?"

"What?"

"Is she dead?"

"No, she's alive and still trying to control every move I make."

The bartender gave a meaty chuckle. "She's your mother. That's her *job*." She poked a few more dimes in the paper tube, folded the ends, bemusement softening her hard-living face. "My mom used to visit me in my dreams."

"Is *she* dead?"

190

"Oh, yeah. This is, like, a hundred years back."

"What did she say?" Mimi asked.

"The usual. Lottery numbers. My bra didn't fit right. After a couple of years, she stopped. I miss her like hell." The woman flicked back her long hair, first the one side, then the other, a curiously feminine gesture that made her seem like a cross-dresser.

Maybe Ellen had just been hit by a car in Vancouver. Mimi deleted the thought. "You probably had a good relationship."

"Not particularly."

Mimi lifted the Indian bag onto the bar and sifted for the bottle. *Mabel D'Huet*, she read. It even sounded like a rose. At home, Mimi's prescription was hidden in a box that incidentally smelled of roses. How far she'd come from that frenzied girl who could cry on command in any doctor's office, who'd stolen her sister's health card and impersonated her—*six times!* But at what cost, this long journey? Her whole life had been folded up small enough to fit into a soap box.

"I have a terrible relationship with my mom," she told the bartender. "She was never there for me when I was a kid."

"Where was your dad?"

"*Pfft.*"

The bartender snugged another roll in a compartment in the till. "So it's all your mother's fault? What did she do that was so awful?"

"Slept with my favourite teacher."

The woman's eyes widened, then she laughed with her big shoulders.

Mimi bristled. "I was madly in love with him. Like, *crazy* in love. I spent all my time planning our wedding. Drawing pictures of the dress. Then one night I hear noises in her room and I go and find him in her bed."

The bartender refilled Mimi's cup with the burnt stuff, tsked. Mimi felt belittled and turned away. Outside the window, eighteen garbage bags were piled up on the sidewalk. She counted them.

"And you would trace it all back to that moment?" Kevin had asked her.

"Yes," she'd said, but really Kevin had given her the story of Mr. Clark.

I should have a better reason, she'd thought. They would run out of things to talk about if she admitted, "Actually, this is just the way I am. It's how I was born. A not very nice person."

The true part of the story was that Ellen had bedded Mr. Clark. After Mimi's dad left, a line had practically formed at Ellen's bedroom door. She must have snared Mr. Clark on Parent–Teacher Night. Mimi knew she was seeing him. Ellen had told Mimi, "Guess who I'm having dinner with?" and Mimi had approved. She'd imagined Mr. Clark in a candlelit restaurant, holding hands with Ellen across the table, murmuring, "Mimi, Mimi, Mimi" adoringly.

Now, so many years later, if she closed her eyes on the eighteen lumpy bags on the sidewalk outside, she could still see Mr. Clark's skinny body. How purple his prick had looked when she'd snapped on Ellen's light. Like a giant, disgusting crayon. Mimi snapped off the light again. She really did not want to marry him after that.

She'd shuffled back to her room and lain in the dark. A bustling came from the hall, Mr. Clark hurriedly leaving. Then Ellen had stood for a few minutes in Mimi's doorway with the hall light on, trying to figure out if Mimi was awake. She was just a black shape, a mother outline that Mimi saw in reverse when she closed her eyes.

After that, Mr. Clark's favours left her cold. She had scribbled a big purple X across his face.

The bartender palmed open a jar of olives, held it out. Mimi declined. "What did your mother die of?" she asked.

"Cigarettes."

Maybe Mabel D'Huet had too. There were empty ashtrays all over the house.

Mimi closed her hand around the pill bottle, but it felt charge-less, as though the mention of disease had neutralized it. She dropped it back in the Indian bag, saw her tiny, not-nice self making teeny-mouth in one of the miniature mirrors. She leaned closer and closer, her own brown eye swallowing her.

Can you phone me when you get in tonight?
M

Ellen didn't and Mimi freaked out. She e-mailed Yolanda, but Yolanda had two kids and routinely took a month to answer. So Mimi had to phone her, which she hated to do because one of her brats was always howling in the background.

"I don't know where she is," Yolanda told Mimi.

"It's weird. Normally she answers right away. I'm worried."

"*You're* worried?"

The computer pinged and Mimi said, "Never mind."

It's too late to call you now, sweetheart. Can we talk tomorrow?

Mr. D'Huet shuffled into the dining room with an offering of bread and peanut butter on a cutting board. This was the next day, Friday, when the gears of Mimi's life, stuck for so long, finally began to turn.

The front door opened and a man Mimi had never seen before walked in. The suit, his tone, his recently cut hair—everything about him, angular, sharp. "I've been phoning and phoning! Why aren't you answering?"

Mr. D'Huet set the cutting board on a box so he could grip the back of the chair with both hands. Mimi had just accepted a piece of bread. She licked the peanut butter off her fingers.

"People kept calling about the job so we turned the ringer off. I meant to turn it back on."

"What the fuck is going on, Dad? The stuff's still here. All of it."

"No," Mimi said as Mr. D'Huet limped from chair to door frame to kitchen. "The bags are out back. We've got through quite a bit, but there are things he wants to keep."

Brent. Brent D'Huet. Mimi had read it on a third-place science fair certificate.

He faced her now, made a sweeping motion toward the front door. "That's it. That's all we need you for."

"Goodbye, Mr. D'Huet," Mimi called in the direction of the kitchen.

193

"Thanks for coming!" he called back.

"You have to pay me," she told the Brent person.

He reached in close to his heart, where his wallet lived, unfattened it more than he needed to. It was a stupid thing to do, to show how much money you routinely carried around and act like an asshole, waving it.

As soon as the door closed behind her, Mimi took out her iPod. She ducked around the side of the house, keeping low. By the stairs that led up to the deck, close to the open kitchen door, she crouched, listening to everything Brent D'Huet yelled at his dad.

On the walk to the subway, the iPod helped with the rage. She'd downloaded her own songs by then, but in shuffle mode sometimes Ellen's songs played. One did now and Mimi tried to name what she felt. Some unfamiliar feeling on the sunny end of the spectrum. Did a memory of Ellen singing the song trigger the feeling, or the song itself?

At home she recorded her steps in a little notebook she'd bought especially for that purpose.

July 6	4,219 steps
July 7	5,122 steps
July 8	7,340 steps
July 9	9,105 steps
July 10	11,654 steps

She did a little Googling, then dug up Glenna's resumé.

"How did you even get my number?" Machinery sounded in the background. Something grinding. "I should hang up after what you did. I'm hanging up."

"I want to talk to you."

"Fuck you, goody two-shoes. Kiss my ass."

Mimi made teeny-mouth at the phone. She almost hung up herself, but didn't, luckily.

Because, if she had, then what eventually happened wouldn't have happened, and who knew where she would have ended up? Because your future isn't written on the palm of your hand. It comes at you in crots and snippets, in words printed on signs. You have to be ready for it. You have to open your ears and eyes.

"Mr. D'Huet's son wants the house cleaned out because he's going to sell it. Right out from under Mr. D'Huet. You know he doesn't want to go."

"So what?"

"I met the son. He's an asshole."

Brent had power; he was in finance, she'd found out just by typing in his name. But Mimi had powers too. Well, not Mimi per se, not anymore. But Glenna did. And if Mimi could unleash Glenna? She could probably change the world.

She was completely honest: pills, a prescription, money.

"How much?"

"Five hundred and you'll be able to get a lot more from Brent."

"Who?"

"Brent D'Huet."

"The old dude?"

"No, his son. I know where he works. I looked it up."

Glenna yawned on her end of the line. That's what happened when you came down—the yawn-fest. Soon what Mimi was proposing would seem like relief.

Mimi threw in her health card.

"Really?" Glenna said. "Sweet."

• • •

SHE'D unleashed Glenna, but Mimi had no idea what this Glenna would do, not even on Sunday night when she found herself waiting in the dark outside the Old Mill station, listening to the rustling around the garbage bags. They reeked so badly now that Mimi, resorting to mouth-breathing, could taste the smell. Toronto was turning toxic. It was not a good place to be anymore.

Just as she was thinking this, Mr. D'Huet's big bashed-in Cadillac pulled up across the street with Brent in the driver's seat. She probably wouldn't have recognized him out of the suit, in a yellow golf shirt.

She crossed over and looked in the car. Glenna was in the passenger seat. She twisted around with a grin as Mimi squeezed in the back with all the garbage bags. These ones didn't smell. They were the parts of Mr. D'Huet's life that Mimi herself had readied for disposal.

"This is Mimi," Glenna said as Brent pulled out. "You met already, right? My crippled friend?"

Brent squinted in the rear-view mirror. He probably wouldn't have placed her either if Glenna hadn't told him. Now he wondered what was going on, the same way Mimi did. She saw it in his glower.

Mimi asked, "Where are we going?"

"Brent has a cottage. He invited us."

"Us?"

"I suggested two girls and he liked that better."

"Oh," Mimi said to the back of this Brent person's head, the keen line at the nape, the crisp hair lying flat. She couldn't even think of him as related to Mr. D'Huet. How had he turned out like that? "Where is this cottage?"

Glenna answered, "Owen Sound."

Mimi didn't know Ontario very well, but it sounded far. Farther even than Scarborough. Already the city was sliding away outside her window, faster and faster once they turned off Bloor and onto the highway. She watched it go with a curious dispassion, as though she already knew she would never return. But how could she have known that then? All her stuff was still at the co-op.

Brent who preferred two girls was staring in the rear-view mirror. "So you work together?"

"We have," Glenna said, with a smirk back at Mimi. She feigned a long stretch and, while her arms were spread, brushed her fingers along the shaved back of Brent's neck.

He jerked away. "Not while I'm driving."

Signs flashed past; they were heading in the direction of the airport. The highway was wide here—Mimi counted fourteen lanes—trucks and cars streaming both ways.

She considered the possible scenarios. One was when they got to Owen Sound, wherever that was, they'd toss the bags and, during the party, Mimi would slip away. In the other, the one where Glenna aligned herself with Brent because Mimi had crossed her once before, Mimi was in trouble.

Out the window she saw, fleetingly, a green patch bounded by the highway and an overpass. And gravestones. At least they looked like gravestones, but they'd passed in a blink, so maybe they weren't.

At that moment, so late, so long past the appropriate time, Mimi gagged on the garbage taste at the back of her throat. Weird that she hadn't felt afraid sliding into a stranger's back seat. Didn't her mother warn her about that? Never, ever get in a car with a stranger? Yes. Yes, she had. So why had Mimi come?

(Later, telling the story, she would say that she'd felt compelled to, that she'd reached a point in her life where staying was not an option. She would say she'd been *called* to get in.)

A big car. They would have to stop for gas. So she had an out. Knowing that helped her relax. Also, if she was destined to die in some drugged-out sex nightmare, wouldn't it have already happened?

So many clues thrown at her! Like that very morning, waking to realize her knee bent without pain, just a rusty stiffness. The first thing she did was get on the yellow bicycle and ride to Riverdale Park, where a long grassy hill fell away from Broadview. Feet off the pedals, her short hair fluttering, she hurtled straight down and when she reached the bottom of the ravine without crashing, she remembered something—watching *The Sound of Music* on TV as a child. Because of Julie Andrews running down the grassy hill, which triggered another forgotten memory regarding the bike and its previous owner—like Julia Andrews in the movie, she was a nun.

And then the most amazing thing happened. Glenna flicked on the radio and twiddled the dial until she landed on a pop station. "(Everything I Do) I Do It for You" was playing.

They had merged onto a smaller highway with only four lanes and less illumination. The moon and a few stray stars hung above the circuit board of subdivisions on either side. As they sped away from her old life to some ambiguous destination, Mimi listened. Mr. D'Huet was right. The song was so generic, so inexplicit, it really could have been a hymn.

Or a mother singing to her child.

And the snippets, which seemed so random, began to adhere and form a whole. The song. Ellen's fingers moving through Mimi's hair, strand by strand. Mimi tallying her steps in her notebook that morning and noticing what she herself had written on the first page: *Who's Counting?*

Glenna belted out the song. Now Mimi began in a quieter voice, testing out how it felt—until Brent snapped the radio off.

But the feeling stayed.

"Tell me about that feeling," Kevin had asked. "Not the powers. What you feel inside when you take the drug."

"I feel like there's something in me to love," Mimi had said.

She unrolled the window. That was neat—a car with a window you had to unroll. Like turning the crank on the orrery. She saw the moon, the faint stars vying for attention against the glare of human habitation. Pluto was up there somewhere, that small cold outcast planet far away. But there were people who still believed in it, people who wished it well.

199

8

POEM

...

Somewhere Mimi was walking, Ellen's troubled and troubling daughter, placing one foot in front of the other on the tarry side of a six-lane highway. She must be hot. Her feet must hurt. No, let it be some safer road, a rural one, where out of a scrubby ditch a blackbird's sarcastic trill rises. Not that trucker's whistle, the one who ogled her at the rest stop half an hour earlier and was now pulling to the side of the highway, waiting for Mimi to catch up.

Yet even as Ellen fretted over this scenario, a mother's worst nightmare, she sensed that Mimi would be okay. Because if Mimi *was* on the highway with July's eye glaring down on her, slogging through a miasma of humidity and exhaust fumes, aiming her sore feet straight for Vancouver, thousands of kilometres beyond that eighteen-wheeler just ahead? If she *was* about to meet that trucker?

No one knew as well as Ellen. *He'd better watch out.*

...

MATT asked, "What are you thinking about?"

They were spooning together in her afternoon-hot loft, Matt's cheek stuck to her shoulder with the glue of their combined sweat. Sunshine mocked Ellen through the skylight—her loose belly exposed, breasts flopping bedward—while Matt's young arm, tanned and firm as a mannequin's, circled her waist. She reached with her foot for the tangled sheet and, failing to catch it between her toes, suffered there undraped.

"My daughter's coming home," she said. "The one who lives in Toronto? She's walking back."

"The piece of work?"

"Is that how I described her?"

Probably. In Ellen's imagination the scene on the highway was still playing out, the unsuspecting trucker leering as Mimi approached, all shimmery with heat haze. He couldn't guess at her awfulness, could only see the blackening clouds she trailed.

201

Mimi had phoned last night, past midnight her time, to inform Ellen of her plan. She was going to walk all the way to Vancouver, or try to, a benign goal for a girl who formerly went in for darker pastimes. Tongue piercing. Shoplifting. Torturing her mother. It would end badly, this cross-country amble, like everything else the girl touched.

Girl? She was twenty-seven. Ellen hoped she hadn't mentioned that to Matt, who quite possibly was younger.

"She called last night from Barrie, of all places. I've no idea what she was doing there. I said, 'Walk to the airport. Fly home.'"

Mimi had hung up. Anyway, Ellen hadn't meant it. If she were honest, she'd ignore the guilt boring into her and admit that she didn't particularly want Mimi back.

About the walking, Matt expressed neither interest nor surprise. He jiggled and squeezed Ellen's right breast, made it stand up and quack, *But where's she going to stay?*

And Ellen said, "Ouch."

LATER, they went outside where it was cooler, to the triplex's communal backyard—a rectangle of lawn hedged by straggly forsythia. A pair of weathered Muskoka chairs faced each other. In the shade of one of Ellen's half-barrel planters, where she was growing lettuce, Tony flopped down and resumed his nap.

Matt was complaining about his girlfriend again. In the beginning, he never used to mention her, but these last few weeks she kept coming up like acid reflux. Ellen listened, sipping her ice water, touching her breast—the talking one—discreetly through her sundress. It felt a little tender, like it had been overhandled.

"If I leave my clothes on the floor, she puts them in the oven," Matt said.

"That's risky."

The downside of a callow lover: obtuseness. The two Muskoka chairs stood so close together that Matt's and Ellen's knees touched, Matt with his forearms on his thighs, looking not at Ellen, but into her lap, as though presenting for her viewing pleasure his shirtless, muscled back. In a small way it compensated her. And the sun, already slapping its hot hands against his shoulders, pinkening them, offered Ellen a small revenge.

This particular issue, the housework issue, so boring to Ellen who lived alone, was at least less painful than Matt's gripe a few days before. "When I open the fridge, or as I call it, 'the condiment cupboard,' and see that big bottle of cranberry cocktail? That's the sign."

The poor girl suffered chronic bladder infections. Meaning no sex. Did Ellen need to know that? Why had he told her? Even 'condiment cupboard' hurt. Every couple, no matter how miserable, spoke its own private dialect. But for Ellen and Matt there was only body language.

Eventually Matt ran out of domestic grievances to air, as well as other subjects for over-sharing. He went home to Nicole, whose name he only ever uttered by mistake.

Ellen moved inside and ran a lukewarm bath. Just as she lay back, Tony burst in, sprang onto the toilet lid, and stepped daintily across to the tub's ledge. Like an agitated sentry, he paced back and forth, licking his black lips. He hated water, hated to see her in it. When she bathed him, he shivered uncontrollably.

203

Her own complaints Ellen addressed to her dog. "I told him about Mimi. He wasn't interested. He only cared that she wouldn't get in the way. So you see how it is, Tone? He can moan about his girlfriend, but when I moan, he changes the subject."

Tony tilted his black head. Pathos bulged in his eyes.

"Why does he keep telling me these things? It's not as though he's going to leave her and move in with me."

Tony tilted the other way.

"What?" Ellen asked, and when the dog whimpered, she lifted her breast out of the water, imitating Matt. "I wish you could talk," she made it say.

That was when she noticed the bruise and how, compared with the other breast, the right one seemed slightly swollen. She climbed out of the tub, dried her top half with the towel. With her arm raised in the mirror, she leaned in to examine the discoloured patch in a better light. Meanwhile, Tony commenced his relieved devotions, licking the water off her calves.

• • •

CAROL, her doctor, said, "Do you have a boyfriend, Ellen?"

Ellen sighed. "Long story."

"But someone's been squeezing you pretty hard?"

"The brute."

Carol probed Ellen's breasts with her long fingers, but couldn't feel any lump. She flicked through Ellen's file, commenting acidly on her dismal record of responding to mammogram requests. "They're not invitations to some party you can blow off."

"I know that," Ellen said, shrinking down.

"I'll send you in, just in case."

"In case of what?" Ellen asked, but Carol had already swivelled in her chair to face the computer screen.

"How are the girls?" she asked.

"Oh God," Ellen said. "You will not believe Mimi's latest."

Carol inquired no further. She was probably just distracting Ellen, whose suspicions were now fully aroused. Except that Carol had been short with her, sarcastic, and that sarcasm reassured Ellen.

Because really, if Ellen had cancer? Would Carol be so mean?

ON Thursday Ellen found herself in the waiting room of the X-ray clinic, gowned in blue, her purse and everything she'd taken off—blouse, amber beads, bra—in the stackable red plastic shopping basket with metal handles that folded down. Most of the chairs were occupied. The woman beside Ellen looked Arab or Persian with rippling hair and a Nefertiti nose. Another was quite old, or entirely grey at any rate. Worry defaced her.

Ellen probably looked worried. Mentally she put the worry in her basket, but this only made the weight in her lap too much to bear. Yet two of the women, the two who were flipping blasély through magazines, didn't appear worried at all.

Good idea. Ellen reached for a *Bon Appétit* in the pile on the table. She tried flipping, but couldn't keep it up even to convince herself. Someone's name was called. The grey-haired one stood and followed a technician down a hall, toting her basket. Another woman arrived, almost as though to take her place, selected a gown from the pile, and went to change.

Eventually, Ellen fell into thinking. Mimi had phoned again the night before from a motel near Goderich.

"Isn't that on one of the Great Lakes?" Ellen had asked.

Mimi had said she didn't know, she'd arrived in darkness, that she guessed she'd find out in the morning.

"Why are you doing this, honey?" Ellen had asked.

"I'm trying to figure that out."

Though Mimi had sounded more cryptic than anything, Ellen couldn't help hearing malice in her daughter's voice, unfairly maybe, because other than hanging up on Ellen that first time, Mimi was being perfectly, uncharacteristically civil. She was probably too exhausted at the end of her day-long walks to rouse her inner mother-tormentor.

Ellen, so familiar with her daughter's dark side, so long-accepting of her own victimhood, pictured Mimi through her mother-eye again. Mother-eye—the curse cast on every birthing woman, the hex of self-sacrificing empathy. *I will see your pain, but you will never see mine.* Through her mother-eye Ellen imagined the stale motel room halfway across the country, vaguely at first, then distinctly enough to make out Mimi by the window, her dancer's body lithe and tall, her dark hair cropped. Pursed-lipped, Mimi tugged aside the stiff curtain and looked across the near-empty motel parking lot, across the lonely, unseen highway, to where the lake would be.

And Ellen's mother-eye saw what Mimi saw: an appalling blackness, a true void. In her bitterness, Ellen had forgotten to give her daughter stars.

"Ellen McGinty?" someone called.

Ellen rose. A technician led her to a small, dim room with an examining table. "Aren't I here for a mammogram?" Ellen asked.

The technician glanced in the file. "Your doctor phoned in for an ultrasound. And a biopsy."

"A biopsy?"

In obedient bewilderment, Ellen set down the basket and removed the gown. She reclined on her side in the gloom, exactly as she had in the too-bright sunshine in her loft with Matt the week before. The technician was Chinese, her hands a man's. An earlier generation might have called her "strapping."

Ellen cast down her eyes and saw it, seemingly separate from her body: her breast. The same breast Matt had playfully given voice to, that the technician was swabbing with an alcohol pad, preparing to administer the freezing. Syringe packages lay on the nearby tray.

Ellen closed her eyes. "Ouch," she said.

She went numb with the shock of it. All of her floating to the ceiling, looking down, the way near-death experiences are narrated. She saw her own forehead furrow: *Don't think that word. Death.* Then a doctor and an intern entered and Ellen settled back into herself. Smiles and introductions, gel slathered on the insensate breast. The doctor wore pearls, Ellen noticed.

The ultrasound wand was a mere pressure, their subdued discussion jargon-filled. The doctor seemed to be explaining the procedure to the intern. Ellen could hardly understand a word. In and out of the white-coated huddle, biopsy instruments were passed.

"Okay!" the doctor sang, peeling off her gloves. An overhead light came on and the doctor and intern left. The technician fixed a Band-Aid to Ellen's breast.

Ellen asked her, "So I'm okay?"

"No—"

A cry tore free from Ellen, startling them both.

Immediately the technician apologized. "My English," she said, wringing her big hands. What she'd meant was that she couldn't comment. The sample had to go to the lab, the ultrasound to the radiologist. Ellen's doctor would pass along the results.

"When?" Ellen asked.

"Seven to ten days."

ELLEN couldn't shake the first feeling, the blindsiding, at hearing that "No." Because her own mother had died of breast cancer. And look what happened? Ellen was left completely bereft, without love and guidance. Not quite true, she knew now, but that was how she'd felt back then. When she was growing up, people always said Ellen looked like her mother. The two of them had the same long nose and auburn hair. Well, Ellen had quite a lot of grey now, which her mother hadn't lived long enough to earn.

Tears flooded Ellen's eyes.

In the clinic elevator she kept her forearm pressed against her sore right breast. The man riding down with her noticed and was made uncomfortable. That or there was something terrible written on her face. Her mother's death, the tears hastily wiped away. He stared fixedly at the floor numbers counting down.

The doors opened on a scrum of people who then cleaved their ranks for Ellen. They parted, all of them looking at her, looking hard, like they knew something about her that she didn't know herself. They seemed burdened with this knowledge because, uncharacteristically for a crowd, instead of charging right into the elevator, they waited for Ellen to step out.

I'm okay?

No.

How had she got to the clinic? She couldn't remember. Then she did. She'd driven. She pushed through the side door that led to the parking lot, stopping a second time because she didn't, in fact, own a car anymore. She'd sold it after she moved to the studio.

(How odd the way her thoughts were being released, one at a time, like old-fashioned bingo balls.)

She'd borrowed the car from Tilda. Ellen waited for the release of the information she needed next: make, colour.

Things flowed a little better once she found the car. She set the basket on the hood and dug with shaking hands for the keys. It was the correct car, she already knew because she recognized Tilda's things in the back seat. A bag of fleece for one of her knitting projects, the steering-wheel club that Ellen had neglected to use.

Driving was automatic.

At the pay station the attendant also avoided looking at her. Ellen stopped on the other side of the gate, flipped down the visor, and checked her reflection in the mirror. Nothing.

"I'm okay," she said.

Only when she got home and knocked on Tilda's door to return the car keys did she figure it out. When Tilda reached for her. "Oh, Ellen. What happened?"

"Nothing," Ellen said, glancing down to see what Tilda saw.

The blue hospital gown and the red plastic basket still hanging on her arm, her clothing in it, her D-cup bra on top of everything.

THAT same day, Day One, Ellen phoned Carol, hopping mad.

"I did say biopsy, didn't I?" Carol said. "Maybe I didn't. I'm sorry."

"I'm so worried now."

"Don't be. Not until those tests come back."

"My mother had breast cancer."

"I'm aware that, Ellen. So excuse me for saying this, but mightn't that have prompted you to have the occasional mammogram?"

Mean! Even as Ellen shouted down the line, "That's what I thought I was going in for!" she felt buoyed up by relief.

209

DAY Two, Matt came over. Ellen's sign said SORRY, WE'RE CLOSED, but she opened for him when he knocked.

"Just so you know, I don't feel like it today."

For the first time in the ten months of their affair, she'd told him no.

I'm okay?

No.

She assumed he would leave and come back another time, but he settled on the couch beside Tony, who woke long enough to wag. Ellen returned to her dentist's chair and the *Bon Appétit* she'd accidentally brought home in the shopping basket. She didn't mind Matt being there. His carefree, shaggy presence was not unlike Tony's.

"How's your daughter?" he asked.

"What?" Ellen said. "Oh, fine."

A week ago his indifference to Mimi had been Ellen's main irritation. Already the waiting had altered everything.

"You seem sort of upset. Are you mad at me?"

Ellen looked at him, her sweet, rutting lad with his hair in his eyes. (Not *hers*, actually.) His chin was turned away, eyes squinted, as though in preparation for a blow. "Mad at you? No."

"What's wrong, then?"

Until the results came back and she knew she was okay, she couldn't speak about the biopsy. Instead she brought up Mimi's crazy scheme, which had been temporarily eclipsed.

"It's so like her to do this. When she was little her father and I used to joke that we got what we'd deserved."

"What do you mean?"

"Giving her such a self-referential name." Ellen demonstrated those long-ago tantrums, thumping her chest. "Me! Me!"

Matt laughed.

"A woman walking alone on the highway? After dark?"

"Someone could pick her up," Matt said.

"Exactly. Some trucker."

"Or run her down."

Ellen didn't confide her dread of Mimi actually arriving. At her current pace she would be bearing down on Ellen by late fall, the oppressive, grown-up incarnation of that long-ago child Ellen could sometimes only subdue by holding her small, thrashing body tight against her own.

"She'll be okay," Matt said, and Ellen sighed.

He pointed to the *Bon Appétit*. "What're you cooking?"

Ellen got out of the chair, tossed him the magazine. "You choose."

The night before, she'd fallen asleep easily, but had woken several hours later to struggle and sweat till dawn. Her mother had been sitting at the foot of her bed, watching her. Ellen was sure of it. Not her father, who died so much more recently. Only her mother. Why?

Now the terrible night was all but written on the face Ellen saw in the bathroom mirror. She washed and dried it. She touched the breast again, noticeably more swollen today, inflamed around the biopsy incision.

Matt chose Korean. Beef barbecue, shrimp and green onion pancakes, field greens. "We'll have to go to the store," Ellen said.

The red plastic basket was already waiting by the door. They walked down to Fourth Avenue, past the blue-awninged café on the corner. It used to be just one of many cafés on Fourth Avenue before taking on the importance of a landmark—the four walls where Ellen and Matt had met—the smell of coffee wafting out, so erotic. Just a café again now; she barely noted it on the edges of her preoccupation.

They crossed the street, walked a block of irrelevant boutiques.

"I was supposed to go to Korea," Matt said.

"What?"

"Last year. I had a job lined up teaching English. Then she was accepted in the PhD program."

"Nicole?" Ellen asked.

Matt looked around, as though Ellen's shameless uttering of Nicole's name might cause her to appear. Theoretically, she could. She lived in the neighbourhood with Matt. Because of her, Ellen and Matt had never ventured farther than Ellen's overgrown, semi-private backyard. This, too, was different.

"So I came here instead. To the city of a thousand language schools. Except half of them have closed."

"A PhD," Ellen said, shaking herself. She had to reimagine the girlfriend, her rival, hysterical stuffer of clothes in the oven. A girl sitting primly on the toilet, wincing as she tried to pee. A PhD candidate.

"She was mad when I couldn't get a job. Now she's mad that I'm working in yard maintenance."

"Are you sure that's why she's mad?" Ellen asked.

They walked into Whole Foods, Matt carrying the basket, Ellen the magazine folded open to the recipes. Everything glowed mockingly with good health. The other shoppers, too, their baskets abrim with supplements and kale. Ellen would start eating better. She'd sign up for yoga just as soon as she knew she was okay. Go and see Celine for herbs.

At the Meats section, Matt lifted into the basket the steaks she pointed to. He glanced nervously around again. He and Nicole probably shopped here. Maybe Nicole and Ellen had waited in the same line with neither of them realizing their point of commonality.

"Do you want to separate?" Ellen asked.

"I'm thinking about it," Matt said.

"I'll meet you at the checkout then."

Ellen moved along to Seafood, sniffing at some pretty nubs of shrimp. Matt followed. "I thought you meant from Nicole! Separate from Nicole!"

Both of them stricken with confusion in Whole Foods, staring at each other. His complaining monologues over these last few weeks began replaying in Ellen's head.

"You're not asking me to help you decide, are you? Because that would be—" She struggled for something other than *cruel*. Couldn't he see how hurtful this was? Because if he left Nicole to her gallons of cranberry cocktail and her PhD? He'd go and get himself some other girl his age while he kept on visiting Ellen.

"*Inappropriate.* Life advice, I can do. Love advice, no. Excuse me?"

She nabbed someone in a Whole Foods shirt, too aggressively by the way he recoiled. "Do you have Asian pears?"

He gestured to the bins of fruit, pinching his lips the way Mimi always did.

"Go," she told Matt, with a curt, dispatching wave. "And green onions and ginger."

"I'm not asking you to help me decide," he told her, walking away backward.

She searched out the rest of the ingredients—sesame seeds, rice vinegar—before meeting up with Matt at the checkout, still angry.

"I'll take the life advice," he said.

His words and the rueful way he clutched the basket to his chest softened Ellen. "This one time? I'll do love advice. Do you have any money?"

He transferred the basket to one arm so he could pat his shorts pockets.

"I mean in the bank."

"That's the problem," he said. "She pays for everything. She's sick of it."

"How long have you been with her?"

"Five years."

"Five years?" Ellen said. "Longer than I was married."

BACK home, Matt straddled a chair in the doorway of Ellen's tiny kitchen. Tony was more in the way, underfoot from counter to fridge, sitting pretty as a meerkat when she sliced the steak, gulping down the raw shreds she indulged him with.

Matt asked about Larry.

"He's a playwright."

She glanced at him to see if he wanted more. Why shouldn't she talk about Larry, after all Matt had told her about Nicole? She puréed the pear, the garlic, the liquids in the food processor, dumped the concoction over the mound of steak strips waiting in the bowl.

"He *started* as a playwright, then gave it up for TV. Now he's bitter. Be true to your heart. There's the life advice I promised. Anyway, we get along now."

"You're friends?"

Ellen shrugged. "We have children and grandchildren. And a history. That's what I meant in the store. If a person stays in your life long enough, the kind of complaints you've been talking about? Or worse complaints? I won't bore you with Larry's atrocities. Suffice it to say there were many. Anyway, over time, these things don't matter so much."

Matt looked doubtful.

"It's like money in the bank. Your attachment is the interest. It compounds. Do you understand?"

"Not really," he said. "I'm so bad with money."

She started on the salad dressing, grating ginger into the bowl. "One thing I'll say about Larry. When he was around? Which he hardly ever was. But when he was actually with us? He was a wonderful father. During Mimi's Troubles especially."

"What troubles?" Matt asked.

Ellen always thought of that time in capitals, like a kind of civil war, which it was. "She tore her meniscus in dance class. After the surgery, she was in a lot of pain. I should've listened to my instincts, but they weren't as loud as Mimi's screams."

So she had allowed Mimi that prescription. And then the real pain began.

"Mimi would phone doctors all over town impersonating me, giving her permission for the drug."

"How old was she?"

"Sixteen. She stole. My friend Celine was over and Mimi plucked the credit card right out of her purse. She started running with this group of girls, meeting up downtown. They were feral. Once they swarmed a bus driver for the outrage of asking them to pay the fare."

"Whoa. You said a piece of work. I thought you meant, like, my sister."

215

"Then she stopped coming home at all. I caught up with her in someone's basement, dragged her out by the hair. Dragged her all the way to rehab. But you never really get over something like that. Not after spending most of a year wondering where your daughter is and if she's moved on to heroin and is paying for it giving blow jobs in some alley."

Matt cringed. "I'm sorry."

Ellen washed her hands. She looked over, saw he was sincerely appalled. It touched her.

"Of course, Larry didn't pay his share of rehab, claimed he couldn't. But he did fly up to visit Mimi. And afterward, he took her to Paris. Just the two of them, for a week. He paid for that."

"Do you still love him?" Matt asked.

"Larry? I wouldn't use the word *still*." Ellen took up the whisk. "It makes it sound like I'm besotted, which I'm not." But she had been, for years and years. Besotted. "I guess I do."

Matt slumped. "Does he love you?"

"I think so. In his substandard way." She dipped her finger in the bowl and licked it, smiled.

He said, "This is fucked, don't you think? You love your ex-husband and he loves you, but you're sleeping with me."

"I could say the same thing about you and Nicole."

He blushed, and it struck Ellen again how simple the world is for people under thirty, for whom love has barely been compromised by life. Love unopened, still in its shiny package.

"Are you happy?" he asked. "I mean, despite all this stuff with your daughter, are you happy with how things are?"

"What a question! Ask me in a week." She turned her back.

"Why?"

"Ask me that in a week too. Can you light the barbecue?"

That morning she'd almost vomited. It had seemed that she wouldn't be able to bear the wait. But when they finally sat down to eat, Ellen was surprised by the time. Several hours had passed and she was starving.

"It's good," she said, lifting a wedge of the crispy shrimp pancake with the chopsticks, dipping it into the sauce. Sweet and sour, the edges lacy. The lettuce, too, had an intense, almost synesthetic flavour. It *tasted* green, this lettuce that she'd coaxed to life herself.

"It's fantastic," Matt said.

"Just think. If you'd gone to Korea? You would've eaten like this every night."

Matt said, "This is better."

SHE woke on Day Three blinking. There was the actual 6 a.m. light and there was the flash of clarity about how her days would go now

216

until Carol called. Increasingly, dread. She would be made sicker and sicker with it. Stopping herself from Googling prognoses, which she had so far resisted—impossible. By the time Carol called, Ellen would be so convinced she had cancer, a fiercely metastasizing type that had already colonized her whole body, that Carol's reprieve wouldn't at first register. *I'm okay?* Ellen would repeat in the phone, dazed.

And then it would be as if the terrible week and a half had never happened, except that she would be left with this wonderful post-scare gift, the kind of appreciation for life reserved for those whose mortality has been severely tested. Survivors of nautical disasters, people who miss planes that crash. A week from now everything would seem very, very beautiful and precious, like Ellen was living in a poem. The light splashing her face at 6 a.m. would not just *feel like*, it *would be*, molten gold. Fact and metaphor both. She would have it all.

She could hardly wait.

In the meantime, though, Tony had to be walked. She went out with him several times a day, somehow always ending up on the abandoned train tracks that ran from the Fraser River all the way to False Creek, cutting through Ellen's neighbourhood in Kits. Community gardens had sprung up where the brambles weren't too thick. Tony ambled along their edges, pissing on the basil.

Somewhere, Mimi was doing the same thing. Walking. Whenever Ellen thought of it, she picked up her pace to stay ahead. Then her mother came to mind and Ellen wondered, *am I also a daughter walking toward her mother?*

During one of these walks Ellen remembered her previous night's dream. Mimi had been a toddler again, so blond she was almost white-haired. Which she had been in real life, deceivingly

217

angelic at two. The dream child screamed in Ellen's arms. She flailed so that Ellen had to turn her face away to avoid a blow from a miniature fist, which actually hurt quite a bit.

Eventually, Mimi worked out her demon and fell limp. Ellen carried her to the nursery. Not the real one—Mimi never had one—but an idealized nursery from a magazine with a frieze of white bunnies on parade. As soon as Ellen noticed the bunnies, actual rabbits appeared, hopping around underfoot. Somehow she made it to the crib without tripping, which was a feat because more and more bunnies infiltrated the room, a colony of them.

Black bunnies.

Ellen laid Mimi down, careful not to wake her. When she straightened, she saw that Mimi's hair had changed to her grown-up colour and that she had melanized to the colour of pitch. Also, the front of Ellen's shirt was dripping with something oily. Something dark and sticky soaking right through her clothes. Ellen felt it on her skin.

On Day Five Ellen followed the tracks to the end. Until then she'd only gone far enough to know that when the waiting was done, she would pause among the gardens and marvel at how people in the middle of a city still responded to the urge to till the earth. They responded with plots and raised beds along this old allowance, with pretty driftwood trellises where the scarlet runners tangled themselves. They responded with old rubber tires, out of which zucchini fecundly tumbled.

At the end of next week—not that long, really—she would open a gate, the one with hand-carved pickets. The one with the angel ornament.

And boldly enter.

She would pick some stranger's peas and taste it,
    the bright greenness of life.

But not yet.

Today she and Tony continued walking, staying true to the tracks, passing a veterinary clinic and two car lots. Behind the brewery, she came to a narrow gravel road. This she followed too, eventually arriving at an empty expanse under the Burrard Street Bridge.

Above her, a cathedral span of concrete echoed with the metallic clatter of cars. Down here, she stood in a weedy no-man's land—a wall-less ruin was what it felt like—bordered by condos, scrubby woods, and a boat yard behind a chain-link fence. Tony pulled hard toward the woods so she let him have his way. He wanted to sniff. Sniff and pee. It was what he lived for.

She noticed her indifference to harm. They entered the woods strewn with litter, some of it drug related. A blue rubber glove caught up in the salal. A shopping cart half submerged in a mucky creek. A yawning duffel with clothes twistedly spilling out. People lived or partied here. Where was her daughter now?

Yet in this obscure, seedy, non-place she was protected by the wait. Or at least it felt that way. She stood unafraid while Tony splashed his dwindling urine against tree after tree.

The only thing that could hurt her was still days away.

"It's all right," Matt said the next time he came, Day Six, when she refused him sex again. "I've come to cook you dinner."

"Really? I didn't know you could cook."

"I can clean too. There's a lot you don't know about me."

219

"I know there is," Ellen said, tagging along to her little kitchen.

He upended his pack, sending two fist-sized, yellow potatoes spinning on the counter. Bacon followed, the package landing with a slap. "You're going to love it. It's an old family recipe. You won't ever have had it."

"Can I help?"

"No."

"I actually want to."

He allowed her to wash the potatoes and put them in the oven. "Now what?" Ellen asked.

"We wait."

She sat back in her dentist's chair while Matt went through a stretching routine on the floor. He'd mowed lawns all day. Grass mingled with his hair. Ellen would have offered her shower, but how would he explain that when he got home?

Then he was leaning close to her, smelling of sweat and lawn, gently shaking her awake. He left her to gather her wits, returning with the potatoes in oven-mitted hands. He needed two bags, paper or plastic, it didn't matter.

"This is yours," he said, handing her the potato in the Whole Foods bag. "Do what I say or you'll fuck it up."

He pulled out a chair, pointed to the bag, then the seat.

"You want me to sit on the bag?" Ellen asked.

"Yes."

She laughed.

"Go. You have to do it while it's hot."

He muscled her toward the chair. She dropped the bag, plopped down on it. Sprang up. "Ouch!"

"Pathetic. Watch."

Matt thrust out his butt, waved it over his bag like a hen positioning herself over the straw. He flipped his knees to his chest. When he landed, the paper bag crackled and his eyes grew wild. For five or ten seconds his feet pedalled the air, then he leapt up and ran around the room pretending to put out a fire in his shorts. Tony chased him, barking in alarm.

The phone rang. Ellen was waiting for Mimi to confirm she'd received the money Ellen had transferred into her account.

It was Tilda next door, wondering what was going on.

Zerquetschte Kartoffeln they called it, this very special dish reserved for reunions on his father's side, or all-male events. Squished Potatoes. Matt fried the bacon, then fried the flattened tubers in the leftover grease.

"And?" he asked as they shared the first crunchy, salty pancake with its surprising softness in the middle.

"I like it."

"Good. That's the first part of the test."

A test? What was he up to? Ellen wondered. What did this odd behaviour mean?

"Part One is do you like my *Zerquetschte Kartoffeln*? Part Two is can you say *Zerquetschte Kartoffeln*?"

"No," Ellen said.

"Try. *Sa.*"

"*Sa.*"

"*Sa-kwetch-ta.*"

"I'll bet that's the squished part. It's—what's that word?" A poetic term. She remembered. "*Onomatopoeic!*"

Do you have dimpled, bruised, and/or puckered skin on your breast?

Yes > Skin changes to the breast could be the sign of a serious problem. > See your doctor.

No> For more information please talk to your doctor.

Day Seven, 3 a.m.

The phone rang. Ellen, who was already awake and sitting at the computer, turned and stared at where the phone lived on the corner of her desk. She actually gagged. It stopped, only to start up again ten seconds later.

"Mom?"

"Mimi?" Ellen said. "Where are you, honey? What's wrong? What happened?"

"Are *you* all right?"

"Me? What do you mean?"

Ellen heard a ragged exhalation, but couldn't quite believe the veracity of Mimi's tears. Tears she could manufacture on command.

"I had a dream," Mimi said.

"It's three o'clock in the morning."

"It's six here. This is the time I start."

"Well, you scared me. You're scaring me."

"Mom, I love you."

Ellen sat blinking for a moment. When she finally spoke, it was in the level, calm voice Mimi would recognize even three thousand kilometres away, a voice from the past.

"And I love you, too, honey. More than you'll ever know. But I have to ask you something. Try not to get mad." She took a fortifying breath. "You're not using again, are you?"

There were rustling sounds. A tissue?

"No," Mimi said.

So matter-of-fact was this *no*, so unfreighted with overreaction, that Ellen only grew more suspicious.

"Sure?"

It was the middle of the night, the only light in the large studio room coming from the laptop on her workbench, Ellen washed in the pink glow of the breast cancer website. All at once the computer went to sleep.

And night threw its hood over Ellen.

She sank inside herself. Over the years things had been said on both their parts—insults, accusations, threats—that Ellen wished could be unsaid, so many things. Now, to this long list, she had added, *Sure?*

A dream, Mimi had said. Ellen's own returned in a flash, the one where holding Mimi had stained her shirt front black. There was another interpretation, of course—that Ellen's breasts had been filled with the toxic stuff, that she'd been nursing her daughter with it all along.

"Mom?"

"I'm here."

"I'll let you get back to sleep."

"Wait, sweetheart." Ellen stood up, steadying herself against the bench. She touched a key to bring back the light. The screen bloomed again with its ominous statistics. "Did I talk much to you about my mother?"

"Your mother? A little, I guess. How she died. You told me that."

"I've been thinking about her a lot lately. Thinking that if she'd been around—" Ellen pressed her eyes, one and then the other, with the heel of her free hand. "Why even think this way? She wasn't. Have a good walk, sweetheart. And be careful, right?"

"Okay."

223

"All day I'm worrying," Ellen said. "I'll be glad when you're finally home."

MATT came by the same day to tell her he'd decided. "Could I stay here?"

"Here?" Ellen said.

"For a while. Until I find a place. Or forever. Whatever. When your daughter comes, I'll get lost."

He said he loved her, and Ellen was truly alarmed then. "So why does everybody love me all of a sudden?"

What had life done to Ellen that she couldn't see this love coming? Life had tested her. It had made her a woman who could be hard on the outside. Ellen counted on her fingers. Seven, Eight, Nine, Ten. She pictured herself four days in the future, standing in a place she didn't know. She would be okay. She and Mimi would be okay.

This was the final test, these four days, and when she'd survived them, she would accept into her soft centre this young man who had made the last ten months of her middle age fly, who was at this moment kissing each of the fingers she had counted on, separately, like people do in poems.

But Carol called earlier than expected
                    and asked her to come in.
Ellen went
and was comforted.
And from that undoctorly embrace Ellen said,
Excuse me,
I have a call to make.

Larry said he would come
tomorrow
        on the morning ferry.

Act Two

9

STAGES

...

In the airport Larry's mother seemed shrunken, her skin a desiccated brown against the glare of her hair, like something left out in the merciless Florida sun, but with purpose to her walk. When she got near enough to recognize Larry, she stopped. Stopped and released the handle of her wheeled carry-on, her baggage, and waited for Larry to come and pick it up. He did, kissing her paper-bag cheek and leading her by the arm out of the terminal into the summery, contrailed air.

In the car she kept sifting through her purse.

"What are you looking for, Ma?"

"I want to show you something."

Eventually she found it, found two, but kept the second—packets they offer on planes in lieu of meals. She pushed it at him. "Open it."

He fiddled with it as he steered, gave up, and tore it open with his teeth. Mini pretzels strafed the dash. "Sorry," he said.

Esther leaned back and closed her eyes, finally at ease. After a minute she raised a finger, righteous and crooked at the top knuckle. "And the orange juice was warm."

"We're going straight to a restaurant."

"I'm not hungry. I'm trying to make a point."

"Which is?"

"Never mind. My disappointments are my own. What about Ellen? Is she coming with us?"

THE last time Larry saw his mother was a total disaster in all senses of the word. In the practical sense, the sense easiest to cope with, there was Tropical Storm Fay tearing up the panhandle, triggering an Enhanced Fujita Level 2 tornado outbreak and biblical flooding. But the millions of dollars' damage, the loss of life, the beach holidays washed away, were nothing compared to Esther's non-reaction to Amber, Larry's latest wife. Outside Esther's condo the long-haired palms whipped back and forth like heavy-metal guitarists riffing. Stop signs behaved like weather vanes. Inside, Esther wouldn't speak to either of them. A stillness had descended, as appalling as Fay's empty eye.

Larry had assumed long, condemning silences. He was well acquainted with the skillful, sometimes devastating, way Esther deployed them. The neutron bomb of her silences. But after two days Amber cracked. As soon as it was safe to, she fled the vacuum of the condo, sobbing. For several hours Larry didn't know where she'd gone or if she knew her way back. He blamed himself for bringing her, though not enough to go looking for her beyond the condo's secure gate. He tried, stepped out the door and gingerly around the fronded wreckage—an uprooted palm had narrowly missed their rental car. He saw the sunken, toothless maw of the collapsed swimming pool and retreated back inside.

She had real physical presence, that size-twelve wife of Larry. Whenever there was something heavy to be lifted, Amber did it. Larry's back was shot. That day, just as he was about to call 9-1-1 and report her missing, she bounded back, trembling and radiant.

"Larry! Half the streets are under water!"

The bottom of her skirt dripped with the proof of it and pooled around her sandals, the rubber-soled kind, designed for deluge.

"And guess what I saw? An alligator! An alligator swimming down the middle of the road. I couldn't believe it. Oh, Larry. I tried to grab a stick and touch it. I wish I had."

As Amber was telling him this, miming the paddling legs, Esther hobbled out of her room. Terror replaced the thrill and amazement in Amber's eyes.

Esther didn't ask about Amber now, left behind in a hurry on Cordova Island. How she was, where she was. No. Two years ago in Florida she had foreseen Amber's irrelevance. Esther asked about Ellen, to whom her son hadn't been married for a quarter century.

229

WHAT a force a mother is! A case in point: the Chinese restaurant. Here in his adopted city—adopted then abandoned, for Larry had mostly lived elsewhere and only returned to Vancouver to be with Ellen during her treatments—Chinese food was ubiquitous. Sometimes three restaurants in a row. In one particular suburb a diner would be hard-pressed to find anything but. The entire Sino-spectrum spread out for the intrepid omnivore, from Szechwan to Cantonese, Hot Pot to Dim Sum, even Hakka, Chinese-Indian. Tripe, bitter melon, live squirming shrimp. But in the company of Esther, Larry, who on his own would choose scalding long green beans stir-fried in shirt-staining curry, made sure to take her to a bad one. Bad as in the Chinese she was used to, the Palm Bay, Florida, Dinner-for-One variety.

She said she wasn't hungry, but how couldn't she be? At home she ate at 5:30 on the nose. Even during a tropical storm she ate at 5:30. It was already 7:00 for Esther, 4:00 for the unhungry Larry, when the waiter set the teapot down between them and listlessly unstacked the little cups.

Esther said, "We'll see Ellen after this."

Larry opened the clichéd menu, read the stock choices. This to win him some time before Esther unpacked her metaphorical baggage. The real suitcase was in the trunk of the car.

"I came all this way," she said.

"It's very generous of you, Ma." He'd told her not to, but at six that morning she'd phoned with her flight times. "How about Lemon Chicken?"

"It's the least I could do for the poor woman."

The waiter shuffled back with a sleepy face and an order pad. The pinkie nail on the hand that held the pad was long and smoothly filed, reminding Larry of the coke habit he'd had once upon a time when he lived in TV Land. The waiter's nail, no doubt, was for spooning out the MSG.

"And the least she could do," Esther went on, "is see me. Or does she still bear a grudge?"

Larry closed the menu. "Do you see anything you want?"

She adjusted her lips and looked away, so Larry went ahead and ordered from the somnambulist, unable to suppress his own yawn.

"I've got you in a good hotel."

She turned back and with the blank-eyed expression of a Roman bust stared straight over his shoulder, out the restaurant window behind him.

"Remember when I took Amber down to meet you? Amber, my wife? During that storm? She saw an alligator swimming down the street. I just remembered that."

He pictured the creature's yellow eyes, its peculiar writhing progress, the warty back, as though he'd actually been there with Amber knee-deep in the receding waters. Then the Fried Rice came, glistening with oil, and the dun turds of Lemon Chicken. Larry served. Esther poked at the frozen peas with her fork and sighed.

He couldn't ask outright what she wanted from Ellen. That never worked. As far as Larry knew, they hadn't been in touch for years. When Mimi and Yolanda were kids, of course Esther and Ellen had communicated. Ellen would put them on a plane to Florida. There were pickup arrangements to discuss. But once the girls were older, they dealt directly with their grandmother. No doubt news shuttled back and forth, complaints about Esther to Ellen, and vice versa. But that was the extent of it as far as he knew.

But before that? Before Ellen and Larry's divorce? Not many silences between mother and daughter-in-law then. The grudge Esther referred to was over some subterfuge that Larry had once involved her in. He'd asked for her co-operation. "If Ellen calls, make like I'm there," he had told her long distance, L.A. to Palm Bay. "Would you do that for me?"

Of course she would, and Larry assumed she agreed without asking any questions because she so disliked Ellen. It was a prickish thing to do, the sort of thing Larry specialized in when he was young and horny all the time. But now he was fifty. Or past fifty.

He asked Esther, who of all people should know. "How old am I?"

She lifted her white, brooding head. "Did you even tell her I was coming?"

231

Larry reddened. "The thing is, Ma? You weren't so nice to Ellen back then."

Esther patted her lips with her napkin and folded it in half. "She raised those girls on her own. They turned out okay. Not brilliantly, but better than I expected, especially Mimi with her drugs. Her mother pulled her through that. And never once did they— Mimi and Yolanda, I'm talking about—never did a bad word about you cross their lips."

"Really?" he said. "I'm surprised."

"And Larry?" she added. "How was I supposed to know Ellen would be the best of a bad lot?"

232

HE'D planned a long pretense, a calm, sightseeing type of drive to Esther's hotel, which was about ten minutes away by the direct route. By then exhaustion would defuse her. In Florida, Esther retired at nine after an hour bathing in milk, or whatever she did.

In the parking lot behind the Chinese restaurant she placed her whole crabbed hand over his. Her several rings cut his knuckles.

"She doesn't feel good, Ma," he said.

"Neither do I."

He drew back and studied her. His indomitable mother, his abominable mother.

"Okay. But if she says no? That's the end of it. Right? Right?"

He stepped out of the car, punched Ellen's number into the phone. Esther reached over to turn on the ignition so she could lower the window and listen.

"Hey, babe. It's me. How're you feeling? Ah. Really? Ah." He nodded several times. He had not pressed send to complete the call. "That reminds me of. Okay, a rabbi, a guru, and an air-traffic controller walk into a gym. The trainer goes up to the air-traffic controller and says—" He had no idea. He tucked his free hand into the opposite armpit, leaned against the car. The smell of burnt garlic wafted over from the restaurant's rear door.

"'Can I help you?' And the air-traffic controller says—" What? What? "'I brought two friends. They want to learn to fly.'"

The words came all on their own, naturally, the way they never did anymore despite his head-bobbing and hand-wringing before the Wailing Wall of the computer screen. Or when he wandered around making voice memos on his iPod. Afterward, when he listened to those memos? Moses wept.

"So the trainer gets the guru lying on a mat. Instantly the guy starts levitating. Then the rabbi climbs up on the StairMaster— What? No, babe. There's no point. I'm just trying to make you feel better. And guess who's here? Esther's here. She's asking to see you. What? No, no. Of course she'll understand."

He stood a minute to let this sink in for Esther before pocketing the phone and brushing the crushed pretzels off the seat. Back behind the wheel, he said, "Ma, listen. I'm sorry you made the trip for nothing. But I did tell you. Didn't I say?"

Esther leaned back and shut her eyes.

Across the Burrard Street Bridge. Right turn to loop back to Beach Avenue. The moseying summer traffic suited his purpose. It took a quarter hour just to get to Stanley Park.

Inside the park the seawall swarmed with fitness freaks, with tourists, with gays. Larry chose a runner, not entirely at random— he liked the way her ponytail and other parts swung—and matched her pace. Then the road veered from the shoreline and they were driving through forest. He didn't need to look over at Esther. The whole car had filled with her discontent. He sniffed a few times,

233

wondering if you could actually smell discontent. And if discontent was available in one of those cardboard air fresheners that dangle from the rear-view mirror, what shape would it be? Nice, but he couldn't voice-memo it with Esther beside him. He was mostly collecting these thoughts for Ellen now, to distract her from the general shittiness of chemo. What was that other thing? What?

The rabbi. The rabbi on the StairMaster. Larry could see him now, climbing, climbing in his suit and yarmulke. His sad, sweat-beaded face.

After he ran out of park, he inched the length of Denman Street to the Coast Plaza. By then, he'd killed an entire hour.

A bellhop materialized and stuck his smiling face right in the car window. "Checking in?"

Esther clutched the belt where it bisected her bosom.

"I'll come up with you, Ma. Get you settled. We can have a drink in the bar. Let's have a little visit. You came all this way."

He was amazed how dignified she looked with her eyes squeezed shut. Her hands were turning white.

"Ma?" he said, gently.

She spoke to the bellhop. "Tell him I'm here to see Ellen. Tell him I get out of this car for Ellen and only Ellen."

"JUST what do you want to see her for?"

They were driving back over the bridge, away from downtown, Larry unable to conceal his anger now.

"Buttinsky," she said.

Yet there was a time when Esther aired her grievances freely. About Ellen she had opened all the doors and windows. Ellen had deliberately ensnared Larry with her pregnancy. Then Larry left

Ellen to marry Amy, who was not a shiksa, but that had not gone well either.

"Two months from now would have been better," he said. "This is not a good time. Three months, better still. When she's well again."

Esther nodded the slow nod that actually meant no.

He parked in front of the corner store, its brick-and-board shelves frilled with plants. Across the street, three small, lacy pots stood on pine boxes in Ellen's window, a white curtain behind them. Ellen was probably in her dentist's chair, where she often spent the night because she felt better when she wasn't lying flat. Larry slept on the foldout couch, or the floor, and all the next day his back reminded him that these arrangements were less than ideal. There was a bed in the loft, but he didn't want to climb down the ladder in the dark if Ellen called for him in the night. He had other complaints, as well. Too many visitors. The graveyard odour of Ellen's clay, the dust.

Esther said, "Where is she?"

Larry gestured across the street. "The middle one. Let me go in first and talk to her."

"No!"

"You can't just ring the doorbell."

"Why not?"

"Ma, she's having treatments! She feels like hell! Can't you understand that? We got about four hours sleep last night!"

Esther exhaled. She made her impatient lip movements. "Phone her again."

After several rings Ellen answered.

"Sorry, babe. Were you asleep?"

"When did you go out?" she asked.

"Listen. I have a surprise for you. I'm just outside. With someone."

Esther made a break for it. She must have mastered the seat belt on the way because it in no way impeded her now. And the car door, so heavy, flew open, as though she'd karate-kicked it. Both the surprise of her escape, and his fear of her falling and breaking a hip, leaving him with two invalids, rooted him in his seat. He remembered her purposefulness in the airport, how she'd stumped along, not slow at all, until she saw him. How could he have doubted her strength, gathered now for this final sprint? His eighty-two-year-old mother was actually running across the street, and by the time he found his voice again, it was too late. She was pounding on Ellen's door.

"It's Esther!" Larry yelled in the phone.

He didn't get out of the car. Because Ellen did bear a grudge. Larry knew for a fact that she did. From where he sat, he couldn't see Ellen when she opened up, only the back of his mother packaged in her pale blue pantsuit, her hair like icing. It seemed they were talking. Then the door opened all the way and Esther stepped inside and the door closed again.

Larry snapped the phone shut. He gave them five minutes, max.

He reclined the seat while he waited and, though he tried to rest his eyes, he kept glancing over to see if Esther had been expelled yet. Gerhard's video installation played in a continuous loop on one side. (Larry pictured the oft-visiting German, shuddered.) In the window to the right of Ellen's, a life-sized knitted raccoon crouched. It was both demonic and kitsch, though Larry was beholden to the woman producing this bizarre menagerie for taking Ellen's dog at this difficult time.

And in the middle were Ellen's pots, which he'd looked at many times without really seeing. Even when Larry and Ellen were married, Larry had paid no attention to Ellen's pots. He remembered eating out of them—at that time they were much chunkier vessels—but he couldn't recall any specific one because they were unremarkable. If one fell to the floor and broke to pieces, not even Ellen cared. She gathered up the shards and flung them off the back stoop, which overlooked a sheltered cove. Those were their hippy years, living on Cordova Island, when Larry was writing plays. The broken pottery landed on the rocks and became even smaller pieces that were then washed away—like Ellen and Larry's two-and-a-half-year marriage.

At some point between then and now, when, Larry couldn't say—he hadn't even known Ellen was turning pots again; she'd mostly worked as a publicist all these years—Ellen had had a breakthrough. Something to do with the airiness of the pots, their uselessness. Too small to be practical, not to mention full of holes, this was what gave them value. Yet he'd always considered himself the artist, even after he'd gone in the other direction, leaving theatre for television because at least his scripts got produced. Ellen's pots sold for as much as two hundred now, though the ones in the window she wouldn't part with.

He rubbed his eyes, blurring the three white pots. Ellen's pots that were, practically speaking, priceless.

Eleven minutes. Ellen and Esther made Gerhard, the gay German skinhead, and Larry, the Jew with a backache, look like a love match. Yet they'd been in the same room for eleven—*twelve* minutes now. Soon there would be shouting. Larry would have to rush in. And who would he placate? Back then, there was no question he would run to Mother—but now?

Esther was probably unpacking. "Here," she was saying, "remember this? Remember when you phoned? When Larry was supposed to be staying with me?"

237

"When he was really in L.A. with Amy? And I was pregnant?"

"Yes. Here. Take it," Esther was saying and she put the thing in Ellen's hands.

Ellen held it up at eye level. It was dense, like a fossil. Larry couldn't quite visualize it, but he could see Ellen with the scarf tied around her head, her face gaunt and beautiful. She'd lost so much weight she was as thin as when they'd met back in university.

ESTHER: All I ever wanted? What any mother wants.

Larry scrambled through the glove compartment for something to write on. He wouldn't remember. He'd already forgotten the idea he'd had driving through the park. Something about the shape of a feeling. Under the insurance papers was an old mileage log. He found a pen just as the thing in Ellen's hands transubstantiated to nothing. To air.

But Esther's baggage does not lighten because it contains something that can't be easily lifted out.

ESTHER: I know we don't have the same God.

They argue about this while Larry takes it down. Ellen doesn't believe in God, of course. She tells Esther she has proof.

ESTHER: What proof? What?

ELLEN: Esther. It's in your purse.

Esther digs down until she finds it. She finds it and blinks back tears. And all she can do now is concede the truth of Ellen's position. Because no just God would ever allow it, that his people would hunger and all that would be offered to them were little packets of pretzels impossible to open.

He wrote down other things. For example, that Ellen said he, Larry, was incapable of happiness. Untrue! He'd felt happy the last few weeks. Ever since Ellen had phoned him on Cordova Island and explained her diagnosis—inflammatory breast cancer—and the grim treatment options. They discussed whether or not to tell Yolanda and Mimi. At first Ellen didn't want them to know. Yolanda was busy with her kids—and Mimi? Who knew how Mimi would react. A week later Ellen did tell them, but during that first phone call, Larry had stopped listening. Because he'd already decided he would go.

Anyway, how happy could he be when Ellen was wretched? So not happy, no. Rather, he felt the way he used to in the middle of a play, as though life were dropping into his lap everything he needed to write it, and if he could just keep up his intensity of focus these gifts would continue flowing. Despite the fatigue, or because of it, he'd lived these last weeks in that same state, loving Ellen again, loving her all the way to remission.

239

Then he really had to get out of the car because reclining the seat hadn't worked. Sit too long and you shall spasm: these were words he lived by. And if it happened that he spasmed, relief came only in the form of a small child walking on his back, preferably his grandson.

He stood beside the car to stretch and fiddle with the iPod. The store's closing ritual had begun. The owner was moving the plants inside. The woman, Vietnamese probably, recognized him because Ellen insisted he buy something there every few days, as though she were personally responsible for keeping the seedy little place solvent. Larry voice-memoed this while the woman was inside. When she came out again, she smiled.

Esther spoke again and Larry repeated it into the iPod, adding his exegesis.

"'Such promise he showed.' Her point being that the only time I wrote anything worthwhile—the plays, I mean—was when I was with Ellen. As if *she* had thought of that. I told her as much myself."

He crossed the street hoping to get a look in the studio, but the white curtain prevented him. Now he was close to the pots, face to face with them. She carved out the patterns freehand. With a tool, she'd told him, or a pin.

What you take away is more important than what you leave in.

He'd go around the block.

A lane ran alongside the row of studios. Larry had got that far when he heard a door opening behind him. It was the neighbour, the knitter with the forgettable name from next door, leaving with Ellen's dog, a shin-high, black thing that reeked whenever it was brought to visit and barked in the night, always when Larry was just on the point of falling back to sleep.

"She didn't even like *Talking Stick*," he told his iPod. "Every time I mention it, she does that thing with her mouth."

He tried to describe Esther's mouth movements that had irritated him his whole life. According to Ellen, Mimi had inherited a version of it. Ellen had a term for it. What?

Later, when he replayed this monologue, there would be stammering and the sound of traffic on Fourth Avenue, where he was walking now among the flip-flopped mob streaming up from the beach to fill the restaurants and pubs. They looked so young, and were, he knew from their piercings and tattoos. Amber had a bruise-like mandala on her left shoulder, and in her right nostril, a stud. Once Larry had come across her in the bathroom with the stud out, picking snot off it. *What have I done?* he'd thought.

It was vaguely insulting, their youth and robust good health. "Speaking on behalf of pain sufferers everywhere," he said into the iPod.

When he reached the end of the too-long block, he turned and left them to their pinkening sunset, their rosy futures.

Now a residential street lined with apartments. A woman three floors up was watering her plants. A man stood shirtless, in shorts, with a long fork in his hand, before a barbecue fixed to the balcony rail. Surely, surely, Esther and Ellen would be finished talking about whatever they were talking about, which Larry was beginning to suspect wasn't him, after all. And as he walked he heard the laugh tracks of all the TVs surreally overlapping. Who was laughing? This was something he ought to know. Were there professional laughers? How much were they paid? And what was their suicide rate?

Ahead of him the weird, frizzy-haired knitting woman was returning with the dog. Larry deliberately slowed to prevent meeting up with her. Last time, he'd incited tears.

"What will I do?" she'd asked.

"When?" Larry asked.

"I love Ellen so much."

"She's going to get better," Larry said.

"From Stage Four?"

And Larry lost it. "Have you ever been to a restaurant?"

"A restaurant?" she said. "Yes."

"Have you ever ordered steak in a restaurant?"

"Not recently."

"But you have."

"Probably." She brought her chapped hand up to her throat. "I'm confused."

"Medium rare? Well done? Well done, I bet."

"Maybe I haven't ever ordered a steak."

"Well, I have. I've ordered a steak many, many times. Rare. A hundred times. A thousand times. Yet how many times have I received on my plate, in a restaurant, the rare steak that I ordered in good faith?"

"I don't know where this conversation is going, Larry."

"Never! Never! They say rare, but they don't know what they're talking about! Do you get it now?"

Behind the googly glasses, tears. "No."

"Well done. Stage Four. *It's just a thing they say!*"

She ran off sobbing. That was two or three days ago. Now the dog arabesqued against a light post. They moved on and Larry, still halfway down the block, walked normally the rest of the way back to Ellen's.

Maybe he should go in and rescue her. The thing was, he really needed to lie down before his back seized up. If he went in and lay on the floor of Ellen's studio it would seem attention-seeking. He'd find some grass and lie there until Esther came out. The grass in front of the studios was a mere strip. If he lay there, people would think he was drunk and call the cops.

Across the street, behind the corner store, a monster of a laurel hedge towered. He crossed and went over to it, checking underneath it first for dog shit. Got down on his knees, crawled under the branches, positioning himself so he was at least partially covered. From the fiasco of his marriage to Amber he'd salvaged at least something. Some useful yoga exercises. His back settled into the hard ground.

Corpse Pose.

AND his eyes flew open. He was back with Amber. No, he was in Ellen's loft. No. He'd been interred in some dark, loamy place, unable to move. When he did, when he attempted to sit up, he got a stinging face full of branches.

He pulled himself to his feet grabbing handfuls of leaves. His back screamed.

242

Night. The house the hedge belonged to, the apartments—all of them unlit. The corner store, closed. Then he remembered Esther and quailed, a boy again, terrified of her wrath, yet unable to resist provoking it. Crippled, Quasimodoed with stiffness, he limped around the front of the store. Across the street, light bleeding palely through Ellen's white curtain.

And something moved in his peripheral vision. Something lumbered. Down Ellen's street it came, a shape. A shape or a feeling? He couldn't tell in the dark, could only make out its long squat form, a blacker shadow, a sort of nullness in the night. If Larry dashed across—presuming he could move that fast—he'd more than make it, but fear gripped him. Fear, then strangely— What? What? Because, could it be that all these notes and scraps of conversation, these half-formed jokes, his pensées for Ellen, were actually—? Finally? A play? A *devastating* play, the kind an audience crawled away from and sat in silent commiseration, never to be the same again?

He turned to look at the thing. Gone.

Larry crossed over. He crossed over and opened Ellen's door.

She'd left a light burning in the kitchen, the one in the range hood. The large main room, scant of furniture, looked like a stage. On it Ellen reclined in the dentist's chair, her bare feet sticking out her pyjama bottoms, her bruised arms limp at her sides. Her head was twisted awkwardly, the kerchief half off. Not a comfortable position. He'd taken it for sleep but now he froze. And there was Esther, laid out on the couch with her hands folded on her chest. On the floor beside her, her shoes and handbag, neatly lined up.

Act Two.

And the black dog next door barked. Which was when he noticed, thank God, the breath rising in them both.

243

THE SOMETHING AMENDMENT

. . .

I can't go," Georgia said.

This was the night before the Bentall Four memorial. Gary was sending last-minute e-mails from bed, confirming the details, the laptop open, not exactly in his lap—he didn't have one. When he looked at Georgia, his eyes rivalled an upturned baby seal's in the shadow of a club.

"You didn't go last year either, hon."

"I have this healing thing with Ellen, remember? Ellen and Celine. I told you about it."

On the bedside table Georgia kept a pot of beeswax-scented cream, which she applied nightly to her face. By lifting her chin and working on her throat she could evade Gary's hurt. "And even if I didn't? I don't think I could. Not when I'm so sad about Ellen."

An incoming e-mail pinged, acknowledging her winning response. What could he say? Cancer trumped everything.

He leaned in to comfort her, his beard rasping her honeyed cheek. It smelled, by contrast, sourly of the tacos they'd eaten that night. While managing not to recoil, Georgia did stiffen like a toy soldier in *The Nutcracker*, the way her little community centre troupe had last month when putting on their Christmas show.

Gary said, "I understand."

But, of course, he only thought he did.

FOUR men were working that day, January 7, 1981. Four men on Tower Four. (Only later, in labour circles, were they referred to as the Bentall Four; it made them sound like terrorists, Georgia thought.) Donald, Gunther, Yrjo, Brian. Ordinary working men standing on the almost-finished roof. A sunny day by all accounts, the sky mirrored back in Towers One through Three.

Georgia was eighteen in 1981 and dancing for Judy Marcuse. Gary was in law school. They wouldn't marry until the next year. And Ellen, who was so much in Georgia's heart these days, who seemed so intrinsic to her life, her right-hand friend, amazingly Georgia didn't even know Ellen then. Ellen was living on Cordova Island.

The four men were pouring concrete when the fly form—a sort of movable construction mould—collapsed. In all Gary's twenty-nine years of organizing the annual memorial, he used the same words to describe the accident. The men had "trusted" the fly form. They'd been working on it for months. Apparently people in the building trades had relationships with their tools and equipment despite the fact that the very screwdriver snugged in its leather loop, the fly form they balance on, verged daily on betrayal. And while Georgia didn't know anything about such bonds, she couldn't help thinking that neither did Gary. Not first-hand anyway.

She would never make light of the accident; it was a terrible thing. But the steady pitch of Gary's earnestness over the last twenty-nine years had left her just a little bit sick of it, especially now that Ellen was unwell. Gary had never even met those men.

Besides, all over the world, possibly every minute, people fell.

THE next day Georgia waited in the rain outside Ellen's studio. Celine's car wasn't there yet and Georgia didn't want to intrude until she had to. She should have stayed in the car, except sitting was not her forte. She needed to *move*.

She did some side stretches in front of the studio window, her five-foot reflection seeming more diminutive under the sunflower-patterned umbrella, hair massed in grey shoulder-length helixes. The window itself was empty, all Ellen's beautiful pots sold or, knowing Ellen, given away.

Then the door opened and Larry stepped out counting a handful of change. For a second Georgia saw Larry, but not vice versa—baggy jeans, flapping shirt, silvering curls ebbing at the hairline. A melting weakness overtook her and she remembered all those years ago, not here but in Ellen's North Vancouver kitchen, how he had glissaded out of the way so Georgia could set down her platter of blintzes.

He stopped short of a collision. "Georgia. Go in. I'm just getting some milk." And he dashed across the street, hunched to delay the wetting, feet moving in comical side-to-side jetés.

Georgia stepped inside the studio. It smelled of clay, lilies, the sickroom. Ellen reclined on the couch surrounded by pillows, wearing a brightly patterned kerchief, which seemed to match the vases of flowers, fresh and unfresh, all around the room.

"What's wrong?" Ellen asked before Georgia had even slipped off her rain boots.

"Nothing."

Georgia hung her raincoat on the rack with Ellen watching, took a breath, came and perched on a chair across from her friend, her back to the door.

"Did you see Larry?"

"Yes. Just outside." Georgia cleared an obstruction from her throat, a hard bead of emotion. An image popped into her head—a jawbreaker. The different layers of colour as you sucked, the anise seed in the middle, which, as a child, she'd spat out because she hated it. She was always surprised it was there, like the grain of sand in a pearl of sweetness, so bitter.

"Did he say something to you?"

"He said to go in. Why, Ellen?" Her hands flew up on their own, like flushed birds, so she sat on them.

247

Georgia had been about to change the subject, to ask Ellen how she felt about this healing thing with Celine, when the door opened behind her. Larry back from the store. Distracted by the heat coming off him as he entered, by the flustering air, her tongue stalled.

Larry headed to the kitchen. Ellen followed him there with her eyes and her besotted smile. The two of them, Ellen and Larry, giddily, show-offedly, in love.

It occurred to Georgia then, horribly, that Larry was going to stay for the healing meditation. Even his ensuing kitchen noises incapacitated her. How could she meditate with him in the room? She looked up and saw on Ellen's face a subdued version of the smile she'd given Larry. Ellen seemed to be offering it, love's residue, to Georgia as they waited for Celine.

More and more these visits trickled into silence. Even when Larry brought from the kitchen two mugs, which he set on the coffee table, toppling the get-well cards, none of them spoke. He kissed Ellen's mouth, kissed the kerchief on her head, went for his coat. Came right back and kissed her again while he was putting it on. Celine knocked. Of course Larry wouldn't stay; those two couldn't stand each other. He let her in, squeezed past. Gone.

Georgia untensed with relief. Her whole little body had been coiled like her hair.

"Is that coffee?" Celine whisked it away to the kitchen, calling over her shoulder, "No coffee, Ellen. I've prepared a remedy. I'll leave it on the counter."

She bustled back, kissed Ellen, then gestured to Georgia to lift the vase of flowers while she pulled the coffee table away to make room on the floor. "Cross-legged," she said.

First, the trial of sitting up. Georgia dashed over. After three tries Ellen managed to stand. "Can't she lie down?" Georgia snapped.

"I'm okay sitting." Ellen sank back onto the couch and let Georgia buttress her with pillows.

Normally, Ellen was the skeptic. Last summer when she announced her illness to them over lunch, she'd ended up savaging Celine, who did espouse some offensive beliefs, such as negative thinking caused cancer. Something turned that day in their stunned conversation. Ellen started hissing accusations—that Celine was glad she had cancer because it proved her dingbat theories. Now Celine could give her *herbs*. Ellen kept saying *herbs* derisively over and over until Celine fled the restaurant in tears, leaving Georgia to mediate their reconciliation with a dozen phone calls back and forth. Since then Ellen had submitted to the savagery of chemo and radiation and been rewarded by a seemingly miraculous remission. Then, at Christmas, back pain—the cancer resurrected in her bones. Now, with more chemo ahead, Ellen had opened herself to dingbattedness.

Georgia and Celine got down on the floor. Celine asked them

to close their eyes, to bring their attention into their bodies. "Feel the body you're sitting in."

Georgia opened her eyes to see if Ellen's were closed. They were. She looked beautiful in the gypsy scarf, her skin tanned-looking, darker around the eyes. Celine wore a pale grey drapey sweater over leggings, her near-white hair gathered in a clip.

"Feel the substantiality of your physical body," Celine said. "Its weight. Feel gravity acting on that weight. Pulling it down."

Which reminded Georgia of what gravity had done to those four men. She checked at her watch; the ceremony had started. Gary would be lining up to lay a rose on the memorial plaque. Rain would be spattering the lenses of his glasses, concealing the fact that he was crying.

She glanced at Ellen again, hoping their eyes would meet this time, that Ellen might roll or cross hers so that Georgia could gently rebuke her with a furrowed brow.

"Receive the solidity of the body," Celine said.

During the years of their friendship, Ellen had always been the solidest. Lately, though, her extra flesh had fallen away. She'd stepped out of it and kicked it aside as she undressed for death. What a terrible image. A burlesque.

"Breathe in and sense the strength and mass of your different parts. Head, shoulders, arms."

When Celine referred to the body as "earthen," Georgia suddenly smelled Ellen's clay again. Then newly cut grass. She felt herself pressed down, only partially by gravity. This naturally made her think of a grave and how Ellen was probably going to die, and that she, Georgia, was bewildered by the specifics of it.

"Feel the torso, its mass and weight. The earthen quality of this body in which you live."

249

The body, the body. The body on top of hers.

The meditation took half an hour, then Celine had to meet a patient. "I'll call tonight, Ellen. We'll set up another session. I love you."

"I love you too," Ellen said, stretching out on the couch and moving just her fingers in that air-grabbing way babies say goodbye.

Celine and Georgia hugged at the door. By the time Georgia turned back, Ellen was asleep.

Georgia lifted her raincoat off the stand, slid into it. And Ellen spoke again. In a soft, slow voice, eyes still closed, she said, "Thanks for coming."

"Oh, Ellen. Do you think it will help?"

Ellen turned her head. The colours in her scarf seemed to bring out the blue of her eyes, sharpening them. She looked right into Georgia.

"It will help Celine," she said.

GEORGIA decided to take the Lions Gate Bridge on the way back. Their house in North Vancouver was almost due north of Ellen's studio in Kitsilano, equidistant to both bridges. Gary only used the Lions Gate to go downtown; otherwise, out of principle, he went by the Second Narrows, which he always referred to by its newer name, the Iron Workers Second Narrows Memorial Crossing.

She chose perversely against Gary's principles (her choice of bridge being, in her opinion, unrelated to her stance on workers' rights), then ended up driving right past the Bentall Centre at noon. As the clot of cars she was trapped in inched forward, she glanced up and saw, reflected in the curved glass wall of a much taller tower on the east side of Burrard Street, a familiar building wavering like a mirage. And forgot to turn. The Bentall towers were of unequal heights, but all of them were surfaced in black glass with vaguely Doric concrete friezes. Starting with recognition, Georgia looked from the mirage, across to the actual Tower Four. If anyone remained from the memorial gathering that morning, they blended in now with the ordinary, ungrieving passersby.

With the thought of grief, Ellen's words came back. *It will help Celine.*

But what would help Georgia?

Craning to take in the whole height of the tower, she nearly swooned with vertigo.

251

IF Ellen hadn't been pregnant the first time Larry left her, she and Georgia and Celine would never have become friends. They were too different—Georgia shy; Celine, at that time, before her baby died, glamorous; Ellen so Ellenish, with her long, bedraggled hair and her long, sacklike skirts and her desperation to tell her sordid story, over and over.

The details of Ellen and Larry's breakup shocked Georgia. Then, after Yolanda was born, Georgia watched Ellen scramble. She bore witness to Ellen's bitterness. Some people thought Ellen drank too much. Georgia thought so, but would never say it because, who wouldn't in those circumstances? All Ellen had got out of the absconding Larry was the North Vancouver house. Georgia was lucky, married to the kindest man in the world, a man with principles who had sunk onto the delivery room floor and sobbed because he was implicated in her pain, then sobbed for joy with his first-born son in his arms, ruining all the pictures. Sixteen years after Jacob, when Maximilian was born, Gary repeated this performance.

Back then, during their early years as friends, Ellen would phone and Georgia would listen. Late into the night, Ellen would slur her explanation of what had attracted her to Larry in the first place.

"I'm from Calgary. The closest I'd come to a Jewish man was *Annie Hall*. How is Calgary different from yogourt?"

Georgia yawned.

"Yogourt has culture," Ellen said. "I'm surprised *Annie Hall* even played in Calgary."

And Georgia would look over at Gary gurgling in his sleep, her very own Jew, but a *nice* one, and be suffused with gratitude.

This went on for years, close to eight years. Then one night Ellen called to say, "Guess what? Amy kicked him out."

"Who's Amy?" Georgia asked.

The hundred pounds of overwrought actress that Larry had married after Ellen.

Ellen's elation was pure of tone, unsoured, which surprised Georgia, into whose listening ear Ellen had regularly poured her nighttime poison. Ellen should have been cackling with vengeful joy. So Georgia's suspicions were aroused, for good reason.

Next Ellen announced, "Georgia? He's coming back."

"*Larry's* coming back?"

Gary seemed to have heard her in his sleep because he suddenly convulsed, flipping onto his back.

"I know, I know," Ellen moaned. "I retract everything I said."

Ellen didn't call again for several days. When this stretched into a week Georgia broke down and picked up the phone herself. She assumed Ellen was too embarrassed to call, but it turned out that she was busy. The four of them, Ellen and Larry and the girls, had escaped to Salt Spring Island for the weekend. Now Larry was working on the house.

"What do you mean, working?" Georgia asked.

"It's falling apart. The deck railings? *Completely* rotten. And Georgia? This is the really wonderful thing. He's writing a play. He's finally quit TV. Come over, all of you. Will you?"

Gary wouldn't, not when for the last eight years he'd been listening in on Ellen's grievances. Gary was unimpressed by the prodigal husband's return. But as much as Georgia herself was appalled, she didn't want to hurt Ellen's feelings.

Also, she was curious.

Only when Ellen answered the door a few days later did Georgia get it. Ellen looked so different! She'd long ago morphed from a hippy to a professional woman who could dress her excess weight into an asset, complaining all the while that she hated to shop. Georgia had always been in awe of Ellen for pulling this off. Nothing flummoxed Georgia more than fashion.

The difference now was Ellen's bright face, the relaxed sweep of her movements, which had always been so rigid, as though she were in the death-clench of a barely suppressed rage. In one glance Georgia understood that Larry's presence was transformational. *Physically.* Strange that she, Georgia, a former dancer, a dance teacher, had never experienced this. Because in her house it didn't happen. She adored Gary, but he was bulky and overwhelming and only grew more so; her instinctive reaction was always to shrink away from him. Early in their marriage, he used to pick her up and carry her under his arm, a tradition continued by Jacob, who, when he was home from university, would tote his shrieking mother around the house while his little brother paraded behind them banging a pot.

"Oh, Ellen," Georgia said, reaching for her friend. "You look so happy."

And Ellen, that much taller, wept with relief all over the top of Georgia's curly head.

They dried their eyes and went to the kitchen where, beaming, Ellen made coffee. Overhead an intermittent grating sounded, which Georgia would have asked about except she couldn't get a word in.

"Mimi and Yo?" Ellen babbled. "They're *thrilled*. Thrilled to have their father back."

Ellen, wandering out the French doors with their coffee, pointed with a mug. The railings around the deck had been removed. "See? Next up, the hot tub. It's *never* worked. Larry!"

She set down the mugs on the patio table and, walking closer to the open edge of the deck, leaned back to see onto the roof. "He can't hear me."

Georgia went and stood beside Ellen.

Larry. She had pictured him bigger, hairier. Horned. Instead she saw a wiry man, almost a small man, with dark, attractively disarrayed hair and a Discman on his belt. He straddled the roof and, though the headphones detracted somewhat from his cowboy mien, her overwhelming impression against the towering cedars in the yard and the big sky hanging over the mountain was masculinity and sweat. He was running some kind of tool back and forth.

"What's he doing?"

"Demossing! The roof was practically thatched. Never mind. He'll come down."

"What if he falls?" Georgia asked.

Remembering how close she was herself to the edge of the deck, she glanced behind her. It was only about three feet down to the grass. The stairs were to the right, the safe route to the yard, which sloped downward to a rock garden. Then the unfurling view.

Years later, that view would enable Ellen to follow her postponed dreams all the way to that little live-work studio in Kitsilano. An eight-hundred-thousand-dollar view with everything in it: downtown, Stanley Park, the ocean.

They went back to the patio table. Ellen talked, but Georgia, distracted by Larry's scraping and his unsafe position, barely listened. After a few minutes hedgehog-sized tufts of lurid green began tumbling onto the deck right beside where Ellen and Georgia were sitting.

"Larry!"

Ellen leapt up and marched over to the edge again, waving her arms, the old, quick-to-annoy Ellen whose brusqueness Georgia had many times had to make excuses for. *That* Ellen, Georgia's dear friend, was still alive inside this gushing, maritorious wife, thank God.

255

The cascade had already stopped. Ellen beckoned to Georgia, who got to her feet.

Still riding the roof, but more uprightly, Larry was jotting something on a pad. He slipped the pencil into the coil, tucked the pad into his shirt pocket.

"His play," Ellen said. "That's his process. A million little notes to himself and one day he sits down and bangs the thing out in a week. Bangs it out. And Georgia? It's going to be *brilliant*."

"So what's he like?" Gary asked that night in bed.

"Good with his hands," Georgia said.

"I'll bet."

She giggled. Gary was, practically speaking, useless. He lumbered through the house breaking things. The knob to the back door detached regularly. Gary would leave it on the stove. Contracts he was good at. Negotiations. Making the bosses bend.

"We have to go, you know. Ellen's my best friend."

After several weeks of their own negotiations, they reached a compromise. Georgia would make blintzes and Gary would be allowed to eat as many as he wanted with no furrowed brows on her part. This would happen at Ellen's house.

The agreed-upon evening arrived and they trooped into the kitchen—Gary, Georgia, and Jacob, who, born three days after Yo, was practically a brother to both girls. He scampered off to find them, as though to flee the adult tension.

While Gary bear-hugged Ellen, Georgia approached Larry with the blintzes and an open smile. On the ground he was taller, taller than Gary anyway, and about half as wide. He seemed almost shy the way his hands were shoved deep in his front pockets, his eyes downcast as he nodded hello, how, instead of accepting the platter, he stepped aside for her to set it on the counter. And in this act of stepping Larry Silver performed a perfect glissade—first position, *demi-plié*, glide—in his socks on the kitchen floor.

Georgia almost cried out to Gary, "Did you see that?"

She'd given up trying to explain a movement or a gesture, the same way she'd given up dragging Gary around to dance performances for him to fall asleep in. "But what does it mean?" he used to ask, and be baffled when she couldn't translate, when she pounded her fist to her heart instead.

Larry Silver's glissade was a handful of ice crystals dropped down her back. She set the platter on the counter, leaning into it until the feeling passed.

By then Ellen had introduced the two men. They'd shaken hands, Gary frigidly, though Larry probably couldn't tell. Gary's reluctance to meet Larry wasn't only out of loyalty to Ellen; he didn't approve of Larry's line of work. But with his round, bearded cheeks, wire-framed glasses, and moist rosebud mouth, Gary looked disarmingly like a youthful Santa, which was part of his success as a negotiator. He seemed to twinkle at you even when he loathed you. The only indication of his true feelings came when Larry and Gary unclasped hands; Gary wiped his on his pants.

"Beer," Ellen commanded, and Larry grabbed two bottles from the fridge.

"Give him a glass," Ellen said.

"He doesn't want one," Larry said.

"How do you know?"

"Ellen, Ellen," Gary said, patting her shoulder.

"So you work for a union?" Larry said.

"Proudly."

"Know anything about the Winnipeg General Strike?"

Twinkle, twinkle went Gary. "A thing or two."

"I'm writing a play about it. I've never tried anything historical before. Maybe I can pick your brain."

"You should put on the steaks," Ellen said. "The kids are starving."

Larry opened the fridge again and tucked his beer under one arm so he could carry the two plates of meat. Gary relieved him of the bottle, leading the way to the barbecue. Georgia could have pointed that out, too, that the way Gary pulled on the neck of the bottle, so gently, communicated something. Already, he was softening his stance.

"You didn't introduce me," she told Ellen after the men left.

"You met. A few weeks ago, remember?" Ellen said.

"We didn't," Georgia said. "He was on the roof."

After helping Ellen with the salad, Georgia went downstairs to the rec room to check on the kids, who were heaped like kittens in front of the TV. Georgia and Gary didn't own a television, which made it especially hypnotic for Jacob. So deep was his trance he didn't notice Georgia's foot on his bum, jostling him.

Back upstairs, Ellen poured Georgia's wine. They moved to the deck, where Larry and Gary hovered by the barbecue several feet away, their backs to the women. Far beyond and below them, the summer city glinted. The islands organized themselves in gradations of grey and green.

"How's it going?" Georgia whispered with a glance at Larry.

Ellen smiled hugely.

"Everything fixed up?"

"Us, or the house?"

"Both," Georgia said.

"We are. He's lost some steam on the house."

They could talk like this, Larry within earshot, because his conversation with Gary had already reached that oxygen-sucking stage other men quickly get to when they talk about hockey, each voluble point adamantly agreed upon so that if you didn't understand the language you'd think they were arguing. The way some of Gary's older relatives slipped into Russian and their venomous exchanges prompted Georgia to ask Gary, "What are they talking about?" Hitler, usually, or digestive troubles.

It turned out that Larry Silver knew quite a lot about the Winnipeg General Strike. He mentioned something called "the Fowler Amendment" and Gary roared out, "The Fowler Amendment!" Larry went back inside, passing Ellen and Georgia at the patio table. He smiled at Ellen but ignored Georgia. He had yet to make eye contact with her. During the brief time he was in the house, the two men continued yelling to each other.

"The Fowler Amendment was why my great-uncle left the *Winnipeg Free Press!*" Larry stepped onto the deck with two more beers. His eyes glided unseeingly over Georgia.

Not shy. Rude!

Georgia turned to Ellen for some explanation, but Ellen hadn't noticed. She sipped her wine and gazed at Larry with an expression not unlike Jacob's. Jacob couldn't believe he was actually watching *Rugrats.* Ellen couldn't believe Larry was back.

By then the vegetables were grilled. Larry started on the steaks, lifting the first one, stabbing it with the two-tined barbecue fork, dropping it hissingly on the grill. He gave Ellen the five-minute warning. She snapped to, rose, called the kids.

During her bitter years, Ellen had failed to mention certain things about Larry, like how funny he was, how charming. Except to Georgia. Mimi and Yo burst upstairs and ran to him, shrieking, "Daddy sandwich!" themselves the two pieces of bread hugging the meat that was Larry. They all took their chairs, Georgia directly across from Larry, Gary at the far end of the table.

Larry asked Gary if he'd go to a play called *The Fowler Amendment.*

"You bet I would," said Gary, who hadn't been to the theatre in at least a decade. "

What's that?" Mimi asked.

"Something bad," Gary explained. "It took away the workers' right to strike."

"It's maybe the title of the play Daddy's writing now," Ellen said.

Yolanda asked, "The DBP?"

"That's how we refer to it," Ellen told Georgia. "Daddy's Brilliant Play."

Georgia was actually angry now that she was sitting across

259

from Larry, angry and quite miserable. She bowed her curls over her plate and poked her food, but no one noticed; she wasn't a big eater anyway. Before dessert, she excused herself and went to the bathroom, where she peed in wrathful bursts. As she washed her hands, she studied her furiously furrowed brow in the mirror. Only her head floated there, seeming buoyed up by her hair. Was that what made her so ignorable? Her size?

Then, as she reached for the towel, as her own insignificant profile flashed in her peripheral vision, she remembered something. The first time she saw Peggy Baker on stage she, Georgia, had to watch from the corner of her eye, otherwise she would be overcome. The way Peggy Baker moved, even how her hands fluttered, was too beautiful for a direct regard.

Georgia returned to the table, where Ellen was passing around the blintzes, Larry asking as he filled his plate, "What's the worst thing you'd do for a blintz?" The kids were shouting out their answers. Jacob would eat a worm. Mimi would dye her hair green.

"You'd dye your hair green anyway," Ellen told her.

Georgia stared at Larry.

Larry said to Gary, "I believe the Fowler Amendment also took away the right to eat blintzes," and Gary threw back his head and laughed, showing the blintzes and strawberries chewed to a uniform pink.

The way Larry kept turning his head to talk to Gary presented Georgia in a side-view.

"THIS was so great. This was so fun," Ellen told them at the door as they were leaving, the wine making her effuse. "This was The Larry and Gary Show!"

She hugged them all, Georgia, Gary, and Jacob, and then Larry did. Just before Larry took Georgia in his arms, he looked. It was like two tines penetrating her.

NOWADAYS they had TV. Gary had relinquished that principle long ago. (In fact, they possessed most every digital gadget available, all of which Maximilian, seven now, had taught them to use.) And not just any TV: a fifty-inch HD flat-screen mounted on the wall where previously there had been a framed movie poster for *The Red Menace*, a gift to Gary from Larry Silver before he absconded the second time.

The Bentall Centre Memorial made the news that night. Gary called to Georgia, who was loading the dishwasher after dinner, "Honey, it's on next! Come see!"

She did, hovering in the doorway, watching the actors in the muted commercials stretch their faces and mouth their lines. Maximilian texted Jacob in Montreal. Gary worked the remote, turning on the sound as soon as he saw the grainy footage.

"Twenty-nine years ago. January 7, 1981," the announcer said.

Tower Four, its last few floors not yet dressed in glass, appeared leached and dreamy, like in an old Polaroid. The camera travelled down to the site below, to the jumble of fencing and containers, the crew milling in shock. Hats hard, shirts plaid, faces blank.

Then a closeup of a boot jutting from a sheet. The camera panned out, revealing the whole draped body before retracing the plunge, reversing it, travelling up, up thirty-six floors to the top of the building again and pausing there for a pregnant second.

"Georgia!" Gary called. He turned and, seeing her in the doorway, patted the place between him and Maximilian.

Georgia shook her ringlets.

No blood on the ground, or did they just not show it? She'd imagined a bloody mess.

Maximilian shouted out, "There you are, Daddy!"

Georgia, who was pressing her forehead against the door frame, looked up just as Gary flashed by. TV, she remembered, adds ten pounds.

The footage from today was crisp and bright, the way more recent memories are clearer. Four symbolic coffins painted black, each bearing a white rose and a white hard hat printed with a name. *Donald. Gunther. Yrjo. Brian.*

"Mommy's crying," Maximilian told Gary.

"It makes her very sad the way those men died," Gary told him. "Do you remember what they're called?"

"The Bentall Four."

"Good. And why did they die?"

"Because of unsafe work conditions."

"Good boy."

They had agreed not to tell him anything about Auntie Ellen until they had to.

AFTER that first dinner, Gary admitted that Larry seemed okay. Later, when The Larry and Gary Show had been happening regularly and Georgia had fallen for Larry, he said, "Anyway, we don't really know what went on between them. Ellen can't be the easiest person in the world to live with. She's not like you."

"Don't say mean things about Ellen," Georgia told him.

Every Saturday the two families got together, always at Ellen and Larry's. Georgia brought along Jacob's toothbrush and pyjamas in case the evening stretched into night, which it usually did. They would carry their sleeping boy out to the car, limp from the rigours of playing with two girls, sated with TV, and lay him on the back seat with the lap belt secured around him. Usually Georgia drove because she drank less. Not that Gary would be drunk. Ellen might be, but not Gary or Georgia, who never forgot that the night would end with a drive home on a mountain highway.

Georgia chauffeured her significant others, the two people she loved most. But did she still love Gary? She glanced in the rear-view mirror, saw him in the strobe of the passing highway lights, watching over Jacob, whose head lay across his thigh. Yes, she did. Of course she did.

But she also loved Larry Silver. She loved how he would play with the silverware as he talked, or nab Mimi running past and very tenderly pick a leaf out of her hair. With Georgia, Larry barely interacted and his every non-look, everything he didn't say, thrilled her. By their second or third get-together she began to experience their avoidance as a sort of reverse *pas de deux* that the others, Gary, Ellen, and the children, were completely blind to. Georgia sat down, Larry stood up. Georgia came into a room, Larry immediately left. And as they passed each other sparks flared in Georgia's peripheral vision. Larry's too, she could tell. If they happened to accidently touch feet under the table, or hands when a glass of wine was offered, they both leapt back. Two nice Bordeaux glasses had been shattered this way on two different occasions.

Gary noticed. He said, "You look beautiful, honey." Of course, that intensified her guilt on two counts, Gary and Ellen. Not that she intended to act on her feelings. She never would. But she loved toeing that line, reaching with one pointed foot toward it and applying the slightest pressure.

263

"You've never said anything about Larry," Ellen mentioned one night.

How wonderful to be able to speak out loud about him, how terrible that it should be to Ellen. "Gary likes him."

"I didn't ask what Gary thinks."

"He's funny. He's wonderful with the girls. Also, a man who's handy? That's pretty sexy."

"Oh, he's sexy all right. But he leaves everything half finished. I finally had to call someone about the hot tub. Just in case you think he fixed it. And *I* paid."

264   "ARE you coming?" Larry asked.

This was after dinner, after the men had cleaned up and were sauntering through the dining room with towels around their necks.

"Sure," Ellen said.

"This baby has a whole new motor," Larry told Gary. "They put in the Bugatti of hot tub motors."

Gary hadn't brought a bathing suit, but that didn't faze him. He marched out and dropped his clothes on the deck. So did Larry, either to keep Gary company or because he always went in nude.

Ellen said to Georgia, "Come on. It's dark." She said, "If anyone should be shy, it's me," and grabbed a handful of flesh that happened to be hanging around her middle. "If it's Larry you're worried about, don't be. He doesn't care. Or we can go in in our underwear if you want."

Ellen left, then returned in bra and panties, pinning up her auburn hair. Despite their years of mutual confiding, there were things Georgia didn't know about Ellen. She didn't know about her underwear, for example, which seemed of such tissuey construction that it might have been stitched by elves. Georgia normally felt sorry for full-figured women and the double burden they were cursed to carry, but Ellen's breasts, supported by this fairy-tale garment, could cast spells. Even her pearlike bottom-half barely dressed in ivory lace could. As Gary liked to say: hubba-hubba.

Georgia said, "Go ahead. I'll be right out."

She checked on their sleeping children. In the bathroom she stripped to her high-rise cotton panties and dingy sports bra. When she saw herself standing there like Cinderella of the Victoria's Secret catalogue, she quickly peeled them off and tucked them inside her clothes.

No towels. They must have brought them to the hot tub. Ellen kept the clean ones in the spare room closet, but that was where the kids were. Georgia didn't want to walk in there naked in case one of them woke up.

She padded on cat's feet to the kitchen, dimly lit by the bulb above the stove. The air stroked her. Outside, Ellen was crying out, "It's too hot, Larry! It's soup!" He said something Georgia couldn't hear, something about his mother's borscht, and Ellen laughed with snorts.

Soundlessly, Georgia stepped onto the deck, into the cooler air. Her nipples hardened and she crossed her arms. Did she want to see Larry Silver naked? She wasn't sure. All she knew was that she would rather he didn't see her, but if he looked now while she was close to the kitchen window, he would. This prompted her to take a few rushing steps into the moonless obscurity before her eyes had fully adjusted. She could just make out Ellen and Gary sitting with their backs to her. Larry was facing Ellen. He was also facing Georgia, but she couldn't tell if he saw her, he was just a shadow.

The only visible thing was Ellen's squashed white ass perched on the edge of the tub.

Georgia squinted and took another step, the wood of the deck rough under the soles of her feet, then not.

August 25, 1991. Georgia fell.

She landed flat on her back without making a sound, or not a loud enough sound for the others to hear over their conversation rising to a drunkenly boisterous volume. They had got onto sports cars, which Gary disdained but Larry loved. Probably Georgia had grunted when she hit the ground. Nothing hurt—the deck was only three feet up. Nevertheless, she lay there mortified and praying that none of them had noticed. They hadn't, or they would have rushed over to see that she was all right. She was fine. She would just lie here for a minute until she thought of some way to save herself.

"Say my play's a hit. Say I make millions and to repay you for your help, I give you a Bugatti. You wouldn't drive it?"

"Nope."

"Where's Georgia?" Ellen asked.

"Modesty delays her," Gary said. "I would sell it and give away the money."

"My God," Larry said.

"Modesty?" Ellen asked. "She has the body of an eighteen-year-old. Georgia!"

Georgia, lying three feet below them and eight feet to the right, heard sloshing. Larry asked, "Another one?"

"I'm okay," Gary said.

"See what's happened to her," Ellen said.

"Would you sit in it?" Larry asked.

"Nope."

She was cold. The grass prickled her back and buttocks. The smell of it and of the dirt under the deck intensified the longer she lay. She calculated her distance from the deck stairs. She could crawl over to them, drag herself up onto the deck and over to the hot tub, then pop up just beside it. They would never suspect. Or she could go in the French doors that led to the basement rec room and pretend she was only coming out now. Except that those doors were probably locked.

She heard a click, like a door unlocking.

"Really, though," Ellen said. "She never put on a pound when she had Jacob."

"I put on a lot of weight when she had Jacob," Gary said.

"You were doing your part! Unlike someone else."

Georgia sensed his approach—a very slight trembling of the earth. And then she saw him, a shadow crouching low, almost running, hurrying to her. He landed on his knees and bent over her, dripping. He found her mouth and kissed it. She didn't resist—the opposite. She breathed in and welcomed first the pressure of his mouth and then his whole weight, so much less than what she was accustomed to. She considered the strength and mass of his shoulders and arms, felt herself pressed down into the earth as he swung his leg across her.

From that position, curled above her, he stirred. With his long, thin cock, Larry Silver stirred up her life.

INSENSITIVE maybe, for Georgia to link these two events in her mind—the Bentall Centre tragedy and that night at Ellen's. But there were tragic consequences that night too.

First, The Larry and Gary Show was cancelled. Ellen called the next week to say that the DBP was not going so well and Larry was in a funk. "You don't want to see him like this. I'll let you know when he gets to the end of Act One."

School had started by then and all of them were busy anyway.

Six months later Larry left and everything returned to the way it had been before, with Ellen calling late, slightly drunk. What she told Georgia was that Amy had originally kicked out Larry because he'd been seeing another woman; now that other woman had sounded her siren again.

"You're sure about that?" Georgia asked.

"Yes," Ellen said, and maybe it was true. When she cried on the phone now, her tears were for Mimi and Yo, devastated by their father's departure.

"I could tell you didn't trust him," Ellen said. "I wish I'd taken the hint."

Thump, thump, thump went Georgia's little fist against her chest. Also, Ellen had discovered she was pregnant, but the fetus shrivelled inside her and died. Georgia accompanied Ellen when she had her D&C.

A bloody mess.

And now this, the most tragic thing in Georgia's opinion, the thing she thought about every time she visited, the reason she couldn't look at Larry—that Ellen had ended up living so much of what turned out to be her too-short life without Larry Silver, who anyone could see, anyone who had eyes in his head, was the love of her life. Georgia bore some responsibility for this.

The two events had twisted tightly together. Georgia wanted to unply the strands and release herself before it was too late, but in a way it already was. Ellen was dying. Georgia should have told her years ago.

• • •

THE next time Georgia visited Ellen, bearing a pot of borscht, it was standing room only even without Larry. In the kitchen, someone was using the blender. Ellen's sister, Moira, a stouter and gruffer version of Ellen, had arrived from Calgary. Gerhard from next door stood around taking up space.

"You are enjoying this too much," he told Ellen. "If we all went away you would get bored and go back to work. Your art is calling you. Can't you hear it?"

Ellen laughed. She seemed ebullient, like she was holding court, alarmingly, after how subdued she'd been two days before. It reminded Georgia of the day before she'd gone into labour with each of Jacob and Maximilian, her sudden burst of energy that had sent her down to her basement studio, where she'd tried to work out a series of steps. She hoped this didn't mean Ellen was about to die. She hoped it was the morphine.

"Georgia!" Ellen called out. "Moira! This is Georgia!"

Moira, sitting at the table with a pair of reading glasses clinging to her nose as she scrutinized the labels of Ellen's pills, smiled a tight no-nonsense smile. A nurse, Georgia remembered.

"I was telling you about Georgia last night," Ellen told Moira.

Georgia had some idea what Ellen had said. That Georgia choreographed dances for preschoolers; that she could, the night before a recital, single-handedly whip up enough tissue-paper flowers to decorate an entire gym; that her closet housed every possible colour of Crocs; that she had worn her hair the same way since Ellen met her despite the counsel of many, many black women who would sidle up to her with the name of the best salon for straightening; that she was "sweet," "elfin," a "pixie," all things that outwardly were true but that belied the bitter seed in her centre.

Mimi was there too, back after several years in Toronto failing

269

to establish herself. Two years older than Jacob, but far behind him in so many ways, she'd been a troubled girl much of her life, though had now sorted herself out enough to be of help. She brought from the kitchen some kind of chlorophyll drink that Ellen tried to wave off.

"Drink it. Mom. Drink it."

Seeing Georgia with a pot in her hands, Mimi floated over. She'd inherited her grace from her father—Georgia could picture her as a long-ago butterfly. She'd taught dance to both Ellen's daughters, but only Mimi had talent.

"I'll come back another time," Georgia said, offering the pot to Mimi.

"No, stay," Ellen said. "Mimi and Moira are going out in a second. Gerhard's leaving too."

He showed some surprise, rubbing his ringed hand all over his shaved head.

"Come back later," Ellen told him. "I need to talk to Georgia."

To-and-froing. Kisses, partings. Then Ellen and Georgia were finally alone. Ellen pointed to the green drink.

"Please pour it down the sink. She won't let up until it's gone."

When Georgia returned, Ellen said, "She's found God. Or something like that."

"Mimi?"

"Ten years ago, if you'd asked me? I would have predicted she'd find Satan. Anyway, she's more pleasant to be around, except for her concoctions. Sit here. Sit beside me." Ellen patted the place. "How is Gary? Is he ever going to visit me?"

"He'd love to. You know that."

With a nod Ellen acknowledged the principles that precluded Gary from ever being in the same room as Larry Silver. The man was loyal; no one could deny it. Ellen reached for the box of tissues on the coffee table, plucked one free and handed it to Georgia even before she started crying.

"You always look so sad. Tell me what's bothering you. Besides me."

Georgia looked at the ceiling, but this only made the tears stream faster. She staunched the flow with more tissues that Ellen passed her. "Gary," she admitted. "I just don't want to be around him. It's terrible. But I can't help it."

"Did he do something?" Ellen asked.

"Him? No," Georgia said. "He didn't do anything. Yet I'm so angry with him all the time."

"He's so fat now," Ellen said. "Are you mad about that?"

Georgia didn't think so. It didn't make sense even to her. If she was going to blame the victim, she should blame Ellen too. But she didn't. Why not? Back then, after Larry left, she'd put Gary through several hellish years that really only ended with Maximilian's birth. But now Larry was back, reminding her of everything that had happened.

Reminding her right now.

When the door opened, Georgia sprang to her feet automatically, like in the days of The Larry and Gary Show. "I brought soup," she told Ellen. "Borscht. Mimi put it in the fridge."

"Borscht!" Larry said, stepping inside.

"Don't run off," Ellen said.

But that was exactly what Georgia did. She pushed past Larry, pulled on her boots and bolted. Out the door and down the drizzling street, sobbing now.

After a few blocks, she leaned against a tree, searched her pockets for one of Ellen's tissues, resorted to her sleeve. Stupidly, she'd

271

run in the opposite direction of where she'd parked the car. Also, she'd left her umbrella and coat. Never mind. She'd go home and phone Ellen later to apologize. She'd pick up her things next time.

She'd just started back in the direction of the car when she saw Larry walking toward her. She recognized his springy gait, so odd in a moody man, and stopped. As though turning and running again weren't an option.

He crossed the street, not hurrying, simply coming to meet her with a perplexed expression on his face. As he got closer, she noticed the dutiful set of his jaw. Ellen had sent him. People used to say that Ellen had wasted her life in the service of Larry Silver, but now Larry was serving her and no one said it was a waste.

He took her in his arms like he'd done that night, August 25, 1991, after they'd made love on the grass a stone's throw from their trusting mates. That night they'd run inside, stooped and hand in hand. In Ellen's basement rec room, Larry had enfolded Georgia against his bare chest. The flesh of her cheek pressed its wetness and felt the rebel thing inside him kick. He kissed her again, then signalled that he would go ahead. In a daze, she'd watched him go, naked, taking the stairs two at a time. She'd waited, then gone as well, up the stairs and through the kitchen and outside to the deck. When she slid into the scalding tub, the others applauded. It seemed hot enough to sterilize her, but wasn't.

Now Georgia looked Larry in the eye. "I need to get it off my chest before it's too late. Is that selfish?"

"What?" Larry asked.

"You didn't leave because of me, did you?"

"When? The other day? I can't meditate. My back's shot. Also, you know." He made claws at his forehead and shook them, signifying, Georgia guessed, mental unrest.

She placed both hands flat against his chest, pushed.

Larry staggered back, surprised, then offended. She could tell he wanted to storm away. But he'd been given his orders and now he scratched his head where the curls were thickest, wondering what to try next. Something that had probably worked a thousand times before: an arm around her shoulder, a reassuring squeeze. He guided her into taking a step. In her confusion, Georgia responded. Could it be he didn't remember? Or was he pretending?

"The Larry and Gary Show?" she tried.

"How is Gary?" asked Larry, steering her on toward Ellen's.

"He was helping you with your play. *The Something Something.* About the Winnipeg General Strike."

"Please," Larry said, sounding genuinely pained.

They walked the remaining block in silence. The only way a man could screw his wife's best friend right under her nose, *literally*, was if, afterward, he just put it out of his mind. The solution was almost more audacious than the crime. Larry had probably behaved like this his whole life—but here was where he stopped. At Ellen's door.

He gestured Georgia inside. "Ta-da," he said to Ellen, before leaving again himself.

"Better?" Ellen asked from the couch.

Georgia nodded, though she wasn't sure.

"Did he say something?"

"Larry? No. Not really."

"Maybe that's better?"

Georgia came over and looked down at Ellen. *What do you mean?* Georgia wanted to ask, but when she opened her mouth, "Borscht?" came out.

"That would be wonderful." Ellen sighed.

273

Georgia went to heat it up. Every time she peeked out of the kitchen, she saw Ellen lying in the same position on the couch, half asleep. Once their eyes did meet (those blue, blue eyes!) and it seemed like Ellen was about to laugh, but she simply fluttered her hands and amended her expression.

11

ABSENT

...

Mom brought the Tech Deck mini skateboards from Vancouver when she went to visit Nonny Ellen. She got them at Toys "R" Us. There were two Shark decks in the pack too, and an ATM Click deck with a skull that's Eli's second favourite. But now Tru has the black Zero Cole Tech Deck with the cobra logo and it's Eli's. It is!

At recess Eli follows Tru around the side of the school to the skate park, the one they made themselves. Some of it's Playmobil, some cardboard. The rails are chopsticks. "It's mine," Eli says, but suddenly Tru's way ahead. He's practically at the park. Then he is, squatting in the dirt playing with the Zero Cole Tech Deck with the cobra logo that he took from Eli, saying, "Awesome! Backside three-sixty kick flip!" though no way can he do these things. He can hardly ollie, even with his fingers. Also, he says his T-shirt's camo when it's tie-dye.

"That's my deck," Eli says.

"You're an alien," Tru says without looking up.

Everybody calls him that. Eli's dad said, "Cool. Alien Workshop, right?" which is a skate brand. Eli felt good about it then, but now

he doesn't because Tru means something else, plus he has Eli's black
Zero Cole Tech Deck with the cobra logo.

Use your words, Eli, Lindy, the teacher, always says. Well, Eli just
tried and his words failed. He stalks over to where Tru squats with
the mini skateboard, spinning it in the air about two hundred times
and making jet noises so that spit comes out.

And Eli kicks him. Kicks hard.

But his foot doesn't connect. He kicks the air and almost lands
on his own butt. How messed up is that?

WHEN Mom picks him up with Fern, Lindy says, "Yolanda? Can we
have a little talk?" So they all go into the classroom. Fern screams to
be put down, then runs around looking for things to mess up. Mom
has to follow her, taking stuff out of her hand.

Lindy says, "The first place to start is a hearing test."

While they're talking, Eli sneaks over to Tru's table. Fern
breaks free and makes it to the art centre, spills the paintbrushes
on the floor.

Then Mom's saying, "Honey, you've got to listen to Lindy, right?"

Eli's hand is in the book slot where Tru sits, feeling for the
Tech Deck. Tru didn't put it back in his case. Eli stopped him after
school and checked.

"His dad's dreamy too," Mom says.

Books are in the book slot, and something old-sandwichy. A
pencil case. Balls of worksheets. Eli crouches and looks.

"Eli? *Eli!*" She's pulling on the neck of his shirt so it chokes him.
"I said we're going now."

As he follows Mom out, Lindy says, "See you tomorrow," and
smiles like she's not mad at him, though she is, she's mad all the
time. She's had just about enough of him two hundred times a day.

Eli runs ahead and climbs in the truck. Then Mom's buckling Fern in her seat and Fern's saying, "Me want! Me want!" and grabbing at him.

"Stop it, you two," Mom says.

Fern bites Eli on the shoulder and he smacks her one.

Mom leans on the horn. *HONNNKKK!* "I can only take so much more! Do you hear? Then I don't know what I'm going to do!"

She hardly ever yells and never has she honked. Both Eli and Fern stop fighting and stare. Mom starts bawling and so does Fern.

"Me want!" she cries like the two-year-old that she is.

"What does she want?" Mom asks, all watery, like she's drowning. "Eli, please. Just give it to her."

And he looks in his hand and sees it, the black Zero Cole Tech Deck with the cobra logo. He has no idea how it got there.

277

"WHEN I call you, buddy, you come, right? Supper's ready. How did you get wet?"

He's playing down by the water, turning over the stones. Living under each stone are mini camo crabs. Crabs have outside skeletons, like armour. They're soldiers and each is a different camo colour. If you take a mini camo crab from under one rock and drop it in a tide pool with a bunch of mini camo crabs from under different rocks, they battle. Eli's not allowed guns. "What's the worst thing in the world," he asked his dad. "War," Dad said, but Mom said, "Cancer."

Now his dad's here telling Eli he called and called, but Eli heard nothing over the sound of the mini camo crabs in the tide pool blowing each other up with the bomb-stones Eli threw in.

"You're all wet and there's mud on your face. Eli, buddy. We're about to eat."

First he was kneeling beside the tide pool, then he was lying beside it with his face on the barnaclely rocks.

"Your cheek's bleeding," Dad says.

Eli wipes the side of his face with his palm, proud to see red smears. He didn't even cry, just like a real skateboarding soldier wouldn't.

He walks with Dad up the path to the cabin, his rubber boot making sucky sounds because it's full of water and trying to pull off his sock. They stop outside at the hose for Eli to wash.

"Mom's not feeling so great today. Let's try not to upset her even more."

"Is she sick?"

"No, she's sad about Nonny Ellen."

Last time Eli saw Nonny was at Christmas. Her hair was different, wispy like Fern's when she finally stopped being bald. She didn't smell like Nonny anymore.

"Come on, buddy. Don't just stand there."

"I'm sad about Nonny too," Eli says.

At supper he announces he's not going to school anymore. "Everybody calls me alien."

"Cool," Dad says.

"What do they mean, alien?" Mom asks. "Does Lindy know?"

Fern keeps spitting out her tofu and squawking like a crow.

"And today? Tru stole my black Zero Cole Tech Deck with the cobra logo."

Eli's in the middle of telling them how they played together before school, sharing their Tech Decks, but then Tru took the black Zero Cole. Tru said if Eli was Nyjah Huston then he couldn't ride a Chris Cole deck, that was the rule. Tru has a real Tech Deck case with a see-through lid and Eli saw through it. Eli keeps his decks in an old *Toy Story* lunch box he got at the Free Store. They rattle and tangle. Tru's don't, they snap in.

Dad's shaking his arm. "Buddy! Buddy!"

"What's happening, Eli? What's wrong with you? What's wrong?"

They're on either side of him, grabbing him, and Mom's crying again, but probably about Nonny, he knows now.

AND the next day he doesn't have to go to school! Easy-peasy! He makes a skate park on the examination table with some Dixie cups and the thing that's for looking in ears. The tongue thing is the rail. The paper crackles when he ollies and grinds.

"Mid-sentence he stops and sort of stiffens, staring into space. He was holding his fork so tightly I couldn't pull it out of his hand."

"How long did this go on for?"

"Forever! We yelled at him, but he wouldn't snap out of it. Finally, he did."

"And then?"

"Nothing. He just seemed confused."

Only when the doctor says, "Eli, do you remember Mommy and Daddy shouting yesterday?" does he realize that Mom's talking about him.

"Yes."

"Do you know why they were shouting at you? Do you remember?"

"Yes."

"Why?"

"Because I'm an alien."

279

But that's not what Eli thinks about himself. He thinks he's a soldier who really can backside three-sixty kick flip.

THEY take the ferry to Vancouver Island, where a machine is going to draw pictures of what's happening in Eli's brain. There are waves in your brain like the waves the ferry rides on. He counts twenty-six seals on the trip. Their heads pop up, black and shiny, then duck under again. Under the waves. Seizures are when it gets so wavy inside your brain it messes you up.

Fern makes stinky-butt on the trip. Dad decides to wait till they dock to change her because the bathroom's too small on the boat. Everybody jokes about it. They say Fern's cute but she stinks, and she laughs because she doesn't get it the way Eli gets that *alien* is mean. It stinks so bad by the time they dock Eli wants to throw up.

"Honey, are you okay? Honey?" Mom asks.

They find the car. It's Mom's friend Amber's car that she leaves parked at the ferry. Amber used to live with Grandpa. But now Grandpa lives with Nonny. Dad changes Fern on the hood and poop gets on it.

They drive Amber's poopy car to the hospital. "Are you scared?" Dad asks.

He didn't know there was a reason to be, but now he does. "Will it hurt?"

"Eli? Are you scared, buddy?"

Didn't he already say?

"WHAT grade are you in, Eli?"

"Two."

"Lie down. Nice. Do you see these wires? And this is glue. I'm going to stick these wires all over your head. Isn't that funny? Yoohoo, Eli?"

"What?"

"Isn't that funny? Are you ready?"

Mom stays with him while Dad takes Fern for a walk around the hospital. Mom promised that after they finish they can go to a restaurant and Eli can have meat like a real skateboarding soldier. While Eli lies there deciding what kind of meat, the nurse fixes the wires to his head. The machine takes forever and the whole time Mom watches and cries. She's vegetarian. It must be drawing a hamburger, Eli thinks.

When they pull the wires off, his hair is full of goop.

Dad and Fern go into a room with Mom, but Eli has to wait outside. They let him buy a drink. The machine's claw hand shows Eli the can, then drops it. *Thunk!*

There aren't any drink machines on Cordova Island.

Mom and Dad and Fern are in the room forever. Eli's almost finished the Coke when they come out. He's burped nine times. Mom's crying harder and Dad's hugging her and carrying Fern.

"I want bacon," Eli says.

Dad high-fives him.

"WHERE do you go?" Nonny asks him when he and Mom get back from Children's Hospital.

She's in her new bed with buttons. No more old-fashioned dentist's chair. Eli loved playing with the levers on the chair, but the bed's better, it's electric.

Eli pushes a button and Nonny on her bed rises up, up toward the ceiling. "We went to the children's hospital. They put me in a machine. Boing, boing, boing! I had to wear earplugs. I have more than one hundred seizures a day."

"When you have the seizures where do you go?" Nonny asks. "I can see on your face that you're not here."

"Really?" Eli says. Then he knows where he must be. "I go to outer space. It's where I'm from."

Nonny laughs and laughs.

"I'm bringing you back to earth now, Nonny." He pushes the button to lower the bed and only then does he get it. They're called absent seizures, the doctor told him. Absent means you're not there. He's absent from school. Yay! When he has a seizure, he's present and absent at the same time.

"It was nice up there," Nonny tells him. "Looking down on you. When I'm not here, that's what I'll be doing."

"You're not going anywhere, Nonny. You can hardly get out of bed."

Nonny pees in a bag now. Eli doesn't know how, but the bag's hanging on a hook at the side of the bed. Lines on the bag measure the pee. Every time Eli checks, there's more yellow. And she has a tube in her arm. Grandpa puts a needle in the tube and squirts in her medicine. That way it doesn't hurt.

They're staying with Nonny while they go to the appointments. Mom is happy to be closer to Nonny, happy that they've found out what's wrong with Eli. He could've had a tumour in his brain, but he doesn't. Tumours kill you so epilepsy's better. They sleep in the little room under Nonny's ceiling that they climb the ladder to. Grandpa has the couch. Auntie Mimi's here too, helping Nonny, but she sleeps next door where the man who made the movie of Nonny lives. Gerhard. He wears earrings.

Appointment, appointment, then Toys "R" Us. Eli picks the exact same pack so he owns two black Zero Cole Tech Decks with the cobra logo that he won't ever let Tru touch.

One hundred seizures means one hundred times a day Eli shoots into outer space. He's an alien. The thing about being an alien? Whenever you're on earth, you can't remember anything about being in outer space.

He tells Mom and Grandpa and Auntie Mimi this at supper in Nonny's studio. Nonny's not at the table. She's lying in the hospital bed watching them.

"There," Mom says. "You just had one. I can tell now. It's so obvious once you know."

"I did?" Eli says. "I just flew to outer space and back?"

283

Everybody laughs. Then Grandpa sees Nonny's awake. He goes over to hold her hand. "Ellen? Do you need anything, babe? Are you in pain?"

"No," Nonny says. "What would I need? We're finally all together."

"Dad's not here," Eli tells Nonny. "Fern's not here."

"Well, they should come," Nonny says. "They should come."

After supper, Mom and Auntie Mimi wash the dishes. Auntie Mimi says, "She's been talking to her mother."

"To her mother?"

"Who's Nonny's mother?" Eli asks.

"Someone who died a long time ago."

"Then how does Nonny talk to her?"

"Shh," Mom says.

But Auntie Mimi says, "She talks to her on the phone."

"What?" Mom says.

"That's what she told me. I asked if her father phoned too.

And she said no. She said he never phoned. She would have to phone him."

Because Nonny's dead mom phoned, Auntie Mimi starts calling all Nonny's friends so that they can say goodbye. And Mom phones Dad and Fern.

ELI isn't ever allowed to be alone, not until they know the medicine works. The medicine's pills you have to be a skateboarding soldier to swallow.

"Remember how I found you playing in the bay?" Dad told him. "You were wet. You cut your cheek on the rocks. You're lucky you didn't fall face first in the water. Because if that happened while you were having a seizure, you would drown."

There are so many things he's not allowed to do now, like ride a bike or skateboard or go down the slide. Not the slide because to go down, first he has to go up. If he has a seizure on the ladder, he could fall and bust his head.

It takes Eli forever to swallow the pill. He gags and gags. When the cats get sick, Dad holds their sharp mouths open and Mom pokes the pill down. "I'll do it myself!" he yells.

Now Eli, Dad, and Fern sleep at a hotel with a drink machine on every floor. Eli's allowed a Coke if he swallows the pill. Fern's allowed to make the ice clatter out of the machine beside it. They ride the elevator up and down ten times to outer space and back, then take the bus to Nonny's. You can pull the cord as many times as you want, but the stop bell will only ring once. Fern doesn't get it and cries.

Because of Fern, Dad doesn't hang around too long at Nonny's. He asks if Eli wants to stay or go with them.

"Can we go to a skate park?"

"We could watch. You can play with your Tech Decks."

Mostly Eli stays because he can be a skateboarding soldier at Nonny's. Mom says no, but Nonny lifts one finger, which means: *let him.* He's even allowed to make machine-gun sounds going up the half-pipe with the new black Zero Cole Tech Deck with the cobra logo. The half-pipe is Nonny's foot under the sheet.

Nonny has a sign on her door with COME IN, WE'RE OPEN on one side and SORRY, WE'RE CLOSED on the other. There's a clock, too, to show when Nonny WILL RETURN. The sign's for Nonny's pots that she sold before she got sick. Dad lifts Fern up when they leave and she twirls the clock hands to a messed-up time.

Now Nonny's pots are gone. Instead there's a TV in the window playing a movie of Nonny. Her hair is to her shoulders, red-brown except for the silver hairs she used to pay Eli ten cents each to pluck out. He plucked and Nonny ouched and Fern laughed. In the movie Nonny's doing ordinary things like making her pots and sometimes holding out her hand to say stop filming, except there's no sound. Her face says stop.

She wants the sign left to OPEN. "If you're not too tired," Mom says.

Everybody who visits writes a message to Nonny on coloured squares. Auntie Mimi puts them in the window with the TV playing the movie of Nonny. At night, she reads them out.

"'I love and admire you.'"

"'God, that time on the ferry? Do you remember how we laughed?'"

"'Ellen, you sat on my guitar. I was angry. I'm not anymore.'"

The next-door neighbour from the other side brings Nonny's dog, Tony. The neighbour is Tilda. "Tilda and Tony have the same hair," Mom whispers to Eli. Tony whines until Tilda lifts him up to lick Nonny's face. Then his tail slashes around and he goes crazy kissing Nonny. The nurse says not to let him, his claws might scratch her, so next time Tilda brings a Tony that she knitted with his fur mixed in. The knitted Tony isn't sad.

"Two days? A week?" the doctor tells Mom.

"A week what?" Eli asks, and Mom shushes him.

In a week the messages on coloured paper will overflow the window. They'll fill up the studio like water in the bathtub and drown everybody visiting Nonny, drown them in goodbye.

Eli can't even take a bath himself.

He can't ever be alone.

286

A woman sits by Nonny's bed. She has a frog face except with teeth. She talks and talks to Nonny until Auntie Mimi says, "I think she needs to sleep. Mom? Are you tired?"

Nonny nods. She wrinkles her nose at Eli while the frog woman kisses her hand.

"May I?" Frog Woman says, and snatches a tissue from the box to dry her bulgy frog eyes.

After she leaves, Nonny laughs. "I did some work for her. She never paid me. We'd see each other at events and she'd snub me."

"Her number was in your book!" Auntie Mimi says.

"She hates me," Nonny says.

Eli asks, "Do you hate her, Nonny?"

"No, no. What would be the point? Come here."

Nonny folds Eli in her sharp arms that seem weak, but are really strong. Nonny is powerful in her electric bed. She doesn't need guns to make her enemies bow down.

Auntie Mimi is mad she phoned the frog woman because that's the last time Nonny really talks. Auntie Mimi says the frog woman stole from Nonny again, stole her energy. But if that's true, it was Eli who stole it. Eli was the last person she hugged.

Because after the frog woman leaves, Nonny sleeps for a long, long time, not waking up until they turn her in the bed. Then all she wants is for them to leave the sign at OPEN. Grandpa tries to feed her ice chips. Her lips pull in.

Mom calls the care team. They bring an oxygen tank, attach the tubes with a strap around Nonny's head. Eli doesn't like the feeling of anything but a finger up his nose. He inspects the tank next to the pee bag. Today Nonny's little bit of pee looks brown.

The nurse says nothing hurts Nonny now.

287

Grandpa lies on his stomach on the floor and asks Eli to walk on his back. Nothing hurts Nonny, but everything hurts Grandpa. His bones say ouch.

That night, when Dad brings Fern, Mom says to say goodbye. Dad lifts Fern up to kiss Nonny.

"Bye-bye, Nonny," Fern chirps, because she doesn't get it.

Eli does; he's a skateboarding soldier and he says he's not going back to the hotel.

Dad starts to cry. He passes Fern to Mom and bows over Nonny with his head on her chest. "Ellen," he says. "Ellen, you saved my life."

"How did Nonny save your life?" Eli asks when Dad finally lets go of Nonny.

"Shh," he says. He takes off his toque, dries his eyes with it, kisses Mom when she hands Fern back. "I'll tell you another time. Be brave, buddy."

While Dad's hugging him, Fern kicks Eli in the head.

One nurse is Nonny's sister, which Eli only finds out now. She sings to Nonny about getting a coat and a hat. She sings *tisket* and *tasket*. *Tomayto, tomahto*. "Do you remember?" she asks Nonny. "Do you remember Mom singing?"

Nonny's breath stops and Auntie Mimi throws a fit. *No, no, no!* Nonny hears and sighs and the air moves back in.

"Don't," Nonny's sister says. "Let her go."

"Who are you to tell me that?" Auntie Mimi yells. "After how you treated her?"

"After how *I* treated her?"

"What are you even *doing* here?"

Mom and Grandpa take Auntie Mimi to the backyard for a timeout. Eli can still hear her crying and Grandpa saying, "Stop it, stop it right now." Next door Tony barks and barks.

Nonny's sister lets go of Nonny's hand, tells her, "Please wait." She goes outside to calm everybody with soft words Eli can't hear. This is how they all miss the very last thing that Nonny says and does on earth.

There's a knock. Nonny's eyes open and her head lifts off the pillow. Her hair looks like Eli's did with glue stuck in it. "She's here," she says.

The door opens. Next-door Gerhard steps inside. He's a giant with a baby's bald head and earrings. Gerhard's crying like a baby, too, his face squinched and wet.

"Ellen? What's happening? How can I help?"

"Oh, it's you," Nonny says, and her head falls back.

Mom takes Eli up the ladder to bed. He sleeps, and when he wakes he sees night through the skylight. Weak stars mean it's not late. Something stinks. He peers over the edge. Down below, they're changing the sheets. Nonny made stinky-butt in the bed. She groans when they roll her onto her side to pull away the dirty sheet.

Eli calls and Mom helps him down the ladder.

Nonny's a fish sucking the air. Short, short, short, long, sucky-mouth sounds, then she stops. Everybody holds their breath with her. Her foot feels cold through the sheet. Eli lifts it to look. Her foot is blue.

Nonny's sister sings the coat-and-hat song, the sunny street song so quietly. The part about the dog, she sings over and over. *This Rover, cross over.* Everybody sings with her. Everybody tells Nonny to go. *Cross over, Ellen. Cross over, Mom.* Except Auntie Mimi can't say it. So Mom hugs her and strokes her hair the way she does for Eli. She rocks her like she rocks Fern when Fern's messing everything up and can't stop. Fern only stops when Mom's *I love you, I love you, I love you* gets too strong for her to fight. Now Mom's saying, *she loves you, she loves you,* and finally, after forever, Auntie Mimi gives up and tells Nonny *okay. Go.*

Right away Nonny starts gurgling. She wants to cross over, but can't. She can't because Eli's still holding her foot.

Gold dust at my feet, Nonny's sister sings.

And Eli lets go.

HE'S in outer space, except the stars are so weak. That's messed up. He must be on earth, otherwise he would be absent, right? The medicine's working. On Cordova Island the stars are bright explosions, but he's in Nonny's loft, staring up through the skylight, Mom asleep beside him.

289

He peeps over the edge. Everybody's lying around like dead soldiers, Grandpa with Nonny in the hospital bed. Nonny's sister on the couch. Auntie Mimi on the floor curled up in a ball. And he remembers the sign on the door nobody turned to SORRY, WE'RE CLOSED.

Where are you going, Eli?

Nonny said when she was gone she would still be there, looking down at him. She would be present when she was absent. But how could she be, if she doesn't have epilepsy? Also, it's messed up, the way Eli's looking down at her. Looking down at Nonny standing at the bottom of the ladder. It's Nonny even though Nonny's in the bed with Grandpa. Even though the sheet's over her head the way she made a tent to read them stories in bed. Like she's dressed up for Halloween.

"I want to change the hands on the clock. So you'll come back sooner. Fern messed it up."

Eli, no. She lifts the sheet now so he sees her face. No oxygen tubes, just Nonny's smile. She's blocking the ladder. *Eli. You stay right there.*

12

ELLEN IN PIECES

...

The yawning beigeness of the room. Beige walls, beige booths, beige floors. Matt is so head-bobbingly tired his chin keeps sinking to his chest. Every time, he remembers more.

How, for instance, he smelled smoke a moment before the detector did. Before it started shrieking, so inhumanly and at so piercing a decibel that the smoke became secondary to the sound. He staggered out of the bedroom holding his hands over his ears like in that Munch painting, wide-eyed, the detector screaming for him, thinking, *this is it, this is the end.*

Every time the number on the pixel board changes—Beep!—it startles Matt, who jerks upright in his chair. The same coarse beep as in that Operation game he played as a kid, trying to tweeze out the dude's broken heart and accidentally touching the metal rim. He looks blearily around the room, wishing stupidly for a certain, familiar face.

Confused by the alarm, *alarmed* by it, he did a dumb-ass thing. He opened the oven door and looked inside so that the clothes smouldering there received a sudden, nourishing dose of oxygen. Shorts, a couple of stinky tees, grass-stained ball of tube socks all ignited in a *whoosh*. Hot fingers of flame reached for him, grazed his shirt front.

He was lucky to leap back in time.

Two seats over a young woman in red leggings and a short flowery dress wrests papers from her Ziploc bag. Smooths them in her lap. Her number flutters down, alights under her chair.

So he ran for it, burst into the hall where the *a cappella* shrieking of the smoke detectors had tripped the sprinklers. One glance back through rain and thickening smoke. The last thing Matt saw of the life he'd lived with Nicole, which had started out so promisingly but had steadily sickened, was the frozen pizza on the counter, soon to be unwrapped by fire and consumed whole.

Across the hall, a stout, grey woman was backing out of her apartment. *Lottman* was the name on her mailbox, but she was crying, "Mr. Muldoon! Mr. Mul-*doon!*" Matt remembered her with a cane and rushed to hold the door, saw the tabby writhing in her arms.

He ended up walking the whole cacophonic length of the hall beside the old woman and her cat. He bent lower than the smoke and got her to too. Someone from their floor with bushy, ironic sideburns banged on doors. "Fire! Fire!" Laptop clutched to his chest, he streaked right past them.

It took longer to evacuate with an unsteady elder and a terrified cat drawing angry red lines on her arms and neck. When they finally stepped outside, both of them were hacking. Between her convulsions, the old lady shot Matt a look of undying gratitude he truly did not deserve as the person who'd set fire to the building.

He picks the number off the floor—A058. Glances around the room again. At breakfast in the hotel restaurant, he'd done the same thing, studied everyone in line at the buffet.

What would Ellen be doing at a downtown hotel at seven in the morning?

293

THE tenants assembled on the sidewalk in front of the apartment, two storeys of faux Spanish with wrought-iron railings. They were a miscellaneous, dampened lot, all of them coughing up smoke— Matt and Mrs. and Mr. Muldoon, the Quebeçois couple from the first floor, mountain bikers who rinsed their armour in the laundry room sink and left it full of grit and leaves like the bottom of a tea leaf reader's cup. The sideburn dude with the laptop was talking on the phone. "As we speak. Smoke billowing out." The woman who'd escaped last was the wettest, seaweed hair hanging down, a candyfloss kind of dog shivering in her arms. It was a no-pets building. Love had outed two tenants; Matt had nothing to save.

"They always say 'billow,'" said the sideburned irony-meister. "Or 'belch.'" He broke off coughing.

Closer, the shrill proclamation of sirens. Then the trucks arrived, firefighters spilling out, tromping everywhere in their yellow coats and heavy gear. One cumbersomely directed them to move across the street, where a crowd had formed, neighbours and passersby, people interested in tragedy or mesmerized by it, on this warm August evening.

"You're getting scratched up pretty bad there, ma'am. Can you drop the cat?"

"No!"

Matt was helping her hold it, one arm around the old woman's shoulder, the other hand on the cat's rumbling back. Under all its fur, it felt half the size it looked.

"She should sit down. She walks with a cane."

"You saved me," she told Matt just before a paramedic led her away.

The firefighter in charge of wrangling the tenants questioned Matt. How many apartments, how many people accounted for? Eight or ten apartments, Matt said, coughing raggedly into his fist. He didn't know anyone in the building except by sight. Vancouver was beautiful but she had a cold shoulder. Matt had lived here almost a year and had only made one friend, Ellen. Through the summer he'd worked in lawn maintenance, had beers after work a few times with the crew, but he wouldn't call them friends. He looked around for neighbours, pointed out the Quebeçois couple sitting under a tree. At the same time he wondered, dully, if he would have to pay for all this.

"There's Nicole," he said.

Running toward him on her toes like a ballet dancer, purple yoga mat rolled under her arm, her shocked expression directed not at Matt, but at the balcony of their apartment from which flames were now earnestly shooting.

• • •

Beep! He starts, rubs his face. Glances over and reads the name the red-legged woman two seats over is writing on her form.

"Oh my God," Nicole said, breathless from running. "I saw the smoke. My laptop's in there. My thesis."

Matt said, "I hope you backed it up."

He probably sounded callous when really he was in shock. Shocked and afraid that he would be held responsible. It didn't occur to him to blame Nicole for stuffing his clothes in the oven. He should have known to check before he turned it on. His fault, then. But here was the really irritating thing: when Matt *did* clean—which he did, a lot, way more than if he'd lived alone—she never seemed to notice. Matt would say, "I cleaned the bathroom," to let her know he was, in fact, doing his fair share. And she would reply, "What do you want? A medal?"

Now she was crying. Matt hugged her, but she made herself stiff and unreciprocal. The rolled-up foam mat was between them.

"I thought you were at the university," Matt said.

"I went to yoga." She shoved him back, brandishing the mat. The twist on her face wrung out its prettiness. "Who is E. McGinty?"

Matt said, "What?"

"Who is this E. McGinty you made fifty calls to this month? I saw it on your phone."

His phone that was inside, melting.

Matt bent over and coughed till he nearly puked.

Beep! The numbers keep changing without getting any nearer to Matt's A067. And the woman's name elongates letter by letter. Matt sits up straighter.

M–C–G–I–N–T–Y S–I–L–V–

• • •

THE fire seemed to be squatting on Matt and Nicole's balcony now, a zoo animal behind bars, raging against the tormenting hoses, smoke amassing above it. A city bus turned onto their street, which seemed apocalyptic too. When had that ever happened?

The firefighter returned and directed them to the bus. The others filed toward it, the play-by-play of the irony-meister adding to the surreality of the scene. "Now they're asking us to get on a bus. I don't know why." The Quebeçois couple, the woman with the dog, a bearded man in sandals with fletched arrows of celery jutting from his Whole Foods bag. He must have come home from the store to find the building on fire. Mr. and Mrs. Muldoon were either on the bus already or in the ambulance.

Nicole was still weeping quietly next to Matt, rejecting his comfort. She asked him straight out, "How long have you been see-ing her?"

And Matt walked away. Away from the fire and Nicole's ques-tion, the first of many he would be obliged to answer if he stayed. Every one would hurt her. He bumped through the crowd of gawk-ers and, feeling the propulsion of a release, broke into a run. For so long he'd dreaded Nicole finding out about Ellen that now all he felt was freedom from that dread, at least until he reached Ellen's studio five blocks away and saw the sign on the door. SORRY, WE'RE CLOSED.

He knocked with his knuckles, then his whole fist.

Ellen's dog barked.

Matt made blinkers with his hands to see past the window where her pots were, hoping for a gap in the white-curtained back-drop. He tried the door. He coughed and coughed.

"Ellen!" he called through the mail slot. "Ellen! I have to talk to you!"

The dog commenced howling.

Ellen's neighbour opened his door and leaned out, his ear-lobes aquiver with rings. Normally, Gerhard smirked or was flirtatious with Matt, but now he was clearly telling him to fuck off, making broad, shooing motions with hands like those of a merciless giant.

It takes a moment. He looks at the pixel board again while his subconscious sorts the clues. McGinty-Silver Michelle.

He had no phone. Even if he found a pay phone, he had no money. He skulked back to Fourth Avenue and stood on the corner until a pair of teenage girls came along. "Hey. Can I use your phone?"

The girls stopped. Dusk was hanging on, splashing their faces with pink light. One said, "Sure!" and took it from the little purse that hung across her shoulder on a long buckled strap. The other twirled her hair, shifting from flip-flop to flip-flop.

Matt turned to face the wall. "Ellen, it's me. Maybe you didn't recognize the number, but it's me. Please pick up. Something's happened."

Could she even interrupt a message on the phone she had? Yes, it was an actual machine. She was wacky like that. She had a cassette player, too, and an old dentist's chair to read in.

He hung up and called again. "Ellen, it's Matt. Can I come over?"

She could be out. She didn't have a cell phone. Who didn't have a cell phone?

"Are you there?" he asked the third time.

The bolder girl whose phone it was said, "Isn't she answering?"

297

"I'll wait five minutes."

"But, like, I'm going to need my phone back."

MATT *turns his head, openly stares.*

Ellen had talked a lot about her daughter. The daughter she was always worried about. She had two and one was good, the other bad. She didn't phrase it that way, but that was what she meant.

298

FOR hours he walked around feeling like his whole life had gone up in flames, which it had. Like his heart was fixed on the outside of his chest with its claws stuck in, which it was. It freaked people out the way he was carrying his heart on the outside, so that hardly anyone he stopped would make eye contact with him, much less let him use their phone. Night came and he was still wandering past Ellen's studio in widening loops, pressing his heart—which was smaller than he had thought. There was something wrong with it, not just its bizarre external placement, but in the way it was beating, syncopated at first, then the stronger beats weakening too, until he realized the strength of the second beat corresponded to how close or far he was from Ellen's studio.

His heartbeat was a form of radar, guiding him back to Ellen.

• • •

THE pixel sign is flashing Mimi's number in all three slots—

A058!

A058!

A058!

—and beeping like a heart monitor during a cardiac arrest. She only notices now. She was thinking about the play, how nervous she is.

Onto the empty seat beside her, Mimi dumps her documents and paperwork. Madly, she sifts through it, yanks her handbag off the floor, burrows down, searching for the flimsy tab. *Beep! Beep! Beep!* goes the sign.

"Oh. Is this yours?"

She looks up. The guy the next seat over, about her age in a grey Hugo Boss jacket and black Nikes, holds out a paper number.

"Thank you," she says, plucking it back. "You saved my life."

He laughs, first a whoop of surprise, then a quieter, private chuckle, which makes her suspect that he was holding onto her number the whole time. Quickly her fingers find her cross. *Think kinder thoughts.*

All the way to the counter she keeps fingering it, and while the poker-faced clerk questions her, too, flipping through the old passport to compare who she is today to how she appears in the five-year-old shot—not so different on the outside—and finally, finally bringing down his rubber stamp.

Though his number was called after hers, Mimi and the guy in the grey jacket end up walking out of the passport office at almost the same time. Mimi senses his steps quickening behind her. By the elevator, she reaches back and flaps the hem of her dress as though it's stuck in her crack, just to show she knows he's staring. The elevator doors slide open.

"Mimi?"

She swings around making teeny-mouth, which is another thing she's trying to let go. "First you had my number, now you know my name!"

"I read it on your form."

Now and then people pop up from Mimi's unsavoury teen years, probably more than she knows because there's a lot she simply can't remember from that time. These are the very people she should reach out to, but it's hard. This guy doesn't seem like one. He smells of an MBA, splashed on after he shaves, but with a sweetness in his hazel eyes so that when he points and starts for the stairwell, Mimi hesitates only briefly, then jerks forward, as though they're connected by a string.

"I was there for almost two hours!" she complains on the way down. "Then I get the third degree. Do I look like a terrorist?"

It's a beautiful stairwell, with oak banisters and placid cherub faces looking out from sculpted balustrades. Angels are everywhere. Open your eyes. Going down, Mimi brushes her hand across one, says her silent prayer. *Thank you that I might get through this day without being a bitch.*

"Where are you going?" he asks.

"On a cruise."

"Where to?"

"I'm not sure yet. It's a job. I got hired as a dancer."

Matt opens the door to the main lobby.

"What about you?" Mimi asks. "Where are you going?"

"Back to Korea. I've been teaching there the last two years."

"Korea?" She stops. "I heard about this place. The penis park."

"Haesindang Park. I've been there."

"Oh my God," Mimi buckles, laughing. "I thought he was making it up! Well, have a great trip."

"You look like a dancer," he says.

She laughs again, then kicks one black flat in the air behind her before skipping off, dodging the people coming into the Sinclair Centre, giving him the slip.

Gerhard was the one who told her about the park. There was

some sad story connected to it. A drowned virgin. Mimi's forgotten. She and Gerhard lived together for a year, while Ellen was dying and afterward. Then her childhood friend Jacob came home from Montreal and she moved in with him. Less cramped. Mimikins, Jacob calls her. *My little Mimikins, when are you going to be finished in the bathroom?* She'll see them both tonight, see everybody, at the play.

Mimi stops then. She's supposed to live for these moments, these insights and openings. But truthfully, she hates them. She hates having to go back and figure out the right thing to do. The right thing is always the hardest thing. (It's never going home and taking a bath.) If she ignores the feeling, it just builds and builds.

301

She walks the half-block back to the Sinclair Centre. And he's still there, standing on the stone steps, looking lost. "Who are you?" Mimi asks.

When he turns, something happens on his face. A lifting-off of some burden. Mimi doesn't know what yet, but she knows she's done the right thing, returning. Her bag is weighing down one shoulder, the way a bird feigns a broken wing. She hoists it and says, "I didn't write *Mimi* on the form. I wrote *Michelle*."

"I knew your mother, I think."

His name is Matt. He walks her to the SeaBus terminal, buys her a tea in the café there.

"I can't believe it," Mimi tells him when they're seated across from each other. She blots her diluting mascara with a napkin, feels for the silver cross. "It's amazing."

"It is," Matt agrees. "I was just thinking about her in the passport office."

"How long are you here for? Do you have plans?"

"I have a thing I have to go to in a few hours." He takes out his phone to check the time, leaves it face down on the table. "Less than that, actually."

"Tonight?"

"I'm pretty bagged, to tell you the truth. And I fly out tomorrow morning."

"Back to Korea?"

"No. I'd need the passport for that. I'm going to visit my folks for a few weeks. In Alberta."

"How are you getting your passport then?"

"They'll courier it."

302

Mimi performs a delicate hand-dance, prying the lid from her cup, extracting the tea bag with the stir-stick, plopping it on the inverted lid. A wraith of steam rises from the paper cup. The bag bleeds. A woman, fiftyish with red hair, sweeps past their table. They both glance at her, as though they're looking for the same person.

Mimi is tormented by these vague resemblances. At least once a week she sees Ellen. The other day, at the grocery store, she turned a corner with her basket, froze. Froze because, there, mid-aisle, was Ellen, her back to Mimi, in adamant conversation with some other shopper about Shredded Wheat. Suspended in the moment, Mimi ran through the possible explanations for Ellen's cruelty, prepared her accusations according to their old pattern—*we had a funeral! what were you thinking!*—until the woman who was decidedly not Ellen, who looked nothing like her in fact, turned. Her scarf had deceived Mimi, or her too-loud laugh. And Mimi crumpled there by the instant oatmeal and the breakfast bars, crumpled inside, then moved brokenly past the imposter of grief.

(Only in dreams is it really Ellen, plopping down next to Mimi on the bus, crowding her out with a surfeit of shopping bags. Mimi glares out the window, refusing eye contact, until Ellen's humming clues her in.

Weak with wonder, Mimi turns. "Mom?"

Ellen laughs and pulls the cord.

"I'll get off with you. We can walk together."

"Sweetheart," Ellen says. "This isn't your stop.")

Mimi asks Matt, "How did you meet my mom?"

He runs a hand through his hair. Longer, it would probably break out in curls. He's quite cute, Mimi decides. Soft featured. Much cuter than in the passport office, where he seemed a bit of a stalker. Now a nervous edginess has infected him.

"We were neighbours, sort of," Matt tells her.

"Do you know Gerhard?"

He blanks, then says, "Next door? Sure. It's funny."

"What?"

"How I met her. I was standing in front of her in a line. She tucked in my shirt tag. I'd only been living in Vancouver a few months. It was the first nice thing anyone had done for me. Then I walked past her studio. Same thing again. She was friendly."

"Sounds like her. Not great at boundaries or personal space. I used to hate that. How she'd talk to strangers as if they were intimate friends. Give them advice. Oh, cringe."

Matt lifts his coffee, sips, then sets down the cup as though it's too bitter. "How is she?"

"Who?"

"Ellen."

Mimi pulls back.

"What?" Matt asks.

303

"She died."

"*What?*"

"I'm sorry! I assumed you knew." Mimi reaches across the table for his hand, but he snatches it back.

"When?"

"Almost two years ago. I'm sorry. I feel terrible."

For a moment neither speaks. Matt gazes at the table between them while the outrage slowly fades.

"I thought you knew," Mimi says.

"How?" he asks the table.

"Breast cancer. It's awful not to have a mother anymore. I can't tell you how lost you feel."

304   She watches his face, which seems almost childlike now. When her nephew Eli puzzles over something, it plays out across his features like this.

Abruptly Matt snaps to, pockets the phone, stands. "I'm sorry. Sorry for your loss. I've got to go. Nice meeting you."

"Sure," she says.

He leaves her sitting there, wanders across the marbled expanse of the station on what seem like semi-drunken steps. Stops and checks for something in his pocket.

When Mimi finishes her tea, she'll get on the SeaBus and go home. Get ready for tonight. Except she's rattled by what's just happened and, now, jealous too. All this time Ellen was alive for Matt. She only just died. For two years Mimi's been staunching her severed umbilical cord. But see how she broke the news? How she said, "She died" for the first time without tearing up?

She remembers her newborn nephew, the thick black rind at his navel. Eventually the scab fell off. He didn't even feel it.

• • •

MIMI spots him on the corner of Hastings and Seymour. Pedestrians cluster, waiting for the light to change. What to say? What would Ellen say? How she yearns for that advice, craves it, when she once rejected out of principle all motherly guidance.

"Matt?"

He turns and sees the scrap of paper she's holding out.

"My number. My dad has a play. It opens tonight. I thought you might want to go."

Matt takes her number without looking at her, stuffs it in his jeans pocket. This seems to remind him of something, because he pulls an open envelope from his jacket, removes the folded pages, the top sheet a flowery piece of stationery, handwritten. He shuffles through them.

305

"Heatley Avenue? Know where that is?"

"Chinatown, I think." Mimi points east. "So, will you come?" Then, because he looks to be swaying, "Are you okay?"

"I'm on Korean time. There's a seventeen-hour difference. It's tomorrow there. Ellen. I can't get my head around it."

Mimi sees the City of Vancouver letterhead. "What's happening on Heatley Avenue?"

"I'm not even sure. I got this letter." He waves the pages in his hand. "In Seoul, forwarded by my dad. From the daughter of this old lady who used to live across from me. Thanking me for saving her mother."

"You saved someone's life?" Mimi asks.

A woman in an electric wheelchair forces Matt to step aside so she can motor down the cutaway curb. One of her legs is elevated. Footless. Matt does a double take and, for a second, Mimi thinks he's going to cry.

"No. Long story. But I needed to come back to renew my passport anyway so I thought, okay. I'd do the passport in Vancouver. Get that lady off my back. But last night?"

He stuffs the papers back in the envelope, jams it in the side pocket of his jacket.

"In the hotel? I couldn't sleep, right? I'm all fucked up with the time change. I thought, maybe tomorrow I'll give Ellen a call. Or just go to her studio. Why are you smiling?"

"Sorry," Mimi says, covering her mouth.

Across the street, the little white man signals he can cross. Matt steps into the intersection, Mimi too, keeping pace with his angry strides.

"I wasn't smiling because it's funny. I was smiling because it's amazing, don't you think? That we ran into each other? Why do you think we did?"

Mimi stays stubbornly by his side. She knocks shoulders with a texting passerby, manages to dodge the next person.

Finally, he shoots her a sidelong look. "I'm just heading to this thing now, okay? Take care. Your mother was a wonderful person."

"She was and she wasn't. Like anybody," Mimi says as they pass the grim sameness of a car rental agency. "We found it hard to love each other. I wish more than anything we hadn't."

A Starbucks, then an alley. Why are alleys so sad?

"Can I tell you about my dad's play? First you have to know that he basically abandoned us. My mom, my sister, me. He married again. Twice."

Her fingers discover that the fastener on her chain has migrated around to meet the cross. She makes two sharp, throat-slashing movements to send it back.

"But when my mom got sick? He just rose to the occasion. He

ran around and did every little thing for her right until the end. And she let him. She let him come back and do the first unselfish thing he probably ever did in his whole life."

They've reached the next intersection. There's an old brick pub on the other side, the walls on street level painted red. A vortex of pigeons swirls above it.

"All those years, whenever he saw my mother, the next day he would write something. But none of these things ever fit together, so he put them in a folder. Then, when she was dying?"

"Please," Matt says.

"People wrote messages and put them in the window of her studio. *Get well* or *I love you.*" (Also *I still have your anus, Ellen. I keep it on my desk.* She doesn't tell him this.) "Memories they had of her. I kept them. And the speeches from the memorial. I gave them to my dad. And one day, maybe six months later, he sat down. From all those pieces, he wrote this play."

"I can't!"

Mimi raises her hands in surrender. "Okay. I know it's hard."

"What's hard?"

"Doing the thing you're meant to do."

He turns on her. "Why would I be meant to go to your father's play?"

"He says it's not just about Ellen. It's about how every person who comes into your life gives you a piece of themselves. And vice versa. I still forget she's dead. But soon I won't. Then how will I keep her in my life?"

"How do you think I feel?" Matt says.

Mimi stares. "I have no idea. I just met you. You're acting like more than a neighbour, if you don't mind my saying."

307

Matt swings around. With the pedestrian light going his way, he charges across, leaving Mimi standing on the corner.

"You've got my number if you change your mind," she calls.

. . .

THAT night, almost three years ago, Matt circled Ellen's studio. Darkness had tucked the city in long since. Finally, a light.

A man answered his knock. He was shorter than Matt, with greying waves of hair and glasses he peered over. Briefly Matt was surprised, then he disregarded him and craned to see inside. Only the floor lamp next to Ellen's dentist's chair was on, the working space in the far corner where she carved her pots shrouded. The dog came to life on the couch, lifting its black snout in the air. He must have smelled Matt, because he wagged.

"What?" the man asked.

"Is Ellen here?"

"She's busy."

"I need to see her."

"Like I said."

The door began to close. Matt, who was wearing Tevas, reacted with his foot. "Ow! Ellen! Ow!"

"Stop that right now!"

The man raised his hand as though to clap it over Matt's mouth. Matt stopped yelling and the man shut his eyes instead and pinched the bridge of his nose above the glasses. He had to be her ex. Ellen had talked about him. She had grandchildren, too, but that seemed impossible. Really, they'd talked so little.

Ellen appeared, coming up behind the man who was probably Larry. "What's going on?" Seeing Matt at her door where he had stood so many times, on the verge of tears now, she put a hand on Larry's shoulder. "It's okay."

308

She stepped outside, closed the door and leaned against it, a woman wide of hip with shoulder-length hair dyed a reddish shade, breasts large and relaxed, a woman too old for Matt who had nonetheless welcomed him into her life. Something was wrong. Her face was puffy, like she'd been crying. And a memory loosened in Matt—a day in his childhood when he came home from school and found his mother like this. Because her mother, Matt's grandmother, had died.

"What happened?" Matt asked, thinking of the daughter. The daughter she was worried about.

"Listen, Matt," Ellen said, reaching for his hand. She kissed the back of it, turned it over and kissed his palm. With her head bowed, he could see the lighter line of her greying part. "Thank you. Thank you for everything. But something's come up for me. I'm sorry."

"Did somebody die?" he asked.

She did the same thing Larry had done, closed her eyes, so Matt recognized the totality of their mutual exhaustion. "Nobody died," she said.

"Is that Larry?" he asked.

"Yes. You have to leave, Matt. This is a bad time."

He stepped back. "Can I phone you?"

"Yes, phone. Give me a couple of days and then we'll talk. And take care, Matt. You're a wonderful, wonderful young person. I wish you could see that in yourself."

"Why do you think I can't see that?" he asked.

"Thank you," she said. "Goodbye."

She let go of his hand and went back inside, shutting the door behind her.

• • •

AND now Matt knows the something that came up for Ellen, the unthinkable something that had been circling her all that time.

IN her letters, Cindy Tomchuk (née Lottman) had written that the ceremony was really for her mother, not Matt, who was obviously "an extremely modest person." All Mrs. Lottman wanted was for him to receive the recognition he deserved. On behalf of her mother, Cindy had nominated Matt for the award. The whole family was thrilled. Thrilled.

Matt spots Cindy puffing at the regulation distance from the front entrance, eyeing his approach, while nearby a cherry tree releases its nostalgic perfume. There's no place with springier air than Vancouver. It's been connecting Matt to these memories of Ellen ever since he flew in the night before.

Cindy bustles over. "You're not Matthias, are you?"

In admitting that he is, Matt's chance to escape is annulled in her fleshy embrace. Finally, she releases him, drops the butt. Her nicotine-tempered laugh devolves into a cough.

"How are you?"

"Okay. Jet-lagged." Devastated, actually.

Cindy leads him by the arm—tightly—into the firehall and to an auditorium-like room half filled with people. There's a carpeted platform up front, and a podium flanked by flags. The civic coat of arms hangs on the wall behind it, the heroic lumberjack and brave fisherman. *By land and sea we prosper.* The stage faces a bank of windows that looks out to where Matt was lurking a minute ago. Across the street, a dreary mildew-streaked social housing complex.

"Don't be alarmed if she starts talking about dying. She doesn't mean it."

The old lady is sitting in the front row of plastic chairs. Mrs. Lottman, not Mrs. Muldoon, so much older Matt is shocked. White and dwarfen and wearing what seems like a pyjama top to which a corsage is pinned, a walker parked in front of her.

"Here he is, Ma. At long last. I found him outside standing all by his lonesome." Cindy laughs, coughs.

The old lady looks up blankly, also expecting to see the old Matt, not his slick, shorn man-self in a Hugo Boss jacket, purchased at the Dongdaemun Market at 3 a.m. The way he expected to see his old neighbour who once cruised the halls planting her cane.

"I cut my hair," Matt says. "It was longer before."

With surprising quickness, she snatches his hand.

"Sit beside her," Cindy says. "I want a picture."

"How are you?" he asks Mrs. Lottman. "How's Mr. Muldoon?"

"She's in a home now," Cindy answers. "I'm stuck with the cat."

Cindy pulls a camera from the purse on the chair next to her mother, takes a few shots with a flash, then asks them to stay right there while she rounds up the rest of the family, who are the majority in the room besides the firefighters standing around in chummy circles talking shop—relatives of Mrs. Lottman. Many relatives of all ages, teenaged and middle-aged, a few younger kids, all dressed in Winners finery, including a little girl in a tiara and a party dress made of shiny pink material. These people, maybe a dozen of them, start coming at Matt, introducing themselves or being introduced by Cindy, wanting to shake his hand and thank him.

"This is Rod, my husband," Cindy says, pulling forward a bald man broadly noosed in a striped tie. "Carrie, our granddaughter." The princess.

"Beth," says a Chinese woman with feather earrings.

Another woman shakes his hand, younger, about Matt's age, in a denim skirt. A reporter, she says. She picks up Cindy's purse, drops it one seat over, settles beside Matt. "I already spoke to Mrs. Lottman. Can I ask you a few questions? What made you decide to stop and help Mrs. Lottman?"

Meanwhile people are gathering at the podium, checking that the mike works.

"What made me decide?" Matt rubs his face. "I didn't. I just. I stopped. Who wouldn't?"

A Lottman who looks like a construction foreman or a prison guard, Mrs. Lottman's son, he guesses, Cindy's brother—they all have the same wide-set eyes—says, "One guy ran past. Right, Ma?"

Mrs. Lottman leans close to Matt. She's going to speak. Though Matt just met these people clustered around him, he's already figured out Mrs. Lottman is their revered matriarch. They shush each other to hear what she's going to say. The little girl in the tiara pushes through until she's right in front of Mrs. Lottman, staring at her great-grandmother with oceanic eyes.

"I just wanted your address. To send you a card. Cindy gets her hands on things. Always, it's a big production."

Some Lottmans laugh. Several object. "He saved your life, Grandma!"

"He came all the way from Korea!"

"I had other things to do too," Matt says, meaning the passport, which reminds him of Mimi. He glances around, having briefly forgotten her while the whole walk here he couldn't shake the feeling that she was following him. He kept seeing the red of her leggings in the corner of his eye, like a raging sty. Only vaguely does she resemble Ellen. Ellen's eyes were blue. Mimi's hair is darker, too, feathery and cropped short. A long neck and pronounced collarbones where Ellen had been soft, body and heart.

Had been.

"Thank you," Mrs. Lottman says with dignity. She puts her hand over Matt's. "Can we go now?"

First there is the ceremony to get through for both Matt and Mrs. Lottman, whose fates intertwined the day of the fire when they had remained separate for all the months they'd been across-the-hall neighbours. The last day Matt saw Ellen. Because when he did call Ellen two days later, like she asked? Over and over? Ellen didn't pick up. He never spoke to her again.

And all this time he's been furious. Hurt. In a serious, fucking funk over how Ellen had wrung out his heart. Ellen, who, in hindsight, was completely unsuitable. Too far ahead of him in life.

Matt got on with it, his life. Got on really well, actually, both financially and in the way Korean women are nuts for every *wei-guk-in*.

The fire chief penetrates the scrum of Lottmans and suggests they start. Most of the plastic chairs get sat on, even by a few people unrelated to the Lottmans. They aren't dressed up. People, Matt supposes, who came from across the street for the free coffee and Chips Ahoy! laid out on a table at the back.

Speeches: a city councillor, the fire chief. Then Matt is called to the front of the room to receive his plaque. His stomach twists. What would they say if they knew he was the one who started the fire?

Close by, a seismic rumble sounds, deep enough to cause the floor to shake. It's one of the trucks. A couple of the firefighters leave the room and Matt turns to face his mostly adoring Lottman audience.

It's obvious what they would say. So you messed up? Who cares? It's not as important as what you do to set things right. And here he is, doing just that.

313

He'll never see these people again. Before today, he didn't know most of them existed. Not even Mrs. Lottman has earned more than a walk-through in his memory. Still, every person who comes into your life gives you a piece of themselves. And vice versa. Well, here's proof of that.

What did Ellen give him? What gifts has he denied receiving since she closed her door to him that night? Can he even count them? Her kindness and her time. Her cool fingers at his nape, tucking in his tag. Food, advice, languid, secret afternoons. What did he offer Ellen in return? He looks around the room still hoping she'll be here. Hoping that's her in the chair close to the window, backlit, an aura around her. Her hand lifts discreetly, just a jiggle to say, *here I am*.

An empty chair.

When the plaque is in Matt's grasp, when the little tiara girl dashes up to present him with a Bristol board card she made—it's almost as big as her and all the Lottmans have signed it—when she says, loudly, her obviously rehearsed sentence, "You're my hero," and hugs him around his waist, everyone claps, even Mrs. Lottman with a weary expression on her face. Some of his grogginess lifts and he feels something like a reprieve. And more.

He actually feels the thing they've asked him to come here to feel.

Because of those times he left Ellen in her loft—sated with their lovemaking and calling down to him, "Thank you! Thank you for being born!"—and paraded his aliveness down the hill, the view opening up to him. If it was evening, he saw the city's illumined parts—the lights of West Vancouver concentrating near the shore, gold and amber in the bay, an aquatic aurora borealis, the freighters waiting at anchor with their decks lit up. He couldn't stop smiling

314

and everyone smiled back. It spread around in his peacocking wake, from person to person. *Behold the mighty pleasure-giver, the bold lover, the hero of the loft.* A slam-dunk at the bus shelter; he hung onto the roof, swung to and fro, startling everyone waiting for the bus.

Thank you, thank you.

When the Lottmans find out he's in a hotel, that he's alone, they're incensed. He must come with Cindy and Rod at least for supper.

"I'm not alone, actually." He checks his pocket. A scrunch of paper.

The curious thing is, Mimi doesn't seem the dark person Ellen talked about. Strange and intense, yes. Even a bit wacky, like Ellen. Was Ellen jealous?

315

Matt glances across the room, feels the plastic ache of two dozen empty chairs.

Amazing that he and Mimi ran into each other. (*Why do you think we did?*)

"I can't," Matt tells them. "I'm sorry. I'm meeting someone. We're going to a play."

Acknowledgments

Shaena Lambert

Patrick Crean   Jackie Kaiser   Franny Brafman

Chris Casuccio   Ingrid MacDonald   Dan Wells

John Metcalf   Richmond Public Library

Douglas Glover   Kathy Hunt   Jacquie Harrison

Dr. Jane Donaldson   Dr. Kong Khoo

Kim Jernigan   Lynn Coady

Curtis Gillespie   Bruce Sweeney

Patrick Sweeney

I give you stars.